DOUBLE SHOT

Indigo City Darker Book 2

A.J. DOWNEY &
JARED KINGPACAL LAIN

COPYRIGHT

DEDICATION

To Jared once again, for keeping me on track and relatively sane. I can't wait for the next one. And to Mary and Carrie for all the encouragement through this process and particularly this set of novels. I'm going to miss these characters like I've missed no others. -A.J.

There are a number of people that I need to take a knee and thank. None of this would be possible without A.J. pitching me this idea – hitmen and romance, a globetrotting adventure, and steamy romance. It has been a fantastic time writing up the lads and Sadie, and now that this book is done, is this really where I have to say goodbye to them? Without my wife, Heather, who has been supportive of me through this from the first page, this book wouldn't have happened. And there are a couple of guys, Llama, Ilya, and Ole, you've had my back for years, always hitting me with the 'why haven't you gotten published,' and now I have. Thank you for having my back when I doubted my ability to put words together. - Jared

CHAPTER ONE

*L*achlan...

Federal agencies are now reporting that the events near Indigo City represent the culmination in a week long confrontation between multiple criminal organizations that ended with an explosion powerful enough to be felt across the entire city and even to the far side of the bay.

The video was grainy and low quality, but the fact that the news helicopter camera had shown anything was proof that their gear was good, but not military grade. I could make out the hulk of the house, but there were almost no details. Even the holes torn in the side were nothing more than dark spots in a shadow. Then there was the 'puff' as the first stage of the weapon fired, reducing the fuel to a vaporized cloud. The second explosion ignited the aerosol and smashed the house like it had been made of match sticks.

The camera swung violently away, as the concussion wave threw the helicopter up and away like a child's toy. A second feed started – security footage from a distant location – only catching the flare of the second main explosion.

State and Federal agencies are asking people to please stay away from the historic Bootlegger Head area, as the investigation into the explosion and the apparent underworld battle that occurred continues.

A reporter interviewed a man in a drab off-the-rack suit. Her pluck and use of sharp words bothered him. He responded to her questions with a deadened monotone. He said that everything was under investigation, and people with information were being asked to come forward, and that the *"goshdarn med'ya"* needed to stop running off at the mouth.

I hit the pause and rewind button. The video zipped back to the start and began playing again, and I watched the house vanish in a puff of flame. It looked like such a small thing, nothing like the explosions in movies. There was no giant churning pillar of black smoke and flame, just that intense fireball, and then everything was dust and shattered ruin, over and over again.

"You're just torturing yourself, stop," Sadie said in her characteristically soft voice.

"I can't accept it," I said, pressing my hand against the side of my face.

The last six months had been nothing but hell, and the only thing that had gotten me through it was the angel with her hand on my shoulder. Sadie had more experience than I did surviving this sort of loss; this hardship.

In a way, she rescued *me*.

It was fair, I had picked her up off the side of a highway, and she picked me up off the floor of the bedroom in a house I had hated. I turned the laptop off and put it back on the desk.

"There was nothing we could have done differently." She gave my shoulder a firm squeeze, a gesture of her support. "You know that."

"There was, there had to have been." I looked up at her. "We played the game for years and never lost, not even once."

"That's the thing Kyle; eventually? Everyone loses."

She was right, and Roan knew it, too. Otherwise, he wouldn't have gone through all the preparations, and there wouldn't have been those videos on the recovery drives in our bags. I suppressed a shudder. She wrapped her arms around me, and I could feel her face against the back of my neck, her warm breath against my skin.

"C'mon, how long have you been watching that?" she asked.

"Too long," I admitted. Watching it was almost an act of penance. Maybe if I watched the house destroyed enough times, the damned fireball, and everything blown to fuck all, it would either make sense or the ache in my heart would go numb from it. Six months hadn't done it, but I had the rest of my life to go.

It was hard to believe that six months had even passed since the battle on Bootlegger Head. Six months since everything went up in flames and death. The bullet wounds had healed, and the stitches were long gone. Doc Max had shown up after I passed out, but Sadie had let her in, and had helped the doc take care of me. We had only stayed at the Daughton house for three days. I spent most of that time in a painkiller haze.

She took care of me after Doc left.

After I could move on my own again, we restocked our bags and left. I didn't have a way to blow the Daughton house, but starting a fire was easy enough. We stayed and watched long enough for the blaze to fully engulf the structure, flames billowing out of the windows after the heat broke them. Even if it was declared arson, it would be chalked up to vandals and not an insurance scam. The house was owned by a real estate holding company, legally. There were loops and tricks in the paperwork that had made the house ours until the moment something went wrong, and then it would be in the portfolio of a multi-million-dollar shell company.

Roan's legal sorcery at play.

He was a fucking wizard, the things he did. Even the way he did them.

A week after the bomb, we had been in much more comfortable housing. The Eastermont Hotel sat high in the West Virginia mountains, not far from the shadow of Raven Rock. In decades past, when Cold War tensions had run high, VIPs and dignitaries had frequented the hotel. That way, if the bombs flew, they would be close enough to the Doomsday bunker under Raven Rock, where the president and all of his men would seek shelter.

That was where the two of us started picking up the pieces of our lives. The Recovery Drives had all the data we needed to do that – a ton of foreign bank accounts, dossiers of contacts and potential associates, the sundry people and agencies that held all of our finances and holdings, completely unknowing of who we were and what we did, and something we didn't expect.

There were videos that he had made, contingent upon his demise, on how to go through with getting back everything we had built. Some were harder than others to watch. The easy ones were the older ones, financial fallout plans that had been laid months or years before, before Sadie had come into our lives. The hard ones were the new ones, the files he had recorded in the last few days. He knew that something was brewing and had gotten everything lined up, fully prepared for any possible outcome.

"Aye, mate," he had said, wearing the purple tie Sadie had gotten for him at St. Henri. That trip felt like it had been in another century. *"Down here, updating some of the bug-out and recovery stuff. The last few days, yeah? You were there."* He sat back, brushed the front of his tie, and took a breath.

The video had jumped. He'd stopped recording for some time before jumping back in.

"So yeah, the last few days, we all know something is going to go down, so I'm putting this into the bug-out, if everything goes completely tits up, there is a chance that one of us won't make it out of the house. With my leg being the way it is, I would put odds on me holding the line while you get Sadie to safety. If you're watching this, I'm going to assume that is what has happened." He paused and took a drink. *"Because if I got out, I don't need to watch my own video on the recovery drive."* He had laughed a little about that.

"Take care of her, mate; Sadie..." He paused, his face grim as he tried not to choke up, I think. *"Take care of her. She's the best thing that has ever happened to either one of us. If the worst has happened, I hope she knows how much I love her, and care for her... and I swear,"* he jabbed a

finger at the camera, *"if you let anything happen to her, mate, I'm going to haunt your sorry ass."*

Sadie had been watching over my shoulder the first time I had been running through his tutorial videos. She had needed to hear the sound of his voice, to see him even if it was a just a recording.

"Sadie. Love. Poppet." He paused the recording to collect himself. *"If you have to see this, I am so very sorry. We've not known each other long, but you have meant the world to me, and I know you mean the world to Kyle too. I hope that you're alright. I hope you both are safe, away from whatever happens."* He wiped at his eyes with his sleeve.

"You'll need to take care of Kyle too, Sadie. He's a hard-ass, and hard-headed, and he doesn't listen for shite. Don't deny it, mate." She had broken into sobs by that point. *"Take care of each other, and I'm sorry, if you're watching this."*

There was a long pause.

"I love you both more than I love my own life. It has been an honor to serve with you, Lachlan, and I haven't words, Miss Brooks. Good luck, Godspeed. God Save the Queen and you both."

The video had ended there.

It was like having the bomb go off all over again, being forced to relive that great ginger moose slamming the door and facing the elite of the Escadrille alone... I shuddered, and it was all I could do to not break down then and there, sitting in front of the laptop with Sadie holding me like a life preserver.

A part of me that I hadn't imagined could even be vulnerable had died – it was shaped like him. Roan had always been burrowed into that fortress on the Head, surrounded by his guns, computers, and all the drones and remote-control things that I barely understood. This was not how it was supposed to have gone down. He should be the one sitting here, taking care of Sadie, not me. I didn't deserve her, and I sure as shit didn't deserve the sacrifice that he'd made for me.

That had been months ago, and the emotional wound still felt just as raw and just as bloody as the day it'd been dealt. The bullet wounds had healed much faster by comparison, the cracked ribs as well. Now, the physical injuries barely bothered me unless I went all out in the gym. That was something I had been doing. I needed the physical pain. It let me fool myself into thinking I could drown out this emotional shit… but I couldn't.

I remembered Roan, when everything went south the first time after he lost his leg and was discharged from the Royal Marines. He had fallen into the bottle, packed on weight, and almost ended himself with those shit life choices. But then he had pulled himself around, quit drinking like he had joined one of those twelve-step cults or AA. Except he hadn't. It'd been all him.

He gave all of his stress and frustration to the iron in the gym, first at the rehab center, then when he moved into my apartment, the apartment complex gym. One of the first indulgences we had bought ourselves was a fully kitted-out home setup – treadmill, elliptical, a weight bench, several specific machines for different muscle groups. He threw himself into it, and it was his cathedral of self-inflicted pain.

He also took over the finances, and I found out how much money I had been wasting on renting things, leasing cars, and all the rest. I pushed him, kept him from giving up. He pushed me and kept me from just settling in.

How close had I been, back in those days, to give up on all the life skills the army had taught, all my experiences in Afghanistan and half a dozen other miserable third world countries, to just go back to being a civvie? What would I have done, become some gym-stalking fitness trainer, worked in some corporate backed self-defense dojo, ended up in some dead-ass dead-end public sector job sitting at a desk or in a cubicle? I could have done paperwork until I broke inside and went on my own personal Project Mayhem where my lurking issues and documented rebellious disorders came to a head with something – a mass shooting, a bomb and manifesto jag, a highly public suicide. He fucking saved me like I saved his ass.

Working out was *cathartic*, and so was the work that we were both trained for, he liked to say. That was a Roan word for things that hurt like hell at the time, but you feel better afterward. There was some truth in that. While I was running, or pushing iron, I didn't have time to think. Everything was concentrating on my breathing, on muscle control, keeping count of the reps like a Catholic counting the penitent prayer out on their rosary beads.

Cathartic things kept you from going nuts or joining nuts.

The alternative was picking up the bottle and letting it finish what Chauvignon had started.

I did break down one time. Inside my bug-out bag there was, of all fucking things, a sampler flight of artisanal gins, each with a different sprig of some herb in each glass bottle. What had he imagined, that we would take the *Rum Runner* out on a leisurely loop around the bay while everything went up in flames?

He probably fucking *did* think that, having cocktails while we were whisked away in that beautiful, powerful, sexy boat he had purpose-fitted for just that very thing. I think the thing that actually broke me was realizing that all those little surprises, those little Easter eggs were done. There would be no more topflight booze from places I had never heard of, no more pairs of the most amazing leather shoes from places in Europe. He knew my goddamn shoe size in different countries, and now that he was gone, I was going to have to buy my own goddamn shoes and I realized I didn't know. I didn't know my own fucking shoe size. I mean, *what the fuck?*

I was glad that Sadie had been asleep when that dam broke. That she didn't have to see me lose it. She was counting on me to be the strong one… *Roan* was counting on me to be strong for her…

For the first few weeks, we both slept a lot. We were both broken. I don't know that I could have hidden it any better. I know I wished to, but a wish in one hand and shit in the other and you tell me which filled up faster.

We left the Eastermont Hotel and ended up taking a train across the country, leaving the DC area, heading north to pick up different rail lines that ran west, until we ended up in the location that he had designated as Safehouse Omega. The safehouse to end all safehouses. Our most fortified one.

Safehouse Omega was buried under yards of Montana soil, hundreds of miles from any other vestiges of civilization. The surface was a small observation hut, and some facilities for gardening and ranching. If we wanted to bring in livestock, or plant seed, we could have. The place had been some sort of vintage fallout bunker that had been built back in the paranoid '60s when the entire western half of the world had lived under the menacing red shadow of Russian nuclear war. There was the Wolf Fork Creek that fed into the north side of the property, and the Dry Wolf Fork that wrapped around the south and west sides. It was a frozen fucking wasteland when we arrived. It was nearly zero, and snow had blown into piles taller than our heads.

The winter had buried us under a hell of snow and ice.

There were some creature comforts – television, radio, computers, all of it several years behind the curve. The television was barely forty-five inches, but the place had no Wi-Fi. Everything was still wired in. The important things were there, armored doors, a secret location, pantries full of the supplies we could live off of for a long time.

At first it seemed odd that there were three snowmobiles. There was no way he could have guessed about Sadie when this place had been set up, but then it was Roan. There were three, so if one went down, we would still have had two to work with. I had not known about this place, but from the notes he left, Safehouse Omega was a hitman time-share. I saw the list of other professionals who had access to this place and had also footed some of the bill.

Some were retired now, some were dead, others were still working out in the field. I didn't worry about any of them. There were less than a dozen of us, and we all knew each other. Our backgrounds had overlapped – we were all ex-military, or ex-intel. We knew who we were and what we wanted and were as close to a fraternal order of assassins as you could get without it turning into a goofy over-the-top action movie with a five-star Hollywood-leading man.

Stuff like this and his investment gaming must have taken up his time when I was out in the field, capping mafiosi and shagging escorts.

I was thankful for him, for everything he did, even as I was cussing him while doing bicep curls, or push-ups.

I started slow; the first month had me seldom moving unless it was to check on the generator or the solar panels. The wounds were still fresh, and the ribs killed me. After I could move without popping painkillers, I started working out again. Just the treadmill at first and then adding weights. That second month, I felt like a crippled old man, working with the lightest weights.

Sadie followed me. She threw herself into the gym. The weightlifting didn't really appeal to her, but the cardio routines and the elliptical did. I started teaching her what I knew. There were plenty of weapons in the safehouse arsenal, so we started with stripping and cleaning literally all of them. Then we set up an improvised shooting range up on a ridge near the surface shed. She was a passably good shot, and with practice she could be good. If she wanted to be.

I also taught her some hand-to-hand, being careful to not repeat my mistake in our first lesson, where she had kicked me in the balls and left me on the ground.

It had been a good month of this, more than three months after the battle and our flight up the bay, when we came together again. It had been a mundane day, pancakes and bacon from the pantry, pistol practice, then we both did our cardio. After we were warmed up, I'd had us working on grappling and wrestling. I was showing her how to break out of holds when we kissed.

It wasn't love or passion, it was just... *need*.

The kiss was short, and there was almost no foreplay. She slipped from my hold like I showed her and executed the reversal perfectly. Then, she was straddling me. We both became aware of it, both sweaty from effort.

She grabbed me through the shorts I was wearing, and her hands were not gentle as she pulled my cock out. She pulled her own shorts and panties to the side and sat down on me, driving my cock up into her. I made a grunt, and then she was riding me like I was some rodeo bronco.

It didn't last too long. Her intensity, me being caught off guard again, I blew my load quickly. It was agony, the pain that throbs in a way that makes it feel so good, as she rode me after I had come. When she ground out her own orgasm, she stood up fairly quickly, dripping my own cum down on my shirt. I felt a little used, but at that point, just having that physical connection was a gift enough.

While I was lying on the mat, listening to her walk away, I was struck by a thought – *was this what it was like for her, in the living room, pressed against the glass?* It had been completely impulsive and insensitive. I felt a weird sensation in my chest. *Guilt?*

The feeling was fleeting, and for that, I was thankful.

I let her shower alone. That seemed like what she wanted. I threw my spunk-stained shirt in the corner and spun the pedals on the exercise bike until I heard the shower cut off. Fifteen minutes on the treadmill, and I knew she would be out of the bathroom by then. Then, thank God, I was able to shower myself.

This place was no resort, it was a bunker. The shower didn't have the same pressure or heat as the old bathroom in Indigo City had, and the hot water didn't last as long. Washing the funk and sweat off me felt oddly purifying. How had we gone so long without each other's touch?

"THE NEWS SAID THAT SHOULD BE THE LAST SNOW OF THE WINTER," I said, picking through a frozen dinner tray. It was some tragedy of chicken and rice that was a disgrace, but most of the good MRE packs were gone. The winter had felt like it lasted a lifetime.

"That will make shooting easier. My hands won't go numb as fast," she said, obviously disinterested in her microwaved calories. Unlike me, she had eaten most of it already. She knew what it was like to be hungry, and I had long been spoiled by the pretentious fare he loved to make.

"Nothing has happened. No one has made a move against us. No one has been chasing after us." I looked up.

"No one," she agreed.

"That means that they aren't looking." I pushed some peas into a wad of potatoes. "Which means they aren't worried about us now."

"So, what does that mean?" She stood up and carried the tray to the compactor.

"That means it's time to get back to work."

"What, just start taking contracts like you used to?" Her tone was incredulous.

"No, not that." I frowned. "Not at all. We have plenty of money and places to go. I'm talking about a different sort of work."

"I don't know that being a jet-setting assassin is really in my future," she said with a twist of her lips.

"Yeah, I don't really see it either," I agreed. "But I want revenge." I pushed the tray away from me. "I want their heads on a stick and their blood watering the ground."

"Revenge?" she echoed. She was hesitant, but I could see something in her eyes, that old mettle.

"Oh, yeah." I nodded. "Specifically, against the Escadrille Cartel. I couldn't care less about the Russians and the Triads."

She stared at me for a long time and finally set herself back on her heels.

"What if the reason they aren't after us is because they're all dead?" She crossed her arms over her chest. "That was a massive explosion, and what if they *all* died in it?"

"Come on, Sadie," I chided. "We know for a fact they didn't."

"How?" She was being stubborn, her chin raising, that glint in her warm brown eyes, the fire I used to love to warm myself by when we were teens.

"If a drug lord like Chauvignon was killed or arrested, it would be all over the news. The only thing that was on any of the major outlets was the explosion and all the low-level assholes the ICPD and Department of Homeland Security picked up, and the body count of how many were carted off to the morgue."

"I saw the news, too." She scowled. "They didn't name names; the investigators said the heat of the explosion was high enough that a handful of bodies they identified were only through dental records and that some they couldn't identify at all."

"I know." I looked away. I didn't want to think about Roan, charred to the point of being unidentifiable…

"If they were in the room with that fucking bomb, where he was, there's nothing left of them. They're just memories and… and… and fucking tomato sauce!" Her voice cracked and she left the room, hands over her face.

I sat back heavily in my chair. That didn't go how I wanted it to go.

THE NEXT DAY, WHEN WE HAD OUR SPARRING MATCH, SHE TOOK MY LEG out from under me and put me on the mat again. "You know what this means?" she asked.

"That I am going to be making dinner tonight and probably doing the laundry for the week?" I asked.

"Well, yes." She smiled. "But I was more thinking about your suggestion, revenge…" she trailed off, growing quiet and staring up and away from me, eyes distant.

I waited her out and finally with a shuddering breath she said, "I want it. I want it so fucking bad… but not at the cost of losing you, too."

She looked down at me and I smiled, raising my hand to cup her face like I'd seen Roan do I don't know how many times.

"I'm not going anywhere, baby. I promise."

Tears brimmed on her bottom lashes but didn't spill as she choked out, "He promised me, too." She squeezed her eyes shut, her face a study in agony that mirrored my own, but I steeled myself. "He promised he would never lie to me, but he did. He looked me in the eye and said he would be right behind us and he *wasn't*." She opened her eyes, tears spilling crystalline down her smooth skin, and fixed me with those deep brown eyes of hers and said, "So don't, please don't. Don't you lie to me too."

I felt my face go as serious as it'd ever been and I nodded, smoothing one of my thumbs through those tears. I brought it to my mouth and sucked it clean and nodded.

"Okay," I said. "Okay, I won't lie."

She nodded and sniffed and got up off of me, pacing several steps away and then back about half the distance away again as she took in deep breaths and got herself under control.

"So, what now?" she asked. "What's next?"

I sat up sharply and rested my forearms on my knees.

"We start looking up the members of the Escadrille that we know of, and we start taking them out, one by one," I said. "We make them pay."

"Do we know who they are?" she asked and gave me a hand up.

"We know who a lot of them are; he did background research and we have a dossier. It's in the recovery drive. I've looked at the list of them and I know the ones we have to kill, and those that would be good practice." I considered the expression on her face. "But you realize that this is killing people."

"They deserve it." Her voice was ice.

"I'm glad we're on the same page then." I assumed a new stance. "I'll need to make a few contacts, see about getting us some new body armor, and some weapons newer than the stuff hanging in the arsenal here. I want Berettas back in my hands."

"I want to break someone's neck." She stared at her hands.

"The neck snap is actually pretty hard. Nine times out of ten you're going to just give them a neck sprain, or release a lot of tension they're carrying," I said. Roan would make jokes when we sparred, so why shouldn't I?

"I want to choke the life out of them," she said, and her fingers flexed.

"That might be the hottest thing I've heard come out of your mouth," I said with a laugh. "I will mention that is also harder than it looks, but yes, it is as satisfying as you are imagining."

"I want to do it." She advanced and struck at my head. It was a good feint, and I blocked it, but she put some effort behind it. I deflected and blocked several more strikes and then caught her in a judo throw. She hit the ground with a grunt.

Could she kill? It wasn't something everyone could do. I had seen soldiers in the field completely fail, unable to take the life of someone who was intent on killing them. I had also seen green hitmen, fresh from the military, or some intel background, completely balk the first time they were confronted with a non-combatant kill. It was different when your target wasn't a person from another culture, ethnicity, and linguistic background. When you were drawing down on a fellow American, things changed.

I had had my own moment. My first balk had almost cost me everything. I didn't know her name. She had been some blonde-firecracker aide to a man I had been hunting. I ignored her, thinking she would duck and cover when the guns and blades came out.

She put me on the ground with a kick to the leg. I had rolled, got a bead on her and froze. How could I shoot a woman that at any other time I would have bought her a drink in an effort to get into her panties? I laid there as she drew her own pistol, and if Roan hadn't put a shotgun round into her chest, she would have popped me between the eyes.

Would Sadie freeze up? Would she be able to pull the trigger and not melt down afterward? How hard could she be? I didn't know if she could do it… but then again, if I were being true to my word and my promise to Roan? She wouldn't have to. I would keep her safe, and out of as much of the action as I could. I couldn't keep her out of everything, though.

There were parts of this that would definitely be a two-man job.

CHAPTER TWO

*S*adie...

"I'm sorry," I murmured late one night as I sat on the edge of the bed running a brush through my long hair. I'd gathered it over my shoulder and brushed it every night before bed like this. Tonight, it was no different, except for the fact that I was lost in reverie.

"Do what now?" Kyle asked, looking up from whatever printouts he'd been reading and over at me.

I didn't see him move, but rather felt it through the mattress below my butt.

"I said I was sorry," I said softly.

There was a rustle of papers as he lowered them to his lap.

"Look at me, Sadie."

He hadn't called me Shady in a while... I swallowed hard, afraid to turn around and meet his eyes.

"Sadie..." His voice was gently chiding. I sniffed and set the brush aside and twisted, adjusting my seated position so I could look at him. He was lying on his back atop the covers in his usual tank top and lounge pants, all in unrelieved black, of course.

"For what? You've not done anything wrong," he said.

I bit my lips together.

"For that time in the gym a while back," I whispered, the guilt eating me alive.

He turned and tossed the papers onto his bedside table and sat up, resting his forearms atop his knees.

"What about it?" he asked.

"I…" I didn't know what to say without sounding pathetic. I mean, I didn't know when he had stopped wanting me, and I felt so *guilty*.

"Sadie, look at me," he said, and his tone was uncharacteristically gentle.

I looked at him and his eyes searched my face.

"Closed mouths don't get fed," he said, raising his eyebrows, and I flinched.

It was something Prissy would say, except she hadn't meant it the way Kyle did now. She usually meant that if somebody didn't come clean about whatever business she was on about, none of us got to eat.

"You didn't want it," I said and swallowed hard. "You don't want me—"

He snorted.

"Don't say shit like that," he said softly, and I felt my mouth drop open.

"But—"

"But nothing," he said. "Don't you ever say shit like that. You're all I've *ever* wanted."

I shook my head, mollified. He raised his eyebrows and jutted his head forward slightly, as though expecting me to say something or argue, but I was honestly too confused.

"I don't—"

"Understand?" he finished for me.

"Yeah."

"It's not you," he said with a shrug, and I frowned. "It's me… I think."

"Okay, um, elaborate."

"About the only thing that gets me worked up right now is the thought of Gwendolyn Kaijin's severed head on a pike."

I jerked back as though he'd just slapped me.

"It's about all I can think about. When I sleep, I go through the last minute in the Bat Cave, and I see their faces, and I know their names. I want every last one of them dead, choking on their own blood. I want them to *know why* I'm killing them in the most violent and personal way I can imagine."

"I-I care, but I don't care about *that*… does that make sense?" I asked.

He shook his head, and I flicked my tongue against my lips, wetting them.

"When it's just you and me, like this… I-I can't do this cold impersonal thing anymore, Kyle. I need more," I said. "And I know it's selfish and I know it's wrong, and I—"

"Shit, *please* don't cry again," he said, sitting up a bit straighter. "Just tell me what you need. I hate it when you cry and I can't seem to fucking stop it and it happens so much now."

I closed my eyes and said, "I need you to *love* me."

"I *do* love you."

"Are you sure?" I asked, looking at him, feeling my face start to crumble. "Are you sure you don't blame me?"

"*Blame* you?" His voice rose. "For *what?*"

"For Conan…" I choked. "For Conan dying."

"Holy fuck, is that what you think?" he asked, and *he* jerked back as though I'd just slapped *him*.

"I feel like it's all my fault," I said, clutching my hands in my lap to belay their trembling.

"No." The word came out with such a savage fervency. His hand lashed out, quicker than a viper striking. He snared my wrist and pulled me to him and I went, desperately needing to be held, to be touched.

He held me tight and said, "That's total bullshit."

He swept a hand into my hair and pressed my head to his chest, holding me so tightly as though desperate to hang onto me. As though he thought that he was somehow going to lose me, which could never happen.

He tugged on my hair lightly and I looked up. His night dark eyes bored into mine and he dipped his head, capturing my mouth with his.

The kiss stole my breath away, and I melted into his warmth.

"I'm sorry," he whispered against my mouth. "I'm not good like—"

"Shut up and kiss me," I begged, and he smiled then lowered his mouth back to mine slowly.

He was hesitant, almost shy with the way he kissed me, and I didn't know what to make of that. Kyle Lachlan had never kissed me like that before, not even when we were teens – not the first time, not the last time before he'd gone off to basic training. I was confused by it, but seized the moment for what it was worth because how many times had I dreamed of this? How many times had I closed my eyes in the last few weeks, and wished for Kyle to kiss me like this, to lay me down gently like he was doing now? His hand was on my waist, the other untangling from my hair to caress the side of my face while he kissed me so gently, so sweetly.

"Is this okay?" he asked.

"Yes," I whispered back. It was more than okay; his attention made this cold and dreary place suddenly more bearable.

"Okay," he murmured. "Good."

His lips were soft and sweet against mine as he gathered the hem of my flannel nightshirt, sweeping the soft material up my legs. I arched my hips when he reached high enough with the cloth and he worked things up and over. I sat up and raised my arms, breaking the kiss just long enough for him to whisk the offending fabric separating us away.

I put my hands to his hips and slipped them beneath his tank top, pulling gently. He smiled distantly at me and lifted his arms as I'd done for him and let me take the material from his body. My gaze was drawn to the fresh pink scars among the old white marring his skin. My fingertips went to one, tracing it lightly, and Kyle shivered and shied away from my touch, laughing almost nervously.

"Feels funny," he told me.

"I came close to losing you," I said with a sad smile.

"I'm still right here, baby…" He touched my face, and I looked up at him from beneath my lashes. His touch became slightly more insistent, and I raised my chin. He let out a sigh and murmured, "God, you're so fucking beautiful."

I smiled then; I couldn't help it. There was nothing beautiful here, and I didn't feel it. This was close to how I had lived in the warehouses, but with a more persistent chill, no one to laugh with, or joke with.

He brought his mouth to mine again, moving over me, laying me back into the sheets.

His body was warm over mine, his hands gentle where he cradled my face between them, grazing my cheeks lightly with his thumbs as his mouth moved against mine, so soft, so sweet, so kind and gentle. He moved down my jaw, my chin, pressing a light kiss to the hollow of my throat and I sucked in a deep breath, arching lightly. His hand trailed lightly down my side and I giggled. He chuckled against my stomach, rolling his eyes up to look at me as I watched him down the length of my body, between the valley of my breasts.

He fixed me with his wickedly dark stare, his eyes twinkling with that mischievous glint I remembered so well – the one that said he knew he was under my skin and what he was going to do next? Well, I was going to like it.

I closed my eyes and tipped my head back, my breath falling from my lips in a rushing sigh as he went down on me, his mouth warm, his tongue like velvet against my pussy.

"Oh, God, *Kyle*…" My voice was throaty, appreciative, and I gripped the sheets at my hips and rocked them against his mouth. His arms went around my thighs, hands holding my hips, reminding me to be still as I let him work his unexpected magic on me.

He went slow, gentle, working me up at a sedate pace out of character for him. I ran fingers through his dark hair gently, and he moved his eyes up to look at me. I watched him, my own gaze heavy lidded with love and lust as he worshipped me with his mouth.

He brought me right up to the precipice but didn't let me go over. Instead, he stopped and climbed my body, pushing his black pajama bottoms out of his way and slipping into me with careful, measured consideration.

I gasped, my arms going around him as he started at a slow, steady pace. He wrapped his arms around me in return, holding himself up, gazing into my eyes from inches away, his expression unreadable. It was so unlike him, but everything I had thought I wanted… but now that my dreams were coming true, I realized I would give anything to have the old Lach back. For as strange as loving and being loved by a man such as Kyle Lachlan was, he was all I had left, was everything, and I was desperate not to lose *everything* again, even this way.

THE NEXT MORNING, I WOKE ALONE, AND I FELT MY FRAGILE HEART grow thinner and more fragile still. As fragile and insubstantial as a soap bubble. I stared at the ceiling and pressed a hand to my forehead, frustrated with myself for pouring my heart out to Kyle the night before only for him to be gone…

I didn't know what I had expected, really… it'd always been this way – three steps forward, two steps back. I just wasn't sure my heart could take any more of it.

Be careful what you wish for… I thought bitterly to myself. I mean, I *had* wanted *Lach* back.

"Sadie?"

I dropped my hand and turned my head, sitting up when I saw Kyle in the doorway to the bedroom we shared, a bowl in one hand and a steaming mug in the other.

"Yeah?" I asked.

"I brought you breakfast," he said, and I frowned slightly and pushed myself into a better sitting position. He came over and sat down on the edge of the mattress and handed me the bowl, setting the coffee on the bedside table.

"You didn't have to do all this," I said gently, feeling guilty for all the unfair thoughts from a moment before.

"Yeah," he said, tracing some of my hair back from my face. "Yeah, I did."

The oatmeal in the bowl warmed my hands, and I stared down into it for a moment before looking back up into Kyle's sincere dark eyes.

"I need to do better," he said.

"So do I," I said gently, and he huffed a laugh.

"No, no, you've been great," he said, and I bit my lips together and searched his face. He leaned forward and pressed his lips to my forehead and I closed my eyes, my body losing eighty percent of the tension it held.

"I'm just not *him*," he said, and I smiled sadly.

"I don't need you to be," I said gently. "I need you to be you. Especially for what's ahead. Right?"

His obsidian dark eyes roamed my face, and he took in a slow deep breath, exhaling it quickly before he asked, "I don't know, you tell me, Shady Brooks… what's ahead?"

"Revenge," I said quietly.

"Are you sure?" he asked.

"I'm sure," I said steadily, and he nodded, the glint in those dark eyes one that said Kyle Lachlan was galvanized. Diamond hard, wicked sharp, and ready.

"I'm going to ask you some shit, and I'm not going to tell you where I'm going with it but I need you to answer me without thinking, okay?"

I nodded slowly and took a bite of my oatmeal, smiling a bit. He'd tried. He really had, putting all the things I liked into it, just not nearly enough of any of it.

"Good?" he asked.

"Perfect," I said. "And I understand to all that other stuff."

"I mean it, Sadie. No trying to spare my feelings, no lying, no trying to sugarcoat or minimize anything. You got it?"

"You know me so well," I said and nodded. "I've got it."

"What was the worst thing to ever happen to you?" he asked.

I dropped my spoon with a clack against the side of my bowl, and suddenly couldn't look at him.

"Sadie…"

"I'm thinking," I said, and he sighed theatrically.

"See, I didn't think this would work." He put his hands on his knees and pushed up, standing, but before he could walk away from me, I blurted out the first thing that came to mind.

"Which one? There are two." He froze and looked down at me.

"Both," he said, going still. He sank down onto the side of the bed and I set the oatmeal aside and immediately regretted it for the shaking in my hands. I clutched them together until the knuckles mottled red and white, but it did nothing to stop the shaking in them. If anything, it only made things worse.

"You can talk to me," he murmured, and I nodded.

"First one, the not so bad one… I was in love with an addict for a while. His name was Simon…" I told him. I told him everything – about how I'd slept with his dealer so Simon could score. After Simon had begged me.

"Simon have a last name?" Kyle asked, and I shook my head.

"He's dead," I murmured. "Overdosed six months after I finally broke up with him."

"What about the dealer?" he asked.

I breathed in through my nose and out through my mouth slowly.

"They called him Turk. I think you and Roan would call him a low-level dealer. Last I heard, he was still dealing out of the tenderloin district of Indigo City."

"Okay." He nodded slowly. "Not sure what could be worse," he said, and I took a fortifying breath.

"As much as I didn't want to do anything with Turk…" I said. "I *did* consent… for Simon, to stop his pain to—"

"What did I say about sugarcoating and minimizing?" he demanded, rising to his feet again. "Don't make excuses for either one of those pieces of shit, Sadie… *fuck*." He raked a hand back through his hair and let out an explosive breath.

"I'm sorry," I murmured.

"Do I even want to know what's worse?" he asked, hands on his hips.

"Probably not, no… maybe it's best I keep that one to myself."

He shook his head. "Not how this particular game is played, baby girl."

"Then could you sit down?" I asked. "It's hard to talk about these types of things when you're looming like that."

"Yeah." He took a seat, and I hugged my knees. "I'm ready," he said, and I shook my head.

"No, you're not—"

"Sadie, just tell me."

"After Simon, I lost everything, and it was the first time I was homeless. I was twenty-three and…" I stopped, hating that I had to drag out old pain and heartache atop all that was fresh and new.

"Take your time," he said gently and perked up slightly.

"These two guys, they uh dragged me off the street into the abandoned YMCA and down into the bottom of the empty swimming pool." I swallowed hard and rubbed my lips together. "They took turns," I murmured and I couldn't bring myself to elaborate beyond that.

"You know who they are?" he asked.

I shook my head. "The cops never found them," I said.

He leaned back and sighed out, covering my shaking hands with his. I glanced up and his intense gaze snared mine.

"This Turk guy, you hate him?" he asked me. I nodded slowly. Not just for what happened to me, but also for what he did to Simon, to *us*. I most assuredly hated him. How many other Simon and Sadie's had his poison ruined?

"Enough to kill him?" he asked me, and I froze. I had to think about that.

I thought about it and he let me, but he'd captured my eyes with his so thoroughly that there was no breaking eye contact while I did.

I thought about Simon, I thought about me, and I thought about all the other nameless, faceless victims of the garbage Turk slung for them to inject into their veins. I knew, deep down, it didn't matter –

that as soon as Turk died there would be another to take his place to pedal whatever poison he'd had the occasion to broker to the desperate... but still...

"Yeah," I answered him, and I began to sweat, knowing that once I took this step, there would be no going back. "Yeah, absolutely," I said.

Kyle nodded and hooked a hand behind my head, pressing his lips against my forehead like he had earlier, only this time it didn't have the restorative power that it had before. No, it took him wrapping his arms around me tight and holding me close for a *while* for the tension to leave my body, and even then, I felt the stain would never come out of my soul.

What was I doing?

CHAPTER THREE

*L*achlan...

Our departure from the Wolf Creek bunker felt like walking into a new world. For six months we had lived a stark lifestyle, with the minimal offerings of the bunker, and our own company. There was internet and television, but there were no other people, no restaurants, nothing like that. There was a township that we had ventured to a handful of times, but paranoia made those trips few and far between. The people that owned and ran the shops didn't know us, but they knew the type. Hyper-survivalists and preppers were as common as cattle in Montana. They didn't have to know us. We showed up, bought a vehicle load of supplies, and left after paying cash.

The only real indulgence on those trips was stopping at the diner and having eggs and sausage that Sadie and I didn't have to cook.

Buttoning up the bunker and cleaning up after ourselves didn't take long. We hadn't made much of a mess, and there was little enough left to take care of. Our last trip into town was to replenish non-food consumables that we had used during our stay – toiletries, detergents, batteries, and the like. There was a list, and it even indicated which places in town carried the various required items.

As we drove from the bunker down to the rail station, I was hopeful that I would never see such a miserable place in my life again. I couldn't understand how people could live here deliberately. The island of civilization there was, was full of yeehaw and cheap beer, too much red meat, and guns. I knew I was shallow, but there was more to life than bloody red steaks, brown liquor, and collecting guns.

Riding on a train for three days to get back to Indigo City wasn't my ideal mode of travel, but it was cheap. Our cash on hand was limited, and I wanted to get boots back on our home turf before cracking into our more extensive resources.

The time on the train gave me the opportunity to call and message the people I needed to deal with. There was our gun guy, and our other gun guy, my tailor, that I hoped to God he knew my shoe measurements; sneakers were just fucking awful. Then there was the armorer, and our car guys. They had all been used to working with Roan, not me, but thankfully they *did* know me. All of this would have been a lot worse otherwise.

I was thankful that they were professional to the level of not asking about him. That was part of the job – you didn't ask about someone if they had gone missing. If they were missing, that meant that they were dead, and it was just a factor of the job.

Despite that professional courtesy, it was still awful. I could feel that space, the verbal space where they paused, knowing me, and knowing my partner handled everything, and that we'd been off the grid for half a year. They fucking knew.

I would spend what felt like *hours* sitting on my phone, talking through a headpiece. Sadie would occupy herself with books, or streaming things to watch on the Kindle tablet I'd gotten her. I could tell that the length of the trip wore on her. Hell, I felt that as well. Some of the conversations ran longer than I wanted, and part of me wanted to just yell at some of them to just fucking handle some of this shit on their own. There were nine million fucking questions, and even on things I liked, guns and cars, it *still* wore me thin.

How did he fucking do this?

How did he have the patience?

I guess Sadie saw that I was getting frustrated with some shit spit asshole over some bullshit renting a furnished house, so she changed seats and laid down next to me, her head in my lap. After a few minutes, my tone softened, and I was toying with a twist of her mahogany hair. I finished my last call for the day, a very eccentric person named Guy, and our final arrangements had been made to procure our body armor.

"Did you know this train has a dining car and a smoking car?" I asked my beauty.

"If the car is smoking, they should probably take it to the train shop," she said.

"It's a car with a bar and allows smoking," I said. "I don't smoke, but maybe a few drinks? Neither one of us has to drive, and there might be other passengers, or maybe none. Who knows, it's a train."

"Hello, 1850 called and they want their transportation back." She laughed and gave a stretch in my lap.

"I know planes are faster, and more convenient, but look at how much room we have in here, and privacy." I gestured to the door to our cabin. "It's no mile-high club or anything."

"Maybe there is a mile-long club?" She tapped the end of my nose.

"There will be if we make one." I gave her a kiss as she sat up. *Keep it light, keep it funny, and don't be intense.* That's what Roan would do, so that's what I was going to do. "Come on, let's put on the best clothes we've been wearing the last six months, and go find out what they pretend food is on a train; maybe have some cocktails."

"You know how to sweet talk a girl, don't 'cha Kyle?" She smiled.

Half an hour later, we were seated in the dining car, watching the nighttime scenery of the Great Plains roll by. She looked radiant in a tee shirt and jeans, and I wasn't half bad myself in my own ensemble of a button-up shirt and khakis. We were models for discount outlet shopping.

We had dinners that were on par with franchise microwave hot plate and cold beer dives. The drinks were slightly better, but only with an almost insulting upcharge. It wasn't that we couldn't afford it, but places were not far from charging extra to use a clean glass, or not spitting in the muddle. It was insulting.

I escorted my chardonnay-and-cheesecake-sated darling back to our cabin, and as soon as I closed the door, I pushed her against it, my lips on hers. I felt like I was pulling back on my own reins, not going too fast, too hard. I had to restrain myself.

"No, no," Sadie whispered. "Don't start pulling your punches, now."

"I don't want to force this," I said.

"I want you to," she breathed, twisting her hands into fists, clenching the front of my shirt. One of the buttons popped off; I heard it bounce off the floor and roll away.

"I want you," she said more urgently and pulled hard, popping more of the buttons off. She had a moment of hesitation, surprised by her own actions. She looked up at me, gauging my reaction, her bottom lip caught in her teeth. I smiled, and that was all she needed. She pulled one last time and the last buttons gave up. I could feel her breath against my skin as she pressed her face to my chest, raking her nails down my sides.

"You doing okay there?" I asked.

"Maybe," she said, and started undoing my pants. My cock was out of my pants and in her mouth before I was completely hard. I groaned. She was meeting me the way I had liked my escorts, already primed, champing at the bit. It didn't take long before I was fully erect, and she was doing things with her hands and mouth that I didn't think she knew about.

"That's a new trick, I like it," I said, my fingers in her hair. She went all the way down on me, and I forgot how to breathe. "And that trick too. *Oh my God.*"

"You like that?" she asked, gasping a bit.

"Where in the fuck did you learn that?" I asked.

"I've been bored and horny for the last six months; I've had time to think about it," she said, and went back to giving me the sort of head that I used to pay top dollar for. I closed my eyes and started moving my hips with her. The trick was to start slow, and gradually go faster, and deeper. With any other woman, I would have ended up with her head buried in my crotch, fucking her face, while she made the sloppy wet choking sounds that really got me going.

If this had been an escort, I would grab her hair and hold her down on my cock as I came, forcing her to swallow it. Some charged for that, some preferred that to the mess. Other times, I would release the escort and then just paint her face with my jizz, like an Andy Warhol painting. There was also just splitting the difference, the first shot or two in the mouth and then pulling out, the rest right in the middle of their expensive makeup. I could feel my balls getting tight, and it didn't help that part of that was her pulling on them, squeezing them.

I stepped back, and she followed as far as she could before I managed to escape her delightful mouth. "Easy, easy," I said, and pulled her back up to her feet. Then I had her tossed back on the cabin's bed. I had her jeans halfway off before she had a chance to unbutton them, and she was still trying to get them off of her foot when I spread her legs and went down on her.

This is *certainly* what Roan would have done, and it was a good way to let my balls loosen up. One day, I was going to have to let her suck me off completely, start to finish, but not tonight, not now. I parted her pussy's lips with my tongue and teased her clit until she was moaning with pleasure. She was wet before I went down on her, but by the time I came up from between her legs, she was a lake of desire.

It was probably the messiest kiss I had ever given, but it didn't matter. Her kiss was mingled with the taste of her pussy as I buried my cock in her. There was no going slow, I needed her too badly, and she wanted me, maybe even more than I wanted her.

"Fuck me, hard and harder," she whispered in my ear. "Make me scream."

If there was one thing that Roan wouldn't do, it was tell Sadie no. And I certainly wasn't in the habit of denying beautiful naked women the things they asked for. I held her by the ankles and fucked her like she owed me money.

She was on her knees on the bed, my hands holding her hips, hammering that pussy like I was mad at it, and then there was someone beating on the cabin door. I opened the door a crack. "Everything okay?" I asked.

"There have been some complaints," a woman in a smart uniform said. She tried to look into the room, over or under my shoulder and called out to Sadie, "Ma'am, are you okay?"

"Fuck off my honeymoon!" Sadie gave a terse shout, but at me she was grinning with a wink. The woman in uniform looked back to me and finally noticed that I was half concealed behind the door, and wasn't wearing any clothes. There was a flush of color in her cheeks and I gave her one of my tactical smiles, turned up to a high level. She took a step back and stammered an apology. I nodded politely and shut the door.

When I turned to face my love again, she hadn't waited, and I was struck for a moment. I watched as her hand danced between her thighs, her fingers moving quicker than I would have guessed.

I took her again, and the pause at the door let me go a little bit longer.

A soul-clenching force wrapped around the base of my cock, my balls drawing tight. I pulled out, and a second later, unloaded on her belly and breasts. Sadie gave a breathy laugh as she held up her hands to stop any errant spunk from getting her in the face. "Oh my God, I hope this train has a shower or something. Holy fuck."

"Yeah, they have a dressing car, there's a shower," I said, lowering myself to kiss her. She kissed me back and pulled me down onto her. The mess was squished between us.

"Now you need a shower too." She wrapped her legs around me.

"Oh, that's terrible," I said theatrically. I was able to get the angle right, and I was still stiff enough to slide inside her again. "Oh no, that's just terrible too." She gave a laugh, and we laid together for what seemed like the longest time that I had spent with her in entirely *too* long.

The shower facilities on the train were equal parts amazing and incredibly disappointing. For one, they were showers, on a train, so that was the pretty amazing part. On the other hand, they were small, and everything was depressingly plastic. The actual experience was purely functional – modestly hot water, a drain, soap, and just enough of each to get clean. We had a quick nightcap and then went back to our cabin.

We fucked again in the morning. There wasn't much in the way of foreplay, certainly no romance, and I wasn't sure what was going on, but when a lady grabs me by the cock and tells me to fuck her, who am I to deny her?

There was a nagging feeling about it, like there was something… *off*.

Part of me wanted to just hang it on the train ride being boring, part of it was maybe we had some breakthrough by simply getting out of the bunker, or maybe something was *wrong*. Now probably wasn't the time to try and figure it out. My answer had been the same for almost every problem I had run into, throughout my life. Advance. Attack. Action. Actions were always worth more than words.

I gave her what she wanted. I enjoyed giving it to her, and by every measure I could see, she enjoyed getting it. After the long drought of the bunker, this was fantastic. I wasn't my old self, not the Lach before she had come around. I fucked her like I had fucked the escorts, wringing orgasms and moans from her, but I didn't play my usual finishing moves. There was nothing that was a *display of dominance*, that's what Roan had called it. When I did degrading things to the escorts, the things that made my dick hard when I thought about them, that had been for me.

Not when it came to my Sadie, though.

I kissed her. I went down on her.

I think he would have approved. I wished to God that he was still here so I could have him unpack this mess for me, tell me what I was doing wrong, or right. I probably would have been an asshole about it, but would have followed what he said. He was smart, and somewhere between boot camp and my first trip to Iraq, I realized that the harder I wanted to fight someone, the more likely they were to be right.

If he were still here, we wouldn't have gone to the bunker. We would have gone somewhere nice and lived like tourist royalty in another country. Roan and I would have shared Sadie, and I had ideas

– things I had seen in videos, things I had paid escorts to do to each other. I liked those ideas, and then there was the stab of pain in my chest.

Revenge wouldn't bring Roan back, but putting some corpses in the ground would make me feel better.

I had the Escadrille dossier, and there was something like seventeen names on the list of people that we were going to send to Hell, postage due. At the top of that list was the frog general, and his inner circle. The rest were higher echelon members of the Cartel, the sort who handled data, were leaders, the ones who had contacts and connections. There was no point trying to go genocidal on the Cartel. There were thousands of members, from gun-toting thugs keeping the most destitute people in the world under their boot, harvesting poppies, to low-level dealers, couriers, and basic gun-toting thugs.

We were certainly going to take a chunk of them out as well, but once the rampage got rolling, I was expecting to see a lot of desertion in their ranks. A lot of rats were going to bail on that ship before we were done with it.

By the time we disembarked from the train at the DC terminal, I was glad to be free from the damned thing. The room had been plenty nice, but I was tired of everything being cheap, plastic, and barely meeting the basic requirements. I was tired of this fucking peasant shit.

Three hours after escaping the train, we were escorted through the front door of a rental house on Phoenician Boulevard. The house was everything that I had longed for over the last six months. Three stories, a baroque red front door, verandas, a hot tub, and a tankless water heater.

"Is that a dragon carved in the door?" Sadie asked as the rental agent left.

"Yeah, probably," I said. I took her hand, and we took a brief loop through the house, taking in the opulence of the place – stained-glass windows, a backyard greenhouse and solar, an elaborate and well-equipped kitchen. Made me wish I knew how to cook. The bathroom was the sort of thing I was really aching for. The floors were fitted river stone, and the shower stall itself was hewn from polished blocks of sandstone streaked with white and pink. He would have loved the textures and colors, the polished copper fittings, and there was even a bench that he could have used.

We took turns showering. It wasn't a lack of interest; it was more a deep and urgent need for a shower so hot and strong that it bordered on punishing.

When Sadie finished – *ladies first* – she was scalded like a lobster and had a contented smile on her face. "I ordered delivery," I said with a smile. "Fantastic place that does a killer veal marsala and an olive tapenade appetizer. A couple bottles of wine, and we can pretend like everything is okay." Her smile toned down slightly in its wattage and she gave me a kiss.

It felt like a Sadie kiss, not like the earlier kisses, not as urgent or demanding. Softer, more… I don't know.

I liked it, though. I didn't really know how to handle aggro Sadie. I *liked* aggro Sadie, but that was going to take some getting used to.

"The rest should start arriving tonight. There should be a few deliveries, some clothing, and some other special things."

"Special things?" she asked, arching one dark eyebrow.

"Guns, guns are the special thing," I said. My phone rang, and it startled the shit out of both of us.

"Hello?" It was a very polite young lady. She worked for the old man who made our body armor, reinforced vests, and other combat-tailored clothing.

"Yes, of course. That's excellent." I nodded to Sadie. The woman on the phone was going on about what we had purchased and how everything had just come together.

"Late is fine, nine will be perfect." I gestured that she was going on and on, and Sadie gave me an exasperated hand wave. Then the woman on the phone said something that hit me in the solar plexus like a police-issue battering ram.

"What?" I grabbed the back of a chair and sat down in it hard. "No, no, please repeat that."

I gripped the phone tight.

"I haven't, no." My heart had lurched to a halt. "We need to talk. In person."

She tried to tell me there was no need, that it wasn't important, but I cut her off.

"No, it's very fucking important, *please*." My voice cracked on the last word.

Sadie had gone very still, her eyes locked with mine, her face a mask of curiosity, her mouth poised to speak but waiting me out.

"Are you sure?" I asked, my empty hand clenched into a fist. Sadie's eyes glittered and I could tell she was on the cusp of saying something. I held up a finger and asked the woman on the phone, "Can we meet sooner?"

I tore my gaze from Sadie's and I ended the call. I stared at the phone but just held it in my hand, watching the screen go dark.

"Kyle? What is it?" Sadie asked, her eyes wide.

"That was Jocelyn, Reynaud's personal assistant." I tried to get more words out, but it seemed like the connection between my mind and my mouth had burned out. I took a moment and tried to force my thoughts into coherent words. "Reynaud made all of Roan's prosthetics."

"And?" Sadie asked, giving me a weird look. "Why would that come up?"

"She asked if he found his replacement acceptable." I let my breath out slowly. "Roan hasn't had a replacement made in five years, maybe six. They made a replacement for someone in the last few weeks."

"Prosthetics like Roan's need to be made to specification," she said, sitting up straighter. "They're made to fit the user. He told me that. Does what you're saying she said mean…?"

"It might, I don't fucking know how, but it might," I said. "Those things are *very* specifically made, like it's way more involved than a custom suit." She put her hand over her mouth and I saw something like fire light up in her eyes.

"We have to go," she said.

"We have to wait. She's going to come here with the stuff we ordered. When she gets here, she might bring the old man. We're going to find out everything we can," I said.

At five 'til nine, a large white SUV rolled into the driveway of the Phoenician Blvd house. Jocelyn pulled a large rolling luggage bag behind her, and the old man who followed her must have been Reynaud. I had never met him. Roan had handled all of this, and my first contact with any of them had been through the phone on the train.

I let them in, and we spent a good half hour going over the body armor, ranging from the actual vests and conventional armor, down to the discrete armor that can be hidden under regular clothing. The dragonscale required little demonstration, I was intimately familiar with it, and the old man knew. The vest and suit cut to fit Sadie did take a moment, because it had been made with something most people who wear dragonscale don't have; tits. His assistant was pleased with it, and I could see that she wasn't just a niece or personal assistant, she was his apprentice. When he retired, she would be the master armorer who held our accounts. She probably had made her set, the way the old man inspected her laying it out.

"I want to know about the prosthetic," I said, almost interrupting Jocelyn.

"Ah, yes. Mister Roan's prosthetic. I am still concerned about how he broke the last one I made him," the old man said. "It was titanium and carbon fiber; it should have been very damage resistant."

"Where did the new prosthetic go?" Sadie asked.

"Mont Saint Chauvignon," he said and smiled. "And the only reason I tell you this, is because I can see that you have changed, Mister Lachlan."

"Pardon?" I asked.

"We have met once or twice, I think. Definitely once." He gestured, and his assistant helped him to his feet. "And you struck me as very much a black heart."

"A black heart?" Sadie looked back and forth between me and the old man.

"Yes, a black heart – an evil man of violent disposition." He smiled at her as she shook her head in silent denial before turning his attention back to me. "But you have changed, sir. I see you, and I think that you may be more of a black knight. Yes," he nodded judiciously, "you are a black knight, and I have brought you your armor. I hope that you have someone to help you find a horse and a sword."

"We don't need either of those things," Sadie said softly, refusing to look at any of us. She glanced in my direction; her deep brown eyes wet with unshed tears. "We need our *shield*," she murmured, and I didn't say anything. What could I say? She was right.

CHAPTER FOUR

*S*adie...

I couldn't sleep.

I stared at the ceiling of the canopy bed, Kyle asleep beside me on his stomach, his back rising and falling gently in the dark. Typically, his deep and even breathing lulled me into a security enough to sleep. In fact, I *needed* him to sleep, as much as I hated myself for it. I couldn't fall asleep or stay asleep without him beside me... but now? Tonight? With the information that had just come to light? There was no sleeping.

I sighed softly and slipped out of the bed careful not to wake him. Padding barefoot in only Roan's shirt, I went out into the house, to the pile of bags out in the living room, to the black tactical backpack I had carried since leaving the *Rum Runner*.

I unzipped the narrow back pocket and slid the laptop I had liberated from the Daughton safehouse. It was set up so you didn't need do anything special to log in to it. Or, it had been... I'd put a lock on it when I figured it out. I had found things on it. Could watch old footage from the mansion on Bootlegger Head's security cameras. I had copies of the images from my past that Roan had put onto a flash drive for me... and the most precious thing about it? I had found Roan's email address.

I'd signed out of it; I didn't want to read anything. No, I created my own email address using the same service and I sent him things. I had been sending him things for the last six months. One, sometimes two emails a day depending on how I was feeling.

Lach didn't know about it. I kept it from him. I was worried that if he knew, he would be angry, would destroy the laptop and my last link to Conan and I couldn't bear the thought.

I was careful. As careful as I could be, and nothing bad had happened yet, so I didn't think it would.

I opened the laptop and took a deep breath as I connected to the house's Wi-Fi and waited for my email to come up.

Letting out a shuddering breath, my fingertips hovering over the keys, I let it out.

From: *lostpoppet@cryptomail.net*
To: *redroan@cryptomail.net*
Subject: *This can't be real...*
Message:
Dear Conan,

I've been writing you these messages for months, thinking they've been lost in the ether, and I guess they have been... except now I'm faced with the fact they won't stay that way. We don't know where you are. We don't even know if you're still alive, but I'm daring to hope. I'm so scared to dream, but the alternative is the yawning dark behind me. The pit of despair I've been living in since, well, since you died.

The only reason we even know you might still be on this earth is a complete fluke. Purely an accident, and I... I don't know. I don't know what I'm more scared of. That you were still here and now you're gone again and we might not know it, or that you're still here and that you might find these emails... read them... I didn't count on that. I'm not sure how I feel about it.

Scared, for sure. Not all of them have been kind, but they've always been what they are. Raw. Honest in the moment they were written.

Lach is asleep. I am trying to claw my way out of this void I've been living in, toward the light of possibility and I can't sleep. I'm trying to be strong. To be more like Lach, and it doesn't feel right. I'm trying to be strong in ways I've never contemplated before. I'm trying to adopt being more like Lachlan – not Kyle, but Lachlan, and I don't know how I'm doing or if I'm even close. All I know is the more I tread that path, the less like me I feel and it already feels like I'm drowning.

Where are you, Conan?

It doesn't matter, really. We'll find you. We're determined. We need you back. Wherever you are, dead or alive, we'll find you. We'll find you and bring you home or we'll die trying and if you're gone? That means that we'll join you. We love you. I know he might not ever say it, so I'll say it for him. You know how he is; you know how he does... well know how I am, and how I do. I won't rest. I won't let him rest. Not until we find you and bring you home. I realize now that home isn't a place. Real home is with the people you love. Just hold on a little longer. Trust us, believe us... we're going to bring you home.

Yours always,

Sadie.

I swallowed hard, hit *send* and closed the lid to the computer. I slipped it back into the pocket that it came from and made sure the charging cable was still in the bottom of the same pocket knowing if I lost *it*, I would lose my last link to him…

I closed my eyes and hugged myself, breathing carefully around the emotion swelling in my chest, pushing out my air.

I needed to go back to bed before Lach missed me.

CHAPTER FIVE

*R*oan...

There were a few things that I knew, and these things sustained me. I knew for a certainty that I was somewhere in France, most likely the south of the country. There was almost no commercial fast food, and everything was familiar. I imagined that other people might consider this incarceration intolerable, but the bread was exquisite, and there was wine at most meals they brought me. The first of many non-sequiturs came when the old woman who handled most of my food and care asked me, the prisoner, if I preferred white wine or red wine. Being the polite person I am, the answer was whatever she felt would best go with what she brought me.

I imagined myself like a white-collar criminal, an insider trader, or a corporate embezzler. I was doing hard time in the south of France, where stoic Frenchmen were feeding me the rustic foods that I tried to make myself. My French was improving, and for the most part, my treatment was well enough.

Cassoulet, Provencal roast chicken, brioche or baguette?

My captor wasn't following the line of interrogation and detention that I would have done were our roles reversed. I would have put myself in a black hole, used sleep deprivation, sound and music blasting, and lines of questioning involving disorientation, and dislocation. That wasn't even digging into the ugly underbelly of enhanced interrogation, where the pain-inflicting tools and waterboarding equipment is brought out. They had done almost none of these things.

They did some physical restraining, and there was some questioning along with body punches and face abuse. It was the easy sort of thing to get through. I had the training from my years with Her Majesty's Royal Marines. I had been taught what to expect if I had been caught by religious zealots and terrorists, and how to get through questioning techniques that were outright and evil torture.

They were softballing me, playing a long game and trying to befriend me. Good cop, good cop, and all of that.

The problem with that was that I knew I only had to wait. I knew without a doubt that Kyle was still alive, and if he was still alive, Sadie was too. In one of their more vigorous questioning sessions, I gave them a soft lead. They accessed the database I gave them the key to, and the key was rejected.

The database has a revolving encryption sequence, and it changes on a random trigger generator. If access is refused now, there is no way to access it, I had told them, and they went after the database. It had been at least a week since the house had been flattened when I told them, and they didn't know it had been a gambit. If Kyle and Sadie had gotten out and he had accessed the Recovery Drive like he should have, the key would be rejected. If he was dead and hadn't touched the drive, it would have been granted access.

It had also been the kill switch entry, and after granting access it would have dumped some very expensive custom-made viral weaponry into their system, and wiped the database they accessed. Interpol and other international police agencies didn't storm the keep, and the query was kicked back.

Kyle and Sadie had gotten away. They were safe.

And if they knew I was alive, these assholes were fucking doomed.

That was what carried me through the actual bad parts of this incarceration.

And those came from Gwendolyn Kaijin.

Certainly not the Escadrille lieutenant I expected to handle my detention. I had expected Ajahi, the big black guy to apply the brutal techniques that the African warlords had become infamous for – vicious animals, hot brands, and stinging insects. That would be hard to resist. The narrow-eyed Aryan would have been my second guess, but that was mostly because he struck me as the sort who dressed in Nazi regalia and engaged in sexual self-humiliation. That was the sort of person who could do abominable things to people, horrific things, and not lose a wink of sleep.

But I got Gwen.

I almost wished that I had one of the others. There was something just insidious about the blonde Asian woman with the cutting French accent. She liked to make me wait, which was why I was restrained on what amounted to a sex bench. It gave me time to think. There was nothing else to do when I was tied up like a literal rib roast, completely naked, staring at the ceiling.

"Allo, lover," she said, finally walking up to her play session. That's what it was, it wasn't torture, it wasn't questioning, there were almost never questions.

"Nice weather we're having today," I said politely.

"You are such a model prisoner, *oui?*" she asked.

"The longer we're here, the more artificial your accent sounds. Maybe you shouldn't force it so much," I suggested.

"Maybe you should remember to be polite. You are very vulnerable," she said, dropping the accent. She patted me between the legs, enough to make me draw up, but not enough to really hurt. "And this is how I like you, big man."

I sighed. There was no telling which way she was going to take her play today. She could be cruel and abusive, or she could be cold and strange; there was seldom any rhyme or reason to it. It hadn't escaped me that this wasn't entirely unlike what had happened months before when Lach carried Sadie into our house. It had been Gwendolyn who technically saved my life at the manse.

She was the one who figured out the warhead configuration and realized what it was. She had shouted orders, and after having shot me twice, she made sure that I was dragged to safety. We barely made it to cover before the timer ended and the Soviet fuel-air warhead leveled the property values on Bootlegger Head.

We had still been caught within the radius of the blast. The fire had roared over our heads, but the car we sheltered behind took the heat and force of the blast. Gwendolyn's hair had been burned away, and there were many burns, lacerations, and bruises from flying debris, and worse. We were thrown into an SUV, where I passed out.

Then it had been a boat, blurred impressions of an airplane, and needles in my arm, keeping me sedated.

There had been a hospital ward, or something that looked like one. There was some concern over my leg before they realized it was an old wound and a missing prosthetic. The first few sessions I had endured with Gwendolyn were what I had expected – questions, basic violence, some willpower eroding techniques, some humiliation techniques.

Then she saw me naked, and everything changed.

The next session involved blindfolds, some naked beatings, and then things took an unexpected turn. While blindfolded, she put some sort of tension bands around my manhood, and simple biology and hydraulics took over. She did things to me, and I don't know where all it went, but those places were hot and wet.

I hadn't been prepared for this. There was no training from the academy or advanced courses on how to deal with being tied up and molested by technically attractive women. I treated it like any other torture. Pleasure and pain were closely related, and I started putting the sensations she had generated in me in the same mental box I would have locked agony in. Controlled breathing, meditative techniques, recitation of lists and other minutia, so that when I finally came, it was less a sexual act and just the reaction of biological function.

I almost preferred it when she brought sadism and pain. She would have her minions wrestle me down and tie me to a whipping post, or some piece of sex furniture, and she would come after me with whips and lashes, or canes and paddles.

She took a perverse delight in this. Once she was sated with her violence, she would put the bands around me, and would have her way with me.

The things she did.

The things she fucking did.

I found solace knowing that Lach would eventually find me, and that they would all pay. It was easier when I had a croissant or cassoulet. It was harder when that sadistic bitch had something up my arse and was whipping me like a lunatic.

Or biting me until she drew blood. Her teeth were so bloody sharp.

I could put on a good show, keep that upper lip stiff and unyielding. I could also take some satisfaction knowing her hair was a wig, and that her vanity had been deeply gouged by that loss.

"You seem content today," she said. "You know that irritates me."

"Sorry, *lass*," I said.

"I think that we need to have an attitude adjustment." She checked the ties holding me down, and took a minute to give my cock some rough tugs and a few full hand slaps, certainly enough to hurt. As much I wanted to give her no satisfaction, the wee bastard had its own will. "Do you remember that last session we had?"

"How could I forget, visiting the Louvre and then the boulangerie afterward with that hot bread and the brie?" I said in a mocking tone.

"Always the comedian." She pulled out a blindfold. I gave a theatrical sigh. "Just like in my last visit, when you came so quickly, I might have thought you some eager teenage boy."

"Sorry, I was thinking about someone else," I admitted. I had closed my eyes and imagined Sadie in her place, and rather than keep that control, I let everything go. Princess Kaijin didn't even have a chance to settle into a good rhythm riding me before I was trying to go soft.

She tugged the blindfold tight and gave me a few open-handed hard slaps to the face. This was her foreplay. "So here are the rules for this game." I heard the soft metal on metal sound of a safety being clicked off and the slide of a pistol being racked back. "This is a

Walther PPK, with a platinum finish. It is a very pretty gun, and I think a man of your worldliness and attention to detail would understand what it could do."

I felt the cold barrel of the gun pressed against my forehead.

"I'm going to have my way with you, and if you come, I'm going to blow your brains out."

"Shoot me in the head and you'll not get anything from me," I said, my teeth gritted.

"What makes you think you are anything more than my plaything?" she asked. There was a tugging sensation and then I could feel the tension band snugged around the base of my cock.

"I was under the impression that I was a prisoner of the Escadrille," I said. "And this was some sort of strange *Fifty Shades of Interrogation*." Her laugh was haughty and sharp.

"You great stupid English-American. You, belong…" I felt her teeth biting down onto the head of my cock and I hissed between my teeth. "To me," she finished. "You are mine to do with what I want. The Escadrille doesn't give a *fuck* about you. Chauvignon doesn't care about you at all. The only reason you are still alive is because of how much *cock* you've got between your legs." She worked me roughly, using strokes and a hard grip to emphasize her words.

"Do your worst, you bloody whore," I growled at her.

"Oh, I'm going to. Do you know what the great sport of the world is, Mister Roan?"

"Football," I said. I could feel her straddling me.

"Killing Englishmen," she said and slowly impaled herself on me. "I fully intend on killing you, Englishman. Maybe today, maybe tomorrow, I haven't decided." The entire time the weight of the pistol against my forehead didn't change.

"You'll get yours," I said. I was digging down into my bag of tricks – meditation techniques, controlled breathing, flexing the muscles of my thighs and keeping my stomach as relaxed as possible. If I could short circuit the blood flow through my groin, I might be able to lose my erection. That was close to impossible with the tension band wrapped around my tackle.

This seemed to excite Kaijin, and she rode me hard, quick, and then she would stop and just roll her hips and clench. She was sopping wet, and it didn't take long for her to start a series of orgasms. Each time she came, she would let out these loud, dramatic screams, and then there would be claws in my chest, or she would move the pistol long enough to slap the hell out of me again and again.

My control was starting to falter.

When she leaned forward onto my chest, and my cock finally slipped out of her, my relief was audible. If she had kept at that slow grind much longer, I was going to lose it. My muscles burned from stress, from the way I was tied, and how many times I had struggled against the bonds. The worst part was that I could feel my heartbeat pulsing through my member, and could only imagine how enlarged it must look, the blood flow constricted as it was.

I gasped when something else wrapped around me, something softer. It was her lips.

She started sucking me off, and her hand worked my balls over. I bit the inside of my mouth until I tasted blood and tried to focus entirely on that very specific bit of pain. "Please, no," I hissed out in a strained whisper. I didn't know if I was talking to her, or telling myself.

I came.

It seemed like my balls wouldn't drain until the pulses subsided.

There was no gunshot, but if she shot me in the head, would I even know it? Would I have time to register the sound of the gun before the bullet ended me? The tension band came off me and she tapped me between the eyes with the barrel of the pistol and gave a laugh.

"If you could only see your face, right now." She undid the blindfold and tossed it on the ground. The light was painfully bright for a moment, and then my eyes were able to adjust. She stood over me, and I could see my spunk on her neck and down into her cleavage. "Don't worry, I recorded it, so I can watch it later. I'll make sure you have the option to watch it."

Then I saw the gun. It wasn't a platinum-chrome-finished Walther; it was just a pencil flashlight. I surged against my bonds and this just amused her again. She didn't say anything, but she took my cock in her hand and slapped it. The pain jolted through my oversensitive member, through my body, and then into the crown of my head. Several more strikes had me howling in agony, and she laughed with sadistic glee.

"You get to live another day, Englishman."

CHAPTER SIX

*L*achlan...

The information about Roan changed everything. I'd initially planned on a shorter revenge run, a trial by fire in a more controlled environment to get Sadie's feet wet and used to the notion of pulling the trigger. There was no time for that now.

"So, here's the plan. First thing, fuck Turk, we're not wasting time going after him," I said, wishing that I had some sort of map, or chart, or one of the glowing floating screens they used in the techno-action movies. "The woman with the old guy said that they shipped the prosthetic to Mont Saint Chauvignon, in Languedoc, France."

"It's not a very well-hidden place. I mean, the guy's name is literally on the map," Sadie said.

"He's French. There's nothing bigger than his ego. But yes, the place isn't hidden. I wikied this place and they've lived there for a few hundred fucking years, so this is like the ancestral home of these guys, or ancestral summer home. From what Roan had on the Escadrille file, their full-scale base of operations is somewhere in Afghanistan or Pakistan. Lawless, poppy fields, machine guns cheaper than chickens, but we aren't going there."

"The two of us couldn't go after some crazy heroin terrorist base, not even if we had Roan." She looked frustrated. "I mean that part of the world is still at war. Even living in a warehouse with no electricity I know that."

"And that's why we aren't going to worry about it," I said. "I can make a few phone calls, wire some money and within twenty-four hours I can have a military bombing raid dropped on their heads. We might have to deal with that later, but right now, I only care about getting Roan back." She nodded firmly.

"So, pack your clothes, and let's see which passports will get us into France with the least amount of attention, and maybe make sure you pack a bathing suit." I gave her a smile.

"What in the hell will I need that for?" she asked, sounding a little hot.

"Easy. After we spring Roan from the frog house, we are striking distance from the French Riviera, and even if we need to make a quick escape, it is a densely touristed area, so flashy cars don't stand out, there are tons of witnesses, and that sorta thing. They can't swing heavy without drawing the French police and maybe even the army down on themselves," I said.

"So, your plan is to go in, guns out, rescue Roan, and then drive to the French Riviera?" Her expression made it look like she didn't fully believe this plan.

"I'm more action than planning, so I'm doing the best I can," I admitted. "And *I* will be the one going in, you'll be hanging back, staying safe."

"He's as important to me, as he is to you," she argued.

"You're right, but look, if I let anything happen to you, he would never forgive me."

"And if something happens to *you*, I'll never forgive you either." She was smolderingly defiant.

"Nothing is going to happen to me," I said.

"Did you forget the house exploding half a year ago, having a black-market doc pull bullets out of you, or me tending to your stitches while we were buried under a ton of snow and misery?" There was a flash of anger in her voice.

"No, I didn't forget any of those things. When we rescue Roan, it's not going to be me going in alone. I have some people I know, professional contacts." I made a peace-making gesture.

"I'm a little low on trust," Sadie said and looked unhappy about it.

"Then give me all you've got, baby. I promise, I'm not going to let you down."

We stared at each other, a long moment of silence stretching between us, but she finally nodded.

We packed our bags, and took two ride shares and a train to get to BWI, and then first-class accommodations to cross the ocean. Sadie was tense, and it was taking all of my composure to keep cool. I didn't have a ghost in my ear telling me what to do and keeping an eye out for me. We had to fly legit, so there were no weapons in my bags, none on my person, and nothing in the checked bag. She complained the entire time – getting back on a train, worry about getting on another plane, and that was fine.

One of the things that we said in the military was that as long as the men were complaining, everything was fine. It was when they stopped bitching that there was a real problem. I let her vent and gave some of mine as well. The first-class seats we had on the Air France Airbus A380 were almost as spacious as the suite we had shared on the train crossing the country.

Once we were in the air, and Sadie had her first Moscow Mule, a lot of the tension went out of her. We were flying with a sense of purpose that was greater than just surviving. There were more mules for Sadie, and she alternated between playing on her phone or the laptop I hadn't known she had until it came out at security. I didn't care that she had it. I worried vaguely about why she had kept it from me, though. The rest of the time she spent watching the in-flight movie options and sitting and staring out the window. It wasn't scenery, there were only scattered clouds and the seemingly endless Atlantic Ocean.

I could sometimes make out something of her reflection. There were quiet tears in her eyes, and I think she was keeping them to herself. He would know how to reach out to her, to sooth her hurts and calm her heart. I used to… but it didn't feel like I knew how anymore.

I sighed to myself and went back to my work. I had conversational French playing in my earbud. I wanted it to be fresh and sharp for working in France. Then there was the matter of finding guys on the ground in France that I could get to Languedoc, and that I could trust. That second thing? That was the sticking point.

The list kept getting shorter and shorter, and I was starting to run out of options.

Shit.

We landed without incident, after a nearly eleven-hour flight, at Paris Charles de Gaulle Airport. It was dark, and travel weariness was already hanging over both of us. The layover was short, only a few hours, before we had our final connecting flight, taking us south to Montpellier. I had arranged to pick up a car there, so we were ready on that end. There was a house lined up too. It should be a safe place to rest and rally.

When this was all said and done, and we had Roan back, we would have to come back to Paris. Sadie would like to see *some* of the city, the bright parts. Most of my experience had been on the not-Eiffel tower side, where instead of bistros and bakeries on every corner, it was packs of feral dogs, homeless people, and vestiges of nationalist groups getting hostile with migrant fringe communities.

"Um, hello, hi." We were approached by a younger looking man – dyed black hair, lip piercing, tattoos up both arms, and some goofy-looking pair of smart glasses. Those would likely have camera and microphone options, and Wi-Fi connection.

Roan had wanted me to try them and I told him that there was no goddamn way.

"Sorry, no," I said.

"Kyle, Kyle Lachlan, I know who you are." He spoke quickly, nervously. "Sadie Brooks, I know you too. I need to talk to you both and its super important."

"I don't know," I said, keeping my tone even and calm, "who you think we are."

"Oh my God, you don't know me, but I know you. I know Roan. I know why you're here." His words came as fast as the disclaimer at the end of a car commercial.

"Who are you?" Sadie asked.

"My name is Grant, but Roan knows me as DJ Raditz." He gave a very large, very nervous smile.

"How about you calm down and stop acting like a terrified tourist? Let's go have a seat at the café and you say what you need to say without making the guards nervous." He nodded in agreement. We ducked into one of the airport cafes and ordered a polite imitation of breakfast.

"First of all, I'd like to thank you for not shooting me or kicking my ass," he said. I gave him a nod of agreement. "Your reputation is fierce dude, it's fierce."

"So how does Roan know you?" I asked pointedly.

"Yes, that *is* super important. So here it is – we met doing guild raids, we were both in a guild of guys who were all in tech and you know. He was a great controller and knew how to exploit DPS, but didn't have the right macros set, so we start trading macro settings and build—"

"English please," Sadie said, looking a little annoyed.

"I'm sorry, we both played the same MMO, and we started trading game stuff, and then real-world tech stuff. I helped RedRoan set up CryptoMail, and the CryptoCoin index, you know, the place where almost all of your money actually is." He picked up a cup of coffee.

"Okay, that works," I said. "You sure you need any more caffeine?"

"I always need more caffeine," he said, and there was no doubting the New York in his accent. "But you guys are about to drive into a massive ambush, and get all killed and stuff, and if RedRoan is alive, I can't like, let you Leroy Jenkins it."

"How do you know any of this?" Sadie asked.

"You've been using RedRoan's laptop," he said, pointing at it. "As soon as you got off of the CryptoMail server, wherever you were, and tapped into an open ISP, I was able to find you."

"Why were you looking for us?" she asked.

"I wasn't looking for you, I was looking for him. We had ongoing business, some game stuff, and stuff like that, you know. I could tell you specifics but if you blanked on basic MMO stuff, this would just zoom right over your heads." He took a breath. "So, I knew where you were going, which is how I was able to get a flight here, to meet you. Before—"

"Alright, I believe you," I said. "So, you know he's here, and what are you wanting to do?"

"Help you rescue my guild master," he said. "And you know, get to meet you. He's talked about you."

"How about we pick up my rental car, and we carry on this conversation on the road?" I said. Everyone agreed. It didn't take long before we were packed into a Mercedes AMG sedan and blowing down the French A9 toward Nimes. We would cut over to the A7, then southeast to Aix-en-Provence, where we were staying. The rural estate of Mont Saint Chauvignon was not far from there. It was all very pastoral and beautiful.

"I should tell you that your gun guy here works for Escadrille," Grant said. "If you show up, he'll either try to nerf you, or will totally alert the baddies you're here."

"So, no guns?" Sadie asked.

"I got a guy," he said. "Plus he owes me."

"Is he local?" I asked. Grant leaned forward and threw a new address into the sat nav that took us to Marseille, in what looked to be an ethnic enclave.

"Is that close enough?"

After half an hour of strolling through the open-air market of Noallies, we found the place Grant was taking us. I was hesitant since we had to walk almost a mile from where the car was left parked because the streets were narrow and heavily congested with pedestrians. In some places, the vendors and bistros spilled out of their confines and people were being seated in the street. There was even a number of men with food carts set up in the middle of the road. It was nothing like Indigo City, or New York, or even Paris. The people here were not the typical Frenchmen I had expected.

Africa was close and I could see the faces of people who were black, but not in the way that I knew them. Grant told us in passing that Marseille was the tolerant and immigrant friendly port of France, and that these were the people of the Maghreb, North Africa. I felt decidedly out of my comfort zone – the scent of spices was strong, I barely understood what was being said around me, and it was all very strange.

Roan wouldn't like it here. I was starting to get a vibe from the place that reminded me of Kandahar, or *Mazar-i-Sherif*, the babble of voices, how close everyone got to each other. It keenly reminded me of how much space Americans enjoy, and how distant our normal culture was. Sadie seemed to be a rock in the surf, the wave of noise and smells rolling over her, and she carried on a constant conversation with Grant.

"I've been here a dozen times, Barcelona, Ibiza, a bunch of other places," he said as he directed us to an outdoor café that had exploded from its original boundaries and filled the front section of what had been handicapped parking. There were no cars, so no one cared. We seated ourselves. Grant ordered something for us, speaking in a clipped version of whatever French-tinged language they were speaking.

I don't think I could have felt any more like an awkward tourist even if I was wearing a Hawaiian shirt, camera around my neck, and a fanny pack.

The food was strange, but the waiter was surprisingly nice, especially after it seemed, he recognized Grant. We had some sort of weird hot-spiced tea beverage, and similar vaguely familiar food. There was flatbread, hummus, and the familiar taste of cumin in the spice mix, and some heat.

"Who are you, man?" I asked as we waited for our contact. "And why are we here, specifically?"

"My day job is deejaying. DJ Raditz, I thought that was kinda obvs," he said. "And we're here because this is where we're going to meet my guy who has the stuff we need."

"In a street café, in the street," I said.

"Relax, just a little," Sadie said, putting a hand on my arm. "You're really putting off a tense vibe."

"Dude, I'm a deejay. I travel all over the East coast of the US, and lots of southern Europe. I do music festivals, play dubstep and EDM I generate on my computers, and they pay me lots of money to do it. In my spare time, I play video games and do computer shit. My guy's brother, that's our waiter. He's gone to tell him we're here. I think he's a cook here."

"Your guy is a cook."

"During the day, he likes to cook, and the shit is good. You should give it a chance," Grant said.

"Oh my God, this is fucking delicious," Sadie said, tearing into what looked like a ball of bread that was stuffed with heavily spiced meat and sauce. "I think Roan would like this."

"Maybe," I relented. I deliberately checked my body language, relaxing my shoulders and letting my hands go loose. I was on edge and didn't like it.

"There you go, my dude," Grant said. We ate, me sparingly, and Sadie sampled almost anything she could get her hands on. The waiter noticed her enthusiasm and how quickly the American woman had embraced their food culture, and brought her all sorts of small bites from the kitchen. Then the cook, a thick-armed, barrel-chested man, came out. He was carrying a platter of what looked like sliced bread. He placed the tray in the middle of the table. He shook Grant's hand, his left hand placed against his own chest. Grant mirrored the greeting, matching his left hand against his chest.

"Kyle, this is Adnan, head chef here, and he formerly worked in the imports and acquisition business." He turned and spoke in what I finally realized was Arabic, and introduced both of us to the man. He seemed the most pleased to meet Sadie and expressed a great deal of enthusiasm for meeting the lovely American woman who had been so excited to try his food. It was a mess to follow because Adnan didn't speak English or French, so Grant was running translation between us. It seemed that the delay was because he wanted to share his favorite dessert with Sadie – some cookie thing that looked like bread and was spiced with anise, oranges, and honey. She tasted it and urged me to try some. I did, and I liked it.

He was less impressed with me, and apparently there was something of a trust issue to be worked out. He had fought before. He had the cautious and wary eyes of a man who had seen combat, and then the café made sense. He fought, he smuggled weapons, and then he turned enough profit to go legit and get out of the business.

"Yeah, I told him that you were ex-military, and were freelance," Grant said. "He wants to know where you served and what branch."

"Why does that matter?" I asked.

"Because if he doesn't like your answer, we leave," he said.

"Honestly, mostly Afghanistan. Some Iraq, that's it. And army." Grant shared this with Adnan in Arabic.

"He asks, no Air Force, no North Africa? No Saudi Arabia?" I looked at the man and shook my head no.

"Tell him I didn't use airplanes or missiles to fight," I said. Grant relayed this, and Adnan smiled. There was another exchange in Arabic and Grant nodded.

"I'll cover the cost for now," Grant said. "What do you need to get my guild master back?"

"Right here?" Sadie asked.

"Sure, no one here cares," Grant said.

"Pistols, preferably Berettas, semi-auto or auto, 9mm or .45, plenty of ammo for both, armor-piercing or rhino rounds. Automatic rifle, I don't care what kind so long as it isn't trash, plenty of ammo for it too. Two automatic rifles." I looked over at Sadie and the only thing that would make Roan angrier than me dragging her into a firefight was to do it unarmed.

"That's all?" Grant asked.

"What, I don't need RPGs or a gunship," I said, but I did really want a gunship; even if it was a shitty Soviet surplus Hind helicopter. Grant relayed what I said to Adnan, who was apparently pleased by my request, though Grant seemed less pleased by his response.

"We can pick what we need up this afternoon. We can come back after *Salat Maghrib,* and it will be waiting for us." He gave me a look. "It seems like it was kind of pricey."

"So, what is Salad McRib?" I asked.

"Evening prayer," Grant said. "And show a little respect. They've been very nice to us considering its really obvious we're Americans."

"What does that mean?" Sadie asked, picking up another cookie and smiling at Adnan.

"Our government bombs their countries as a hobby," Grant said. "They take it a little personal."

"Oh," she said. "I didn't think about that."

THAT EVENING, WE PICKED UP A NON-DESCRIPT PILE OF BOXES, ALL marked food donations and cooking supplies. We carried the boxes to the car which thankfully we had found a way to move closer. With the afternoon open, we had indulged in some recreational shopping, which Sadie enjoyed, Grant curated, and I paid for.

The rental house in Aix-en-Provence was a historic home, several hundred years old, or something like that, and there was a vast amount of history tied to it, including ancestral ties to Avignon and Mont Saint Chauvignon. We settled in and started the process of deciding who slept where, who had first crack at the showers, and going through the produce boxes of weapons.

"Fucking AK-47s," I said, picking one of the guns up. This was some bullshit. I was a professional, and I didn't use the official firearm of terrorism.

"What did you expect, dude?" Grant asked, looking at the other guns in the crate. There were more AKs, and several Russian pistols and a few black-market looking, more mundane guns.

"I didn't expect flea market firearms, and you said these were expensive?"

"Yeah, a little bit." Grant glared at me.

"I guess this will have to work." I started stripping down the rifle to make sure it worked.

"You're in France, dude, they aren't really keen on guns here. It's not yee yee, like back home."

"Fuck," I growled. "And after this, I have to go into this job blind, and with no backup."

"Nah, my dude, I'll have you from above," Grant said. He pulled the largest of his bags into the spacious living room of the house and opened it. Inside he had a large quadrotor drone, and the gear to go with it, including cameras, and a pair of headsets. "I was working on this for Roan – all sorts of smart systems, adaptive flight – it can almost fly itself. The headsets let you pull the eyepiece down to see what the drone is seeing even without a monitor. You could fly this thing by yourself and have it following you around and only control it when you need it to move."

"Well, that's more goddamn like it." I looked at the pile of carbon fiber and silvery metal struts. He continued setting the thing up, but decided he needed some music to work, and started playing what he called vapor wave, or something like that.

Sadie finished her shower, and I went next. The music and the addition of a third wheel took out the option of spending some quality time with her, so I opted to go over the garbage rifles we had purchased, as well as getting her set up with one of the pistols so she could have some mode of self-defense.

There was little sleep that evening.

Nerves were frayed, the difference in time zones had us all jet-lagged, and the sudden influx of spicy North African foods into our soft American bellies was not without minor incident.

The sun rose without us, and it was nearly noon local time before we woke. The sleep, late coming, had been needed. Sadie set to making us coffee, while Grant showed his chops with a computer. In a few minutes, he was laying out maps of the Chauvignon estate, the roads, the approaches, where shelter was, and more. The place was enormous, and there were a large number of out buildings, and houses besides the main estate, which was a miniature fortress unto itself, with a stone tower and curtain walls.

I was not equipped to deal with that.

"We use the drone, and scout it from the air," Grant said. "I've got IR on this, so we can see where people are, and more importantly, the places they actually use. Old buildings like those, they only worry about keeping the parts they use comfortable. A few months ago, when it was cold as shit, this would have been a walk in the park."

Scouting the Mont Saint Chauvignon grounds took the better part of two agonizing days. The worst parts were when we had to bring the drone back in and wait for the battery pack to recharge. But it was worth it. Between the drone and Grant's computer wizardry, he built us a map of the grounds, and using night flyovers, he picked out what buildings were occupied and which were just there, and how well guarded the place was.

Another point in our favor, there was almost no security, but there were a large number of people present. Mont Saint Chauvignon was an active vineyard, and they made wine on the grounds. There were also a number of horses, and some other livestock that seemed more recreational than being raised for meat. The place reminded me of the parts of *Beauty and the Beast* I vaguely paid attention to.

We laid out a plan. There were three potential buildings that had constant heat signatures that were human. The easiest to get to was attached to the main house, but it looked like a recent addition. The others were an apartment attached to the stables, and then there was an old stone building that Grant said had been a jail from when the keep was a local seat of government. And then he mentioned a bunch of stuff about French monarchies and musketeers.

"We should check the old jail building first," Sadie suggested.

"Why?" Grant asked.

"If it was a jail, it should already have bars and cells, right?" I nodded in agreement. "And Roan is a wizard. That means they won't let him anywhere near electronics or internet stuff."

"That's true," Grant said.

"And why in the hell would they be doing anything in a place that inconvenient to the main estate? Look at how far from the main building it is. That's where I would keep him. Away from other people, away from modern tech, and in a place with bars and stuff."

"I think that's the first place we should check," I agreed.

"So just the three of us are going to break into this place and get Roan out?" Sadie asked.

"No. I'm going in alone. I won't put you in harm's way and I don't think deejay skills are useful in a break out attempt. I want you guys to work the drone for me and be my air support." They both nodded.

"That works for me. I'm not a fighter. Well, I am in the MMO, but that's not real and I'm not a dragon man either," Grant said.

"Oh, I know who you are," Sadie said, perking up. "You play that gold lizard guy with the giant sword." He nodded and looked confusedly at her. "I watched Roan play some, too complicated for me to keep up with, since you guys are all super good at it."

"It's just a game," I said.

"This is going to go just like a game too," Grant said. "You're going to be my Player One, and I'll guide you through this like it's any other dungeon raid."

"Like hell, mate."

"I'll use the headset," Sadie offered. "And he can fly the drone?"

"That works," I said. "What works better for you, daylight or night?"

"Night, because all of the employees will go home," Grant suggested.

"Good plan," I nodded. "Let's walk through it first, and if we have time, see if we can find any of their security systems."

"They have a basic electronic system on the main house, cameras at the front gate, and three points around the main house," Grant said. "Here, here, and here. I can get you around them by following this hedgerow. You cut under it here behind the stables. From there it should be a covered approach down to the stone jail.

"Perfect. I run into trouble, you spot for me, and I handle it." I left unsaid that if something went wrong, they should leave. Hopefully, they would have that level of common sense.

"Can you hear me?" Sadie asked.

"Copy that," I said, checking the bolt of the AK. What a piece of crap, and not for the first time, I missed all of my guns. An AK and a cheaply made Makarov were no replacement for even the cheapest and worst of my old firearms. I had to work with what I had, though. I could hear a distant murmur of words and knew they were talking; we didn't have the time or patience to do any practice runs with the drone, and her running comms.

I hoped I wasn't relying too heavily on how good I thought I was. I hadn't been rolling into any action in over half a year, and the last time I hadn't fared all that great. But this was different, thank God, this was going to be different.

"It looks like you can go that way, toward the tree," Sadie spoke in my ear.

"That way isn't a direction," I said softly.

"Yes, it is." She was curt.

"Left or right, north or south, nine o'clock, three o'clock, those are directions," I almost hissed.

"Fine, go left. No! The other left."

"I only have one left," I said.

"My left, not your left," she huffed.

"Put Grant on the line," I said and then I waited. Ahead I could hear the rustle of leaves, and the crunch of someone walking not ten yards from my position.

"I need better direction." I was calm, the lull before a storm.

"Do you have any guild raid experience?" he asked. "Run any FPS?"

"Definite no to the first, I don't recognize the second."

"First-person shooter games where you play what you're doing right now." He sounded annoyed.

"Yeah, you can safely assume the answer to any video game question is no," I whispered. There was someone approaching my position.

"Horse, eleven o'clock, three meters," Grant said.

"A horse?"

"Yes, big four-legged animal, suitable for riding on. You know what those are?"

"A comedian," I said and looked where he indicated, and there was a large gray horse who had wandered over to where I was. It had large eyes and seemed to be inspecting me. It came closer and gave me a large sniff, and I seemed to pass whatever test that was. It moved on.

"How do you feel about walking cover?" Grant asked.

"You want me to follow the horse?" I asked.

"No, I think we can *Metal Gear* this situation. There are at least a dozen horses, and it looks like your buddy there is wearing a halter. He's been turned out, so if you grab him by the halter, you can lead him where you want." Grant seemed pleased with this.

"How do you know about horses?"

"Mounts are a part of the MMOs, dude. I raised and bred them in one of the realms I play in. I sold an epic mount for a few hundred dollars last month."

"You *bred* a horse in a *video game* and sold it for real money?" I asked.

"Yeah, I did, so grab the nose band of the halter in your left hand and walk in a leftward sweeping arc. There should be an outbuilding to your left, and a fence to your right," he said.

"I've got it." I took the noseband of the horse and it seemed to be okay with this. "You seem alright," I said to the horse.

"Thirty meters, you're going to make a left-handed turn," Grant said. I could hear the whirr of the drone as it passed over me. "There is an open barn on the left, then a flagstone path, and what looks like an orchard to your right."

"Got it," I whispered.

"There are two heat sigs in the barn. You should be fine though."

"Thanks."

I wished I had more gear, something more than the bulletproof vest and AK. I could have done so much more with a set of night vision goggles, my actual combat armor, and a real rifle with a scope. I could have rained death down on them from afar, like a gunship but with much better hair.

We kept trading information – Grant throwing out distances in meters, where important things were, picking out potential ambushes, spotting cover, and using his drone to make sure that I never ran into anything unexpected. It was a tense fifteen minutes, moving through green fields, and through collections of old stone buildings and new wooden ones.

I felt a little tug when I turned the big horse loose. I kind of liked him.

Then I could see what I was looking for. The old jailhouse was a long low building made from age-worn stones. As I approached, I could makc out the black iron bars set in the narrow windows. If those walls were thick enough, a few men could hold it against a much larger force, provided they didn't have any explosives.

"Can you give me a read inside?" I asked.

"Three heat sigs, but the sigs are blurry. The walls are thick and I'm getting the readings through the roof."

"I'm taking the north entrance," I said.

"Bird in motion, you're clear."

I shouldered the AK and broke from the meager cover I had and made a line for the north door. It was a heavy thing of pale wood and banded with black metal, and it was open. There were two people standing in the center aisle of the building, one facing me, the other distracted by his phone.

I trembled to squeeze the trigger, spray them both with bullets and find the third sig. That should be Roan. The person facing me went pale. The tray they were holding fell from their hands and clattered against the stone floor.

It was a woman and she spat out a river of panicky French. She was unarmed, and the other person with her looked up from his phone. "*Merde,*" he said softly.

"Hands on your head, don't make a sound," I said, brandishing the AK at them.

"*Eloise, faites ce qu'il te dit, mettez vos mains sur votre tête. Il ne te fera pas de mal si tu n'es pas armé.*" I knew that voice, and a tremor ran through my arm. The woman looked to the cell she was standing in front of. She put her hands on her head, obvious fear written on her face. The younger man with her hesitated, he was also unarmed. I saw it in his eyes, he was going to bolt.

I was faster and put a burst from the rifle into his legs.

He gave a scream and collapsed.

"About time, mate," Roan said as I walked up to the door of the cell. "*Cles,*

S'il vous plaît." The woman moved hesitantly, but pulled the keys from a chain around her waist, and opened the cell. Roan was standing and stepped out.

I don't know who was more surprised, him or me, when I hugged him.

"C'mon, not in front of the help," he said. I could feel knots in my chest. Someone else was speaking in my ear, but at that moment, I didn't fucking care.

"I'm sorry it took so long."

"Kyle? Is it him, is he there!" Her voice was quivering and shrill. "Do you have him?"

"Hang on, Shady," I said. I dug into my pocket and pulled out a second earbud. I gave it a squeeze, and then the small red light blinked on. I handed it to Roan and then passed him the folding stock AK I had slung over my back.

"I hope I remember how to dance." He gave a laugh, popped the bud in his ear, and racked the AK.

CHAPTER SEVEN

*R*oan...

"Merci pour votre gentillesse et le pain, restez ici et vous vous serez en securite," I said, giving Eloise a polite nod of the head. She nodded in wide-eyed understanding. I knew she wasn't a part of the Escadrille. We had spoken enough that I knew she lived here, and had always lived here, and had almost no knowledge of what the Chauvignons did for a living, and she had no liking for that *putain* Kaijin. I didn't want anything to happen to her.

"Hello, Poppet, are you there?"

"Sorry, my dude, this is DJ Raditz," the voice in my ear spoke.

"Raditz, Grant, are you really here?" I asked. "And where is Sadie?"

"She's right…" There was a crackle and scuffle sound.

"Conan! Conan, are you okay?" Her voice was going from shrill to thickening with emotion.

"Hello, Poppet," I said, feeling a crack in my voice. She let out several sobs, and then I heard Grant take the mic from her.

"Bogies inbound, my dudes." Grant was in my ear again, and I assumed, Lach's. I looked at him, and he nodded, two fingers to the north door, and then two fingers to south door. I understood and headed toward the south door. I was slower than normal, but the replacement prosthetic they had given me was a poor one, quickly made and compared to my old one, it might as well have been a wooden pirate leg.

"Three inbound south, one north," he said. I could still hear Sadie making noises in the background.

"Would you compare this to the Fortress of the Frost Lord, or the Lair of the Deathless Dragon?" I asked.

"Fucking *what?*" I heard Lach half-bark.

"Totally Deathless Dragon, but put it in Elfenwood, wood instead of stone," Grant replied.

"Fantastic," I said, and dropped to my one good knee, shouldered the AK and fired three quick shots. The action of the gun was flawless, the accuracy of it was as rusty as my practice. Two of the approaching men went down to body shots. I aimed low. I wanted to put the bullets through their bowels. That would hurt more, and last longer. I knew them, and their fists and boots. They were the ones who handled the leather straps and gags before Kaijin would come and play.

The last tried to serpentine, and I put the round higher. His neck came apart at the shoulder and he fell backwards.

I rose to my feet and started advancing again. "Grant, give me directions to the motor pool area," I said.

"On it, my dude. Looks like three hundred meters to your south-south-east. Pathway, ornamental stone wall with open gate, six bogies, two are dogs."

"Fucking dogs!" Lach growled.

There was a burst of gunfire, several three-round bursts in close succession. I moved forward. The men ahead of me were already turning to face the louder threat of the guy firing off bursts. That was fine with me. "They're breaking toward you, mate," I said.

"Let 'em come," Lach said. There was another round of rapid fire. He was lying down suppressing fire, and it was keeping their heads down, and drawing them toward him.

"What's the count?" I asked.

"Looks like nine, now," Grant replied.

"Be careful!" I heard Sadie yell so we could hear her. I advanced again, quick and low. There were shouts, and I knew that whatever guard detail *le putain* had would be completely on its feet and responding. I reached the door to the main garage which looked like it had been a livestock barn, or perhaps part of the keep that had been changed over. I opened the door and stepped into darkness.

"I can't follow you in there, dude!" Grant complained.

"Keep on Lach, he's drawing the heat right now," I said softly. I pulled the door gently shut and kept to the wall as I moved to the doors at the end of the room. There were a half a dozen vehicles inside – most were labor vehicles and such – the place was a working vineyard and did some other agricultural activities. Eloise had told me about the annoyance of going past where the wannabe soldiers were mock-barracked, between the jail and the main kitchen.

And that the arsenal was attached to the barrack hall.

At the front of the motor pool.

I kicked the door of the barracks open. There might have been a few stragglers left inside, the last to hear the call, and the slowest to pull on their boots and grab their guns. I sprayed the room with the AK, putting bullets through thighs, groins, hips, and knees. They screamed, some tried to draw weapons, and they were the ones I gave a second splash of hot lead.

"Giuseppe? You bloody wanker, I told you I was going to do this." I raised the rifle and pointed it between his eyes. The gray-headed man snarled at me; hands clamped over the shredded ruin of his left thigh. He started to scream a litany of obscenities at me, but I cut him short, shooting him between the legs.

He made the motions of a full scream but no sound came out of him.

I put the last round in the clip through his chest. He collapsed backward and painted the wall behind him with a fan of blood. The door to the arsenal was open, and I turned and faced the kid standing in the doorway. He was holding a FAMAS F1 rifle, and I could see his hands trembling.

I stared him down and advanced; his eye twitched.

With deliberate intent, I lifted the rifle to my shoulder, feeling that cold rush of adrenaline. I had been out of commission for too long, on my back for too long, and too long before that, sitting in just a chair. I advanced on him, with an empty gun, but he didn't know. He stumbled back, giving ground. His face became a mask of fear and the last few strides were at a near run. At the last moment, I swung the rifle and bashed him in the face. He fell with a crunch and a spurt of blood from his nose.

I grabbed the FAMAS from him and jammed it in his face. "If you bloody well live through today, go home to your mother, and you kiss her bloody feet." He shuddered, and his pants went dark as he pissed himself.

He curled up into a ball and sobbed. I stepped over him and went to one of the racks that still had guns. I grabbed several magazines for the FAMAS, and a pair of pistols. "You there, Deej? Bring Lach to my location. I have access to weapons and ammo."

"He's moving your way now, but could use some support, no god mode IRL," he replied.

If this had been the arsenal on Bootlegger Head, there would be strange, exotic weapons, fun explosives. This was a barracks, so there might have been three or four different guns, but twenty or thirty of each. I saw something that gave me a special feeling, a long barrel shotgun with a pistol grip. I hefted the powerful gun, racked it, and started stuffing shells into the tube.

"How's the weather, mate?" I asked.

"Raining," Lach responded.

"He's pinned behind a stone wall, ninety meters west of your location," Grant said.

"Not for long," I said, and slid the last shell into the gun and pumped it into the chamber. "It's a shame we can't run music through the comm."

"Are you fucking nuts!" Lach grunted.

"What are they doing?" I heard Sadie demand.

"I can," Grant said. "What do you think we are? Noobs and savages?"

"Lay me down a beat, something heavy."

"I'll lay you down something fat," Grant said, and a few seconds later the channel was flooded with a throbbing base beat. It was the battle theme from the *Volcano Dungeon*. It was perfect. I was free, Lach was back and Poppet was here. Well, hopefully not too close to here, but close enough. I took a deep breath – spend gunpowder, blood, piss. I was back in the game.

I had suspected they were alive, but now I knew they were, and it was time to pay back some debts that had been racked up since we took that last job. The shotgun spoke, its voice thunder. A man fell, some of his features reduced to red gore. I moved position, and the big gun spoke again. The body armor the man was wearing took most of the hit, but still knocked him to the ground.

His struggle ended when I bashed him in the face with the heavy stock of the gun.

"Helo inbound, helo inbound," I heard Lach on the line. The stroke of the rotors had meshed almost flawlessly with the sound of the music, and I let it carry me. I flanked the men who had Lach pinned down and pumped rounds through the Benelli as fast as I could. It was carnage. It was also taxing, and I could feel the sheen of sweat on my brow and knew that my endurance was nothing like it had been before.

I almost stumbled when I reached the wall. Before the surviving house guards could respond to that, they were cut to ribbons. Lach was up and advancing. Then there we were, side by side. "How long has it been since we were both in the field?" he asked.

"Too long, it would seem," I said. There were no more rounds left in the shotgun, so I dropped it in the grass. I would use the FAMAS from here on. The helo was getting dramatically closer. The sound was unfamiliar. Whatever it was, it wasn't a Blackhawk or any other American helo. I gestured toward the main building. Kaijin would be in there, and I wanted to put a few dozen rounds through her. I wanted to hurt her.

She had spent six months making herself the focus of my hatred, the scapegoat for everything that had gone wrong in the last half a year.

I saw her for a moment. She came out of the main building with four or five of her closest. The helo cleared the tree line and revealed itself to be a EuroCopter Panther, and a well-armed one. The door gunner leaned out and sprayed the field where we were with his large machine gun. Avoiding his aim was easy enough, it wasn't a precision weapon. It was a devastating one, getting clipped by a round from it could easily be life ending.

The wounded men of the estate took the worst of it. They didn't know who we were, so they were just shooting everyone. I grabbed cover and braced myself as a stream of lead shredded into everything around us. The low stone wall that had previously sheltered Lach now protected us from the opposite direction. The helo stopped shooting as it rotated and touched down in the grass.

Kaijin and her retinue were boarding the craft and for a moment, she met my furious gaze. I raised the rifle and emptied the entire magazine in an entirely too short buzzsaw of bullets. I was certain some struck the helo, and aside from a few people who were dragged in through the door, they left no one behind.

Lach fired several rounds with his AK. Where I had fired in a moment of passion and wasted my ammo, he took calm and cool aim and clustered his rounds into the engine of the helo. It powered up and lifted into the air, and as quick as it had come, it was gone.

But it was trailing a cloud of black smoke from the engine he had pock-marked with old Soviet ammo. "Good shooting," I said, and clapped him on the shoulder.

"The car is the opposite direction. Why did we go this way?" he shouted over the fading roar of the helo.

"Because she was this way, and I was going to shoot her," I said.

"Who?" he asked.

"Gwendolyn Kaijin, mate. The things that bitch did to me, I'll kill her with my bare hands if I get the chance."

"We'll kill her," he said. "And all the rest of them. They fucked with the wrong people."

"I checked the radio, there are all sorts of people speaking really fast and angry-like. We should probably get out of here," Grant said. Lach nodded in agreement.

"We only came here to get you. Revenge can wait," he said with a degree of calm and cool that I found surprising. The hug from him earlier was almost the same as a full-on emotional meltdown from a normal person; sobbing and blubbering on the floor. He had been shaken. Fuck all, *I* was bloody shaken.

The two of us fell back, tracing a path that Lach seemed to know, clearing several low walls, and then vaulting a fence. The estate was out in the rural part of the country, so it was a two-lane road, and parked close by, concealed by the boughs of old trees, there was Sadie and a skinny guy with long braided black hair.

Sadie.

If I could run, I would have.

My legs were trembling, and the stump of my bad leg was throbbing furiously. It was going to be bruised as bloody hell after this, but I didn't care. I limped toward her as fast as I could.

"Get in the car, I'm driving," Lach said. No one was going to argue. "Grant, you get shotgun. Give him the rifle, mate." Grant looked worried but there was no room for argument. We quickly threw ourselves into the seats, and Lach didn't even wait for the doors to be closed before pulling away. As soon as the last door was shut, he put the hammer down, and the big German sedan revealed its secret weapon, a massive 500 horsepower motor, and one of the best non-F1 drivers in the world behind the wheel.

The tires screeched in protest, and Sadie squawked as we took the first hard turn. The country roads were narrow, and few were straight, so he was limited to hard technical driving, and had few opportunities to unleash the power lurking under the hood of the car.

"Why are you driving like an absolute madman?" Grant asked, exasperated.

"Because they have a helicopter, and there's a chance we might be chased," Lach said, hurling the car through another turn, and then another. I took the opportunity to wrap Sadie in my arms. Was this a hallucination, like *The Occurrence at Owl Creek Bridge*? Had Kaijin finally succeeded in killing me? Had my heart stopped, was this mad rescue and flight from the stone prison the delusional response of my brain starving for oxygen? If it was, there was no reason to not steer into the skid.

I inhaled the scent of her hair, and it was somewhere between internalizing an orgasm and doing a line of coke. That I knew what some of that was, was beside the point, and just her being there was infinitely better than either of those other things. I kissed her forehead, and then her lips, and for a long moment, nothing else existed.

I could have wept with joy.

I didn't, though. Maybe it was still the sense of disbelief, maybe the fact that I was still riding that adrenaline high and hadn't come down yet. Fuck, it could be that I was just goddamn dehydrated and didn't have the moisture to spare. The engine roared and there was the distant sound of traffic. We had left the country roads and had joined the A9.

The A9?

The A51 would take us to Marseille, or north into the south of France.

The A9 didn't go anywhere but…

"My dude," Grant asked, looking over at Lach. "Are we going to Monaco?"

"Yes, yes we are," he said, his eyes darting from the road ahead of us to the mirrors. "And we have a tail."

"Oh shit, that's bad," Grant said, turning and looking through the back window. I looked too and saw it – a trio of cars in hot pursuit – a pair of doughty Renault sedans, and a much-abused Citroen hatchback. The Merc we were driving had a more powerful engine, and a better driver, but these assholes lived here, and while Lach was executing corners with precision, this was his first time seeing most of them. They lived here and could probably drive most of these roads in a wine-soaked stupor.

"They won't try anything, this is a major road," Grant said.

The first fusillade of gunfire peppered the arse of the sedan, shattering the back window and causing Grant and Sadie to both scream; Grant in fear, Sadie in anger.

"Shoot at them," Lach said, grabbing Grant by the collar of his shirt.

"I don't know anything about real guns man, I only do this shit online!" He had a note of rising panic in his voice.

"Give it to me," Sadie barked, and snatched the FAMAS from him. She turned in a fluid motion and dropped the barrel through the shattered back window and drew a bead on the lead car, one of the Renaults.

Nothing happened.

"Safety's on, love," I told her. She saw it, shouted a foul word, clicked it and then put half of the clip into the A9, the trunk of the Merc, and the Renault that was closing in on us. The Renault jagged hard to the left, slammed into the concrete median, and ground to a hard stop, sparks and a cloud of steam and smoke boiling up from it.

She screamed something inarticulate at them, lost in the roar of the engine and noise filling the car in the absence of the back glass.

"Easy, that's full auto, and that was a lot of ammo," I cautioned.

"Yeah, yeah, I'm not losing you again because I was worried about having ammo for later," she said, and it was almost like hearing Lach speak through her mouth.

The two surviving pursuit cars were upset by the loss of one of their own, the Renault falling back being caught in the snarl and panic of traffic, and the Citroen falling back from sheer intimidation. The driver and company regained their courage and began closing on the Merc again, which was no small task. The German car had a lot more power than theirs did.

When they got close, Sadie would fire a few bursts from the rifle. It was almost surreal seeing that. The stock jammed in her shoulder, and each time the muzzle blazed fire, I could see the shock pass through her, making her flesh ripple. It was almost hypnotic.

It was also insane.

There was no reason that Kyle should have her here. Not here where she was using a rifle to shoot at chase cars while he hammered down like he was challenging the lap time at Le Sarthe. Hell, I shouldn't have been sitting next to her while she was shooting. She should have been taking cover behind me, while I provided covering fire.

"Poppet." I looked at her, her hair waving in a fierce mane around her head. She fired a last burst and then the rifle was empty.

"Got any reloads for this thing?" she asked.

"It's not safe," I said.

"No shit?" She made an open-handed gesture. "Give me another mag if you've got one." I grabbed the spare I had and wished that I had more of them. I handed it to her, and I could feel a nugget of anger starting to glow. I couldn't believe he had brought her. She unloaded another burst and sent the lead pursuit car skittering away from our bumper. I thought that she had missed, but soon steam was boiling out from under the car, she had holed the radiator.

"How's it going back there, Shady?" Lach half-shouted.

"Better for us than them," she said. Her form was good, and she went still, letting the sights on the rifle find their target. She fired a three-round burst, and the last car swung into a hard right-hand turn, and then physics came into play. The center of mass moved above its axis of inertia and then the front wheel buckled under the weight, sending the car into a violent roll. Glass, debris, and smoke trailed behind us. She dropped back down into the seat and tossed the FAMAS on the floorboard.

"I don't like that rifle," she said, nonchalantly.

I didn't have words. My poppet had just smoked three pursuit vehicles with less than sixty rounds of ammunition.

"Do you have us a place yet?" Lach asked.

"Yeah, but it's not cheap," Grant said. "Looks like I can grab you a room for three nights, but it's going to be about nine grand."

"There's a black card in the glovebox," Lach said, moving the car through traffic, trying to put distance between us and the destruction in our wake. "See if there is an upgrade. I am willing to go up to twelve or fifteen large; it's Monaco."

"Done and done," Grant said. "Do you know where the Fairmont is?"

"The hotel that overlooks the Grand Prix course, where Nikki Beach is?" Lach asked.

"The one and the same, have you been?" Grant asked.

"A few times," I offered. I didn't mention why he had been there, or how much he had spent on escorts that weekend. Dropping fifty grand on a weekend didn't matter after a Sultan in a quaint country had paid just over a million for taking out a rival of his.

Lach maneuvered us through the Monegasque Customs station leaving the A9 and entering the sovereign nationality of Monaco. It was most convenient that all of our passports and documents were so cutting edge when I made them a world and a lifetime ago, they were still good. We were waved through with little issue, and I was more than a little thankful that the customs people didn't look hard at the rear end of the car. The bullet holes would have been hard to explain.

"I was going to tell them that French people don't like German cars," Lach said as he flitted us through the narrow streets of the old city, across part of the actual Grand Prix track, and to the check-in counter and valet parking for the Fairmont Hotel.

The massive building was a hallmark of the country, and hundreds of millions of people saw the royalty of racing muscle F1 cars around it, and then under its parking garage facility every year at one of the most hallowed tracks in open-wheeled racing. I had certainly watched a fair number of races here. It was almost sad that this was my first visit.

The staff were exceedingly polite, and we were escorted up to the room that Grant had procured for us, using Lach's black credit card. That was a sword that cut through all barriers, gleaming black and almost knife-edged in its precision. The car was taken to the valet parking, and Lach told them that they would need to procure the services of a car broker. The mischief on the A9 had been entirely too close to them, and there was no way that they were going to be seen in the Riviera driving a damaged sedan.

The concierge all but fell to his knees.

The room was breathtaking. The southern wall was entirely glassed in, and the view was spectacular. There were yachts and sailing boats in the enclosed harbor, everything lit up in the evening darkness. I felt like a weight had been lifted from my shoulders, and my soul felt light again. Kaijin was still out there, but I was no longer her captive.

She hadn't broken me.

She hadn't won.

"Showers," Sadie said, plucking at her shirt. "I need one. We all need one."

"I'll call room service," Lach said. "Showers, all around. We smell like the locker room at a shooting range. Anyone have any requests?" There were a few sundry requests, nothing that piqued his eyebrow – ceviche, a salmon salad, and then I said something that surprised him.

"A bottle of the house sauv blanc, and find out what they have in American whiskey," I said. I had learned that not only was I stronger than that sadist cunt, but I was also stronger than the devil that lived in the bottle. "Oh, a steak, rare, and whatever their two recommended sides are. I'm starved."

He laughed and ordered.

One by one, we all took showers, and even trying to run the hot water out seemed to be a fool's errand. Even Sadie with her feminine predilection for water temps approaching the boiling point wasn't able to make a dent in it. This seemed to please her greatly.

We all talked for a bit, and there was a good deal of relaxing. The news was left playing on a television. The running shootout on the A9 was the highlight of the reel, but local officials were stymied by the fact that those involved had all had extensive criminal records, and while they were certainly interested in whomever they were pursuing, none of them had spoken. Or at least something like that, the news was broadcast in French.

"Where are you going to stay?" Sadie asked Grant pointedly, and I could detect a tremble in her hands where she clutched them in her lap, her cream satin robe, courtesy of the hotel, shimmering under the overhead lights where it rippled around her.

"Oh, me?" He seemed surprised. "Don't worry about me. I have some friends who stay around here, and they love the DJ Raditz. I'll probably spend the next week doing a tour of clubs and house parties. I won't lie, the last day or so has given me so goddamn much inspiration to work with that I'm sure I can turn it into another bomb-ass club tour, maybe some EDM singles. It will be fucking sweeeet." He dragged the last part out like a hair-metal rocker torturing a guitar string.

"You won't stay here?" Sadie asked and though she may sound innocent in her query to Grant, I heard the apprehension in her voice that he might say yes. He was, by far, too clever for that.

"Nah, I've had too much…" he hesitated. "Fun. I need to go do some industrial-grade decompression and defragging." Lach raised his glass to that, offering a silent toast to the sentiment.

"You're a good man," he said to Grant, and his smile was thin, tired.

"Right now, I'm a fourth wheel. You guys have a blast, and Guild Master RedRoan," he offered me a deep dragon-kin bow, fist clawed over his heart, "I deliver you to safety, blessed be the Guild."

"Thank you, and the Guild will remember and repay this great debt," I said, returning his bow.

"Is this MMO game shit?" Lach asked with a barking laugh.

"It certainly is," I said. "Name your price, sir."

"The Orb of the Kraken-God," he said.

"Done," I agreed. There was a certain paradox – a successful deejay, electronic musician, and club promoter, and still a borderline introvert. His goodbye was brief, and as much as I owed him, I was still glad to be alone with the people who were my family, Kyle and Sadie.

No sooner had the door shut behind Grant than Sadie and Lach turned and the three of us were left, mere steps between us, staring at one another, the silence heavy.

Sadie's eyes filled first. There was a slight tremble, growing to convulse her body into a violent shudder. I went to her without thinking and pulled her into my arms, her slight form crashing against mine a wave upon the rocks, her resolve dissolving like seafoam as the reality closed over all of our heads.

Together...

I felt her reaching blindly behind me to Lach, her small hands that had so flawlessly gripped the rifle in the car opening and closing, grasping at air. There was a clack as Lach set his glass aside and joined us, coming around to crush her small form between us. He hugged me, holding her between us where she was always meant to be and I caught the glimmer of tears and emotion in his obsidian gaze as well.

I buried my hand in her long silky hair, pressed her to my chest and met my partner and best friend's eyes, tears in my own and nodded. He sniffed, and I did too, a slight laugh from him met by a chuckle from me.

We'd never been so free with emotion in front of one another like this. It was… uncomfortable, but right and undoubtedly what our girl needed from us right now as she wept so freely against me.

She cried an ocean, our Sadie did, and with the catharsis came exhaustion.

It was the reunion we had been waiting for. Freed from the constraint of spectators and the threat of bodily harm and death. Her eyes were reddened and puffy from tears and weeping. I felt my own tears freed upon my face, the pure, ecstatic release of finally being out from under the Escadrille's thumb and having them back, and they were *safe*.

I had dreamt of this.

This moment, imagining it, had sustained me when Kaijin had been at her most sadistic.

Then the inevitable event came. Lach was the first to step back from us both. The downside of adrenaline was the crash. Lach seemed nonplussed, but this was old hat to him. His crash usually involved large amounts of gin, and escapades with prostitutes. The thought of that was sour in the mouth. When the euphoria of reunion was faded, I could see the wind go out of Sadie's sails.

We escorted her to the bedroom and stripped her nude, letting the satin of the robe fall away from her smooth skin. I looked, relieved she was free from scar or injury that she hadn't already possessed upon first coming to us.

I gave her a few chaste kisses, while Lach pulled out a simple silk nightie and we slipped it over her head. She made a soft noise at the sensation of the fabric sliding down her body. We all but carried her to the bed, tucking her into the middle.

"Both of you," she purred sleepily. "Stay with me, please? Don't leave me."

"Yes, Poppet," I said. I stripped and took the cloth bits that Lach held out to me, changing into something more suitable for sleep and tried to not look at the ruin of my stump. I made sure she couldn't see it. I had put a lot of punishment on it today, with a less than stellar prosthetic under me. For not the first time, I missed my old carbon fiber and titanium leg that was left under the ashes of Bootlegger Head.

"Got a crutch for you," Lach murmured. "Gonna need to give that a break for a couple of days and get you a new leg."

I nodded quickly and deliberately averted my gaze to Sadie. He nodded and looked… I don't know. I couldn't quite identify the look but it was of no consequence. I got into bed with her as Kyle changed himself, lifting the blankets to slide in between them and to put Sadie firmly between us. It was not lost on me that he took the side of the bed closest to the door to the room.

It didn't take Sadie long to drift into sleep, her body pressed in the midst of ours, her cheek pressed to my chest, her arm around me, clutching me close. If this were a similar thing to *The Occurrence at Owl Creek Bridge,* then this was the closest to Heaven that I could imagine.

Lach and I stared at one another over her sleeping form for I don't know how long. I could practically feel his unrest. His comedown ritual incomplete, I knew he was seriously wanting for a drink.

"Go," I murmured quietly. "Take care of yourself, mate."

"You sure?" he asked, and ran his hand down Sadie's body, over the covers as though she were feline for real rather than in just her grace.

"I'm sure. You're no good to us for what comes next if you can't have this."

He grunted. "You know me so well."

"Aye," I agreed.

"I've got my phone. Call or text me if anything comes up with Shady… she—" His mouth pressed down into a flat line. "She might need us both," he said finally. I didn't know what he meant, but Sadie stirred slightly in her rest and I didn't wish to push it. I simply nodded and held her a little tighter.

Lach rose and dressed. I understood. This wasn't his come down; he had a ritual about him and the call of it was strong. No, this? This he was doing for *her*. He gave me a nod before slipping from the room. He would go down to the hotel bar, get a drink or three, and then who knew what.

I laid with her a while longer before I couldn't. It was the pain throbbing up my leg. The stump was in agony and sliding the prosthetic back on was torture. I didn't know where the crutch Lach had said he'd procured happened to be and I didn't wish to wake my lady in a clumsy attempt to find it, so it had to be endured. I went to the suite's kitchen and had counters and chairs to use which helped. I walked slowly, found the bottle of whiskey room service had brought, and poured myself a few fingers of it in a glass.

I used Lachlan's laptop, sorting through what had happened to the world and our finances over the last half a year, and to determine how safe we still were. Monaco had become one of those Casablancas for the international community. If Gwendolyn Kaijin were staying in the next room, the unspoken rules would demand that we present nothing but the greatest civility and honor to each other.

The powers that existed, and vacations in Monaco would not permit anything but peace and decadence in their grand resort. I was loath to want to believe she or any of her ilk were present in this very hotel, but if they were? I would abide by the unspoken treaty.

"Bugger," I muttered and occupied myself fully in stock portfolios. I didn't even wish to look at what my email held. Not after six months unattended. I sighed and sipped from my glass. Were that I could sleep as readily as our girl…

CHAPTER EIGHT

*L*achlan...

The Saphir, the hotel bar of the Fairmont, was a jewel of smart design and all that hip nonsense. It was pretentious and expensive in all the worst ways. It was the sort of place where people would drop a few dollars on a casual meal to wash it down with wine that was a few hundred euros a glass, some close to a thousand a glass.

It lacked the warmth and character I had learned to appreciate from the big moose. Even his Black-Eyed Susan bar back in Bootlegger Head dripped more charm and character compared to this artistic mess. This was an art gallery without art, but the same utter lack of anything else.

The bartender was multi-lingual, and the bar was well stocked enough to mix me a proper Aviator, down to having fucking vintage crème de Violette. That was at least good.

I let the alcohol soothe through me. I could watch a few ships bobbing in the water, and that would have been dandy if I were a photographer or a watercolor painter.

There were a number of women in the bar, some were obviously escorts, the hour was right, and the day was close enough. These women were the Ferraris and Lamborghinis of leasable vaginal activity.

"Why, I do believe we've met," one of the painted women said, sliding into the seat next to me.

"Oh?" I said, covering with a drink of my Aviator cocktail.

"Do you not remember me?" she asked. She did seem familiar, but I also know pretending familiarity was a basic tactic for getting in close to someone. She was probably just working me like a john.

"I'm sorry, it's been a very long day," I said, not at all lying.

"Mister Newman, from New York, and probably the only person I've ever met who knew that violet crème exists," she said. I recognized the old cover name, and it must have shown as a startle on my face. "My hair was a little different, a little shorter, and you might remember how flexible I am." She gave me a throaty laugh.

"It started with an X," I said. I gestured for the bartender to bring her a cocktail.

"Xaviera, and how about a bottle of wine?" she offered. I knew that trick, and I would only fall for it one time.

"Did I buy a bottle last time we were together?" I asked.

"Sadly, no." She gave me a little pout.

"I tipped you well, you were quite talented." I did recall a certain gymnastic feat she had accomplished, allowing her to go down on herself, while I took her from behind. That had been quite a night, and expensive, as I recalled Roan bitching later.

"You did. Perhaps I can show you something that might make you forget every woman but me." Her smile was genuine, or at least it seemed that way.

I should be halfway hard by this point. I should have already kissed her, or slid a hand under the hem of her dress to feel for sheer panties, or for that most pleasant of sensations, bare lips beneath my fingers.

I didn't feel anything.

Instead, I could only think of Sadie, asleep in the bed upstairs, hair coiled around Roan's fingers, her eyes that stared into mine soul deep and somehow still managed *not* to reflect something monstrous back at me, closed. The brush of her nipples under the sheer fabric, the swell of her breasts, the roundness of her ass, whichever she pressed against me, and the soft sigh of her breathing as she slept.

Today she had wielded a rifle with little initial hesitation, and then to definite effect. I had been able to just drive, not worry about dodging and evading, because *she had us covered*. The one time I had looked back to see that she was okay, the only thing that I had seen was the round apple of her butt pointed at me, and a colorful hint of the underwear she wore riding over the waistband of her jeans.

That was what I was thinking about.

I didn't really want this, and that felt wrong somehow.

Xaviera was flexible enough she could lick her own pussy, and had done it, with my cock in her ass. I remembered fucking her until I came on her face. She had lavished in it, and I had tipped her very well. I had fantasized about her, and now that I could have her again?

There was nothing, zero interest.

"Xaveria," I took her hand for a moment, "I will never, ever, forget what we did, or more precisely, what you did while I was watching. That being said, as lovely as you are, I am going to have to pass."

"What if I offer you… a discount?" She raised an eyebrow. "You weren't unimpressive yourself."

"It's not a matter of money," I said.

"What is her name, then?" she asked, fanning her fake eyelashes.

I couldn't keep the smile off my face, and she smiled too. She knew, without me even having to say it – which I wouldn't. Shady was mine – *ours*, and we didn't share. Not even her name. Not even like this.

"That I'm going to have to keep to myself," I said with a wink, turning my genuine smile to a tactical advantage, turning it up a notch.

"Always a man of mysteries, Mr. Newman." She gave a polite tip of her head, and then she sauntered away. There were other customers to be had, and the topflight escorts were never pushy or aggressive; their time was worth more than badgering men into picking them up.

I finished the Aviator and gave the bartender a tip.

Her eyes bulged slightly as she read the amount on the receipt. She had made the drinks excellently, and that was about the only part of this that had felt right. The elevator was silent as it whisked me back to our floor, and then I let myself into our suite. Roan was up, the lights in the kitchenette dimmed. His face was illuminated by the glow of a laptop, technically mine. I barely used the thing. The phone I carried was perfectly acceptable for anything I needed.

"She still asleep?" I asked.

"Yeah."

"How's the leg?"

"It's been better, a lot of bruising," he said. He had a glass of whiskey close at hand.

"How's the whi—" I stopped. This was fucking small talk. "Conan, are you okay?"

He looked up at me using his first name; we only rarely ever spoke with first names. Years of military work had reduced us to commonly using just last names, the habit of dropping rank in front of that had faded, but the last name thing had stuck.

"I'm not doing well, mate," he said. I could tell that he had a lot to come back from. His time in captivity had cost him a good deal of weight loss. The mass had gone out of his chest and arms – a quick guess was a mediocre caloric diet and no access to weight training equipment. Outwardly he showed no signs of torture – he still had all ten fingers, all five toes, and there was no deformity to his face, so likely still had all his teeth.

"Do you need to talk about it?" I asked the counselor question.

"Maybe, probably, but there are other things we need to talk about first," he said, closing the laptop.

"Shoot," I said, pouring myself some of his brown liquor.

"Why was Sadie there, why did you have her in the line of fire?" he asked.

"What is that dungeon thing, *don't split the party?* Leaving Grant and Sadie at the rental would have kept them out of the danger zone, but it would mean leaving them in a second location and requiring us meeting back up. Sure, I could have tried it alone, Grant could have remoted the drone from the rental, but then there would have been no one else in the car. It was a tactical decision. Fewer loose ends, more resources in one place."

"Sadie isn't a bloody resource," he said in a low voice.

"Yes, she was. Every one of us was a resource in the mission, and the mission was to rescue you. I had to, and when you get on your laptop, you'll see and hopefully you'll understand." How did he drink this brown stuff? Ugh.

"What's on my laptop?"

"She's been either emailing you or keeping some intense personal journal, and I'm doubling down that it's everything to do with you." I finished the glass in a gulp and felt my stomach churn.

"Have you been reading them?" He looked somewhere between surprised and angered.

"Fuck, no." I held up my hands. "I've been forgiven for crossing some serious boundaries, but that's a level of personal that even my sociopathic ass knows not to cross."

"Oh, well that's almost surprising," he said thoughtfully.

"Things have changed, mate," I said. I opened the bar cooler and found a small bottle of gin. It was overpriced but ordering room service to bring me a couple would take too long and might wake Sadie. She had become a notoriously light sleeper since the house fell. "*She* has changed. You might not want to see it but she *is* capable."

"I don't like her in the field," he said.

"That's very regressive of you, sir," I said with a little jest in my voice. "Women are joining the Marine corps these days, and there is a female fighter pilot now." He gave a sigh, and I saw that the point might have been conceded.

"Lyudmila Pavlichenko," he said, raising his glass to a mock toast and throwing the last gulp down.

"Name's not familiar, but she sounds old and Russian."

"She was a sniper for the Red Army, killed a few hundred Nazis. They called her *Lady Death*." He seemed to accept this.

"I'll raise a glass to shooting Nazis, it's on my bucket list."

"Honestly," he looked up at me, and I saw a crack of a smile on his tired face, "mine too."

"You seem interrogation free," I eventually said.

"I was barely questioned, and everything I gave them was dated or the encryption had cycled. I knew that you were still out there somewhere; gave me strength." He smiled.

"So, what happened?" I asked.

"Kaijin kept me as a trophy, a pet." He poured another glass and sat it nearby but didn't pick it up.

"Did she take you on walks?" I asked. This was weird.

"She tied me up, a lot of it had a strong BDSM feel to it, but it was darker." He gave a small shudder.

"Did the anti-interrogation training do anything?" I asked, genuinely interested. All of that had seemed strange, and now I wanted to know how much was legit and how much was smoke.

"It did, well, some of it did," he said. "It prepares you for pain, and sensory deprivation, all that. But if the captors don't take Friday night crime dramas as a guideline, it's not so effective. It's easier to block out pain than it is pleasure."

"Pleasure, what did they do to you, force you to eat baguettes and foie gras?"

"Ha-ha." He gave a mock laugh. "They fed me very well, the bread was amazing, Eloise made it, the woman who was there at my cell. She took care of me, and that was the other thing that held me up. I knew you and Sadie were safe, and Eloise was keeping me up with fresh bread, cassoulet, and all that rustic French food, and a fair bit of seafood."

"Bless your heart." I gave him a smirk.

"I really *really* want a greasy cheeseburger now, actually. A Burger World number four, with the double meat, double cheese, and bacon," he said.

"Sure, when we get back. I don't think they allow Burger Worlds in the European Union – too aggressively American and zero redeeming nutritional qualities."

"There is one in Paris, at the airport," he said. "But no, I want the real thing, back home. Maybe go over into the Carolinas where they haven't banned half of the stuff that Burger World uses for cooking."

"That's a lot of self-destruction coming from you, mate." I felt a bit of concern. "Are you sure you're okay?"

"I'm not," he admitted. "That sadistic bloody cunt tied me up like some animal and did whatever she wanted to me." There was a flush of color in his face that wasn't from the booze. I stepped over to him and put my hand on his shoulder. Part of me had the notion of mentioning that some people paid top dollar for that sort of treatment.

"We'll take her down." I gave his shoulder a squeeze.

"I don't want to take her down. I want to murder her. I want her to die with her eyes open, terrified, knowing that she's going to die and there is nothing she can do about it. I want to cut her bloody head off and stick it on a pike and leave her for the crows."

"We can do that. The hard part will be finding a pike." I nodded.

"Sharp stick will do." He gave a small laugh. "Some of what she did was just for her own fancy, sometimes what she did was just fucking sadistic. She would bite me, she would draw blood sometimes." He gave a small shudder.

"I assume I don't want to know, and you don't have to say." I offered the best support I could. I felt like I was doing fucking horrible at that. Fuck this caregiver role, it was so goddamned hard. "I'll do anything I can, and I won't even be my usual sarcastic asshole self."

He laughed.

"God, that sounds dreadful. Did you get promoted while I was a way, you a full bird colonel now?" He snapped me a salute.

"Major General, and you've been demoted to potato peeler." I laughed.

"That's what I need. I need you to be you, and Sadie to be herself." He leaned back.

"What if we've both changed? What if we've all changed?" I asked.

"That might be the most introspective thing I've heard you say." He sounded thoughtful.

"Easy, I'm still who I am." I held up my hands in a defensive gesture. "We're not going down to the town for manicures and to go blouse shopping."

"Mate," he said softly. "You do get manicures, I've seen the receipts."

"And you'll take that secret to your grave." I pointed a finger at him.

"Probably not, Sadie knew before everything. The pedicures too." He smiled.

"You bastard." I gave a laugh that was louder than I intended.

"So, we need to plan what's next."

"First thing, we need to rest. As far as I know, *Pax Sicari* is still in place, so we're safe here," I said. No one would try anything here in Monaco. This was a safe space, a reservation of peace. "Get you a new prosthetic, get some clean clothes, and spend a day or two without a high-speed car chase, gun battle, or assault on a defended location."

"Those are good ideas…" he said. "The leg especially. I'm no good hobbling on a cane, and if I do too much damage to the stump, there could be a chance for a blood clot."

"We don't need you stroking out," I said. "Sadie hasn't forgiven you for dying at Bootlegger Head."

"If I hadn't slammed the door, they would have had all of us," he defended.

"That's true, but you promised her that we would all be okay, and she's had six months to be mad at you about that. I'm sure it's all in your laptop, that's the one she's used this whole time."

"Fair enough," he said.

"I'm glad your back with me," I said. "I don't think I said that earlier. I've been… just making this up this whole time."

"All I've done is just endured whatever that sadistic bitch could throw at me because I knew you'd come and find me." He pushed the chair back and stood hesitantly. He was off-balance, exhausted, and probably more than a little buzzed.

I hugged him.

"You're more than a brother to me," I said. I looked up and saw her standing in the hallway. The only thing missing from her messy hair, slack nightgown, and sleep-marked face was a stuffed animal being carried by a leg.

"I love you," he said softly. "Brother."

"We're being watched, and yes," I spoke. I could feel those doors inside me closing, what emotion I had retreated. "What are you doing up?" I asked as she walked over to join our hug.

CHAPTER NINE

*S*adie…

"*Do you know what the most powerful piece on the board is?*" *Hal Jefferson asked me.*

I looked up from where I trailed light fingertips over the stone pieces in his most prized possession – a chess set from before he was homeless. The timing clock was in his hands, worn and tired, a bit of duct tape at the corner, but it still worked.

I looked back down to the stone table with the chess board etched in it. Hal could be found all day every day at Winthrop Park in central Indigo City under the row of maple trees at the chess tables.

"I'll give you a hint," he said. "It ain't that big fat tower you're eying."

I smiled. "You can't fault me for thinking that the biggest piece would also be the most powerful," I said, lifting the ivory tower piece from the shabby blue felt.

"The bigger they are, the harder they fall," Hal said with a laugh. He was a light skinned black man. His skin tone was the color of good strong tea with a hint of milk, darker freckles in a smattering over his nose and cheeks which were etched with deep smile lines. His light gray eyes smiled too when they looked up at me, roving my face as I returned his smile and put the tower piece back down in its place.

"It wouldn't happen to be my favorite pieces would it?" I asked, lifting the white and black horse's heads from the felt, one in each hand.

"The knights?" he asked me, casually, setting up a row of white pawns in front of himself.

I dropped my eyes to the white and dark knight pieces in my hands, the dappled sunlight coming through the trees shifting over the pieces and frowned.

It was as if the dream slowed here, my waking mind nudging my sleeping one as if to note this moment right here was a significant one, and I should pay attention.

"I could see why you would think that," he said, leaning his arms against the edge of the stone chess table and looking up at me plaintively. "But no, it ain't them either."

"So, it has to be the king then, am I right?" I asked, setting the two knight pieces on the table and reaching for the black king piece.

"No, it ain't him... you see the king is weak and vulnerable. No, when the shit gets real and starts to hit the fan," he picked up the white queen, "it's all on his lady to save her man." He held it up into the light and ran his thumb over a smudge – real or imagined there was no telling with Hal. He was a paranoid schizophrenic and today happened to be a good day for him. Or it seemed so. Even in the throes of his paranoia, when the voices were their worst and he kept rocking, people lined up to try and beat him.

He was the Indigo City Chess King.

I picked up the black queen and he handed me the white one.

I shifted along the high thread count sheets and moaned, Hal's voice echoing in my mind from that long-ago summer day.

"No, if I had to pick the most powerful piece on the board, I'd have to say it's the queen. All women are powerful, the Red Queen in my head proves that... if women ever realized just how powerful they are and really got together, I'd say they'd be running the world in no time..."

I winced and moaned, sliding my arm out in front of me, reaching for Kyle, except he wasn't there. That more than anything tore me from the dream. I twisted and put an arm back for Conan, except he wasn't there either.

I moaned, more of a groan, and let my head fall back to the pillows.

I wondered if that was why I had really woken. I feared I wouldn't be able to sleep without them, that any time one or the both of them got out of bed without me, I would wake. In fact, with how the fission of anxiety coursed through me, with how afraid I was, I was sure that it was true.

This had been an ongoing theme with Kyle over the last six months. It was like my body knew my lover had gone and my poor brain just couldn't handle even the subconscious thoughts of his absence. Invariably, these thoughts and worries built and built and built until I was so very afraid, I just *could not* go back to sleep. Not without knowing where he was. The anxiety building and building, my panicked mind thrusting me from the warm nest of blankets to seek Kyle and now Conan – *praise everything* – out. To make certain they were okay. *We only just got him back, and already it's starting,* I thought.

I didn't know how long this symptom of my poor mental state would last. I worried it would annoy one or the both of them beyond measure quickly, but I needed to tell them about it. I feared they would discount me. That I would be told I was being too clingy… except, didn't I have a right to be?

I was the girl who consistently lost *everything* with great regularity, and I was so fucking *tired* of it. A soul-deep wearied worry that just kept abiding no matter what.

We'd only just gotten Conan back. That third of my soul I'd thought I'd lost forever, and I was utterly desperate not to lose him again, just as I was absolutely desperate not to lose Kyle.

I loved them both so much it hurt. I knew what that phrase meant now. I literally loved them so much that when I thought of them, my heart swelled so big in my chest the constriction of the cage of my ribs around it was a physically painful thing. My heart was so full when I was with them, it barely left me room to breathe and likewise the thought of losing either of them without fighting my hardest not to? Well, it stole my breath for a very different reason.

I threw back the blankets and slipped from the bed, the marble floors that were supposed to be heated chilly under my bare feet.

The light silk of my nightgown slipped off the bed as I took a step away from it and whispered against my legs. I hugged myself and gritted my teeth in slight frustration, tired beyond measure. I went on a miniature scouting mission to find my errant men who should have been in bed with me but weren't.

I heard them before I saw them; they were having a deep conversation from the direction of the living area which was open on one side leading to an outdoor living space on a sweeping and magnificent veranda. I padded up the hallway and Kyle looked up from where he stood in front of the kitchenette, hugging Conan. He fixed his attention on me in the shadows of the hall, the ice clinking in his glass as it settled on the stone countertop nearby them.

"What are you doing up?" Kyle asked me and Conan startled, perking up. I came around the hallway and went to them, their arms opening to pull me into their embrace. I noticed a second glass of amber liquid and ice sitting beside the open laptop, but the screen wasn't one I recognized. He hadn't read the emails. Not yet. I shuddered in their embrace and sighed out. I wasn't ready…

"Come, let's sit." Roan gestured to the living area and took up his glass. I laced my fingers in his and Kyle went around to refresh his drink as Roan led me to an armchair in front of the glass wall that took in the night-darkened view of the harbor in Monaco.

He sat with a grunt and some difficulty and I didn't hesitate; I simply crawled into his lap and settled myself, resting my head on his shoulder, pressing my lips to the crook of his neck, his arms sliding around me as a contented hum escaped his not quite as broad chest.

He'd lost some of his size while in captivity. Had traded some of his bulk for being shredded. Had toned down but was no less strong. I could feel that strength in his arms as he held me.

"You alright, Poppet?" he asked.

"I don't think I can sleep without you both," I murmured and sighed out. "Go ahead and keep talking about whatever you were talking about." I felt them trade a look, the silence heavy with all the things they didn't want to say in front of me. Kyle came around and stood at the windows in front of us, sipping from his glass. I sighed and cuddled closer to Conan and he smoothed a hand over the outside of my thigh, lingering over the curve of my hip.

"You can't keep hiding the rough stuff from me," I murmured. "Not anymore. I won't have it."

"Poppet…" Conan's voice was reluctant, worried, and dare I say, resigned.

I pulled back, fixing his keen green eyes with my own.

"I know you don't want that," I said. "I know you want to protect me." I looked to Kyle who was staring at me with his guarded obsidian gaze. It was the way a predator eyes what they think might be prey but aren't sure. The way they look at something and try to decide if it is something to be eaten or that will eat them. That last was different, that last was new, and I welcomed it.

"I know you want to protect me, too," I said, not wishing to discount the feelings I knew he had for me. "But this?" I waved my hand in front of me. "Keeping things from me? No, I won't tolerate it." I looked back to Conan and laid my hand gently along the side of his face, his eyes slipping closed and he looked so very tired as he turned his face into my light touch.

"I've had *everything* taken from me. Time and time again. I was there, in the thick of it, and you can't take that back from me. Just like I won't let anything take you from me again." I kissed him then, lightly, gently, a chaste press of lips.

"I'm done with being the sad girl with nothing," I whispered against his mouth, still loud enough that I knew Kyle could hear it. "I won't lose either of you," I said. "And if there's a risk that it might happen, then damn it, I want to be there. I want to share in that risk too. It's only fair."

"What, one for all and all for one?" Kyle asked with a sarcastic smile. "You think we should be like the three musketeers?"

"One, I'm kind of surprised you know any classical literature references at all," I said dryly. "And two, *yes.*" I tore my eyes from

Roan's questioning and calculating gaze and faced Lach's predatory grin.

He pointed a finger past me at Conan and said, "You've been a bad influence on her, mate."

I looked back to Conan who was smiling softly. "I'm alright with it in this particular instance," he said. "It's about time I had a point over you."

"Ha!" Kyle gave a mock laugh and took a sip from his glass. "Never happen," he half-sighed, half-muttered. Conan's smile broadened slightly; he had scored a point there.

"You can't keep cutting me out of the dangerous stuff," I argued, ignoring their banter, letting my eyes drift to the coffee table in front of us. It was a piece of oval glass set on a red and blue patterned rug against the darkly colored tiled floor. There was a chess board frosted onto its surface, a box underneath presumably holding the pieces. I thought of Hal and my dreams.

"I've spent all this time thinking you're my knights, white and black," I said softly, my gaze unfocused, my mind conjuring up the scratched and chipped stone table on that summer day in Indigo City. "But I think I've been wrong, maybe you're my kings," I said, looking up to consider the both of them. My gaze met Conan's because I knew he would be the one that would take the most convincing.

"The queen *is* the most powerful piece on the board," I said and Roan's gaze softened, his arms tightening around me just that little bit more as he looked me over.

"They'd never expect it," Kyle said, rattling the ice in his glass. Conan took a sip from his own. Whiskey of some kind or maybe Bourbon by the smell of it… I didn't know. I couldn't tell. I could never afford that kind of expensive liquor. What liquor I had was either scavenged from the dregs of a label-less bottle, or shoplifted from the bodegas – cheap vodka samples in a hundred flavors, discounted wine coolers in open top bins – and I shuddered at the thought of the oversized cans of malt liquor that were so painfully cheap that I *had* been able to afford them.

I didn't know if I should be worried that he was drinking, but by the same token, I think I should have worried more if he hadn't been. What, with what he'd been through… with what we'd all been through in our own ways…

"Expect what, mate?" Conan asked distractedly, his expression one of precise studiousness as he searched mine out and I tried valiantly to keep my expression neutral. I wanted to win this argument, after all.

"Her as part of the team," Kyle answered.

"They're already scared shitless of what the two of you can do, could you imagine if there were three?" I asked.

Conan smiled, and I looked up to Kyle who held the mirror of it on his own lips.

"I doubt we'll be able to train you up *that* fast," Conan said.

"I already know some of it," I said defensively.

"We can split the difference," Lach said assertively. "She's a great shot with a rifle. I trained her myself, sure, but some of that was God-given talent." He fixed Roan with a look and raised his scarred eyebrow. "You want her as far from the action while still in it? Teach her how to snipe. She can be our angel from above."

Roan looked a little startled, as though the suggestion was some sort of revelation. We sat patiently and let him think about it for a time and finally he dragged in a reluctant breath, letting it out in an explosive whoosh and said, "Aye, I think you're on to something there, mate." He paused a moment the wheels turning and murmured, "Our very own Lyudmila Pavlichenko."

I didn't know who that was, nor did I care when I appeared to be gaining ground. I ignored the name for now and I nodded. "And no more cutting me out of the rough discussions and planning," I said. "I know you want to protect me, and part of that is you teaching me how to protect myself and keeping me informed on what to expect. I think we've already proven prior methods haven't worked." I said the last gently, without reproach, but it needed to be said.

Roan nodded a little sadly and sighed. "Agreed," he said and while he didn't sound exactly *happy* about it, he didn't sound completely miserable either.

I snuggled into him and laid my head back down on his shoulder and murmured, "Now go back to talking about whatever you were talking about before I came in here." Kyle looked down into his glass, his smirk growing into an infectious smile that spread to my face.

"So, where were we?" He cleared his throat and raised his eyebrows at Conan.

"Bugger all," Roan muttered, and he knew he'd been defeated on this one. He took a fortifying breath and downed the last of whatever was in his glass and set it aside on the flat arm of the chair, freeing up that hand again to hold me close. "I suppose we should discuss a training regimen for our little Poppet, yeah?"

"I suppose you should," I said with determination. Kyle laughed.

"Now whose been the bad influence on her?" Conan muttered darkly, but he took any sting out of the comment by turning his head and pressing his lips to my forehead.

The magic of his forehead kisses was absolutely unmatched thus far, and I felt myself relax with victory when it came to this little argument about my involvement firmly in my grasp.

I drew in a slow breath, breathing him in and smiled, a careful tremulous thing as he traced some of my long hair behind my ear. The ice rattled in Kyle's glass as he slugged the remainder of what was in it back. I straightened in Roan's lap and turned my attention to Kyle, the set of his shoulders, stiff as he stared into his empty glass with something akin to disappointment.

I saw the echo of the long-ago boy I used to love in the man who stood before me now, and I felt myself soften, my heart leaping and grasping at the nostalgia offered up by memory.

"What's wrong, Kyle?" I asked softly.

Roan's hands slid along my silk-clad body, urging me up off of his lap, to go to my other lover. I stood and went to Lach, letting my arms drift around his waist.

"After intense situations, like combat, or a long mission, everyone has a comedown. Civilians aren't trained to handle it or expect it. That's why you see people having these great meltdowns, tears, shakes, the works. They don't know how to handle that much adrenaline and emotional stress," Roan said. I could feel Kyle tense under my arms.

"Kyle and I are no different, and this is his comedown, love," Roan said and Lach gave him a dirty look, as though he didn't appreciate being outed so directly.

I looked up into the impassive face of Kyle and smiled softly, unafraid, unperturbed. I had learned to love this cold side of Kyle Lachlan over the last several months and in a moment of clarity looking up into those glittering obsidian eyes, I knew, there were softer parts to the cold and calculating predator in my arms and those bits were close to the surface tonight.

"What about it?" I asked him softly. His hand rose and his thumb lightly caressed my cheek as his eyes slid over mine. He didn't say anything, but I saw the question in his gaze.

"Ask," I murmured. "Whatever it is you need… I'm here."

Conan grunted, and we both looked to him. "I believe some privacy is in order," he said and he fixed Kyle with a look and a sharp nod. Kyle returned that nod, once up and once down and we watched as Roan limped for the bedroom, a hand pressed to his bad leg. I frowned but Kyle cleared his throat and recaptured my attention.

"Come, sit down with me," he murmured, and I nodded.

He led us to the armchair Roan had just vacated and sank down into it, tugging me gently into his lap. He was tense, a muscle in his jaw ticking.

"Kyle, just tell me what—"

"I'm trying," he admitted. "This… this isn't easy for me. Everything in my life has changed, getting you back after so long, and us getting Conan back from the dead. It used to be simple, tactical. Now it's a puzzle, and I can't see the picture or the pieces."

I twined my arms around his neck and buried my fingers in the back of his hair, massaging the back of his head in that spot where the base of his skull met the top of his neck, the place where stress and tension like to twist into a knot. I searched his face long and hard, willing him to tell me his secrets.

"What can I do?" I asked softly after we went long minutes without saying anything at all.

"I can tell you," he said. "But I'm not sure that you really want to know."

"I really want to know." I nodded.

"I want you to kiss me," he said and then held up a hand to stop me as I moved to comply. "But not how you normally do it," he said.

"How then?" I asked softly.

"Do you remember how you were on the train, coming back to Indigo City?"

I nodded slowly, slightly afraid of that Sadie. I didn't like being her. I didn't know if I liked what I'd become earlier tonight, either… but I couldn't say I regretted it.

"And that's what you want?" I asked.

"My comedown is pretty simple. I want to fuck a beautiful woman. Not sex, not make love, but fuck. Roan calls it *asserting dominance* or *life affirmation*, or some other therapy nonsense. I like it rough, and dirty, the dirtier the better. Some of the things I've done with escorts I don't know that you could handle it, or that I could do it to you. I think you might think less of me—"

"Mister Lachlan, you talk too much," I said, brushing my hands through his hair. I covered his mouth with my own, in a kiss as savage as I could make it. I groaned into his mouth. This, this I could do, I could manage. To be whatever he needed in this moment was definitely something I could handle. That and I don't think he realized, what he was asking wasn't precisely a hardship.

I *missed him*. I craved his body against mine, the feel of him inside me, and while I relished the times that Kyle could and would be gentle with me, there was something to be said about the way *Lachlan* touched me, too. I would take whichever side of the man I could get. Rough? Gentle? It was all the same to me, honestly, as long as he *touched me*.

"Sadie," he breathed my name as I slid around in his lap, shoving off of him to better situate myself to straddle him.

"You talk too much, Mister Lachlan. You're here to fuck, aren't you?" I asked and placed his face between my hands so I could put my mouth over his again.

His hands went to my hips and then down to squeeze my ass, an appreciative noise slipping from his mouth into mine as our tongues clashed. He tasted like something akin to pine needles and turpentine and I tried to ignore it which was easy to do when he started walking the light silk of my nightgown up with his fingers. I slipped out of the straps for him, to bare my breasts should he want them and felt wanton and brazen, well aware we were parked right in front of the windows at my back.

Anyone could look, anyone could see... I thought to myself then, right on the heels of that his words drifted back to me. *The dirtier the better.*

I lifted my mouth from his and leaned back, pulling his shirt off, some of the buttons popping and bouncing off of the floor.

He looked up at me, a carnal smile on his lips that evoked images of crazed serial killers in a slasher flick more than anything romantic or from a rom-com – but he'd said this was what he wanted, what he needed. I would provide anything, in any way I could, to make both of my men okay. Again, this wasn't exactly a hardship; it wasn't any kind of sacrifice even. Not when you loved someone this much.

"My God, look at you, Shady," he sighed, leaning back to look me over, his dark gaze roving over my pale skin like I was a work of art.

"You know, I've missed you calling me that," I confessed, thrusting my hips unbidden over his, grinding against his erection through his slacks. There was nothing between us but the sheer material of the panties that Roan liked so well.

"I thought you didn't like it," he said softly, and dragged me to him, kissing the sweet spot on the side of my neck, over the pulse point. I gave a throaty half-gasp, half-moan, and gyrated against him harder.

"I'm here for you, and right now, I'm here for you to fuck." I gasped, with growing confidence.

He chuckled darkly against the side of my throat and nipped at my skin sharply. I bit down on a different sort of gasp.

"Are you sure you want to do this, you want to be this, for me?" he asked.

"Yes," I answered him truthfully. "Yes, I want to be this for you, because you belong to me. You're mine," I said, and he growled somewhere between pride and possession.

"That's perfect, you're perfect. I am so proud of you." He wrapped his arm around my lower back and lifted me slightly; his other hand he worked between us frantically to free his cock. It took much less effort on my part to ease my underwear to the side. I was already wet, and ready when he pulled me down onto him, plunging himself hilt deep in a sudden almost brutal thrust that went *all the way deep*.

I shuddered, the angle wasn't the best, and I felt crushed between his cock and his chest. I barely gasped out an *"Oh God"* but I wasn't sure if the words actually formed on my lips.

I wasn't sure if I liked the feeling or if it was just finally having him. His face, a reflection of something he'd seen on mine, definitely told me he had *loved* my reaction to it.

"You're going to take everything I give you, aren't you, babe?"

"Yes," I answered him swiftly, unequivocally.

"I don't want to hurt you, but there might be a few moments where this won't be gentle. You're sure you're okay with that?" he asked.

"Yes, whatever you desire, Mister Lachlan." A snake of fear began to uncoil in my belly; its tail up and rattling.

"Thank you," he murmured, and wrapped his arms around me, holding me fast. I stared into his dark smoldering eyes as he set a *punishing* rhythm. He pounded himself up inside me and I let go, surrendering myself to the sensation and shock of him hammering me with every inch he had.

With the sour came the sweet, however, and with patience, breathing, and that surrender to sensation, a wild and intense pleasure began to build.

I stared down into his handsome face, twisted into a mask of concentration as he fucked me, sweat beading his brow, his breath sawing in and out of his tight chest as he locked his arms around me. I felt my orgasm begin to build, my pussy tensing. I bit my bottom lip, and closed my eyes to concentrate more on that warm weight, that golden glow like the sun just pressing at the horizon waiting to make its debut.

"I want you to come on me," he gritted out, and I was close.

"Close, so close," I warned him, breathy, my body taking over, my mind going out to breakfast without me. I wanted it, I wanted it so bad. I wanted to come and feel the coursing impulses of pleasure flit and cycle through my being and let *go*. I wanted the fear inside me to coil tighter and go back to sleep, and I wanted to give my lover everything he asked for and more.

The orgasm hit me with the force of a freight train, my body throwing back over his arm, my hair brushing the floor behind me as I cried out, my position and lack of breath from it cutting off the scream that had been building. I made a strangled noise and stared at our reflection upside down in the glass behind us as Kyle smiled with a savage glee as my pussy pulsed and scrambled for purchase around his cock. All electrical impulses in my body went haywire at his urging.

His savage grin was matched with an equally savage laugh as he took in what a beautiful mess he made of me and after a few seconds, he drew me up back into a proper sitting position in his lap.

My mouth found his, and we kissed as I twitched and pulsed around him, the actions slowing as the orgasm petered out.

"Get up, stand up," he said with a calm I couldn't imagine. "Bend over."

I did as I was told, getting up and bending over the chair, my trembling knees on the cushion, my nightgown forgotten around my waist. He peeled off his shirt and let his slacks drop around his ankles and then shoved his way back inside me. I almost fell as the sensation almost overwhelmed me.

"Now, relax," he said, and I felt the end of his finger, maybe his thumb, start massaging my asshole. The sensation rippled through my entire torso. It was somewhere between disconcerting, and something that I knew I wanted. He pushed the digit inside me, and I let out a groan that came from somewhere deep inside my abdomen.

He rode me harder, and none of the noises I made slowed him

down. They seemed to encourage him. There was another finger in my ass, and I started losing myself, flashing back to when they had shared me. That had seemed a lifetime ago. My eyes were rolling up into the back of my head, and he had reduced me to a pair of holes wrapped around him.

He was talking…

"I'm going to fuck your ass, baby." He slapped my ass, open palmed and hard. I clenched around his fingers and his cock, and the sound that came out of me was a throaty half-moan and a half-wail. I slipped forward, and he was no longer inside me. I ached for him to be back inside. I felt empty without him.

His hand went to my hip and pulled me back into position.

"Are you ready for this?" I could tell he was doing something behind me, getting himself ready, I guessed. I bit my bottom lip as he plunged his finger back in my ass, and then my breath caught in my throat. His fingers were gone and the head of his cock was firmly against my back door. I ached for him.

"Lean forward, stick your ass up, and relax." His voice was firm. Not as firm as his cock. I coughed out a groan as he pushed through, his slippery cock penetrating my ass. I was paralyzed, and it took every brain cell I had to remember vital things like breathing. Then the resistance eased and the bulge of his cock was inside me, filling my ass the same way that Roan filled my pussy when it was the three of us like this.

"It's easier because you've done this a few times now," he said, his breath coming out a little ragged. My own breathing was no more stable. The initial discomfort and the weird feeling inside my gut had vanished and his thrusts seemed to be hitting things inside me that I didn't know I had.

"That's it, yes," he hissed between his teeth. His strokes were fast, hard. The entire time his balls were slapping against my pussy and it throbbed for attention. I was so wet it was dripping down my thighs.

God, I liked this.

I couldn't take it, and buried my fingers in my pussy, fast and frantic. "Oh fuck." I groaned like a husky animal.

"Come for me, come again," he said in that commanding voice, making me squirm, my hand wet with my own juices. The sun rose, and it was beautiful and exquisite, an agony that I didn't want to ever end. He felt me, and held me against him, pounding when my body was trying to get away.

The agony, I shuddered. I came again.

"When I take my escorts, I cum on their faces," he said.

"Is that a – problem – for you?" I put together the words like a stumbling child. Words were a challenge at the moment.

"You're not some escort," he said, and I could feel him starting to tremble.

"Mister Lachlan, you said you wanted to fuck, so do what you came here to do," I said, hoping I sounding sultry and sexy. Part of me hid an ember of jealousy for those escorts he fucked like this, unhindered by concerns and worries that suddenly didn't seem to suit him. Was this what his fear was? After sharing me with Roan, after fucking me in the ass, for what, the third time, this was where the hang-up was?

"If you don't give me a proper facial, Mister Lachlan, I'm going to be disappointed." I hoped that didn't come across as corny or cheesy.

I could see it, his love and concern, his deeply buried emotions bubbling to the surface.

"Do it," I said.

He grunted and pulled out of my ass. I turned to face him, down on my knees, and his hand and cock were inches from my face. That was as close as I would get – there was a line between being what he wanted and just disgusting. He made a noise like a wounded animal and came. It was hot, heavy, and sticky.

That wasn't new, but I would never tell him.

He spent himself with more fury than I expected, and there was a lot more of the stuff than I expected. It was a mess, but thankfully he seemed to have avoided my eyes. I kept my eyes closed, and rode out the last orgasm of the evening, a small pleasant burst against the palm of my hand while his nut started running down my chin. I was melting as quickly as it was.

He sagged back and then sat down hard in one of the chairs. There was a thin sheen of sweat on his chest, and his cock hung down, still dripping cum from the end.

"So, what happens now?" I asked.

"With an escort, I swipe my card and fuck off to the bar while she showers," he said.

I pulled the nightgown up over my head. There was no sleeping in it now, his mess starting to streak the front, and a shower was most definitely in order.

"I'm sorry, I don't accept plastic, Mister Lachlan." He gave me his ruined shirt. Wiping the mess off took a little work, it seemed to smear more than come away on the cloth. I stood up and gave him a smile, turned on the ball of my foot and walked away.

"Shouldn't you be getting yourself a drink, from the bar?" I asked, throwing a little pout into my voice. The acting helped me cover how wobbly my knees were and how easy it would be to just sit down and lean against the wall until it felt like I had bones again.

"That's what I do," he said, protest in his voice. "But you aren't an escort, I love you…" he trailed off. His face was a mask of guilt and agony.

"So, what does that mean, Kyle," I asked, my voice a forced whisper.

"That means I want to take care of you, not treat you like a whore or a prostitute," he said softly and there was something, I didn't know, guarded and at once vulnerable about the look he gave me.

"Okay," I whispered. "And what does that look like?"

"Come with me," he said softly, kicking out of his pants. He took my hand and led me toward the bathroom. We edged through the bedroom, and either Roan was asleep or was playing at it to give us our privacy.

He turned the knobs and started drawing a bath. He gave his charmed half-smile and trailed his hand through water, testing the temp. I twisted my hair into a quick knot. I didn't want to look in the mirror. I didn't want to see what sort of mess he had made, but I wanted to make sure that none had gotten into my hair.

None had, and I was thankful for that. He held out a hand to me like some sort of bathtub valet and I took it as he helped me over the high lip of the whirlpool tub. I lowered myself into the roiling, steaming water.

"Are you going to join me, Mister Lachlan?" I asked, and he smiled. He shook his head and from the edge of the tub took up a washcloth and a bar of soap.

"No, this isn't about me, it's about you and I really prefer showers," he said and wet the cloth and lathered it with the soap. He washed my back and between my shoulders. "How are you feeling?" The gesture was nice but sitting in the water made the places that needed the cloth out of his reach.

"Nice," I said. "But that wasn't for me, it was for you. If you need to go do the thing you do, that's okay. And don't feel bad, I enjoyed it too."

He smiled then and nodded. "Good. You relax here, I'll grab a quick shower, then I'll tuck you in with Roan."

I smiled. "That sounds perfect."

While he showered, I turned the jets in the tub to high, and added more hot water. The only thing missing was a swirl of glitter, or a mountain of fragrant bubbles. He was so – tactical - that I was still just really settling into the bath by the time he was done, toweled off, and returned to deliver me to our emperor-sized bed.

He seemed more like himself, the only thing missing was his signature glass of gin. Maybe he shotgunned one in the time he was gone. He looked perfect, put together, calmer and far more collected than he had earlier. I was a little jealous at how invigorated he appeared, actually. Like he was ready for anything but especially the next thing – whatever that may be.

He fluffed a towel and greeted me as I gave up the bath. I could have stayed longer, hell, I could have lived in that cauldron. He wrapped the towel around my shoulders and helped me out and then dry off. His touch was brisk and a bit rough, but this might have been the first time he had tried for aftercare, and he was clumsy. I did what

I could to keep my expression dreamy and contented and not let him catch me with a smirk on my face.

When done, my breasts and ass were expertly dried, but my arms and my feet were still wet. It didn't matter, the sheer sensation of having this hard and near emotionless man towel me dry, worrying about me, that was almost as pleasurable as all the orgasms he squeezed out of my tender pussy.

I adored this.

"I love you," he murmured and kissed my forehead.

"I love you, too," I murmured back dreamily.

"Come on, babe. Let's put you to bed."

"Stay with me this time?" I asked, and he smiled.

"Promise."

We went into the bedroom and Conan shifted over on the bed, lifting the blankets while Kyle ushered me beneath them. He draped his robe over a chair and climbed in behind me.

"Feeling better, mate?" Conan asked him, taking me into his arms. I heartily welcomed the embrace.

"Much," Kyle agreed with a satisfied sigh, and he pressed his lips to the back of my shoulder in a reverent kiss before cuddling up to my back.

"And you, Poppet?" I looked up and laid a gentle hand along the scruff of Roan's cheek, leaning up to kiss him quietly. He smiled slightly against my lips and cuddled me close. Kyle shifted closer at my back and safe between them, I slept.

When I woke the next morning, Conan stroked one of his big hands along my body, from the back of my thigh over my bum all the way to the back of my neck and back down to my waist. I sucked in a deep shuddering breath and stretched like a cat.

"Mmm," I hummed slightly and a glance over my shoulder revealed Kyle was gone.

"He's safe, Poppet," Conan murmured. "Gone to work out."

"You stayed." I smiled.

"Aye." The light in his green eyes was sparked but so much dimmer than it had been before.

I touched his cheek lightly and sighed, letting my eyes roam his ruggedly handsome features.

We lay like that, in silence, for I don't know how long, me nude and pressed against him in his lounge pants and tank top. Kyle's style on Conan's body… just one more reminder that it hadn't all just been a bad dream.

He sucked in a sharp breath as I pulled myself into him and laid my lips against his, willing him to kiss me back for real this time but leaving the option to him.

He groaned slightly against my lips and opened to me, tentatively tasting my bottom one.

I sighed out and fought back the tears carried on a fresh tsunami of relief that flowed through me. His hand came up and swept my hair, free from its knot, away from my face and when he arched into me, I could feel him hot, long, hard and thick through his clothes.

"Sadie," he whispered, and it sounded desperate.

"I'm here," I said back softly, and he rolled me onto my back. He found no resistance from me. None whatsoever.

We kissed and held each other tightly and I could feel myself growing wet, my pussy throbbing with need, my heart filling with a desire to just be as close as possible with him.

He pressed his forehead to mine and tried to catch his breath and I trailed fingertips over his arms, lightly, a barely there and reassuring touch.

"Nothing has to happen unless you want it to," I whispered thickly and though he didn't open his eyes, he smiled.

"Oh, but I want it to," he said, voice strained.

"Then take me," I murmured. "I'm right here."

"No can do, baby." Kyle's voice made both Conan and I jump and shout, Conan collapsing over me and covering me with his still much larger than mine body.

"Bloody *hell*, mate! Make some bloody noise next time!"

"I'm sorry!" Kyle cried and held up his hands in surrender. "I thought you fuckin' heard me come into the suite. I wasn't exactly being fucking subtle about it."

I closed my eyes and smoothed my hands over Conan's body through the ribbed black tank he wore. When I opened them, he was looking down at me, a slight worry eclipsing his expression.

"Give us a minute?" I asked Kyle, and he sighed.

"I wish I could, but you and I need to get out for a little while. I took the liberty of calling up a tailor and a personal shopper to come up for Roan. They're supposed to be here any minute to take measurements and shit."

"Ah, that I'll bloody well say 'thank you' for, mate."

"Yeah, I thought you might," Kyle said. To me he said, "Come on and get dressed, babe. You and I have some shopping to do."

"I don't know…" I was trying to come up with something, anything, that was better than a petulant "I don't want to" which should have been good enough, honestly, but I couldn't tell if there was something more to things than Kyle was letting on or… *damnit.*

"It's alright, Poppet. Go with him."

"I promise, when we get back here, I'll find someplace to fuck off to and give you guys some space or whatever."

I sat up as Conan moved off of me, "I don't ever want you to feel that way," I said to Kyle and he hung his head and shook it.

"No jealousy or hurt feelings here, Shady. I promise. That didn't come out how I meant it to. I just meant that I had my fun last night, and I just meant to return the courtesy."

Roan sat at my feet and leaned back on his hands nodding. "I knew what you meant, mate."

I smiled and reached out, curling my fingers around his hand, wiggling them beneath where it was pressed flat to the mattress. He looked over at me and I smiled.

"You're sure you'll be alright?" I asked, but he didn't answer right away.

Kyle sighed and said, "Shady, he'll be fine. Monaco is the Switzerland of the underworld. No one can or will touch us here without raining hell down on themselves. It's not worth it. We're safe here for at least a couple three days."

"Go on, Poppet," Roan said gently. "I don't suppose they have in-house barbers here?"

Kyle nodded. "They certainly do, and the hot lather shave is exquisite. As soon as Shady gets her fine ass out of bed and dressed, I'll have one sent up," he said.

I let out an exasperated sigh and got up. I went to my small suitcase that'd been in the trunk of the Mercedes but that had thankfully *not* caught a bullet… *Jesus, the night before?*

"What?" Kyle asked as I shot up straight from my suitcase like it'd electrocuted me.

"It hasn't even been twenty-four hours," I protested, and the men exchanged a look.

"As often happens in this life, love," Roan said gently. "You'll get used to the times things move quickly."

I sincerely hoped not, but he probably wasn't wrong.

"Right," I said and nodded.

"Go get dressed," Kyle ordered gently, and I slipped into the bath-room to do just that. Kyle joined me after just half a moment for one of his ridiculously fast tactical showers and to dress himself.

He finished about the time I put the last touches on my makeup.

"You know, you're beautiful with or without that stuff on your face," he said offhandedly, buttoning his cuff. "Not many women can say the same."

His compliment was both brutal and sweet, like the man himself.

"Are you hitting on me, Mr. Lachlan?" I asked, arching a brow at him in the mirror.

He grinned, and it was one of his panty-vaporizing smiles that sadly not even I could claim immunity to.

"Just calling it like I see it, Shady Brooks." I smiled and got up. He held out a hand to me and drew me close.

"I'm worried about leaving him," I whispered, and he smiled down at me.

"I know, but trust me on this one, okay? I've known Roan a lot longer."

I nodded and said, "It still feels too soon."

"For you or for him?" he asked with a gentle smile and I had to return it.

"For me," I whispered.

"Ahh, see. There it is." He tilted his head back and blew out a breath and when he dropped his dark eyes to mine, he said, "You're a brave woman, Shady. Always have been and always will be. So, let's enjoy this place, take the downtime while it's presented, and do something mundane for a change. I get it, it'll be the bravest thing you do today given the circumstances; but he'll be here when we get back, I promise you, and I'll let you guys have all the time you need."

I nodded and took in a deep, cleansing breath.

"Okay," I murmured.

Still, leaving the suite and Conan behind *was* the hardest thing I had to do that day.

"SADIE!" I looked over and saw Grant raise his hand high in the air. I laughed and shook my head slightly and curled my fingers in a wave. He was on a nearby yacht in its slip, high on the back deck behind a set of turntables. I had to assume he was the source of the seriously sick bass-dropping beats drifting through the warm summer air. He waved at me to come join him and I waved him off laughing. I was waiting on Kyle who had slipped into a spa across from the harbor. I couldn't go in. I had a cone of gelato and no food or drink was allowed inside.

It was fine, he'd said. He would only be a minute. Still, I turned back, chest tight and felt it loosen in relief as he came jogging across the road back to me.

"What'd you go in there for?" I asked.

"Need to know basis," he said and took my hand, bending to kiss me quickly. "How about we go shopping for something for Roan? A present from you is sure to make him feel better." he said.

I smiled. "I like that idea."

"Maybe I'll get him something, too," he said, tucking my hand in the crook of his arm as we strolled.

I finished my gelato before we found the perfect shop. We ended up in a high-end men's boutique of some kind and I do mean *very* prim and proper. Suits, ties, finely made shirts and tailored jackets and slacks. The type of thing Roan would just absolutely adore if he could be with us, which I knew he couldn't now.

He hadn't even tried to put on the prosthetic leg. Instead, he had done something I had never seen him do before – he had tied the end of the lounge pants below his stump into a knot and had hopped around the suite before our departure with the help of one of those canes with the collar that went around your arm.

"What should we get?" I asked curiously.

"Well, I know what I'm getting him," Kyle said, eyeing the wall of shoes.

"I'll be over here," I murmured. The light, pale blue skirt I wore swished against my legs, and I stepped over to the table of ties and kerchiefs, a brilliant purple catching my eye.

It wasn't Roan's style, the purple that had caught my eye. It was really more fuchsia than purple, but it had led me to the table and the table held a matching tie and kerchief in a deep and dusky amethyst that would be just *perfect* with one of his gray suits. I could picture him so easily adjusting both and tugging on his waistcoat that it made me smile.

I bit my bottom lip and picked them up, turning to Kyle and holding them up so that he could see. His eyebrows went up, and he nodded like there was no question. I should absolutely get them.

I smiled, and that's just what I did, pleased when the man at the counter boxed them beautifully for me.

Kyle swiped that black credit card of his that opened doors and made people hustle just that little bit more at its appearance and we were on our way.

The afternoon was starting to drag on into evening as we walked quietly arm in arm, stopping here and there along the way.

I stopped in front of a display in an antique store window and cocked my head.

"What?" he asked. "What is it?"

I pointed at the timepiece that had caught my eye. I'd once told Roan that all he was missing was a pocket watch to make him look like a proper butler and he'd laughed and then had gently taught me the difference between a time piece and a pocket watch and had told me that he wouldn't be caught dead with the latter.

"I need to see how much that costs," I murmured.

"The pocket watch?" Kyle asked, and I shook my head.

"The *timepiece*," I said, trying to make out the little placard in French beside it.

"It's ugly," he remarked, and I smiled.

"It's *British*, I think; and it's old. World War II, maybe?"

"Let's find out," he said.

We went in and found out I was right; it was both British and did harken back to WWII. It was an old GSTP or General Service Time Piece. A timepiece worn by officers in the British Army, mostly.

It was sad, but also no wonder how it had wound up in the south of France.

"Sadie?" Kyle asked.

I nodded.

"I want it for him," I said, and he smiled and the black credit card made another appearance.

We went back to the hotel after that, but not to the room. Kyle said Roan would text him when the tailor, barber and whoever else left. Instead, we went to the hotel restaurant where Kyle ordered himself a gin and tonic and I stuck with just water. I didn't feel like drinking.

We had dinner. He seemed disappointed that with just the two of us, that we couldn't properly enjoy an *omakase*, a chef's choice dinner from the sushi bar. He had a filet, and I kept it light with a fresh salad, my nerves fraying the longer we waited for Kyle's phone to buzz across our table.

Finally, it did, and I tried not to jump and sneak a look at it. Kyle smirked when my eyes met his.

"We're good to go, baby. Come on, I'll walk you up." We returned to our suite and Kyle let me go in first.

"If you'll excuse me," he said. "I'll be right back." He set our bags from our shopping trip on the kitchenette's counter near Roan and walked to the restroom.

Roan looked up at me over his laptop screen, his face eerily illuminated by whatever was on it. I glanced at the glass wall and the deepening dark outside of it, my throat tightening up at the laptop screen and the open and all too familiar email service in the window's reflection. The emails I wrote him...

My gaze flicked back to Roan's, and I opened my mouth, closed it, then opened it again to rush out, "Please don't hate me for anything I said in those emails." I pleaded openly with everything that I was in that moment and he cocked his head slightly and shook it.

"I could never hate you for anything, Poppet," he said, and I knew he meant it. I sniffed and looked away, clearing my throat.

"Come here," he murmured soothingly, and I did. I went to him and he twisted on his stool and wrapped me up tight in his arms. All the cracks I had carefully tried to shore up in my façade widened and my heart came pouring out my eyes.

Damnit.

"Shh, I've got you now, eh, love? I'm here."

"I know, but when I wrote those—"

"Shhh, I know," he whispered into my hair.

"Everything okay?" Kyle asked carefully, coming back out from the bedroom.

"Aye, we're good, mate."

"Good deal," he said and sounded relieved. "I'm going to head down to the bar and handle some business shit."

I felt Conan nod.

"Be careful," I said, sniffing and turning my face so I could see him. "I love you."

He smiled at that.

"I love you, too," he said, and he nodded to Conan. "Same to you, bro. Just shoot me a text whenever I'm good to come back. I don't hear from you by last call or whatever, I'll get a different room."

"You haven't heard from us by last call, mate, just come back here," Roan said and I nodded emphatically.

"I don't want you in another room," I said.

"Agreed," Roan said.

"You got it," Kyle shot back with a solemn nod before he dragged open the door to the hall and disappeared through it.

"What's all this now?" Conan asked, jerking his head in the direction of the shopping bags and their parcels. I smiled.

"Presents for you," I said simply.

He smiled genuinely and kissing my forehead said, "Go wash your face, Poppet. I'll wait for you to get back, yeah?"

I nodded, and I went to wash the makeup off my face and to slip into one of the hotel's satin monogrammed bath robes. When I returned, he had the parcels out of the bags and lined up waiting.

"You didn't peek now, did you?"

"I wouldn't dream of it," he murmured, and I went to stand next to him. His hand automatically went to my hip, his arm around my back.

"Where should I start?" he asked.

"Well, this is from Kyle," I said, touching the brown paper wrapped shoebox.

"And this?" he asked, touching the counter in front of the slim, flat, navy blue box with silver lettering that held his tie and kerchief.

"Me," I said.

He slipped that one off the counter and I smiled at him, excited for him to open it. He lifted the lid.

"Oh my," he said. "Now that's a sight." He smiled in appreciation.

"You really like it?" I asked.

"Aye," he said quietly and looked at me and those eyes of his, something was slightly thawed in them. I smiled, warmed to my toes, and he sighed, picking up Kyle's package.

"What was that for?" I asked with a giggle.

"We'll see," he said and pulled the string on the top. It fell open, and the paper fell away and he plucked both string and paper from the box and set them aside on the counter.

He chuckled and opened the box and then laughed.

"Only Lach," he said, "would buy a pair of shoes for a one-legged man. What's this?" he plucked a card from between the shoes and opened it, snorting and muttering, "Bloody wanker."

I took the card, grinning at the smile that painted my lover's lips and asked, "What is it?"

It was a gift card to the spa Kyle had gone into and written in Kyle's messy handwriting above it? *Half off a spa pedicure, buddy. You've earned it.*

I read it out loud and Roan laughed as though my reading it out loud somehow made it even funnier.

I couldn't help it, I had to laugh too.

"Thank you," Roan said. "The both of you."

"I saved the best for last," I murmured, sweeping the box from the antique store into my hands. I was suddenly nervous, capturing my bottom lip between my teeth and taking a deep breath. I handed it to him.

He looked at me curiously and took the box. Quirking an eyebrow, he lifted the hinged lid.

We'd stopped by an engraver on the way back to the hotel and had a little silver tag engraved and fastened above the watch itself, sort of a key chain for it, only much smaller, riding on the watch chain. Roan read it out loud.

"No more lost time..."

He took in a deep breath and held it, his jaw tightening, eyes misting with emotion. I hadn't expected it to make *that much* of an impact.

He stared at the time piece for a long time and I grew nervous.

"Is it… is it okay?" I asked.

He looked at me and nodded slowly, setting it aside.

"It's wonderful, Poppet."

"I saw it in an antique store window and it was calling your name," I murmured. "It's from World War II."

"Yes, I know," he said with a smile that was borderline brittle.

I gave him a tremulous smile back, and he reached for me. I went willingly, *eagerly* into his arms where he held me tight for long minutes, breathing in the scent from my hair, and kissing me soundly on the top of my head a time or two.

"What would you like to do now?" I asked quietly, and he leaned back to look at me and said, "Right now? I would quite like to go back to this morning," he said, and I smiled.

"I'd like that, too."

So that's what we did – we went to the bedroom, and we got into bed. I slipped from the robe and left it behind and we resumed our positions from earlier in the day, me nude and pressed against Conan tightly in his borrowed clothes from Lachlan.

"Personal shoppers didn't pull through for you huh?" I asked, plucking at the rib knit tank top.

He chuckled and said, "Personal tailoring takes time, Poppet. The clothing will be delivered before we check out."

"Mm," I murmured and turned my face up to his.

He didn't hesitate, his fingertips brushing my chin, his mouth covering mine.

We kissed slowly, sweetly, and I closed my eyes, sighing out.

All too soon, we were back in the position we had found ourselves in that morning and I could *feel* his hesitation.

"It's alright," I whispered. "We don't have to do anything you don't want to." I swallowed hard, and he traced my hair away from my face, back behind my ear, eyes glittering in the dark as they searched my face in the low light.

"Why would you say that, lass?" he asked, and I rolled my lips together and sniffed, trying not to let emotions get the best of me.

"I heard you," I whispered.

"Heard what?"

"What you said to Kyle at Chauvignon… about—" I took a deep breath. "About the things she did to you."

He didn't exactly recoil, but he *did* flinch.

"I-I know what it's like," I stammered and suddenly couldn't meet his gaze, my cheeks growing hot, my eyes hotter.

He touched the side of my face and my gaze went back to his.

"*No*, Poppet," he whispered and sounded horrified. I sniffed.

"It was a long time ago," I said. "For me. Long before you and Kyle." I bit down on my words and thought *way to kill the mood, Sadie*, but I felt as though it needed to be said.

He pressed his lips to mine to silence me and I was alright with that. The kiss deepened, taking on a frantic sort of energy.

I wrapped my arms and legs around him and towed him down over the top of me, holding him tightly, cradling him against me.

"Sadie." He groaned my name into my ear.

"Whatever you want, whatever you need, I'm here," I whispered.

Silently, he reached down between us, capturing my mouth with his again as he shoved his borrowed lounge pants out of our way.

It wasn't neat or precise the way he worked himself inside of me. What it was, was raw and honest. Perfectly imperfect as he slipped his way into me to the hilt to the track of both satisfied and desirous moaning from between us.

He made love to me with slow rolling even motions, his hands finding mine, fingers twining, holding them flat to the bed to either side of our heads as he pressed them into the mattress and rose up above me.

He rocked his hips, plunging in deep and even strokes into my body as we made eye contact and let all the feelings we couldn't express with sounds or words pass between us.

We were like that an extraordinarily long time, quiet, falling into the rhythm of our bodies against one another, soaking up the warmth and the love and showering each other in devotion that felt like satin rose petals falling against our souls.

"Oh, God, *Conan*," I groaned when my orgasm swept through me, taking me by surprise. It was the most delicate, subtle thing. So gentle, sweeping through me suddenly but in such a way that I swear it was a touch of gossamer against the senses; so fleeting and so perfect, you could almost believe it hadn't happened at all.

Conan groaned and bowed over me, releasing my hands and plunging his arms beneath me as he took his own pleasure in my body, and I wrapped myself around him, holding him tightly until he began to shake with silent wracking sobs against me.

I felt an initial surge of panic that quickly subsided as my need to nurture and protect him as much as he had me barged into the fore.

"Shhh," I soothed, holding him close. "I've got you."

The storm was brief, and I let him bury his face in my hair and the crook between my shoulder and my neck for as long as he needed to, simply lying still beneath him, sweeping my palms soothingly over every inch of his back through his shirt.

He pushed up and kissed the tip of my nose gently, making me smile, his eyes red rimmed as he sniffed thickly.

"Thank you, Poppet," he murmured, and I touched his cheekbone, edging around a thin red scar, something new, something fresh, with the gentlest of fingertips.

He'd been through so much...

"Of course," I whispered and his expression changed, growing somber and more serious. He lowered his mouth to mine and kissed me then, and it felt somehow more grounded.

It would take so very much more for the three of us to heal from all of this, but that kiss tasted like progress and hope.

CHAPTER TEN

*R*oan...

With Lach and Sadie gone for most of the day, I was left to my own devices and several appointments. There were things that needed to be handled on my laptop, including the emails, and those I was concerned about. What sort of things had she divulged, what anger and pieces of her soul were waiting in my inbox? I would wait a bit on that. I didn't want to open a bomb that would shatter me while the tailor was measuring my inseam.

The cosmetologist was heralded by a curt phone call from the front desk. She was a stunning raven-haired Spanish woman, with a full kit over her arm. I was seated, and she took six and a half months of missed haircuts off of me. I felt a pound lighter, and younger. The hot shave was everything Lach had said it would be, and it would be the only time a person could hold a sharpened razor to my throat in such a manner that I was close to falling asleep.

I felt like a new man when she packed her razors and scissors away, and brushed my shoulders clean. The style was different from my old efficient short crop. This felt more stylish, rakish, something Lach might have done if he had my red hair.

The tailor and his assistants showed up not long after she left.

The gentleman was older, but had the sharp face of a retired soldier. He recognized me as a fellow one, and his demeanor changed. His gruff attitude vanished, and he was smiles and conversation. He talked about serving with the UN forces, in Cypress, Lebanon, and Beirut, how he was a veteran who fought in multiple battles, yet somehow never served in wartime. I told him about Iraq, Afghanistan, and spending time on her Majesty's carriers and assault ships.

His assistants were much younger – one a young lad with a strong chin and the hard sharp eyes of the Parisian, the sort of man who had no memories of the Nazis, and his only experiences with violence involved terrorists blowing things up, or shooting up buildings until the gendarmes arrived. The final person was a quiet woman with a tightly done bun of black hair. She reminded me of a young Sean Young. Her smile was disarming, and there was something about her eyes that had me relaxing.

While the old man was talking about Cypress, and wearing a blue helmet, I saw something that made my blood run cold. The young woman was an assassin. I saw a glimpse of a tattoo on the inside of her wrist. It was a jambiya, a curved knife that was the symbol of the *Pax Sicari*.

She was one of the peacekeepers who lurked inside the city, making sure that everyone behaved. That I saw her tattoo was no accident, it was something she allowed, almost a professional courtesy. Later, when we were alone, I would have to ask Lach if any of the Hidden Knives let him know they were there.

The fitting went quickly, and it was a measure of my self-control that I kept a calm and collected face.

The personal shopper came while the old man was packing up his kit. I ordered a tea service to be brought up, thankful to live in a place that was nice enough to have such an offering. The meeting with the shopper took a little longer than the tailor, but she was very interested in details and accessories. She reminded me a good deal of the women that Lach would drop large amounts of money on.

They had to have day jobs, I supposed.

Once she was gone, I had a proper English breakfast brought up.

The breakfast anglaise was perfection, down to the imported sausages.

The tea, I shuddered down to the toes that were long gone, was flawless.

That left only one matter, business on the computer. Updating the portfolios and stock options took well over an hour. Most of the good leads I had panned out, and the returns were still in the green, though they should have been much higher in the green than they were. The cost of being on a forced half-year detention, it was what it was.

I found several other distractions that took me through a large slice of the afternoon. I did realize that I was avoiding my emails. I sighed, picked up the bottle of whiskey that I had danced with last night, and it was still half full. I poured a few fingers of booze and sat down. It was time to get serious.

Because juggling a few million in investments and having a Hidden Knives assassin visit you was just any other day for me, I hit the button and opened my email. Unsurprisingly, the box was full. I set to clearing out the junk, and the old stuff, and tagged a few for later review and response.

There was a clear chain of emails, all from Sadie. I clicked the first one.

Dear Conan,

It's been twenty-one and a half days since we lost you. It feels much longer. I don't even know why I'm writing this, except I miss you, and I want to feel connected to you and I don't know any other way to do that now. Your shirt doesn't even smell like you anymore and that hurts.

Kyle and I watch your videos, but with as much as we do, it feels like you're growing ever more distant. I see your face; I hear your words but we've watched them so many times now I have them memorized. So much so, I play them every time I close my eyes. Every time I shower, every night before I try to sleep.

I don't sleep. Not much anymore. More often than not, I wake and Kyle isn't with me. He's working out, or scrolling through screens or watching old footage from the mansion. Sometimes I sit on the floor, resting my head against his knee and watch too.

He doesn't touch me anymore. Not like he used to. Doesn't call me 'Shady' either. I never thought I would miss that... I miss it almost as much as I miss you calling me 'Poppet.'

I won't say where we are or anything. I haven't told him that I'm even writing these. I'm afraid he would get mad at me for compromising us or something... but I need this. I need something.

I love you. I miss you.

Sadie

Six months gone, six months I had lost, lost with her.

Fuck.

This was going to be a rollercoaster of digital emotional trauma.

I needed something to distract me from the knot growing in my chest.

Fuck.

I checked the saved videos, and there were several archived news loops. I clicked on them, letting them play through. The Soviet warhead worked flawlessly, and there had been no incriminating evidence found. The only thing that I could find in several news trawls were reports of military-grade explosives being used, and that for some strange reason, it read an antique Soviet era explosive. Arson wasn't being pursued since such weapons would be almost impossible to get into the US.

The investigation was wrapped, and it was deemed that the Chinese must have been involved, as several ships had been sunk, there were several dozen arrests made, and that there had been some sort of underworld grand melee.

I hit the bottle again, taking a pull from the neck. Bootlegger Head had reverted to state control, and there was no current plan on what to do with the property other than having the wreckage cleared away and the grounds made safe again.

I wiped at my face; I was running away again.

I clicked through more of the emails.

Dear Conan,

Today I'm angry. Angry with Kyle for being so cold blooded, and angry with you which I find devastating but I can't help it.

Whatever happened to your promise? You swore you would never lie to me, but you did. You looked me right in the eye and lied and said you would be right behind me but you weren't and now you're gone and I just can't take anymore.

It's frozen out there, colder than you can imagine. My hands go numb so easily and it hurts with every recoil but it doesn't hurt enough to match what I'm feeling inside. Today is one of those bad days where I feel like I could never forgive you... and I immediately drown in guilt for it.

I miss you.

I miss Kyle the way he was before all of this... but most of all, I miss me.

I wish you both had let me die.

Sadie.

My heart broke for her. I could hardly imagine how it had been for her. They had bunkered in Montana, in the old silo facility, under the snow and ice, with Lach wounded, me seemingly dead, and her all but alone again. I could see how her space in the warehouse might have seemed more appealing by comparison.

There was no hole deep enough to hide the Escadrille bastards from me.

I clicked through more of the emails. I read as she processed through the stages of grief. Laying it out as stages made it seem trite. It took the emotion out of it, reducing trauma and suffering to levels like a game.

Dear Conan,

I woke, dreaming of you.

I dreamed I lay there sound asleep, roused by a gentle sweep of fingertips along my back, and when I opened my eyes, it was you.

God, I can't tell you how much I wished this dream were something true.

I did something today I'm really not proud of. I fucked Kyle on the weight room floor. The first time for anything since... well, you know.

He wasn't into it. I don't know why I did it except for selfish reasons. I wonder if this is what being mad feels like. Mad with grief... I cried in the shower afterward and I feel so guilty. Sometimes I wonder if he blames me for your death. I know I do.

Losing you has broken me in ways I didn't think possible. I hate them for that. I hate myself for it and I want to hate you. I want to hold my anger and wrap myself in it the way I used to wrap myself in you but I can't. I think of you and it all slips away and all that's left is this horrible ravaged wasteland where I feel like my heart used to be.

Kyle is more distant than ever, fixated on some distant point... I can't even say he's Kyle anymore. This is Lach. He's fully Lachlan now, if that makes sense.

I don't know, maybe I'm something different too. Not Sadie, not Poppet or Shady, not even Roan Lachlan. I don't know what I should be called. I don't know what's left. I feel like this hollowed-out shell, a ghost, wandering through – well, I won't say anything about where I am.

I love you; I hate you, and everything in between.

I wish you were here. I wish I were there. Everything in between that, too.

I don't know who or what I am anymore except yours. Yours in life and now in death.

Yes, that's how I'll sign this.

Yours.

The hotel had a very excellent gym, and I paid it a visit.

I wore myself out with steel and sweat, giving myself to the burn of exercise. This was one of the things that I had been denied for months. No one I loved or cared about, no gym, no freedom, no Sadie. Just that sadistic bitch, and her laugh and her teeth.

The whole time Sadie was going through an emotional breakdown.

I pushed, sweat dripping until my eyes were burning from it. That was fine.

I hit my limit on the bench press. It started with sweat running into my eyes, and then once the tears started flowing, I cracked like a dam. Thankfully, the facility was empty, and I was able to limp to the showers and hide my breakdown under a roar of water and steam.

I sat for a while, the hot water not running out, and my leg raw with agony.

Sadie had been sitting in a shower like this once.

I thought about how shite the showers were at Wolf Creek, and wondered if she had sat in one of them and cried her heart out while Lach was sleeping, some IV stuck in his arm, that she had put in.

Fuck all of this.

Fuck the Escadrille, and Kaijin, and *Le Generale*. I wanted to crush them, to make them bleed and scream with the pain that they had put us through, and all because we wouldn't join their fucking heroin Cartel, or that they had hired us for a suicide mission in their petty fucking family dispute.

I calmed down, and had room service for lunch, a round of painkillers, and finished off the bottle of whiskey from the previous night. The suite had been serviced while I was away, and that was a nice touch. Of course, it was a nice touch, the Fairmont sat literally *over* the Monaco Grand Prix track, and faced the Mediterranean. There was nothing about the place that wasn't nice.

Lach had texted me a few times through the day, an unusual change from the usual pace of things. He was going to keep Sadie out and occupied so that I could have the privacy I needed to get my things taken care of. I knew as soon as I sent him the text, they would be in the suite posthaste. I was glad for it. I didn't want her to see me break down, and there was no way I could have worked through the portfolio stuff if she was here. I would have doted on her every second.

Did you have omakase without me? I texted Lach after he sent me a pic of the offering at the in-house sushi restaurant. Ninety-five euros seemed like a surprisingly good deal for a chef's tasting course at a place as posh as this.

Lach: No, mate, made ressies for lunch tomorrow.

Good, room is clear. RTB - I texted. Return to base, we had lived for those three letters to come across the radio, sweeping across the ruined wasteland of the Afghani highlands. We would wheel the jeeps and IFVs around and make for home as quick as we could. There were showers and hot meals, and fewer mortar rounds. RTB was the bell calling us home.

They returned, laden with bags. They had spent a good deal of money, but it was all needed. Not just in terms of replacing missing clothes, but in the basic pleasure of buying things. Everything we had previously owned had been blown to fuck all, why not buy each other gifts and trinkets?

Sadie had been enormously worried over the contents of those emails she had sent me, and I saw that her building tears weren't because I had read something that she wanted to keep private, but that I would see all the ugliness and hurt in them, and I would turn away from her. I took her in my arms, in my lap, and she came close to having a crying jag that might have cleansed her soul, but she wasn't ready for that yet. There was something still unsaid between us, a dam of sorts.

Kyle bowed out, excusing himself for strong cocktails and some distraction. I knew that he was making room for the two of us, and not off hunting for his own sport. She had a number of things for me, and a few joking gifts from him. Those would have to be repaid in kind, but that would take some time to come into my mind. Then there was the engraved General Service Time Piece. Something caught in my throat, and I felt my eyes sting. It was enormously thoughtful.

There was no way she could have known, but I had owned one of these before. It had belonged to my grandfather, and the only engraving on it was a woman's name, my grandmother, Esther. It was gone, lost when the house went up.

Then she all but led me from the lounge, overlooking the sea, to the large bedroom and its waiting king-sized bed. She doffed her clothing with quick efficiency. There was no striptease or attempt at seduction, only the flash of her breasts, the dark triangle marking her pussy, and a slowly growing ache between my legs, and in my chest.

We had been close this morning, before Lach had opened the blinds on the day and swept her from my presence.

He surely had many reasons, I did need my space for the things I had done that afternoon. I knew that the two of them had gone through his game the evening before. I thought about what I knew of that, his penchant for fucking tactically beautiful women in the ass, and how he took pleasure from destroying beautiful things. Was it the same for him, emptying his balls into their perfectly coiffed hair, their precision-applied makeup as it had been lobbing grenades through the arches of brutalist regime monuments and the palaces of warlords?

Another thought started to intrude, I felt Sadie's lips on mine, her hand feeling tiny, tugging me out of my boxers. The remembrance of her lips on mine, groaning as Lach and I took both of her holes, it was violated by the spectre of Gwendolyn.

The desire all but died, remembering her cruel touch, how her hands had felt small wrapped around my cock, and how I never knew if she was going to suck me, or use the damned loop cinched around the base of my business to make me hard regardless of what I wanted. There were flashes of her teeth biting into my tenderest flesh, or her soft breasts pillowing my cock as she brought me to orgasm.

Then Sadie was there, and I heard her whisper that phrase that seemed like the language of the seraphs. *I got you.* And she did have me. We spoke in the shadowy language of lovers, confessing our hearts to each other. She knew what that woman had done to me, at least what I had told Kyle, and that she knew this sort of cruelty.

We would have to find the person who was callous enough to lay hands on my Sadie and make that piece of shit pay. And dearly.

Revenge would have to come later, because there was something much more important at hand. I could feel how wet she was, and her need for me was almost palpable. There was no grand seduction, no acrobatic feat of a gymnast or Olympic lovemaking, like some erotic gods fucking. I was a nearly shattered man, and she was a beautifully broken woman. When I sank my cock into her, it was like something soothed both of us. Her breath was hot against my neck, and my chest. I made love to her, no rush, no urgency.

The only thing that mattered was that we were together again, and there was absolutely nothing left between us, not even space or air. I could die in that moment, or live in it for eternity and it would have been perfect.

Such things, like shadowy languages, aren't meant to last.

When she came, it was such a small and soft thing, I was brought close to tears. This was her, this was the Sadie that I had dreamed of. When the sadist woman had taken every inch of my pleasure away for hers, I had held the thought of this woman, seemingly so small, but so much more important than myself, as an amulet against the abuse.

We rolled, she under me, me buried inside her. A sense of urgency grew in my belly, and my need for her became more intense. I went faster, and she took it. I pushed deeper into her, and her lips and pussy were hungry for me.

There was no anger, no fury, no spite. There was no horrible woman laying into me with a thronged whip, there were no forced positions, there was no fucking pain, there was only the sweetness of her.

The tears fell on her face from my cheeks.

I wept and then lost my rhythm. She whispered magical words in my ear, and it didn't matter. We laid together, and the weight of it came home, I was free. I had truly escaped; I had been rescued.

I was free.

My own orgasm seemed like an afterthought, a bodily function taking care of itself.

It was like an evil spirit leaving my body, purifying me with its passage.

When she kissed me, it tasted like a promise, a promise that the bad things were over.

CHAPTER ELEVEN

*L*achlan...

"The first order of business is that we need to get out of Monaco and back home. The house on Phoenician Boulevard should still be secure, and there's nothing tying it to our identities, as known to the Escadrille," I said. Roan had his laptop set up, and the one that was technically mine, but I pretty much never used, right next to it.

"Aye, but the Escadrille people know we're here," he said calmly.

"Which means they'll be watching the main avenues that any sane person would use to leave the city." I pointed at him.

"Which means that if we get on an airplane, going anywhere in the world, they will have someone on us in a matter of hours, if not meeting us when we land," Roan remarked.

"Who knows, we might have made them angry enough to look into bringing down an airliner while we're on it. No way for us to fight a missile shot at us," I said, feeling a little discouraged.

Sadie's eyes were large, but she had said she wanted to be included, so she was being included.

"Taking a ship is right out. Anything large enough to go somewhere of interest to us would be able to have some of their people on it. As soon as we're out of Monaco's waters, we're right back at the airport problem. Hell, it would be easy for them to put people on almost any boat in the harbor, just waiting for us to try and slip their net." He grimaced.

"Do we know that?" Sadie asked. "That they know we're here?"

"Yes, they know," I said. "Just because there is an enforced peace here doesn't mean there is an order of silence."

"They probably know what room we're in," Roan admitted.

She got a little paler.

"So, what would an insane person do?" I asked. "Outside the box answers only."

"Smuggle ourselves over a border illegally," Roan said.

"Swim?" Sadie guessed.

"Take up residency." I threw one out, but I knew that wouldn't work. Monaco was expensive and eventually we'd go mad cooped up in a single city, no matter how nice it was. And did I mention it was expensive? Like, *really* expensive.

"Attack." Roan didn't look up from his screens. "We attack."

"Like an ambush?" I raised an eyebrow.

"Would they expect that?" Sadie asked.

"Possibly, but not as likely." He looked hopeful. "Hitting Mont Saint Chauvignon really took them be surprise, and literally three and a half people—"

"Four," Sadie interrupted him.

"Four people were able to crack their perimeter security, overwhelm their detail, and then escape, while also forcing their VIPs to bail out in a EuroCopter," he finished. "They were arrogant, but they won't make that mistake a second time. I am willing to bet that that place looks like Charlemagne himself was in charge of defense."

"We don't go back there, no," I agreed. "That's probably where they're staging everything from, and God knows who and how many are there."

"What about the others on the list?" Sadie asked.

"Each of their top people have their own estate, and the *Generale*, he moves around like a third world dictator, there's no way we could get to him, we'd have to bring him to us. Like setting a snare," Roan said. "Mont Saint Chauvignon is apparently where Kaijin lived when not hustling smack and killing people with her poisonous…" he turned and looked at Sadie and stopped.

"Poisonous what?" she asked.

"We don't know, we only suspect she's a poisoner. My guess is that the way she plays the dominatrix vamp card, it's something like a vaginal insert, or weaponized anti-rape tool," I said. Sadie recoiled in horror. I gave her a solemn nod.

"The woman is made of poison, that's enough," Roan said.

"What about the other lieutenants?" I asked.

"Tracking them isn't easy, but it seems like Ajahi spends most of him time either in South Africa, or attending the *Generale*. Malmaison, the little Aryan fart, has a WWII art gallery in Oberhausen, Germany."

"An art gallery?" Sadie sounded surprised.

"Germany has laws about Nazi paraphernalia. You aren't legally allowed to own it, but it can be kept in a museum. I'm guessing he lives above the museum, gallery, whatever, and he keeps his trophy collection downstairs."

"Can we get a viewing?" I laughed.

"Invitation only, it's a private gallery." Roan gave a small knowing laugh. "Probably Malmaison's inner circle of wannabe Nazi circle-jerkers."

"Gross." She grimaced.

"Very, and an odd person to have in the Escadrille considering they seem to be mostly French and have a lot of ties to the French Foreign Legion," he said, clacking out a few notes, or searches, or whatever, in his new computer rig.

"What's his angle, and how can we use it?" I asked. Roan went to work on his keyboard, and Sadie stood and walked over behind him. She put her hands on his shoulders while his fingers relentlessly pounded the keys. There was an angle here, something we could use as a wedge. There was always a way to break through, to break out. The key was finding the weakest point and hitting it as hard as possible.

Kaijin was certainly strong, maybe the second after the old French guy.

Ajahi sweated the pure confidence and arrogance of a man who kept hyenas on chains, and collected skulls and AKs like most people had tchotchkes on their mantles, or forks in their silverware drawers.

Then there was Malmaison, the sweaty little bastard, looking nervous sitting with his own elite. A wannabe Nazi sitting between a half-Asian mock mademoiselle and an African warlord. How awkward was that for his master race fantasies?

"From what I've got, he's not at Mont Saint Chauvignon, he's in Oberhausen. Looks like he wasn't called in," he said after a few minutes. "But maybe his angle is that he is a fence for weapons coming through the Netherlands and Belgium and supplies angry young men for the Escadrille to use as boots on the ground."

"What is the best way to get there?" I asked.

"Airplane; it's almost a straight shot," Roan said. "But way too obvious."

"What's the worst way?" Sadie asked. "Besides walking, or I don't know, fucking swimming."

"There is a bus, but it's more than twenty-five hours," he said.

"Diversion – book a flight, get a ride share to the airport, and after checking in at the counter, we go grab a rental car, and drive out," I said. "What's the drive time?"

"About eleven hours, give or take," he replied.

"We'll take it. Can we use the autobahn?" I asked, with a hint of excitement in my voice.

"Of course, it's not a single road." Roan snorted at me.

"Let's see about discretely renting something stupid fast, and we drive, while the *Generale* watches the airport waiting for us to fly... to where?" I was suddenly drawn to a halt.

"Mexico?" Sadie suggested. "That's where everyone runs to, isn't it?"

"It is, and the Narcos are probably not very happy with what happened before the house went up. A lot of them went to jail or were shot." Roan nodded. "I think that's a good idea."

"Then let's book tickets to Mexico City, make sure that the frogs know about it, and then we drive something loud and obnoxious to Oberhausen. They won't be watching the roads. Especially not the ones running deeper into Europe and not heading to a place that we have no reason to go after."

"Are we going to hit this guy?" Sadie asked.

"I don't know, we could. Take one out while the others are all dealing with diarrhea in Mexico," I said. "I mean, we have to take at least their command structure out."

"Agreed," Roan growled. "They came after us hard, and they will come again, and again until either we're dead, or they are."

ROAN BOOKED OUR TICKETS, MADE THE CALL WHILE WE WERE SITTING IN the hotel café sipping espresso and nibbling at small pastry things. It was inconspicuous, but we had to lay down a trail if we wanted them to follow it. We had a mid-morning spa treatment, and I had to laugh while Roan got his half-priced pedicure. Sadie was uncertain and uncomfortable at first, but either just accepted it, or realized that it was something to be enjoyed. We mentioned a few things about what we were going to do when we got back home and peppered in a few points of interest. Breadcrumbs. Bait.

After the spa, we went back to the room, packed our bags, and made ready for our plan. This was going to involve some sleight of hand. Roan had his crutch, his prosthetic stowed in one of his newly purchased carryon bags. Sadie had a muted lavender and gray blouse and slacks thing going on, and I had a very drab herringbone jacket draped over my arm. We checked into our flight, strolled through security, and then into the sky lounge, presumably to grab drinks before what should be our well-publicized, by now, flight back to the United States and the *California SafeHouse*, in Berkeley.

The flight started boarding, and we went to the airport bathrooms and changed. The herringbone jacket and drab outfit were replaced with a very crisp and sharp black suit. Roan's suit had matching cuts to mine, but he said the color was Supermarine blue. Probably a WWII reference, that was certainly one of his things. When we met outside the bathrooms, Sadie's drab mock pantsuit had been replaced with a Monaco styled dress that barely came to the middle of her thighs.

"You'll need to be careful getting in and out of cars, Poppet." Roan nodded to her.

"Unless you want to make sure everyone knows what color panties you're wearing." I gave her a wink. She blushed. I wasn't sure if it was literally what I said, or the chance that she was going commando and onlookers would see something more than a flash of fabric. There was a good chance it was the second. I gave a laugh.

We left an hour later, following a surge of disembarking passengers who had just arrived from a packed London flight. No crutch, no one-legged man. I walked alone; Sadie walked with her arm in Roan's. He looked like quite the lucky sugar daddy at that moment.

We passed through the exit, down into the parking garage, and the valet brought us up our rental car, a large Bentley Continental. It might have weighed over two tons, but it had a massive twelve-cylinder engine, an astonishing amount of power, and, important for our plan, a huge trunk.

"Are you both ready for this?" I asked. Sadie looked confident, but I could see the worry on Roan's face. "This is a good plan, and we only have to play this game maybe thirty miles. Then, we're free."

He nodded.

I called the escorts, lined up where they were going to meet us, and that it would just be a woman in a blue dress driving the car. She complained a little, still a little sad that I wasn't going to let her show me any new contortions she had learned. I thanked her, and told her she was still going to be paid, just riding in a car to put on a show for the locals.

I went into the trunk first, stripping down to slacks and my undershirt. Roan stumbled in, and then Sadie tucked the last of our bags in with us. It was cozy, real cozy. "If there is a problem, bang on the lid and I'll pull over." She sounded concerned.

"It'll be fine, let's go," I said. The faster we were gone, the sooner this would be over. I wasn't worried about myself, but for him. We knew Kaijin had tortured him, but we didn't know what she had done, or if there would be any lingering triggers waiting to be set off. Sadie was hesitant at first with the car. It was bonkers with horsepower, but was almost the size of a moving truck in terms of weight.

She navigated through the Monaco traffic, and after a few minutes, pulled up to a curb. There was a flutter of female voices, sparkling with laughter, and it sounded like everything was going fine. The car barely shifted as they loaded in. A carload of scantily dressed young women, lots of thigh and chest showing, leaving Monaco in a Bentley. If the Escadrille was watching, they didn't see hitmen escaping their noose, they saw arm candy going home to spend sugar daddy's money.

Sadie must have given the keys to one of the other girls, and the new driver was more confident and assertive. Maybe she owned a car like this herself? There was no telling with their profession, you never knew if the escort was a doctor-to-be, an aspiring actress, or a race car enthusiast. One I knew had a passion for big game hunting and taxidermy and after bagging a few rhinos in DC, she would fly to Africa to go on safari.

We drove through the checkpoint, and the girls became very loud, mocking and braying, and then we were off again. We hadn't been stopped more than thirty seconds; they must have just waved us through.

Well chalk one up to good luck.

The car ride only lasted another fifteen minutes, but the driver wasn't doing the speed limit, either. When we pulled over and were released from the trunk, we were in Le Ponte, outside of the principality of Monaco, and aimed toward the A7, which was the first leg of our new drive. Sadie had three other women with her. Two I recognized as escorts I knew, the third must have been a friend. They all wore similar daring dresses with high hems and low cuts, all bright colors, and they dripped with expensive jewelry.

"How did we get through customs so quickly," Roan asked.

"Like this." The contortionist gave a laugh and popped her tits out of her top. The other two did the same. "All his blood shot right to his cock, and he had none left for his brain." They laughed, and Sadie blushed.

Roan had turned a slightly less striking shade of tomato.

"Well done, ladies, well done," I said. I handed them their payment. There were air kisses tossed about, and a second car pulled up with a dark-headed entirely serious woman driving it. The girls waved, got into the car with the stone-faced woman, and then they were gone.

We wasted no time leaving ourselves.

"They seemed… nice," Roan said.

"They're crazy," Sadie laughed. The two of them were getting comfortable on the couch-like back seat as I pulled us away from the curb and set us off toward Oberhausen.

"You know, it's a shame that we can't take out time on this trip," Roan said. "I mean, we'll be driving through Lyon and Dijon."

"That's a mustard," Sadie quipped.

"And that is where that mustard comes from," he added. "I call for when we eat, we eat somewhere in Dijon. If you say no, I'll never forgive you."

"Yes, Le Clerc, I'll get you a mustard baguette and a rind of cheese." I laughed. He gave me the finger.

I let the Bentley glide as fast as I dared. I wanted to eat up ground, but not be pulled over by any of the police here. We had no way of knowing who and what parts of that system belonged to Chauvignon. The guy was like cancer everywhere he went.

Somewhere between Lyon and Dijon, I was able to see that Sadie had indeed gone the commando route. "Don't make a mess on the seats, the rental company will have a shit fit," I said, adjusting the rearview to face down into the backseat.

Roan gave me the finger again, and Sadie just moaned.

We found a roadside café outside of Dijon to appease our resident Francophile and his sudden renewed interest in bread. Sadie sat in the front seat after that. We were cruising up the A31, and I was enjoying something that was a treat. The challenge of getting road head is paying attention to the road, rather than what your passenger is doing.

Somewhere before we made it to Metz, I blew my load.

"I want both of you, tonight," Sadie said in a tone that brooked no debate.

Customs in Luxemburg was a little tedious, but nothing out of the ordinary. Roan's EU passport smoothed most of the ruffles out. We rested there for a while, letting the vibrations and noises of the road fade, and enjoyed the comforts that a place only as old and small as Luxemburg could offer. We knew entering Germany would be the last real test of our passports and documents for a while, and it was likely that if Malmaison had his own security net, that would be where it should start.

We found a bed-and-breakfast to put us up for the evening. The trunk ride had been literally in another country, on the other side of mountains, and I could smell myself. It was a fact that none of us were anywhere near fresh now.

Dinner was served by the hostess, some traditional meat pie made of pork, with some sort of beans, and copious amounts of wine.

Dessert was served by Sadie, and it was a glorious treat that ended with a mess that required showers for everyone involved, but most of all, her.

I had seldom slept so well.

THE TRAFFIC HEADING INTO DUSSELDORF FROM LUXEMBURG WAS HEAVY, but Oberhausen was a suburb of Cologne, and it was a major important place in Germany. As we made the drive at an annoyingly conservative and not fun pace, Roan told us history, and by history, how the Royal Airforce had bombed the shit out of this place back in the great war, and how we Americans had done the same thing, just raining bombs down on it.

It was hard to tell, hard to imagine. Everything seemed like it had never been touched. He pointed out that the main point was that there were few buildings that dated back to before the mid-1940s. That made sense, and it also made the place feel more like an American city than an old European one.

We drove through the heavy congestion of urban traffic, to the brazen point of passing in front of the doors to the Malmaison Military Archive and Museum – appointment or invitation only. It was a large square building, set with a faux front giving the imitation of Greco-Roman grandeur, white false pillars against a jaundiced yellow exterior. The windows were few and looked to have been blocked up from inside. A paranoid bunker almost in the heart of a major urban area, that was either brilliant, or idiotic.

"The hard part will be getting an invite or breaking in," Roan said.

"I was thinking getting our weapons inside." I shrugged.

"I've been able to see some of the collection. He has a lot of military hardware, lots of guns, ammo, and if the gallery is believable, everything is in working order, even the armor." He took a sip of tea.

"He has armor in that building?" I asked.

"Three armored cars, two artillery pieces, and two tanks," he replied calmly. "In running order, which could be a problem if he decides to pull a *GoldenEye* and chase us through Cologne in a Nazi tank."

"I think tanks are way above our pay grade." Sadie sounded concerned.

"Don't worry, tanks are only good for fighting other tanks. I would be more concerned about whatever security he has, because it looks like he doesn't use any Escadrille sourced men. I'm seeing his electronic system is connected to the local police and a private security contractor." Roan patted her on the hand when she leaned over his shoulder to look at the screens.

"High-end private security means helicopters and good communications systems." I scowled.

"It does, but do you know who else has good security, comms, and aircraft?" he asked.

"Who?"

"The TSA, and we spoof them so often it doesn't even count

anymore." He gave a laugh. "All we have to do is get your phone there, inside the building, and see if I can hack into his security like I do at any other checkpoint. Once I'm in, we can manipulate his system, lock him out of it, keep those external security forces in their barracks polishing their jackboots."

"So how do we get in?" Sadie asked.

"With this," Roan said, holding up the GSTP she had given him just a day ago. "He's a military antiquarian and sufficiently interesting paraphernalia will net us a meeting with him. It has to be juicy, and all we have to do is attach a sufficiently interesting story to this."

"But the guy's a wannabe Nazi, why would he care about a British timepiece?" I asked.

"If you look through the collection, half of it is Nazi junk, and half is stuff that they took as trophies – it's shot up flags, broken officer's swords. It's a collection instances of Nazi victories," he said. "Which means that this GSTP belonged to a British officer who was killed at Dunkirk. A little research, attach a name to it, and see if he takes the bait. I think the only thing that might interest him more would be an RAF timepiece, but they used a different make and model and he'll know that from the picture."

"But he knows me, we've had dinner," I added.

"Aye, you. And I'm sure he knows me, he visited the estate at least once, did some uninspired questioning, and then Kaijin ran him off. There's no love between those two," Roan said.

"What about me?" Sadie asked.

"He's seen you, but in highly stressed conditions, so maybe?" Roan admitted. "I don't like that option, but there is no angle for violence. You would be safe so long as he doesn't realize who you are."

"Disguises?" There was a hint of excitement in her voice.

"Makeup, different outfit, maybe change your hair color," Roan suggested. I must have growled at that because they both looked at me. "Come off it, mate, it's hair."

"I could have it cut into a bob and dyed blonde." She toyed with her hair like it was a Parisian bob.

"Absolutely not." I stood up. "No."

"It's *my* hair," she protested.

"Changing the color is fine, but if there is anything I would forbid, it's cutting it. I want your hair long." I had an unexpectedly strong stance on that.

"You going to dress me too?" Her words were sharp.

"No, well maybe, but that's not the point. You cut that hair off, it will take months, a year, longer, to grow back." I crossed my arms. "I would rather you carry a submachine gun into that building rather than give yourself a buzz cut."

"Think that's a bit much?" Roan asked.

"If it comes down to cutting her hair, I'll just kill Malmaison myself. I'm ex-US Army. Killing Nazis in their own country is in my blood."

"Mine too," Roan said. "Hairstyles can be changed, and the right coif can make her look like a pin-up girl or a bookish military historian."

"This is like listening to people talk about updating the Mona Lisa, defacing art." I felt my temperature rising, a possessiveness that felt unnatural even to me.

"Mate, if we promise that her hair isn't cut, you'll be okay with whatever disguise we come up with?" he asked. I gave a grudging nod. "So, why don't you fuck off to that bar on the corner, and I'll take the lady and come up with a good disguise for her."

"There was a biergarten across from Malmaison's gallery. I can surveil the place while you two play dress-up, maybe get us some more intel." I stood, feeling bristled up like an angry cat.

When I turned from grabbing my jacket and put my hand on the knob to go out, I heard Sadie ask Roan, "What's gotten into him?" and Roan answer, "Haven't the foggiest."

That made three of us.

THE BIERGARTEN WAS RUNDOWN, AND IN NEED OF RENOVATIONS. THE amount of abuse the tables had taken made me wonder if they were left over from when this place had been rebuilt. The pictures inside made it seem like half of this part of town survived the bombing. Malmaison's building seemed to have come through with its walls intact. There was a picture of it as a burned-out stone shell and wreckage everywhere.

There might be something useful in that, so I snapped a few pictures with my phone, and sent them to Roan. Hell, he might just like them for being old war shit.

I wasn't much of a fan when it came to beer, but I took one of the oversized mugs the place offered, along with some sort of appetizer plate. German food, with all of its sausage, potato dumplings, and mustard, wasn't my dream plate either. There was very little traffic going to the gallery, maybe two people, one of whom looked like Malmaison, but it was hard to tell. It wasn't like he would be stomping around in a military uniform with a swastika on his arm.

He had a woman with him; she was an escort. Not one that I knew, but I knew their demeanor. I imagined, for a moment, him and her in some sweaty gross Nazi roleplay, and then felt disgusted and dirty.

The RTB text came a few hours later while I was taking a lap around the plaza. I couldn't get back to the room quick enough. I was ready for action, not this snooping and waiting business.

I felt an upwelling of anger in my chest when I saw what they had done. Her hair was almost gone, and what remained was a bright almost silvery blonde. Her makeup changed the contours of her face, and the lipstick was wrong, too dark. She looked like a completely different person, not my Shady but some bookish dry woman, ten years older, and the outfit was awful. Beige stockings, a twill skirt, conservative old lady's blouse and a button-up blazer to match the skirt.

"What the fuck, mate." I felt my throat get tight.

"First, calm down," Roan said. "It's a bloody wig, nothing's been permanently changed."

"I bet you wouldn't have recognized me if I came and sat at the table next you at the biergarten," Sadie said with a little sass.

"No." I clenched my fists.

"Yes, I sat behind you for a good fifteen minutes. You barely touched your gallon of beer or your appetizer. Not that I blame you, pickled onions are gross." She smiled. "I guess that means that the mission is on?"

"Aye, it is," Roan said, grinning.

I felt the anger subside; this could actually work.

It took less than four hours for Malmaison to respond to Roan's pictures and query to visit the gallery and have him authenticate a British timepiece recovered from Dunkirk. He seemed most interested, and setting up the meeting was astoundingly easy. He made a show of how lucky *Frauline* was that he was even in town.

An hour after that, Roan and I watched as Sadie, *Frauline* Isla Schneider, lately of America, visited the gallery. We were staked out in the plaza, close enough to keep a line of sight to the doors, and stay in range of the earpiece she was wearing. It was Bluetoothed to our earpieces so we could all hear everything that went down. Roan was ready to feed her any information she needed, something he called his millionaire plan; some game show bullshit.

I would have killed for a video feed, but the handful of video-capable devices we could get our hands on were either incredibly obvious, or the resolution was only good enough for filming first-person sex in public videos. Her legs looked great as she mounted the steps to the gallery, and the door opened promptly after her two police knocks. Malmaison greeted her personally and walked her inside.

He spoke a quick and fluid German, but Sadie interrupted him politely to forgive her for being an American and only speaking one language. He himself apologized, no doubt pausing to take in that flash of cleavage visible through the top of her blouse. They discussed some of the art he had hanging in the gallery, and we both listened.

Art was worth more than gold, more than platinum. Some old paintings were priceless, and the Nazis stole a ton of the shit. Roan seemed to be making a catalog of the pieces Malmaison was telling her about. Periodically, Roan would prompt her to stall him, get him talking about a piece while he did more of his computer stuff.

It was maddening. There was nothing for me to do but try to sit and not look like I was ready to attack.

There was a smattering of talk about the guns on display. The pride of the Third Reich, trophies taken from defeated Allied soldiers, commandos, and pieces of destroyed equipment. He mentioned more in his collection, outside of town. That the tanks and vehicles he had here were for general public viewing, but that he had several Allied warplanes and tanks, shot up and left in that condition. He bragged about how the airplane collectors and museums would be sick if they knew what he had.

Roan grumbled in agreement.

He gave a thumbs up, and I saw lights on his screen turn green, and video feeds booted up. I was able to see a CCTV of Malmaison and Sadie standing in front of the intimidating profile of a tank, slab sided and brutal, flanked by flags and stolen artwork.

"How does he not get busted for this?" I asked, out loud. Sadie repeated my question to him. My heart froze, and Roan gave a look that would have curdled milk.

Malmaison laughed.

Then he told us. The people that would be most concerned about this being here, they were always welcome in his gallery. They attended the same monthly meetings and saluted the same flag. Everyone in power was corrupt. The trick was getting them to be on your side, rather than on any side of perceived *good*.

Sadie said that if those fine gentlemen in the Carolinas had such a passionate and intelligent leader, things would have been so much different back in the States. "Don't put too much butter on that bread," I said softly.

Malmaison's anti-Semitic and racist monologue was cut short by Sadie offering him the GSTP. He inspected it, and condemned the engraving on the tag, having defaced a valuable historical artifact, and confirmed that it was indeed a British General Service Time Piece, but that it was not, in fact, from Dunkirk, and made a number of observations that placed it much closer to the disaster that was the Axis defeat at Normandy.

The smile on Roan's face was small, but I knew it went down to his soul.

"I'm getting hard thinking about how I'm going to kill this guy," I said, trying to cover the earpiece so that Sadie wouldn't hear.

He invited her upstairs for some wine and polite conversation. It was so rare that he had the privilege of speaking with an American who had the right side of history in mind. She politely declined, stating that she unfortunately had evening plans with friends that couldn't be put off. I felt my jaw hang open when she suggested that maybe tomorrow, she could wear something more befitting his pleasure, and would take him up on his offer then, if he wasn't too busy.

I was ready to bolt through the door and sock this joker like Captain fucking America.

When we made it back to the rented room, she was already there, wig removed and stripped out of the outfit Roan had her dressed in. All of her undergarments were a uniform beige color and seemed a bizarre mix of practical and vaguely erotic.

"Not now, I have to shower. I feel fucking diseased just being that close to him," she hissed, removing the last of the undergarments and tossing them on the floor. "He tried to kiss me, fuck, *ugh*." She ranted all the way into the shower.

Roan stayed at his terminal, using the new links he had to explore Malmaison's entire setup. "Electronic door locks and mechanical ones, I can pop the electrics, but someone will have to pick the manual ones."

"You know I can do that," I growled, staring at the hacked video feed of Malmaison making a few phone calls and removing his tie. The motions were precise, controlled, and I knew that he could be dangerous in a fight. Taking him out quietly would involve a massive amount of stealth and the upper hand.

"After we take him out," Roan spoke, "I'm going to blow all of this information out so that Interpol and everyone else interested in recovering stolen art and military relics gets these things back where they belong."

"Good."

I exercised – push-ups and crunches – burning off the nervous energy, waiting for night to come. Normally I would have had a few drinks, but I wanted to be sharp, not loose. There would be no need to be smooth or for fast talking, just a need for precision, silence, and absolute focus. Kaijin had been sloppy in her defenses, and the only reason I hadn't blown a ragged hole through her stupid face was her bug-out chopper.

Malmaison was a deviant, paranoid, military fetishist. He had much better guards, much better security.

He was also a pervert. They always were.

"There are no drones now," Roan warned. "And the only thing you'll be able to sneak in is a pistol or a knife."

"That's more than I need. The place is full of weapons if I need one," I said.

Close to midnight, I left the rented room and made my way to the gallery on foot. There was almost no traffic, and most people who were up and out would be on the other side of town where the clubs and discotheques were pumping out loud music. I ghosted to the side of the building, staying to shadows, listening while Roan played the spotter, using Malmaison's own cameras as his eyes.

I reached the main door and heard the electric lock click open and then managed to get the lock on the door to open. If it had been a modern lock, I might have been fucked, but all the physical stuff looked a few decades old. I'm sure he was squeamish about chopping up his old door for a new system. *Idiot.*

I let myself in and eased the door shut behind me. Paintings lined both sides of the building, and there were a lot of them – golden frames, statues, fancy as shit carpets on the ground. The guns and blades were mounted in wall displays, plaques detailing their gory history. I stopped at one, a softly lit cube display that had all of a British commando's kit. The plaque mentioned that the blood stains were authentic and from the commando when he was shot to death, giving the time and place. There was a commando dagger and a garrote. I picked up both, one in each pocket, and left the display open.

At the specified time, Sadie dialed Malmaison and got him on the phone. This would keep him distracted while I moved into place. He was up, and as I approached the back of the main hall, I could hear his voice echoing from above. There was a second floor, and a single staircase going up.

I had to ease around his collection of Nazi armor to reach the staircase, and then I took it as quietly as I could. I could hear him laughing and flirting with *Frauline Schneider,* dropping details about how disappointed he was that her timepiece wasn't what she thought it was, but that he was assured that everything else about her was real, especially those lovely breasts.

For a moment I entertained the fantasy of tapping him on the shoulder, him turning around to face me, an action movie one-liner, a quip, then a nose breaking punch to the face, some hand-to-hand, then the slow Hollywood knife stab down into his chest while he kept looking from my eyes to the knife, back and forth, as the blade penetrated his flesh, slowly, like a lover.

Hollywood fantasies.

I looped the garrote around his neck, twisted the ends together and turned. The wire was wrapped around his throat and with sheer force, I lifted him off of the ground, our backs pressed together. His phone clattered to the ground, the screen shattering, and he thrashed and kicked, but his heels couldn't connect with any meaningful purpose or force.

"Your collection is going back to who it belongs too," I grunted. He gurgled and thrashed. "And this is for blowing up my house in Indigo City, you fucking asshole." He must have realized something about who I was, or who I was with, because he threw a few desperate elbows, and thrashed harder. I could feel the handles biting into my own hands and could imagine what the wire was doing to his throat.

"My brothers, in the US Army," I jerked against his struggle, keeping him away from a wall or anything he could get purchase on with his feet, "killed Nazis with guns." He managed to score a hit with his elbow, made my vision swim for a moment, but I didn't lose my grip. "You don't deserve the mercy of a bullet."

There was a horrible sucking noise, wet and bubbly, and then he stopped struggling.

I dropped his dead weight and staggered at the sudden lightness. He stared at the ceiling of his apartment, his throat a bloody ruin, windpipe torn open and exposed, and a tremendous amount of blood. The wire must have gouged one of his arteries.

I removed the commando's knife and inspected the blade. The craftsmanship was perfect. I put the point just to the side of his breastbone and hammered the knife home, putting British steel into his heart, just to make sure. "I don't know who carried you," I said, looking at the knife. "But you can rest easy now, soldier. One less motherfucker in this world, and your knife made sure he was fucking dead."

I left the gallery. I was vaguely aware of Roan talking in my ear, and after a few blocks, I tucked the earpiece in my pocket. I didn't need instructions; I just needed a little bit of quiet.

I felt a level of calm that bordered on Zen, that felt like the edge of enlightenment.

The air tasted different; the smells seemed sharper.

It was almost a transcendent level of inner peace.

CHAPTER TWELVE

---

*S*adie...

I hated the accommodations. The German bed-and-breakfast didn't really have a bed big enough for the three of us. What they had were these weird beds that were more like two mattresses put together, so if I wasn't sleeping draped over one of my men, I got lost in the crack of the mattresses in between them and woke up pressed to the wood platform that supported them.

The bathroom was nice at least. It boasted a large glassed-in shower and a corner tub.

It was about the only thing nice about the room, though. There was no kitchenette, no real table, just a small corner desk and a couch at the foot of the bed to sit on. It was very utilitarian but then again, I was beginning to get the impression that was how the German people were. Frank, to the point, and utilitarian – but not unkind. Just... I don't know... abrupt.

It took some getting used to, and I was really, *really* hoping we weren't going to be here long enough to get used to it. I wanted to go *home,* and by *home* I meant America. It felt like I knew the rules better on our home turf and I definitely wanted back on the home court advantage.

Roan and I were staring at his laptop screens, me perched on his good leg, his arms around me as he clicked through screens and spoke urgently into his mic.

Lach had either taken out his earpiece or switched us off and that made me extremely nervous even despite Roan's assurances that this was actually a good thing and perfectly normal when a job was well done.

I jumped and bolted to my feet when we heard him at the door. Or rather, heard *someone*.

I very nearly cried out in relief when he stepped through and I went to him, thrusting myself against his lean, hard body, twining my arms around his waist as he leaned back against the door to shut it.

"Hey, what's the matter?" he asked and I looked up at him. He smiled down at me and took his hands from his pockets, capturing my face between them. I made a noise somewhere between surprise and protest as he covered my mouth with his.

I froze, stuck between welcoming the kiss and cringing from the sensation of the thick wet he smeared along my cheeks with his thumbs.

"Mate!" Roan called out with reproach and Kyle drew back, a dreamy look in his obsidian eyes that I didn't usually see until *after* we'd had sex. He let me go and looked at his hands which were covered in thick, sticky, congealing blood and I felt vomit burn the back of my throat. I put the back of my hand to my lips which still tingled with his kiss.

"Aw, shit, I'm sorry Shady. Come on, come take a shower with me, I'll help you get it off."

I nodded and looked back over my shoulder at Conan who nodded, his green eyes shuttered and unreadable, the set of his mouth disapproving, yet softening when he saw the alarm on my face. He jerked his head at Kyle's back and I nodded and trusting Conan that he knew what was up, followed my other lover into the bathroom where I tried very hard not to look in the mirror.

"C'mere, baby," Kyle murmured and drew me into his arms again. I slipped the straps of my satin nightgown off my shoulders and let it puddle at my feet just inside the door.

He took off his black bomber jacket, revealing the plain black fitted tee underneath. He had on black tactical *everything* from pants, to the belt holding them up, to the boots on his feet. I didn't think about things too hard. I tried not to fixate on his bloody hands, I just offered up my lips and murmured, "Please don't touch me until we get that off," and started to work on his belt, peeling the Velcro, slipping the long tongue through the belt loops so I could free it through the buckle.

He groaned, holding his hands out to his sides, the fingers flexing as though he battled mightily with the need to have his hands on me.

His belt free and hanging open, I gathered his tee in my hands and he raised his arms over his head, we broke the kiss just long enough for him to raise his arms to allow me to pull it over his head and once his upper body was freed, I don't know… it's like he lost himself and lost focus, his arms going around me and his hands on my back half grabbing my ass, he hauled me up against his trim, hard chest and God, if he wasn't *warm*.

I worked at things between us. Getting his pants open, sliding his boxer-briefs down, and wrapping fingers around his cock, stroking him.

"What would you have me do, Mr. Lachlan?" I asked him in as sultry a voice I could manage.

"Stop," he whispered. "No games, no Mr. Lachlan… not tonight," he said. "I'm just me this time. Just Kyle and his Shady."

I felt a tremor that went soul deep followed by a wave of shock. I stared up at him and swallowed hard stammering out, "I… I don't understand."

He smiled at me then, his usually hard and dark eyes that reminded me of glittering obsidian, softer somehow. Soft like they used to get when he looked at me when we were kids. I thought that look was lost to me with the man that Kyle Lachlan had become, but it was back, it was here right now, and I felt drawn to him like a moth to the flame.

His arms went around me as I sank against him and into that look gratefully and we kissed for I don't know how long.

I don't remember how he got out of his boots, just that he did, stepping on the cuffs of his pants to get out of them before drawing me into the shower, working the knobs deftly to get the spray going while I stood well out of it as he adjusted the temperature.

He ran the water over his hands, the worst of it coming off, and when satisfied, he held out a mostly clean hand to me. I swallowed hard and took it and he turned me into the spray. I gasped as the deliciously hot water hit me right between the shoulders, the tension that rode there with my uncertainty easing marginally with the onslaught.

Kyle smiled down at me and it was like nothing I had seen by way of expression to date. Soft, gentle, a little boy's smile on the cold hard man's face and I delighted in it. He loaded his hands with soap and got the rest of the blood off while I luxuriated under the hot spray, and when he was done? He soaped his hands again and held them out as though asking. I nodded, and he smiled and smoothed gentle fingers over my face. I closed my eyes as he made small circles with his fingertips, paying close attention to what I assumed were the bloody patches left by his thumbs in the other room. He smoothed those same fingertips along the sides of my neck, brushing my wet hair back over my shoulders and I relished the sensation in the killer in front of me being so gentle, so careful of me.

"Head back, Shady," he murmured, barely loud enough for me to hear over the running water.

I tipped my head carefully back, soaking the rest of my hair and with Kyle looking on, closed my eyes and tipped it back even further, letting the shower spray rinse the soap and blood from my face.

His arms went around me, and his lips went to the hollow of my throat where my collar bones came together. I barely had the presence of mind to tip my face yet further back out of the spray before I gasped.

I tangled my fingers gently in his wet hair as he kissed his way down my body, slowly going to his knees in front of me, looking up at me as though I were the Mona Lisa indeed; the finest work of art that he'd ever laid eyes on. Something special, something sweet radiated from him. A contentment and I didn't know why but it both moved me and bothered me. I thrust the latter aside for now, in favor of reveling in the former as he nuzzled my stomach, closing his eyes and just holding me close for a long moment as I slicked my hands back through his hair, lightly scratching his scalp with my nails.

"God, I love you, Shady my Sadie," he murmured and I smiled, whatever misgivings holding whatever tension in my back and shoulders relinquished for the time being.

"And I love you," I said back softly. He looked up at me then, resting his chin against my chest, between my breasts and looking up at me with such an *adoration* practically begged me, "Say that again?"

"I love you," I told him and I meant it. I loved him madly, deeply, not precisely the way I loved Conan, no, not exactly the same, but I loved him. So much. I loved each of my men equally for very different reasons, but I *did* love them both and losing either of them? I knew it was a risk we took, I had already lived it once, and I knew without a shadow of a doubt that I wouldn't survive it a second time. Not losing Kyle, not losing Conan… they were both now such a part of me but I had to confess Kyle maybe deeper so in one aspect – I had a history with him that ran so very deep.

The second time I told him I loved him I smiled as his dark eyes closed and such a bliss painted his darkly angelic features, as though he listened to the sweetest sound ever made for his ears and it made me smile, too. Just us, just he and I and the endless hot water and steam – not all of which was created by that hot water.

He slid his hands up over my body and went back to kissing me, asking me, eyes closed, lips and teeth grazing the skin over my hip, "You trust me, don't you Shady?"

"Of course, I do," I said and he smiled again like my voice made the sweetest sound and he nudged my legs apart.

He looked up at me and said, "I want to go down on you," and I nodded, breath catching because honest to God, I *loved* Kyle's mouth on my pussy.

"Just relax for me, baby," he whispered. "And remember… I've got you, Shady."

I bit my bottom lip and nodded, not sure what to expect, but then his mouth was on me, tongue delving between my pussy lips seeking out that kernel of pleasure and I gasped, leaning back hard against the stone shower wall behind me as he gripped my sides with his hands above my hips and went to town with his mouth, licking sucking, and I swear to God swallowing me whole.

I tipped my head back, fingers finding his hair, and I moaned.

He took his hands down, caressing over my hips, over the tops of my thighs, taking his mouth from my mound for just a second, glancing up at me before with a swiftness no man should possess matched equally by his strength, he hooked his arms behind my knees and lifted me *bodily* off the shower floor. My arms went out to my sides, palms flat to the glossy stone walls to catch myself as Kyle settled the backs of my thighs onto his shoulders and he put his mouth back on me.

"Oh, God!" I cried, head thrown back, gasping, the shower spray going over us, pelting him in the back as he worked me with his lips and tongue.

"Relax, Shady," he murmured as I trembled in his grasp and I finally did. Relax, that is, letting the wall hold me up at my back, my hands leaving it and fingers tangling in his glossy black hair, hauling his mouth tighter against me. He groaned in delight against my body and I cried out, gasping, panting, as he took me up high and higher still settling me and keeping me on the precipice.

I panted and gasped wantonly, wordlessly begging, my eyes opening to slits vaguely aware of Conan's blurry figure on the other side of the glass shower walls picking up our discarded clothing. He stood and smiled at me, approval all over his hard and handsome face as he took us in for a moment. He nodded and turned, ghosting back out of the bathroom as Kyle tongued my clit, teasing it just right and with a cry I came all over his face, gripping his hair tightly, pulling his head back and meeting his eyes as the orgasm destroyed me from the inside out and remade me.

He smiled and pressed a lazy kiss to my pubic hair, nuzzling my lower abdomen before asking, "Ready for another one?"

I whimpered in disbelief in response, my fingers nerveless now and simply resting against his hair as he chuckled darkly and said, "I'll take that as a 'yes', my Shady girl."

He put his mouth against me and I let out a strangled cry as he started working me up all over again.

I don't know how many times he made me come that way. Twice? Three times? Each more devastating than the last until I achieved that utter nirvana of disconnectedness where I felt as though I were simply floating. He set me down then, keeping his hands on my hips, making sure I was steady as he climbed to his feet.

I trembled against the shower wall, my knees together, feet akimbo, hands wrapped around his forearms to keep myself on my feet and he smiled as though he'd unlocked some sort of achievement or had earned himself some sort of a prize.

I closed my eyes and shook and shook and shook and he kissed my forehead gently, waiting until the trembling subsided to a degree he was pleased with.

"That's my girl," he whispered as I stabilized on my feet, then before I knew it his hands were on the outsides of my thighs, wrapped around the back, pressing me back against the shower wall all over again as he lifted me onto his cock.

I wrapped my arms around his shoulders, fitting my mouth to his as he plunged up inside me, my cry of pleasure muffled by his kiss as he grunted and set his usual, punishing rhythm that I was both accustomed to and absolutely *adored* out of him.

I gasped or cried out with every one of his thrusts as the head of his cock rode over that spot inside of me, stroking me to life from the inside as readily as he had from the outside with his tongue only moments before.

I dug nails into his back and he threw his head back, giving such a satisfied gasping moan that served to turn me on all the more, which I hadn't honestly thought possible.

"Oh, God! *Kyle!*" I gasped his name as I drew so very very close to yet *another* orgasm and when it hit, I wrapped myself around him as my pussy milked his straining cock for everything it had to give.

"God, Shady!" he cried and both of us winded and trembling, he pulled from me and set me down.

He washed every inch of me carefully after that, and when he shut off the tap, we were all but prunes.

He left my side only long enough to grab towels, winding one around his narrow hips and securing it, taking his time to towel my hair from wet to damp and my body from wet to dry before leading me into the bedroom.

Conan lay in bed, his cock tenting his lounge pants, his chest bare and a laptop resting on his stomach. He looked up at me and smiled as Kyle guided me into the bed.

"Lose the pants, mate. You good with Sadie taking you for a ride?"

Conan set the laptop aside immediately and thrust his pants off, down to his knees as I got onto the bed. Kyle whisked my towel away and kissed the back of my shoulder quickly saying, "Ride him, baby. I'm going to grab some lube." I smiled and straddled Conan, leaning over the top of him, his arms going around me, kissing him soundly as I writhed my wet pussy up and down his length, not penetrating. Not yet.

He grunted below me, his hands traveling over my nude body with care and appreciation. I pushed against his chest and looked down at him, biting my bottom lip and writhing some more at a slightly different pressure and pace.

"You good with this?" I asked, double checking.

"God save the queen, *yes,*" he said and I smiled, he moved his hips in counterpoint to mine and slipped inside me. I was wet, primed, and ready to take him. No waiting. No need to ease into things, and God *yes,* he filled me up and filled me out so perfectly.

I sighed in contentment and rolled my hips low and slow, grinding against him, my clit throbbing and a fresh orgasm already building as I heard the cap to a bottle of lube click off to one side and Kyle said, "So fucking perfect watching you two together. Ride him, baby."

I put a little more roll into my hips and kept my eyes on Conan, a smile tugging at the corners of my mouth as I listened to Kyle make himself ready, the sticky sounds of him spreading lube on his cock. I stole a glance in his direction, standing off to the side, nude and perfect, running his cock through his fist, wanting to join in so bad he was crimson and throbbing in his hand. His dark, gleaming eyes roving over the pair of us in front of him as we made love for his eyes and edification.

He got up onto the bed behind me, and ordered us to keep going, spreading my ass cheeks. I expected him to tease my asshole with fingers or thumb but he went down on me back there. Teasing me with his tongue eliciting a gasp from me and a grunt from Conan when my pussy throbbed around him in sheer pleasure.

"Easy, mate. Don't want to go too quick," Conan warned and I felt Kyle kneel up behind me.

"Sorry not sorry," he said and I could hear the smile in his voice.

He used some lube on the pad of his thumb and gently rubbed it against me, slick and cool, the pressure light and pleasing, and I gasped again, panting, bowing over Conan's body. Conan's arms went around me, and he claimed my mouth in a kiss, holding me to him, giving Kyle access as he eased a thumb against my asshole and pressed gently, the first joint slipping into me. I jumped slightly at the sensation and he made a soothing noise and asked, "Too much?"

"Not enough," I murmured and fought not to writhe. He eased the digit in further and finding no resistance and no complaint from me, quickly added a finger, withdrawing his thumb, adding a second finger, and massaging them in and out of me in counterpoint to Conan's slow and careful thrusting.

Conan hissed, and it sounded like it felt so good.

"You good?" Kyle asked and I knew he wasn't asking me.

"Not going to be able to last long. She's so wet, feels so good," my lover beneath me said.

"I'm here," Kyle said and his fingers left to be replaced with his cock. He pushed in so fucking *easy*, sliding into my ass where it felt like he honestly belonged and I shuddered against Conan's chest. The pleasure coursing through me, my pussy lightly grabbing at his cock as he glided through my wetness which felt like it spontaneously doubled.

I screamed, sucking in air as the sound tried to escape, and it ended up being such a sound of pure, breathy delight.

I felt so full, so *complete* and I never wanted this sensation to end as it felt as though my brain clicked off and went into some sort of standby where coherent thought was unnecessary, there were no bad feelings or emotions, and I could just float elegantly between my two men who spoke around and over me though I didn't have a thought or a care as to what they said. Not when they made me feel like this.

WE DIDN'T LEAVE OBERHAUSEN RIGHT AWAY. BY MORNING, ROAN blasted the contents of Malmaison's collection to multiple authorities, including German, Jewish, local news, holocaust groups, military museums, and the rest. It was, by all accounts, an absolute *firestorm* of news coverage, none of which I could understand because it was in German. Still the pictures were universal. Police images inside the museum uncovered the treasure-trove of artifacts and blasted them worldwide. In every shot, there were police everywhere along with censored pictures of the body, roving reporters fighting police for access to the gallery, and at least one thing stood out from the harsh clipped words falling from the reporter's lips. A couple of names: Gustaf Malmaison and Escadrille.

Lach and Roan both seemed well pleased, I just wanted to leave; but when I asked, Roan had kindly explained to me it would look suspicious as hell if we picked up and took off right after a murder as gruesome as that Nazi fuck's. It made sense, but I was restless. Eager to be back on American soil and for sure, back into a better bed than the one the German B&B was able to provide.

I was sleeping poorly, and that was compounded by the anxiety of air travel in general. We had an almost four-hour drive to Paris where we had only two hours before boarding a just over fourteen-hour flight to New York. Why so long? Well, we had yet another two-hour stop in the middle of that before the final leg of our journey back to the States.

Roan insisted on the drive, the whole time he chattered like an excited scholar about how this was a part of Germany packed full of WWII history, I listened, curled into his side in the back seat of the Bentley Continental as he told me and Kyle all about how this area was where the allies penetrated the Rhineland, we stopped for a few minutes near one particular bridge that the Nazis and Allies fought over with epic and heroic resolve; the Bridge at Remegen, and I smiled thinking about the movie we shared before our first time together about another bridge. *The Bridge on the River Kwai.*

I couldn't sleep in the car. I could never sleep in a moving car again after my parent's accident, and I definitely couldn't handle sitting in the back seat by myself while both front seats were occupied. Long car rides were *not* my favorite thing, but Roan's crisply accented voice with its rich, honeyed tone soothed the anxiety of the trip to Paris remarkably well.

When we arrived at the airport, I was surprised twice over. Once that there was a Burger World in the Paris airport, and again when Conan was the one to suggest we eat there. We shared a meal of burger and fries, surprisingly not as greasy as what we got in America, as if France even had the power to refine the worst food on offer from our home country.

Still, thankfully, it wasn't long after that when we boarded our flight.

I couldn't sleep on the plane. Every time I tried; I would wake shortly from a nightmare. Usually the old standby of the car crash that killed my parents. Sometimes, it wasn't my parents, but Lach and Roan in their place. I would wake with a start, whoever was sitting beside me in our first-class seats holding my hand over the low wall between them on the Airbus A340.

I couldn't even imagine what making the trip in the cramped conditions of coach would be like, but I almost longed for it when I saw the seats and how they were set up in first class.

There were four across the plane, window seat, then a fairly wide aisle, then two center lane seats separated by a low wall but at least *next to each other*, then another wide swath of aisle equal to the first and a window seat.

I couldn't really effectively be close to either one of my men, and one would always be entirely too far from me in the window seat on the other side of that damn low wall.

I loathed that low wall between myself and whichever man was sitting next to me, they traded off sitting beside me every two hours or so to try and make things easier, but I hated it just the same. I could never be close enough.

I didn't try to sleep anymore after the first nightmare. I was too restless, my thoughts spinning and whirling, my emotions vacillating wildly between righteous anger and soul crushing guilt over actually *helping* to kill another human being, the pictures – though censored – via the news outlets haunted me. Made it real. There was no out of sight, out of mind for this one and that bothered me, a lot more than I thought it would.

"What's wrong, Poppet?" Conan asked me part way into the first leg of the flight from Paris back to New York. I sighed and shook my head, uncertain how to put any of it into words.

"Feeling guilty, yeah?" he asked and I smiled. I was getting better at keeping things off my face, I mean I had successfully fooled Malmaison, but my men? I could never fool either of them. Especially not Kyle who had known me the longest – even with the gap in our intertwined history.

"I guess, it wasn't really *real* until…"

"Until you were washing the blood off?" he asked quietly.

"No," I said softly, burning with shame at… I don't know, that it wasn't the blood, but a picture on the news? "The photos, on the news…" I confessed, trailing off.

He reached over the low wall with his other hand, the one closest to me already tangled with mine. I looked up and he smiled at me sweetly, caressing my cheek.

"You're not like Lach and you're not like me, Poppet. You're *you* and you feel however you'd like about it. However, do not lose sight;

that man was pure evil and the lot of us did the world a great favor by ridding it of him."

"I know," I nodded, and I *did* know. Malmaison was one of the monsters and you shouldn't feel bad about slaying the monsters but here I was and I *did*. I looked past Conan to Kyle who was watching one of the in-flight movies on his television screen, his headphones in his ears as something exploded on the screen, a small smile playing on his lips.

"I don't understand why he was the way he was when he came back to us this time," I said frowning slightly.

"Ah, that I may have some insight for," Conan said.

I looked back to him and he looked almost apologetic when he said, "The Comedown is typically something cathartic, Love. When the catharsis is in the slaying, the comedown looks a little different, yeah?"

I jolted slightly as the implication sank in.

"You mean he enjoyed," I dropped my voice to a whisper that could barely be heard over the engine noise of the plane, "killing that Nazi fuck so much he didn't need a comedown?" I asked.

"It would seem so," he said with a precision nod. "Were I in his place, I am afraid it would have been much the same."

I swallowed hard and looked past him at Kyle again.

"I don't know what to make of that," I confessed and he nodded his expression guarded.

"Take all the time you need with it, Poppet."

I looked up at him and tilted my head slightly, scanning his face and finally deciding this closed-off ness was a mild *fear*.

"Don't think for a minute that *I* would think about leaving either of you," I said squeezing his hand tightly. "You're my everything. The both of you."

He smiled and it held such a relief, as he raised the back of my hand to his lips.

"Cor, I love you," he said and I smiled and felt the burden my soul contained lighten at those words.

"I love you more than words can say," I said simply.

I tried watching a movie, fidgeting in my seat. Conan alternated between sitting with me and using the plane's available Wi-Fi, which was surprisingly excellent, to work on his reclaimed laptop. He typically reserved this work for when it was his turn to be in the window seat.

I tried to sleep again, I really did, as the light dimmed outside the raised window coverings and finally within the plane itself as people laid their seats back into beds, but I couldn't.

Conan slept in the window seat and Kyle beside me, but all I could do was lay on my side and watch them.

The longer that we were in the air, the more tired I became as the minutes and hours slipped like grains of sand through an hourglass, the more *emotional* I found myself.

I watched both my men sleep as I struggled to reconcile the girl that I had been with the woman I was now and it was *work*… I suppose all growth is painful to a certain extent, but I could do with a little less pain lately and good *lord* all I wanted was some damn *sleep*, which remained so elusive I could cry.

That's what happened as we crossed the Atlantic on the final leg of our journey, the cabin darkened in deepest night. I lay and watched my two men sleep and I cried. I wept with tiredness, with a deep emotional and mental exhaustion and it was my light shaking as I was wracked with silent sobs that woke Kyle, his hand still twined with mine.

"Hey," he said roughly, stretching his other arm out, arching his back. "What's the matter?"

"Nothing," I told him which was true. "Everything," I said which was also true. I sniffed. "I don't know."

"Oh, baby. C'mere," he reached out motioning for me to come over the low wall into his laid-out seat and I sniffed.

"I don't think we're supposed to."

"Shady, I don't care," he said impatiently. "Come here."

I looked up and down the aisle and seeing no flight attendant I went over the low wall and into Kyle's waiting arms. He hugged me through the thin fleece blanket and rubbed me up and down soothingly through it. I rested my head on his chest and closed my eyes, listening to the steady throb of his heartbeat beneath my ear. He kissed the top of my head and sighed.

"I could sleep so much better like this," he said and I smiled.

"Read my mind," I said back with a sniff.

I don't remember doing it but I drifted off, I think Kyle did too, because he jolted awake under me the same time I did, a figure bending over us in the dark, the flight attendant shaking me gently by the shoulder. I saw Roan startle awake just behind her.

"I'm sorry miss, I'm going to have to ask that you return to your seat."

"Just a little longer?" I pleaded.

"I'm sorry, but it's airline policy," she said straightening.

"It's okay," Kyle said over my head and I could picture him giving her one of his thousand-watt smiles. "Bad dream earlier, just let her get her bearings. Two seconds."

I got the vague impression of the flight attendant nodding but she didn't move. Damnit, I hated feeling like a naughty child, her standing there all imperious.

"Everything alright, mate?" Conan asked sleepily from the next seat.

"Yeah, we're good, mate. She just had a bad dream is all."

I pushed off of Kyle awkwardly and with a slight noise of exasperation from the flight attendant went back over the low wall separating the footwells of our seats and back into mine. I guess she wanted me to walk the long way around. No way was I pulling that walk of shame. I had nothing to be ashamed of.

"You alright, Poppet?" Roan asked and I looked over to him and nodded, Kyle was smirking, the flight attendant was pissing off up the aisle and Roan sat just beyond it all looking quite amused.

I felt slightly less bad when the attendant returned with a complimentary hot coffee made just the way I liked with lots of cream and sugar and when I sipped? Spiked with something absolutely lovely.

"I wish I could let you stay," she said sympathetically, "but flight safety."

I smiled and nodded, thanking her gently and Kyle looked up and thanked her too.

None of us went back to sleep, we only had a couple of hours of our flight left, and so I settled in and watched another movie, eyes wide and stinging too tired to feel anything anymore. Conan quietly switched seats with Kyle and reached over to smooth a hand over my hair. I looked up at him and tried to smile, but I think it fell flat, the boys exchanging a look when they didn't think I was looking.

The men made me take the window seat for landing, and I didn't know why at first but then the lights and magic of New York appeared below us, rising out of the clouds like some sprawling fairy-tale castle in the sky and I was transfixed, completely engrossed in the view as we circled for landing, both my men talking and chuckling behind me as I was glued to the window portal.

I could barely keep my feet under me through baggage claim and Kyle turned to Conan and handed off his rolling bag asking, "Can you manage?"

"Aye, with one of those." I frowned perplexed and followed Conan's gaze to the carts lined against the railing meant for luggage.

"Alright, be right back."

"Why do we need one of those?" I asked blearily, swaying on my feet. I'd been up for more than thirty hours by now with only an hour's catnap at most in there a total of maybe twice?

"Because, Poppet. You're dead on your feet," Conan said kindly, tucking me into his side.

"I can make it," I protested.

He simply chuckled in response.

Kyle came back with a luggage cart and loaded it deftly and Conan took over driving it.

"Okay, Shady," Kyle said sweeping me up into his arms. I gave a quiet yelp and put my arms around him. "I've got you," he promised then said to Roan, "Shit, what's my name again?"

Conan laughed and said, "Kelly Gregson."

"Right, thanks." Kyle scanned the men holding signs above my head and I blinked up at him owlishly.

"This way," he said and Conan fell into step beside him.

I only vaguely remember Kyle handing me off to Conan waiting in the back seat of the town car and I don't remember anything but the sensation of floating after that. Blessedly, while I slept, I didn't dream and wherever we were, the bed was much more comfortable.

CHAPTER THIRTEEN

*R*oan...

The news was buzzing when we finally settled into the borrowed apartment.

"In international news, German art collector, historian, and philanthropist Gustaf Malmaison was murdered in his home gallery, with the killers releasing a veritable cornucopia of stolen artwork, Nazi paraphernalia, and in a property associated with Malmaison, human remains put on display, some of the bodies dating back to 1944 and the Allied invasion of Europe during World War Two," the male anchor in the off-the-rack suit said.

"Authorities in Germany and internationally are curious to find out how such a large amount of stolen art, some pieces documented as stolen during 'Die Kristallnacht', the violence against Jews in Germany prior to the outbreak of the war. Several state and local officials in Oberhausen and Dusseldorf have been detained for questioning, and at least two government officials have resigned prior to attempts to question them," the blonde headed female anchor said, the buttons on her blouse pulled as tight as her hair.

"Oh, they're right fit, now," I said. Lach gave a small laugh. He was less distracted now, getting from Paris to NYC had been trying. Sadie had some of the worst emotional fuss I had seen, and couldn't be placated. She had only stopped after we had landed, and she could lay in Lach's lap while I drove the rental car to the apartment. It might have been the longest continuous bit of sleep she had since we left Germany.

"We'll try to not make a mess, we've not rented this unit, the owner is out of town and said she didn't mind if we crashed her," I said.

"Her, who is this mystery woman?" Lach asked, helping himself to the refrigerator.

"She's a driver," I said. "And she doesn't drink, so there's no booze here for any of us."

"Oh, that won't do," he said, closing the door.

"It will have to, unless you want to have it door dropped or walk down to one of the corner stores to get some." I gave him a laugh. "But don't think you'll get anything but overpriced off-the-shelf juice."

"I would kill for some of that black gin, or the Botanical shit you found me," he said. "I missed those small touches while you were dead, I don't even know where to look to find that shit."

"Most of it is all online, mate," I said, turning back to the television.

"State sources have tied Gustaf Malmaison with two organizations: the Deutschland arm of Atomwaffen, a known Neo-Nazi organization with roots in Germany, the United States, and many other countries, and the international heroin Cartel known only as the Escadrille," the spunky female anchor was reporting. They droned on for a while about the sensational part of the story, a Neo-Nazi stabbed, images of Atomwaffen signs and retelling of terrorist attacks, and the rest.

Lach checked on Sadie again and then quieted himself on how to sort out ordering some gin to be delivered to the door. I could have done it in about three seconds, but he seemed intent on figuring it out himself, which basically meant asking me a question every few minutes; *which app, which bank account, what's the address?* I waited, answering distractedly and automatically, absorbed by the news.

"Until recently, the Escadrille Cartel was largely only known to a handful of international anti-drug task forces, and it was assumed that it was a very small operation. The murder of Malmaison comes just a week and half after

what French authorities call a pitched gun battle in the small township of Mont Saint Chauvignon, an ancestral estate remaining in said family's hands for generations. The 'patriarch' of the estate is international fugitive and suspected terrorist Guillame Chauvignon, suspected to be either the actual leader of the Escadrille, or one of its founding members."

"Oh, I bet the General is fit to be trussed and roasted with an apple in his mouth," I laughed.

"Carrot up his ass," Lach agreed. "You want anything?"

"Get me a fifth of Laphroaig, the regular bottle will do," I added.

"Gotcha," he said, "Do you tip in the app or in person?"

"The app, and give the twenty percent, they'll bump you to the front of the line for that."

The view from the seventeenth floor was nice, not Central Park nice, but a good panorama of Queens. Our hostess did have tea, which was lovely. There was no coffee; so Lach opted to just go get some, rather than try to have it brought to the door. The booze last night had had him pacing like a little kid waiting for Santa to arrive. There were things that I could have told him about the apartment's owner, but there was a reason that I had kept the two of them from meeting. Their skills overlapped, that was the main thing. She was a much better driver than him, and he hated not being the best at anything. The most important reason, she was attractive, and single, and I hated to think that a solid working relationship I had with a New York transportation specialist of her caliber be wrecked because of how cavalier he was with his smiles and how many relationships he left smoldering behind him.

The fact that he had not alienated or tossed Sadie to the side was simply stunning. A year ago, I wouldn't have believed that Kyle Lachlan could maintain a relationship longer than a few encounters at the most. Not days, not weeks, just how many times could he be face to face with a woman before he was done with her? His relationships had never been marked by time but rather encounters, until Sadie…

He had grown so much, had changed so much, it was simply astounding when I stopped to really think about it.

Sadie was up before he got back, which I completely expected. I could almost set a clock by her nocturnal insecurities. When she walked into the lounge, overlooking the city, she wiped at her face and made a mumble of words that I took to be a general round of questioning.

"Fifty-three minutes, that might be a new record," I said.

"Fifty what now?" She scratched the side of her head.

"Lach got up fifty-three minutes ago, he went to get us coffees and maybe a spot of breakfast, I told him a box of bagels, or donuts; whatever he found that wasn't a franchise offering." I gestured for her to take a chair. She did so, almost insolently. It was a good thing Lach was away, there was a very definite charm she had, half asleep and sitting at the table in nothing more than a tight-fitting shirt and panties. He would have her over a chair or the table in a moment, if she were ready or not.

"He's coming back?" she asked.

"Yes, he's coming back, why don't you take a shower and wash your hair?" I suggested. The apartment would need to be neat when we left, and I had no desire to clean up any messes I didn't have to. I would rather our Poppet be dressed when he arrived.

"K," she grumped, before getting up and shambling to the bathroom. She was adorable. It was easy to forget that so much of this was new to her, and it wasn't that long ago that she was living in a pile of boxes and never traveled farther than she could easily walk.

Lach returned while she was showering. "How long?" he asked.

"Fifty-three," I replied. "You owe me."

"Fuck all, I was sure she wouldn't sleep more than forty-five after I got up." He dug in his pocket and handed me a crumpled wad of cash. "I got you a regular coffee, cream and sugar, and a box of assorted bagels."

"How do you assort bagels?" I asked.

"Fucking hipsters, there's a green one; they said something about bacon avocado, I don't know. I just got an assortment," he said. "She in the shower?"

"Yeah."

"You have any fun?" he asked.

"Let her shower. She can't seem to take off her clothes without one of us fucking her," I gave him the sternest look I could. He shrugged and went and knocked on the bathroom door. I felt my jaw tighten in slight annoyance, but rather than enter the restroom, I heard him tell her something about vanilla macchiato something or other. I relaxed some. I was beginning to quite prefer the Lach who listened and wasn't quite so insolently defiant on every small thing.

When she finally came out, I was done with one of only two of the plain bagels in the box while Lach was picking at the unhealthy green shaded bagel. He wasn't enjoying it, but he also seemed to refuse to be bested by a strange piece of bread. Sadie picked up her coffee, a towel wrapped around her head, and one around her chest, and she smiled at the taste.

"Are you just trying to bait him?" I asked, but I wasn't annoyed in the slightest with her.

"Maybe you?" She gave a flippant laugh.

"You seem to feel better this morning," I said. She shrugged, looking a bit guarded, and took a bite of the other plain bagel, casting a curious look at Lach and his green one.

"Oh, no, Prince Charming, you don't eat the food if it's green, you throw it back in the dumpster," she said. He tossed it down on the table, and stood to face her. I could see his eyes on her, I knew what he was thinking, because on some level, I was certainly thinking the same thing. What would happen? We would fuck, the three of us, and then half of the day would be gone, or longer.

"Not now, not now," I said. "We need to make a plan, there will be plenty of time for all of that later. Come now."

"Fine," Lach said, sounding a little cross. She wasn't even dressed and hot out of the shower, the thought was damned appealing. I couldn't fault him.

"So, what now?" Sadie asked.

"The best news is that we have plenty of room right now. Everything we did in Oberhausen has completely blown up in the Cartel's face. If you didn't see the news, there are multiple agencies who were suddenly pulled in to deal with them, the DEA apparently didn't even have them on their radar despite them being in the billion-dollar club for heroin."

Sadie's eyes bulged. "Billion?"

"Yes, billion. Looking at what parts of their portfolio I could find, the Escadrille is somewhere in the vicinity of ten billion euros a year in heroin trafficking." Even Lach's eyes grew large at that.

"Fuck," he whispered.

"Yeah, but now they have half a dozen agencies with letters for names on their arses, and it looks like the French have seized Mont Saint Chauvignon as a drug forfeiture. The DEA and State department have jumped on the bandwagon hitting their financial assets in the US, France, and Pakistan."

"Why Pakistan?" Sadie asked.

"That's where the poppy fields are," Lach answered. "That's where the tribal warlords are using twenty-first century slavery to harvest those flowers to make opium and push it out onto the market. Pakistan, Afghanistan, that entire part of the world is the Poppy Basket."

"Poppy, not poppet?" she asked with a wan smile. I stood up and went to her, putting an arm around her.

"Poppy, like the flower, no relation to '*Poppet*,' I promise." I smiled.

"So, what's the plan?" he asked, looking at me curiously.

"We've got some time and room to work, and the things we need to do include getting back home, locating *Le Generale*, and making sure that nothing like Bootlegger Head happens again. That means getting our dear Sadie trained and ready so that if it *does,* happen again, she will be competent and capable."

"I'm not *in*competent." she gave me a bit of a scowl.

"I know you aren't incompetent, Poppet. Lach and I spent longer in advanced infantry training than I've known you. You have survival skills and wits, in spades," I said. "But there's quite a bit left to learn."

"I can handle myself in a fight, I can shoot a rifle, I know how to take care of myself." Her ire was unexpectedly raised. She was almost naked and already stoked to fight.

"Hand-to-hand, knives, pistols, driving, handling vehicles that aren't cars with automatic transmissions, handling explosives, security protocols in electronics systems, there is a ton of stuff that you don't know and before you interrupt, let me add the incredibly important word: *yet*." Her lips were a tight purse, and she didn't seem convinced. "I spent months with a Royal Marine drill instructor screaming in my face, and even longer doing things like running in the rain, at three in the morning."

"In the rain, or in extreme cold, or standing at attention until someone passes out from heat exhaustion," Lach added. "We'll teach you, but it won't be what we went through."

"I don't have any tear gas," I said with a smile, only half serious.

"Oh, I'm thankful for that one, mate," Lach said. "Once was enough of that shit."

"That sounds like a lot of bullshit to go through," Sadie said, running her bottom lip through her teeth thoughtfully as though measuring up the challenge before her.

"That's the point, it *was* a ton of bullshit. A nearly insurmountable amount of bullshit. It's a heap designed to be so much that it breaks you. The training strips us down like a rifle, to our component pieces, and then slams us back together as not a person, but a weapon." I leaned back in the chair I'd taken beside hers.

"I don't know that I want to go that far," she said honestly. "That I want to be a weapon." Her voice was soft at the last.

"You don't have to be," Lach said. "But you *will* be able to take care of yourself, and if the situation calls for it, you'll be able to take care of others."

"Like *us*," I added. Sadie looked highly skeptical, and vulnerable for a moment. I could see the wariness, and the world weariness there too. How long had she been abused, jerked around, lied to, all of those horrible things? "And it is my sincere hope that you never have to use any of those skills, but it's better to have them and not use them than the alternative," I said gently.

"Come off it, mate," Lach said. "You can't white knight her now. She's pulled the trigger; she's seen everything that we do. You never know, she might find something in what we do that really gets her going." I crossed my arms. "Seriously, the woman that owns this place, she's one of us. Didn't take much to figure that out. There are other women in this profession."

"Yes," I admitted.

"And Sadie? She's our equal, that's exactly how we're going to do this," he said and his tone brooked no argument.

Arriving back in Indigo City felt like a real coming home. Putting New York behind us felt like closing a chapter of my life that I was glad to see the final words of it committed to the page. The house on Phoenician Boulevard was splendid, a renovated historic home, with all the accoutrements of modern luxury but the classic styling of wood, tile, and metal that had faded in popularity decades ago. Everything was warm an inviting, which was nice. The bedrooms were also splendid, harkening back to a different era.

I welcomed such a definitive change in decor.

The location in Indigo City was likewise perfect, I was closer to my old pub, and I missed those comfortable seats and now that I knew that I could sit there with a proper pint and not lose myself to the bottle, I was looking forward to returning.

There was a gym nearby, which would be important since the house didn't have a gym in it. That was a luxury I was going to have to learn to live without, at least for a while. The other learning curve was dealing with the massive Alaskan King bed, nine foot by nine foot, all the bedclothes had to be custom ordered, and sleeping with two other people was not something I was used to.

How many years had I slept alone?

That sleeping arrangement made our new training regimen slightly different. The workout routines were easy, cardio and light weight training were no big deal and just left muscle burn and sweat. The same went for firearms training, shooting guns was just that, nothing more. The hand-to-hand and mock knife fighting, those went differently.

Those were harder. Harder for all of us, and a few matches almost turned into actual fights, between myself and Lach, mostly. When the frustration got the worst of Sadie she would lash out, accurate and violent. I am ashamed to admit that there were a few emotional breakdowns. Some bruises – *a lot* of bruises, and an equal amount of hurt pride.

She could kick, so not all of those bruises were hers. She could also take either of us out, her heel strikes and leg sweeps superb. Testicles and fake legs were nowhere near safe when her ire was raised.

But at the end of it, we weren't recruits and instructors, we were a unit – or at least that was the goal.

"So now that we aren't sitting under an Escadrille Sword of Damocles, how and what did you teach Sadie?" I asked. He looked grim for a moment, my question taking him back to the aftermath of Bootlegger Head.

"Basic things at first, she can field strip most any pistol or rifle. She might have problems with anything weird. She can clear a jam and knows when she can fix a gun and when she needs to toss it and pull something else. Only real issue we found there was that a lot of the pistols in the bunker were too big for her hand. She can shoot most of them, but has to teacup hold them, and keeping the barrel on target is difficult for her."

"What did she do well with?" I asked, stirring some cream into my tea, a luxurious feeling, even after Monaco and France.

"There was a PPK she did well with, but you know how small those are," he said.

"Not a lot of stopping power, and that's what she would need, keep her out of CQC."

"She did a ton better with the rifles, mate. Something she can put in her shoulder, pow pow." He made finger guns. "And she can ring the bell damn near every time."

"How much are you exaggerating?" I asked.

"Mate, listen, she's a better shot with an AR than *I* am," he said soberly. "Sadie has my full confidence, not because she's my childhood sweetheart, but because she would have even made Drill Sargent Hartman scream a compliment at her."

"That's gilded praise, indeed. Impressing a drill instructor?" I asked. I thought about my own instructor, back in Manchester. I suppressed a shudder.

He nodded. "After guns, there was hand-to-hand," he said. "It took a while to get to that part."

"What was the problem, did she need confidence or competence?"

"Mate, I had a chest full of cracked ribs that healed *slow*. For a month there, breathing fucking *hurt*. I'm thankful to be alive and not a fucking morphine addict right now." He ran his hand across his ribs, phantom memories of the pain etched on his face. "But that dragon-scale armor held up, just bruises and cracked ribs, no actual holes in me. At least not where the armor had me covered."

"That's good to know; so, it was you holding things up?" I asked.

"Once I could move without screaming, we went to work training. It was stressful. That place up there is *desolate*."

"It is a bunker in Montana, desolate was a feature," I admitted. "So, what did you do for downtime?"

"There was no downtime." He looked down at the floor, at his shoes. "That was a luxury that we didn't have."

"I know the bunker, it had amenities." I scowled. "She's not like us, she never had a drill instructor, you can't run a civilian through that and expect them to be okay."

"I didn't have any choice, mate." He looked up at me, his eyes uncharacteristically sheened with moisture. "Conan, you were *dead*. The house was a burning crater. We were fugitives and not just with the authorities, but the entire fucking underground, and I didn't know how close the Escadrille was to finishing us off. I barely remember firing rockets at boats in the bay, I probably had a concussion, and

Sadie pretty much carried me through the bug-out plan. If they had found us, we would have been killed pretty quickly, and easily."

I didn't say anything and had to look away. I had been captured, tortured, abused in ways that still burned in my dreams. For some reason, part of me imagined them escaping easily, that they were safe and comfortable wherever they had managed to hide. I wanted to hoard the suffering, like it was mine, and no one else's…

"So, we trained, we sparred, and it was bleak as fuck. Neither of us fared well, and that was all I felt like I could fucking do." He let his words trail off.

"She was frayed and about to fall apart when you two found me," I said, concerned. "I don't want there to be a repeat of that."

"Yeah, me either. I'm not cut out to be a drill instructor, and the bunker is a place I never want to go back to, physically or emotionally."

"So, we make sure that this house," I gestured to the Pinterest worthy carved staircase and inlaid walls, "doesn't become a second bunker."

"I don't want this place to be a bunker," Sadie said, drifting into the room like a vagrant balloon. "Is there coffee?"

"Yeah, in the pot," Lach said. "The cream is on the table." She looked at the service I had in front of me and the modern glass teapot among the various offerings of cream, honey, and sugar.

"Why would someone put cream in tea, ugh," Sadie said and poured herself a cup from the coffee carafe. "I overheard some of what you two were talking about, are you hiding stuff from me?"

"Nay, wouldn't dream of it, love." I smiled at her.

"Carry on, then," she said, jingling the spoon in the cup. That was an obscene amount of sugar she'd dumped in.

"We need to do things, things that don't involve being sweaty and tangled up," I said.

"I like some of those things," she said, hiding the gentle curve of her lips by sipping her coffee.

"Aye, as do I," I said. "But all work and no play makes Jack a dull boy."

"I liked when we dressed up and had fancy dinners," she said softly and her expression held a sadness and a wistfulness at the same time.

"Agreed, and we should continue that. Cocktail dresses and fitted suits, dinners out on the town, the fancy places in Baltimore, DC, and here in Indigo, they're all on the table," I said.

"I also liked movie night," she added.

"Does he get to pick all the movies?" Lach asked, hooking a thumb at me.

"Well, no, but he gets first choice, and then we do what we do best." She leaned over and gave him a peck on the lips. "We share."

"The Smithsonian, the other Smithsonian, the National Art Gallery, the National Geographic Museum." I started ticking fingers off.

"The National Spy Museum," Lach added grinning.

"Aye, that one," I agreed.

"Can we go to a theatre?" Sadie asked. "Fancy dress-up like?"

"But we've already got a movie night," Lach protested.

"You mean Broadway, stage theatre?" I asked. She nodded.

"Those seem so fancy, glamorous." There was an almost shy smile behind her eyes.

"What's hot?" Lach asked. "I'm not a Broadway guy, the only play I think I know is the one with all the cats in it."

"You mean *Cats*?" I asked.

"That's the one, I don't want to ever see that again, though."

"When did you go to the theatre?" I asked.

"Mate, on a contract, about three years ago, the Stage Guild guy and the drug pusher?"

"Oh, yeah. I did make you sit through *Cats*."

"There were other options?" He looked at me, his eyes darkening.

"Oh aye, I just thought you would enjoy singing cats," I laughed. Sadie smacked me on the arm and then she laughed. "So, here's what I personally would want to go to, *Hamilton* is still on Broadway, obviously. The Frank Lloyd Wright production of *Phantom of the Opera* is at the Baltimore Hippodrome, including the one-ton chandelier that flies over the audience."

"Wasn't there a *Spiderman* play?" Sadie asked.

"Yes, and if it were still playing, I would still say no." I scowled. "Comic books have no place on the stage."

"What, no *Batman Versus Superman*, the Musical?" Lach asked.

"No, absolutely not," I countered.

"This feels a little bit like the time-share," Sadie said. "But in a better way. I like this."

"I do too, Poppet," I agreed.

AFTER EVERY SPARRING MATCH, THERE WAS AFTERCARE. HAIR WAS smoothed, kisses were exchanged, and we would sit quietly, just touching – back-to-back, heads in laps, sometimes laying across each other when the grappling ended. She was a natural in many things and her skill grew quickly. Confidence bloomed when she learned how to hold her own.

When she figured out how to get inside someone's guard, or how to break a block with a kick, her grin was impressive.

Things started to feel normal again, and the looming sense of paranoia was greatly lessened. It certainly helped that the news had plenty of coverage about the mounting campaign against the Escadrille and the heroin trade in general. They were getting their noses bloodied at every turn, down to local militias taking to storming the Escadrille poppy fields and burning them to ash.

Our schedule turned into a very splendid routine. The first part of the week we would start the days with breakfast then some sort of cardio. Lach liked treadmills and free running, I picked either the elliptical machine at the neighborhood gym or stationary bikes. Sadie alternated between spin with me, or running with him. I couldn't take the impact, even after the replacement prosthetic arrived.

Afternoons were sparring matches, hand-to-hand. We took turns with Sadie, and even Lach and I squared off regularly. The hard part about sparring and grappling with her was the distraction that came. For every match that came up with hurt pride and angry feelings, there was a sparring match that ended in a post-coital shower. Most though, went like any sparring match.

Then it was regular showers and a cultural evening. The museums in DC were close enough to visit in a day. There was no shortage of them, and some were large enough to warrant more than one visit. After wandering through art galleries, and halls filled with dinosaur skeletons or the history of aviation and space, we would find some casual eatery. Burger World, that sandwich place, the little hole in the wall ethnic places where we were challenged by menus that weren't American food, where sometimes the menu wasn't even in the English alphabet.

The end of the week was our formal dinner out. We made a list of the haute cuisine of the area and visited them one by one. *Omakase* at an invitation only sushi restaurant, another restaurant that was only open from eleven p.m. to one a.m., where food courses were prepared in a duel between chefs. Wearing a low-cut dress and sitting at the front row of tables, Sadie received more than one amuse-bouche from the rival chefs.

Other places were the sort with the black menus that told you what you were having, and there were no prices. Those, the art of the food was exquisite, and the ambiance second to none. I could have been lost and become jaded and decadent to this sort of food, but sometimes a day later we would be having food from comfort places that Sadie knew. Having a diner griddle top lunch was sobering after the heady richness of a Nouveau French dinner the night before. There was an art to hash browns that could only be appreciated after foie gras and merlot.

Things became easier after the first few weeks. The tension and worry drained out of Sadie. This wasn't going to be a repeat of the bunker, and there wasn't a sense of doom and dread hanging over us. She learned quickly, and she started to give as good as she got as her confidence grew. This overlapped into other areas. She became more precise at the rifle range. Smaller handled pistols dramatically improved her one-handed marksmanship.

She was more assertive in picking her own wardrobe, not just accepting what I thought she would look good in. Then she was accessorizing *us*, picking colors and patterns that went with the dresses she had chosen for herself. There was a little struggle between her and Lach, but they had to come to their own accord, his own sharp sense of style and her more organic one. The harder he fought against pastels, the more she wanted him in them.

She almost always did our ties for us and her knots were becoming as crisp as my own. God love her for that.

CHAPTER FOURTEEN

*L*achlan...

Life on Phoenician Boulevard was something that I hadn't expected could be possible, it was almost like heaven. Everything had fallen into place in ways I didn't know they could. One of my oldest flaws, my attention span, was even sated. Nothing became tiresome, the sparring matches three to five times a week would have bored me, except that there was still that line that could be crossed where the spar could get real. There was another line that could be crossed, the other way, and the next thing I knew I could be balls deep in Sadie. It was a coin toss what direction that would be from.

The food was the same, we bounced back and forth from Roan's pretentious fancy stuff to Sadie's fast-food tastes, and there was something that just made that fucking work. Even with the week laid out on a schedule, that didn't make it feel rote, or like a trap.

Dancing? Sure.

Dive bars and live music? Oh yeah, we did that too.

One night we could be down at the Yacht Club, eating fresh caught crab and duck filet. The next we could be having a low-country boil on the beach because that's how this new rustic restaurant rolled.

Movie night definitely improved, since we shared the remote. It wasn't always old crusty cowboy movies, or black-and-white movies that people holding trash cocktails bragged about being the best, even though they were hard as shit to sit through. Sadie took it as almost a personal mission to indoctrinate me into Disney, sitting through films that were older than we were, some older than our deceased parents, some older than even our grandparents.

But I got to pick a few movies, and thank God and special effects for that. If I had to sit through The Little Mermaid and Chariots of Fire, they could sit through some high octane bare fisted beat 'em up.

The winner there was a little gem that I remembered from when I was young, one of the few movies that held my attention deficit eyes, *The Professional.* They were attentive and appreciative through the shoot'em-up violence and Jean Reno, the consummate French hitman.

"This movie is one of the things that showed me what I wanted to be when I was a kid," I said, looking over at the two of them. They were both looking at me like I was an alien.

"Mate, where was this movie before?" Roan asked. "I mean, after all of the Michael Bay explosion and computer graphic garbage you've made me watch; and you knew about this movie the whole time?"

"This movie makes me want to wear a choker," Sadie said, smiling at me.

"It's certainly a fashion statement," Roan said. "And an easy one to accommodate. I think there were a few complementary ones in that last personal shopper delivery you got the other day."

"Oh, I *have* to go look." She popped off the couch and vanished into her bedroom. Technically it was *a* bedroom, but for all intents and purposes, it was her large closet, with a bed in the middle of it, since we all basically slept in Roan's master bedroom.

A few moments later she returned, and I heard Roan's suck in a breath. I looked up to see her standing by the doorframe, naked save for a black choker on her neck. In the light of the television, she was lit like some dark goddess. Her skin was as bright as her bush was dark, and her nipples, I felt my own heart give a lurch.

"Boys," she crooked a single finger and beckoned for us to follow her, "your presence is required."

We both came off of the couch and followed her, her perfect ass leading the way.

"I don't want to waste time, so take off your clothes," she said, pointing for us to go into her bedroom. The bed was technically a queen size, more than enough for one, comfortable for two, but for three?

I was the quicker to undress, and for that reason and that reason alone she had me first. Roan was still fighting with his slacks when she took me into her mouth. I wasn't even completely hard; I hadn't had the time to work it up. The sensation was beyond what I had imagined, and she seemed amused by this. She squeezed my balls and pulled on them. I groaned and Roan cussed, finally free of his slacks and boxers. She gestured, for him to come to her.

I was hard when she released me from her lips. This reminded me of the Sadie from the train, but she didn't feel stressed or frayed. She felt excitingly assertive.

She stroked me, and pulled Roan to her, so she could suck his cock too. There was something about watching her take all of him that just made me harder. She made those wet noises, taking almost all of him into her, and I was amazed that she could breathe, it must have been going down the back of her throat. I looked at him, and had to stifle a laugh, his eyes were almost gone into the back of his head.

When she did come up off of him, she looked up at both of us, stroking us both. "I want you both to fuck me." She made the last part of fuck a hard k. "*Both* of you." She looked at Roan.

"Okay," he said.

"Not okay." Her voice seemed richer than normal. "You're not going to make love to me, we're not going to have sex, Mister Roan, you are going to fuck me."

"Yes," he said, a little hesitantly. "Alright."

"You are going to fuck me," she said, glancing in my direction before fixing her gaze on our partner. "And *you* are going to fuck me in the ass." Her voice brooked no opposition.

"Poppet," he said, touching the side of her face.

"I mean it," she said, and then took him back in her mouth.

"Don't argue with the lady, mate," I slapped him on the shoulder.

"You first," she said, before going back down on him.

"Not like this, Shady, let's move you to the bed." She reluctantly let go of him, and I helped her to her feet. "Lay on your back, across the bed, this way."

"Mate," Roan said, looking down at her. She looked up at him, and when he was close enough, she grabbed his cock and pulled him close enough to start kissing the bottom of it, and he groaned.

"Enjoy it, she's not a porcelain doll that you're going to break," I said. Then I kneeled on the other side of the bed and spread her legs. There was something that was just sublime about going down on her. It was something that I never did with the escorts, never. I didn't kiss them, and I didn't go down on them. It still seemed like a splendid and new thing to do. It was also fun feeling her muscles tense and release as I sucked at her clit and eased a finger into her ass. If she wanted Roan to go there, I had some work to do first.

"Poppet, you don't have to do this," Roan said, his voice softer than usual.

"Conan," she gasped. "I want this, I want you, I want *both* of you."

"You can let go a little bit," I said. "If it's too much she'll tell you." He looked a little concerned, his faced screwed into a knot of concern. He was reluctant, but did what she wanted, letting her take his cock. Her head was tilted back, and I could see the choker stretched tight against her throat, and the visual gave me a thrill. I went back down on her, hoping to match the dedication that she was showing him.

She groaned, and there were a few moments where I thought she might tap out, instead she just seemed to get wetter. There was only so much of this that I could stand and it was almost a rush to plunge my cock into her. I half expected something like quenching a glowing sword in water, but it was like sticking that glowing metal into a forge. Her pussy was so hot and wet I almost lost it at that moment.

She wanted it rough, she wanted it hard, and I obliged.

Somewhere along the line, the choker broke.

We made eye contact, Roan and me. A head nod, a gesture, and he knew what my idea was. I took her right tit in hand, giving it a good rolling squeeze, then pulling until I had her by the nipple. He did the same, but with the other one. When she twisted under us, the sensation I felt was nothing short of this side of heavenly.

It must have taken some effort on her part, but Sadie gave us both a push. When she was separated from us, she was panting for breath, and let out this animal like sound, a deep half groan half shriek of pleasure. Laying there, she surveyed the two of us, naked and hard, and this made her smile. There was a cat-like grace to her movements when she rolled on the bed and got onto her knees. I saw her leg quiver for a moment, and was ready to catch her if she fell, Roan had all but mirrored my movement, either way and she would be caught.

She turned her back to Roan, giving him a sultry look over her shoulder. "It's time for you to fuck me," she breathed. "I want you to fuck hard enough that all I can do is hold on to him."

I nodded in agreement. He took her by the hips, and she dropped her back into the perfect arch. Going down on me was easier, and she took to it with enthusiasm, as Roan eased himself into her, slowly at first. That was probably best.

He worked up to what would be a leisurely pace for anyone else but was fairly quick for him. Her moans vibrated from her throat through the base of my cock, and I was living for that.

"Harder, fuck me," she said, her voice demanding. He looked concerned; his eyes momentarily lost. "Please," she groaned.

He did as she asked, and sped up, and was a bit more forceful.

Then a bit more. I gestured for him to bring it up.

And he did. Soon she wasn't able to do anything but hold on to me like I was the ladder on the side of the wave pool. I held the side of her head, present and supportive, and I mimed to him that he should stick his thumb up her ass. There weren't special forces hand signals for that, so I improvised, but he got the point.

She writhed as he slowed his pounding to give himself a moment of focus to start working her ass over. I gestured to her nightstand, there was a bottle of lube waiting. She *did* have this planned out, didn't she? "You want me to go first," I asked her, as she lay panting against the sheets.

"No, I want you inside me." Her words rattled, but there was no mistaking her intent.

"As you wish," I agreed, and she went back down on me now that she wasn't being battered by Roan's thrusting.

He picked up the bottle, and it looked like he was just going to upend it and squeeze a glob out onto her ass. I signaled him to stop, threw a few more hand signs, and he did the task properly. I never met a single woman who enjoyed having cold lube squirted onto their ass. Well, there was that one escort, but she had been from Iceland and something about polar bear clubs. She had a thing for ice cubes, but this was so not the time to be thinking about her.

"Relax, slow deep breath," I said as he worked the lube up over himself. Then he put the head of his cock against her backdoor and gave the smallest fucking push I'd ever seen. "Mate, hold still," I directed him. "Sadie, think you can push back against him, get him in?"

"Yeah, but slow like," she said. I eased back, giving her the room and focus to handle the thing she had wanted. I knew how that felt, how tight she could squeeze, and how it would feel once he penetrated and then I prayed that nothing went wrong.

It took a few moments that felt like minutes for her to get him inside, but when he was in, the sound she made. It was pure delight, and accomplishment. Getting him going was a little slow too, but he was rightly cautious, and once everything was sorted out, and he had his rhythm, she pulled me back to her, and went down on me with a fury I hadn't seen before. It was intense, and soon I was doing all the techniques I knew to keep my control.

I had to let myself float, just be part of the moment, and not think about too much. If I thought about it, it would be over and I would be spent. I was the pro at this, I wasn't going to be the first to crack. Well, I knew she had already had at least one, maybe several orgasms, but that didn't count.

I shuddered at the thought and gripped the base of my cock. A moment slower and I would have filled her mouth, with no warning.

"You fuck me, too." She sighed as I took a small step back.

"Let her up, mate," I said. The look on his face was distant, lost. I knew that, he wasn't trying to lose himself in her either. He nodded, and she made a sad whimpering sound when neither of us were inside her. I popped down on the bed, facing up. Her movements weren't smooth this time, but when she eased down, there was no resistance. She was achingly wet, and I shuddered. I felt him as he took her again. The reentry was again measured and slow, and that was fine, as long as everyone was mostly holding still, it made it easier to bring my cool back down.

It was different this time, I was used to being in the other position, doing the proverbial driving, while the two of them were under me. All I had to do was just, be there, and that was all. I could roll my hips a little, but that didn't really matter.

She howled, and kissed me, and bit my neck and my ear.

She would clench up tight, he would groan, and then she would let out a body shuddering shriek and then I would feel heat trickle down my sides. She was coming all over me.

It got inside my head, everything coming together, all the sensations, all of her energy.

I only managed to make a grunt and I came. She felt it, she had to have, it felt like something more than semen leaving my body. She gave a sob sound, and there was that wash of wet heat again.

"Poppet, I'm spent," he said, and she turned into dead weight above me, her face pressed against mine.

Her bed was too small for the long and close attention that we would share after such a romp, and we were driven to the shower too quickly for my liking. Roan and I had to pick Sadie up and physically carry her to the bathroom. Every time she tried to take a step, her ankle would try to roll, or her knee would fold in an instant.

She started finding a few of her leg bones in the shower, thankfully the shower was ridiculously oversized, one of those installations that gets put on the cover of remodeling and house flipping magazines. Roan held her up first while I soaped and washed her front. Then, I held her while he washed her back.

After the shower was done, we were scrubbed, pink, and smelling of elderflower and some other thing I had never heard of. We carried our queen up to Roan's bed and deposited her in the middle, and gave her all of that soft attention, soft kisses and caresses, brushed hair and half-whispered words.

She drowsed off quickly.

Neither of us got back up, sleep was much more appealing.

CHAPTER FIFTEEN

*S*adie...

It was a rare treat for me to wake still between both of my men and rarer still to do it before them and after such a supremely satisfying night as last night's encounter had been. I hadn't known what'd possessed me but *God*, I wouldn't mind if it decided to come around and visit a little more often.

I smiled and didn't move, just closed my eyes again and drifted somewhere between sleep and awake, warm and satiated between my two lovers. I was half draped over Conan with Lach half draped over my back and I had to confess I *adored* it when I got to wake first, and the boys, uninhibited in their dreaming states had a hold of each other as much as me.

I would never bring it up. I would *never*... but it was nice when they could drop the machismo in sleep and I could catch these glimpses of how deeply they cared for one another, too.

Conan was the first to come up from the depths of his slumber, his deep and even breathing interrupted by a particularly deep breath and an almost startled jerk of his body beneath my cheek.

I felt a hint of a smile tug my lips and I didn't quite want to give myself away that I was awake first. What can I say? I was feeling mischievous.

Roan's fingertips found the side of my breast and drifted slowly in a light caress down my body and I sighed out, melting just a little into him. He chuckled and I must have had him convinced I was still soundly sleeping because rather than say anything or try to wake me, he shifted his arm under me slightly and tapped Lach.

"Mate," he said low and careful and I felt Lach twitch at my back.

"Ungh!" Kyle made an undignified sound and Roan chuckled and made a gesture I couldn't see, his hand coming off of me and then returning.

Kyle chuckled lightly, the sound you make when you see an adorably sleeping kitten and my heart fluttered. "I love it when she's like this," he murmured, shifting slightly and pressing his lips to the back of my shoulder, his breath warm as he breathed me in.

"She's an angel, isn't she?" Roan asked, and it was everything to keep my breath moving in and out at its deep, even, and measured pace.

"She's always been," Kyle murmured, and his voice was heavy with the ghost of memory.

"I've never known you attach to anyone like this, mate," Conan mused, and I could feel his eyes on me.

"Yeah, well, there's nobody else like my Shady," he said.

"Why *do* you call her that?" Conan asked.

Kyle was quiet for a long moment and I didn't expect him to answer. It wasn't his way to open up – not even about the small things and he especially didn't talk about the past. He'd always said *'what's the point?'* and that *'talking about it never changed it.'*

"You know how kids are assholes?" he said quietly. "Back in school they started calling her *'Shady'* to torment her. I didn't like them messing with her, so I tried to protect her. I wanted to kick all of their asses, even the teachers who knew but couldn't be bothered. I know now that they had more to deal with than name-calling and bullying, then. I couldn't beat them all up, but I wanted to, and I tried. Got my ass handed to me more times than I could count, but I always got back up, all bloody nose and scab covered fists."

"I can completely imagine you being willing to fight everyone in the world. What I find hard to imagine is you as a child, and losing fights," Conan murmured, smoothing a hand along my back as much as he could with the arm that was buried beneath me.

"I know it's cliché, but she's different from all the other girls, and that hasn't changed a bit," he said. "I mean, I was this angry, angsty, asshole kid. I was really getting a handle on playing the manipulation game, I could pick out the sheep and the wolves, and was working out how to be the alpha wolf. Then, there she was. This skinny little girl, scared, but absolutely tough as nails, and she didn't know anything about the game. She wouldn't learn the game; she wouldn't play it. Instead, she would challenge it at every chance, you know?"

"Not really. I'm not familiar with the American foster care system and I had most of my family growing up."

"There was this other girl, Tara, she tried to teach Sadie the game but Sadie would point blank say it was stupid and she… I don't know. She just *refused* to play by anyone's rules. You know? Even mine. She moved at her own pace, but at the same time… she never lost that innocence, the kindness. Believe me, I was *The Asshole*. I pushed her and everyone else away but she just… she refused to give up on me, mate. Like you."

I swallowed hard, knowing what that confession cost him and whispered, "How could I?"

Both of them chuckled.

"Good morning, Poppet." I opened my eyes and looked up at Conan, he smiled down at me and brought my fingertips to his lips and he pressed a light kiss to them.

Kyle nipped lightly at the sweet spot on the side of my neck and I gasped quietly.

"I tried, I gave you every reason and opportunity to leave me, like everyone else had," he said.

"I know," I answered and twisted a bit so I could look back over my shoulder at him. His dark eyes held an equally dark light, one that I don't think I had ever recognized before.

"Question really is, why didn't you?"

"Precisely because everyone had," I said softly. "Everyone needs someone," I murmured. "As aggravating as you could get, I wasn't willing to be everyone else. Besides, you looked out for me… and you did it without expecting anything back."

"You sound so sure about that," he said with an almost shy smile and I turned over, he took himself off of me to give me the room to do it. Conan turned on his side and spooned me at my back, propping his head on his hand to regard us, a hand on my hip, thumb smoothing circles against my skin. I tucked my hands beneath my face, Kyle mirroring Conan, laying on his side hand propping up his head, free hand kneading my breast gently but I wouldn't be distracted. I fixed his gaze with mine.

"Aren't I?" I asked.

"The only thing I wanted was everything," he said, voice darkening, growing slightly seductive.

"Maybe then, but not now," I said softly.

"Nothing's changed between then and now," he countered but I could taste the lie. I smiled slowly and shook my head and he cracked first, grinning wide and chuckling, looking away and letting out a breath with an, *"Ohhhh."*

"I don't understand," Conan said, laughing. "Why does it sound like she's just bested you, mate?"

"Because she did," Kyle said, casting me a knowing look.

"Check and mate," I whispered and smiled.

"Enlighten me, if you would be so kind." Conan sounded even more perplexed.

"If he wanted everything from me," I said, grinding my ass softly back into Conan who sucked in a sharp breath. "He wouldn't be sharing."

Kyle let out an explosive breath. "You've got me."

Conan laughed a bit and said, "This is certainly a sort of generosity that isn't much like you. The only sharing I've seen you do before this was magazines in a firefight and when you donated your blood."

Kyle's gaze slid off the both of us and he hooked a hand behind my head, pulling himself to me and pressing warm lips gently to my forehead. He drew back and I smiled. I could see it even through his guarded gaze, and it warmed me down to my toes.

I didn't expect him to answer Conan, but he surprised us both when he did.

"Because I trust you, you're more than a brother to me," he said, hesitantly. "Because I love you. Not in a sexual, romantic way, but platonic. I think that's the word." He looked at me when he said it. His dark gaze flicked back to meet Conan's bright green eyes. "We've been broken, incomplete, for a long time. So, we worked, we made crazy money, and built a fortress. It didn't make us happy, maybe satisfied, but not happy. Then I found her, and I was never good enough for her, I'm not a whole person. But the two of us? How well we work together, how well we complement each other? The two of us *and* Sadie, we're more complete than any couple will ever be capable of. There's no room for my pride, so I did what I had to do to make it happen." He got up out of the bed and looked down at us both. "Best decision I ever made," he said and with a sardonic grin he severed his normally guarded gaze from us and turned to go into the bathroom.

I smiled and turned to look back at Conan who looked shocked.

"And that's why I never gave up," I said and grinned. Because I knew that no matter how broken Kyle felt, no matter how sharp his edges or sharded his personality, that he was one of the best people I had ever had the occasion to meet. I knew it deep down to my very soul.

Conan's gaze roved my face, and I turned over, putting my arms around his neck and kissed him lightly.

"You are so very loved, Conan Roan," I murmured and with no small amount of emotion in his own voice he murmured back thickly, "As are you, Ms. Brooks. As are you."

"Kyle Lachlan, too?" I asked softly, needing to hear it.

"Aye, him too," Conan said without hesitation. I smiled and kissed him and the kiss he gave me was so full of love and light I could taste it.

"Thank you," I whispered finally after several moments of just simply cuddling. We heard the shower start.

"For what?" Conan asked.

"For being brave enough to love us both. Part of the reason I chose to love him all those years ago was because I could hear how they talked about him. You know? Not just Dean and Prissy, but his case workers and the shrinks."

"Oh?" Conan asked, curiously.

I nodded carefully and met his glinting gaze.

"They all called him the boy who could never be loved," I said. "And I knew he heard it. That he believed it. I was determined to prove them as much as I was him, wrong about that. Everyone deserves to be loved."

Conan tightened his arms around me and kissed the top of my head, wrapping me up tight against his chest. I cuddled into his warmth and he sighed.

"You couldn't be more right, Poppet. You couldn't be more right."

It didn't take much urging for me to get the both of us up and to go join Kyle in the shower, even though we had showered just the night before after that phenomenal and mind-blowing sex.

Some showers weren't about washing the body clean of impurities, though. Some were about cleansing the soul. I had a feeling, that for Kyle, this was one of those showers meant to soothe some aching old hurts talking about the past had brought up.

I was a firm believer that there wasn't any ointment or cure for such aches and pains than an optimistic dose of the present and a tincture of our smiling future, so after giving him a few moments alone to collect himself, we went in to hug the man between us briefly, to shower, laugh, talk about other subjects more mundane, and to start our day.

CHAPTER SIXTEEN

*R*oan...

One wise man said something along the lines that the only thing that is constant, is change. And whoever he was, he wasn't wrong. There were people who had entered or left my life and had become catalysts. My father, when he left one day and never came home, two days before the constabulary informed us of his death in a traffic accident. My mother's new husband, the one with the iron fist and xenophobic hostilities. My drill instructor, Lach, and then there was Sadie, the first time, and then the second.

A few men in uniform screamed at me to go faster, harder, and frame every response with a shouted yes drill sergeant or a no drill sergeant. Almost everyone else had been in the camp telling me to be smaller, be quieter, take who I was and turn it down to a muted setting. A lot of my career in the military had been a form of rebellion. No one there wanted me to walk more softly, or keep my voice down. They only cared how my bunk was made, and that I stayed in formation, and did what I was expected to do.

That and I knew my stepfather would have boiled at the notion of serving in a military that wasn't white as the Cliffs of Dover.

Sadie rescued me, and in a seemingly unplanned moment, didn't give me permission to be myself, she demanded it, and she unapologetically loved me for it.

I gave her everything I had, and I didn't hold back, not at the end.

It had been liberating.

I felt like a new person in that shower, all stress and worry drained out of my body.

There was no real and proper way I could thank her. There weren't enough Viennese waltzes, duck confit, or jeweled tiaras in the world that could express that.

I certainly was going to try though.

She was changing me and had changed Kyle. I didn't feel like quite the untarnished white knight. White knights didn't fuck the fair princess up the backside, that was for one thing. But Lach, he wasn't quite the black knight as he had been, suddenly he was applying himself to being attentive and soft, when he had for years been nothing but a shark, a sharp knife.

My dear Sadie had changed too. She had always had a core of sterner stuff, but now she had confidence, and was a lifetime away from the first day I saw her. Her bone thin half-starved body had filled out, and there was definition and tone to her. She found a purpose beyond just surviving another day, making it through another week.

AFTER A THIRD MONTH, HAVING PUT QUITE A DENT IN THE entertainment and humanities offerings of the Baltimore/DC/Indigo City area, we decided it was time to visit a certain memorial. The anniversary of Lach finding Sadie and bringing her into our house seemed like a fitting date to go back home.

The drive from Phoenician, across Indigo, and down to Bootlegger was quiet and somber. Clouds hung over the city like a funeral shroud and the news promised rain later in the day. Breakfast had been light, a scattering of toast, some fruit, none of us had much of an appetite, and we had a lunch reservation at the

Powhattan Hotel. Dressed in black, we did seem fitly dressed for a wake.

It *was* a wake really, for years the House on Bootlegger Head had been an integral part of our lives. Lach and I had turned the place into a fortress, ran the most lucrative jobs of our respective careers there, and amassed the fortune that placed us in the rarified company of the wealthy and the elite, with none of them knowing who we were, and that was an incestuous group of mock blue-blooded bastards.

We were no Rockefellers or Carnegies, but the holding companies I had built through elaborate means and online constructs were worth tens of millions of dollars. The house had reflected that, in our collected art, the cars, and the investments that had danced out of the Batcave and into our portfolios. The carefully manicured lawn, the intricate defenses, the historic stone wall, the jetty to where the boat had been berthed, it had all been by our hands.

The driveway curved up, and sections of the wall were still present, but the carnage of so many months ago was gone. The wrecked cars hauled away, the bodies carted off to the morgue, and the burning wreck of the house had been cleaned away. The basement under it was filled, and there was nothing left of it but a wide grassy field. We parked and then walked the rest of the way to where the front door had been.

The police and federal agencies had swarmed the place, and through cross referencing, they had found all but two of the land-mines. Those would be dead now, once activated they had some sort of clever chemical trigger that would eat the fuse away, after so many days, leaving it inert. The other possibilities were that they had gone off and not been accounted for in the survey, or someone pocketed a pair of landmines, and then the dead fuse would still have happened.

"I really fucking liked that house," Lach said.

"It was nice," I agreed.

"Nice, you two owned a mansion that would have made Bruce Wayne jealous. All fancy and expensive and full of tricks and secrets." Sadie slipped an arm around my side. "I was only there for a few months but nowhere we've been has really matched it, you know?"

"Aye," I nodded.

"That's because he did everything." Lach gave me a smile. "I mean, God knows what asshole decorated and furnished this new house."

"They liked mismatched antique furniture and basic store offerings." I gave him a laugh.

"Did you have all the furniture custom made?" Lach asked.

"Nay, just a few pieces. Most of the stuff I found in overseas estate auctions, and I had a field day when some Silicon Valley wanker bought a castle, hated everything in it, and sold it. I took everything I could get, even tried for the tapestries, but those went, *ouch*, way over my budget."

"What's way over your budget?" Sadie gave me a squeeze.

"I won't pay thirty grand for old wall rugs." I squeezed back.

"You cheapskate, next thing I know, you'll be hitting me up for tips on how to find clean food in the dumpster." She smiled, but there was a shadow over Lach's face. I gave him a tiny shake of the head, no reason for him to jump on that soapbox. She would never eat from a trash can, dumpster, or alley again in her life.

"What are we going to do with it, can we rebuild?" she asked.

"Nay, too many questions, there was a lot of contraband inside that building and they found residue and wreckage but not enough for tracing records. The people who owned that house *died* with it, and as far as the government is concerned, that is that. There are provisions, the city is supposed to take possession of the property, and ideally turn it into a park, at least that's what is in the contracts."

"A park, that's, *nice.*" Lach gave a sneer.

"I think it *is*, nice," Sadie said slightly defensively, knowing Kyle for his penchant of off-color jokes. "A park I can come to and sit and remember the good times? I'd much rather that than some development." She sniffed.

"It is, indeed, the best option," I agreed. "We can't take it back, too many questions, too much heat."

"Still, we're out all of that money." He tucked his hands in his pockets, I knew that annoyed body language, and it sometimes surprised me that even after the amount of money we had, he could be upset by even small losses.

"Nay, again. We're not out as much as you think." I gave him a nod.

"Explain that," he said.

"The place was insured, because obviously, mate. The cars, the art, especially the art. There was a rider on the house as well, nice lump of change, that." He looked unconvinced.

"A lot of insurance companies pay out to dead people?" he asked.

"That's a good question." She looked up at me.

"Well yes, insurance companies pay out to dead people all the time, that's a cornerstone of insurance fraud, and there are a few very wealthy people who built their fortunes doing that sort of skullduggery. But, no, our policy doesn't pay out to dead people, it paid out to the investment and holding company that legally owned the house. You would be mad to think that our real names, or that any of aliases were attached to it."

"I think you might be a wizard, Mister Roan," Sadie said and pulled herself up to give me a peck on the cheek.

"Thank you, Poppet, but when I game, I'm a paladin, actually." I smiled.

"Of course, you are - you big nerd," Lach laughed. With the worry over lost money gone he warmed.

Taking a loop around the head, following the waterline, had the feeling of a funeral procession, the somber pomp and circumstance, a quiet and guarded walk. The sky threatened rain the entire time, and we were left with our memories. The last time I had been here, several of the Escadrille hirelings had been dragging me away from the house, through what had once been a wall but blown to splinters. There had been the stench of blood and cordite, burning rubber and hot metal, and I had a few bullets shot through me. Just under the vest, into the hip.

They had good doctors and the bullets hadn't struck bone. There were things to be thankful for. Lach and Sadie had their own memories. The boat, rockets, gunfire. I wondered where they had been when the warhead went off. I knew that I had been spared a lot of injury because of an array of destroyed SUVs and a stone wall. Some of the men who hadn't had shelter had fallen over dead, organ burst by the pressure wave. Others had been left screaming, ruptured eardrums, bleeding from their eyes, internal hemorrhaging that would take hours to kill them.

It had been an ugly business, but there was nothing beautiful about war. And that was what had happened out on the Head.

"Oh!" Sadie gave a shout and released me to go trotting off toward a new grown hedge of weeds and water grass. "Pspspspsp," she called and then I saw what she had seen before either of us. The amber eyes of a large black-and-white cat. "Come here, Sylvester, come here you." She chided the cat for giving her a wary look and retreating into the weeds.

"Come off it, how do you know that is the same cat you named before?" Lach asked.

"Because I recognize his coat, and he has one white whisker, mister." She kneeled and tried to cajole the cat out of its hiding place, but it was to no avail. The cat had been a feral before, and it was very much unchanged in that regard.

"Come along, Poppet," I said. "He's a wildcat now, and won't come to you."

"I know, but still." She sounded a little crestfallen.

"He's been fine this long, he'll be fine without us," Lach said. "I didn't even know there was a cat on the property before."

"I only knew because he set off the motion detectors," I nodded.

We watched as the cat emerged from the far side of the weeds and then bolted like a black-and-white streak, following an arrow straight path to vanish into a gap in the wall, well away from where we intruded on his domain. Lach helped Sadie back to her feet and swept the fragments of grass from her black skirt.

"Are we going to stay at the new house?" Sadie asked, finally.

"It's okay, but it doesn't have the same charm, does it?" I asked. She shook her head.

"If we build from the ground up, the things we want done will go quicker and easier, plus we won't have to work to preserve a landmark." Lach led us back up the head, to where the new path had been bulldozed through the ruined wall. It looked like service vehicles and equipment had been brought through, and no one put any effort into cleaning up the damage they had inflicted.

It didn't really matter now. The house had just been a place, that was all.

The Powhattan Hotel was waiting, with its dining room overlooking the Chesapeake, enclosed in insulated glass.

CHAPTER SEVENTEEN

*S*adie...

I was battling a bit of this deep seated, I wasn't sure, *rest-less* feeling? It was this phase in my training that I felt as confident and competent as ever, and yet it was *different* somehow in that I didn't feel *confident* in that confidence I felt fidgety, and the routine, while necessary, and the structure it provided that had left me feeling delightfully secured before was now starting to leave me feeling almost *caged.*

I didn't know what it all meant with the front of my brain, not yet, but I kind of wanted to speed some things along and get it figured out. It wasn't the same type of nervous energy spurred on by anxiety. No, there wasn't anything to be *afraid* of, just a feeling like something was *off* and that we needed to be doing something.

It was driving me so crazy that I wanted – no *needed* to do something to break up the ghost of monotony already.

Every other Sunday, we had started doing something on our own. It was past time, Roan had said, that we cut the proverbial apron strings and started doing things that appealed to us individually. He said that we might be a unit, but we were individuals too. We had to reclaim our own independence, or our interests.

He was right. I knew that, and I wasn't at all sad or upset, didn't have an ounce of bad feelings in me when he'd almost nervously suggested it and found it sweet and almost endearing at how he almost stammered it out. Add to that at all the nervous looks he cast in my direction when he brought it up over dinner one evening and I don't think I could be any more in love with the man for caring for me as deeply as he obviously did.

"Poppet!"

"Yeah!" I called out, straightening from where I pulled on my last running shoe from the bench at the foot of the next to useless bed in my dressing room.

Conan appeared in the doorway. "I'm headed to The Black Watch, love."

"Didn't want to miss your kiss goodbye?" I asked.

He chuckled and held out a hand to me, I got up and went to him and took it. He hauled me in close and captured me with an arm around my waist, kissing me soundly.

"Mmm," I hummed out in pleasure and absolutely indulged in that kiss for as long as possible.

"Kyle already gone?" I asked.

"Hardly, just waiting for him to get his big ginger ass out of my way so I can have my turn." He slapped Conan on the shoulder of his overcoat from behind.

I laughed and Conan stepped aside.

"Be careful," I called to him as he retreated up the hall, he waved a hand over his shoulder without looking back.

"And where are *you* going?" Kyle asked me, helping himself to a globe of my ass in each of his capable hands and hauling me up against his hard body.

I put my arms around his neck and sighed asking, "Wouldn't you like to know?"

"Looks like you're headed to the gym."

"Nope," I said, popping the 'p' and smiling at him. "Thought I would go for a run to the bookstore."

"Ah." he pecked my nose and looked down at me.

"What about you?" I asked.

"Just going for a drive."

"Something fast, loud, or both?" I asked.

"Pfft! Both," he said, making it sound like I was crazy for even suggesting that you could have one without the other. I grinned and tipped my head back and with a mightily contented smile my cold-blooded killer dipped his head and heated my blood with one very fiery kiss.

I hummed in pleasure against his mouth and he jerked his head back as though he'd been burned.

"Don't do that," he said, voice low and intense.

"Why?" I asked with a little smile, loving the effect I had on him. The only thing I loved more was hearing it.

He squeezed my ass and let me go and said, "Because you don't want Roan to get too much of a lead on you, too much and it makes it harder to track him. You make mistakes if you put yourself into a situation that requires more than the usual amount of haste. You can't afford to make mistakes if you're trying to get one up on Roan. There is no margin for error."

"*Fuck!*" I complained. "How did you know?"

"Cardio?" he asked. "Baby, you've never run from anything in your life, it's more like cardi-*no*."

"I haven't complained about doing it since the bunker," I said, rolling my eyes. Kyle turned sideways in the doorway to my room so I could get by and gave me a sharp smack on the ass on my way through.

"Which is why he hasn't caught onto you, yet" he called and I rolled my eyes without looking back over my shoulder at him. I heard him chuckle. "I love you," he called.

"I love you, too, babe!" I called back, but still gave him the finger over my shoulder. He laughed outright, and I turned the corner, out of sight.

I set my watch out front, and the timer on it, just as I had been taught. Following that, I did the calculations in my head on Roan's walking speed, the route he would take to The Black Watch, I had never been there, but I knew where it was. I pulled up my hood I set off at a fast walk. I stepped it up into a half-paced and measured jog a short time later after checking my time, rounding corners, waiting at crosswalks, and before long, I caught sight of him – his broad back and fiery ginger hair as he strode with another smart walking cane up the sidewalk.

My chest squeezed tight at the sight of him like it almost always did. I was so grateful to have him back there weren't even words.

I hung back, waited and took the corner in a natural stride. He still moved up the street none-the wiser, or at least pretending to be, and I diverted at the next corner, passing just by him as he waited for the crosswalk signal, looping around the block. The Black Watch was in sight, and all Conan had to do was cross the street, take a few paces up the sidewalk and head through the front door.

I picked up the pace once I rounded the back side of the building and I was obscured from view. I paused and stretched at the next corner up and watched the door of the pub swing shut behind my lover. I caught my breath, waited for the light to change and took my time crossing the street and walking down the length of sidewalk to the banded oak front door. I took a deep breath and let it out slowly, hoping he wouldn't be angry with me for intruding before I dragged on the iron handle set in the weathered wood.

The door dragged open smoothly on well-oiled hinges and I stepped into a world of warm glowing wood and a black-and-white checkered floor. I stared at the floor for a moment as I took down my hood and a man behind the bar called out, "Oi, luv. Bar's closed, private function."

I looked up and met Conan's surprised green gaze and smiled.

"She's alright, William. Poppet, what are you doing here?"

I smiled a little wider and looked back down at the floor, walked up to Conan and took his hand giving it a squeeze before letting it go and said softly, "Check mate."

I stopped my watch. His smile was everything when he realized what I'd done.

"What a clever girl you are," he said quietly, and I tipped my face up for a kiss. One that he gladly gave me.

"Come and meet the lads," he said and drew me up beside him.

CONAN WASN'T AT ALL HAPPY WHEN HE REALIZED I HADN'T BROUGHT MY phone with me. We had a nice visit and breakfast with his friends. The topic of conversation had been somewhat steered by my presence. These men were all veterans, some had scars, and there were a few who were missing pieces. Some wore prosthetics, some didn't hide the loss. They knew who I was, which was a thing.

Although it wasn't precisely a surprise that Conan had spoken of me to his friends, it certainly was flattering and remained somewhat unexpected for parts of me. Wisely, Kyle was kept out of the equation which suited me just fine. While it wasn't a secret, there was no need to advertise our status as a romantically involved triumvirate. Why invite any judgment or conflict where there didn't need to be any?

They had pints of beer, some were eating, most weren't. The conversations revolved around their military experience: Royal Navy, Royal Marines, Royal Airforce. Their pride was a deep thing, like the atmosphere of The Black Watch. Polished, ancient and ageless at the same time. They seem to trade stories of violence for the things they lost, or left behind. It was memories of their sweethearts and wives, how they'd missed them during their time away. Not every story had a happy ending but even with the bitter there was the sweet and some humor to be found with the passage of time in the darker moments.

We rose together after our goodbye's and fingers linked stepped back into the daylight filtered by the overcast sky. Conan turned to me and I smiled up at him. "You're not mad?" I asked, and he smiled back.

"Not at all, Poppet. Still about the phone, though."

I felt my smile grow, and I shook my head slightly. "If I had my phone on me, how could I prove I didn't just use my GPS?"

"Why would I disbelieve you?" he asked and tucked my hand in the crook of his arm.

I felt my smile grow, and I told him truthfully, "Oh, Conan. I don't have anything to prove to you… this was honestly for *me*, I think. To prove to *myself* that I can be capable."

"I see," he said simply, and he looked, I don't know… pleased?

"And what would you have done were it not important to you to prove yourself?" he asked.

I shrugged and said, "Probably would have gone to the bookstore and perused the stacks," I said honestly.

He nodded, and we sauntered along the sidewalk.

I finally asked. "I went right by you, right before you crossed to go into The Black Watch, you really didn't notice me?"

He smiled and shook his head. "You blended perfectly with the public, my darling. I hadn't noticed a thing."

I felt my chest puff with pride and he laughed, putting an arm around me and pressing me into his side.

We went to the bookstore together and spent an hour or so in the stacks selecting a few books. I had my ID and a credit card in a pocket in the upper arm of one of my sleeves but he waved me off and paid for mine too.

I was trying to be better about actually spending a little money and about shopping for myself, but it was hard sometimes. Especially when I passed someone I recognized from the streets. There were times I felt like some kind of a sellout or something and others I simply felt grateful. Then there were the times I was shrouded in guilt right on the heels of that gratitude.

"Shit," I whispered as we passed by Winthrop Park on the way back to the house on Phoenician Boulevard. I drew up short and stopped.

"What is it?" Conan asked, and I thrust my chin at the chess tables.

Hal was in the throes of one of his schizophrenic episodes, rocking back and forth violently as he eyed the pieces on the board in front of him, made his move, and hit the switch on the top of the clock.

"You know him?" Conan asked, and I nodded drifting a step in that direction. Conan hung back briefly, and I looked back at him with somber pleading eyes.

"He's no threat despite all appearances, I promise you."

He inclined his head slightly and came with me. There was a small crowd of spectators around the tables, their hands buried in their pockets against the late fall day as Hal's opponent made a move. The young man paused when I called out softly, "Hal?"

Hal looked up and squinted at me, his head jerking back slightly before recognition dawned and he stood up.

"Sadie girl?" he asked, and I smiled.

"Hi, you remember me?"

Hal lurched on his feet and hugged me, Conan stood straighter and looked like he was ready to step in, but drew up at a stern look from me. I wrinkled my nose slightly at the pungent body odor coming off of Hal and tried not to let it show on my face that it bothered me when he pulled back to look at me.

"You look fine, girl. Damn fine," he said, and I smiled. "What you go and do? Get yourself a sugar daddy?" he asked, eyeing Conan.

"Two," I said giggling, and he laughed at me, his face pinching into worried lines.

"You good, though?" he asked, and I nodded as he said, "'Cause we all thought you was dead somewhere."

"Almost," I told him. "If it wasn't for Conan, I would be."

He looked past me, up at Conan and nodded.

"The Red Queen, the one in my head, she said you was dead." He started tearing up and I put a hand on his arm.

"Oh, no, no, Hal. We've talked about this," I murmured.

"I know. I know what you said. She doesn't always tell the truth."

"That's right," I soothed.

"Sadie, sometimes she can be real mean," he told me and I nodded.

"No, I know, Hal… she can't help it though."

"I know, I know, you said that too. Sometimes people are mean because people are mean to them." I nodded kindly.

"Have you eaten today?" I asked, and he shook his head. "Will you be here? Can I get you something to eat?" He nodded, and I led him back to his seat.

"Right, alright. You play, I'll go get you some food."

"It's so good to see your face girl, the Red Queen," he shook his finger at the sky, "she almost had me fooled this time."

I smiled and nodded. "You play," I told him, and he nodded.

"Come on," I murmured to Conan. "I need to find him something to eat."

Mutely, my lover followed me across the way to a little café. I ordered two sandwiches, waited for them to pack them up with their side of an apple and a bag of chips each and I brought them outside.

"Are you alright, Poppet?" Conan asked me.

"Oh, yeah. Absolutely," I answered, stopping for the crosswalk light. "I know I can't save him, or anybody else and I know in the grand scheme of things that this won't make much of a difference," I said, hefting the bag with its two Styrofoam clamshells. "But it will make today, and maybe even tomorrow a little easier," I said.

We went back and got to the table just as Hal took the young man's king. The small crowd of hipster and nerdy types all mumbled and muttered and there was a small smattering of applause. I smiled when Conan swiftly took the young man's seat and began to set up the pieces. I sat beside Hal.

"If you would like to eat, I'll set the board up for another game," Conan said and Hal nodded.

"Eh, thank you—"

"Conan," Roan supplied.

"Like the Cimmerian." Hal nodded, and I giggled at Conan's silent but accursed look. Hal either didn't notice or didn't care, saying, "Chess isn't a game for barbarians, you know. It's a game of kings – did you know Sadie here is a queen?"

I smiled and opened up one of the containers of food and handed Hal a half of the sandwich inside. He began to chew furiously, taking half of the sandwich half in one bite.

"Indeed, she *is* a queen," Conan said with a polite nod.

"You be white, white boy," Hal said, and I snorted. Conan grinned, inclined his head, and started to set up the pieces the other way around, making himself white and Hal black.

They chatted amicably, Conan very patient with Hal's tics and sudden outbursts. Waiting until Hal had his fill and gave the instruction to begin. I could tell that he had experience with this sort of thing.

"White goes first," Hal told him and Conan smiled again.

"Right you are." He hit the switch to reset the clock and then pressed the switch to start it before moving one of his pawns.

Watching Conan play Hal was a treat. The two of them trading off in swift and efficient movements, the small crowd of onlookers silent. The only thing that you honestly could hear was the rustle of the leaves overhead and the shush of the pieces moving across the board punctuated by the click of the switch as they passed the count of the clock between them.

"Bollocks," Conan finally muttered as Hal put him in check.

"Check," Hal said and rocked harder and faster. He was excited, Conan was providing him a challenge and Hal rarely, if ever, got one of those. It *did* happen, just not very often.

They both went back and forth faster than ever, Hal would move a piece, hit the clock, then Conan would move a piece almost faster than you could blink and touch the clock even faster. I couldn't precisely follow what was going on when it came to the board but several moves and Hal hesitated. He rocked to and fro and his face lit up more excited than I'd ever seen it. He moved, hit the clock, Conan grinned, moved his white queen and declared, "Check and mate, sir."

The small crowd sucked in its collective breath and held it as Hal's eyes bounced over the board and then Hal smiled. It was a beautiful thing to behold, and he stood up fiercely and declared, "You win, white boy."

The crowd applauded, and I smiled and stood slowly.

"You take care of my girl, now," Hal said and held out his hand. Roan stood and shook it and Hal declared, "She's a queen, don't forget."

"That she is, mate, and I won't forget," Conan replied and he held out his hand for mine.

"He's not bad," he told me as I tucked myself into Conan's side, our bag of books around my wrist. I'd held them while Conan had played.

"Oh, I know," I said with a proud smile.

"First time I've been beat this year," Hal muttered to himself. "He's a good one, mister red knight, Golly." He looked up, his eyes sliding over us and he called, "Who's next?"

"That's our cue," I murmured and Conan and I took our leave.

"He's an interesting fellow," Conan declared as we crossed the park.

"He is," I agreed. "Paranoid schizophrenic," I said. "Chess and the streets are his home. There's no real *'helping'* him. He doesn't want a roof, they come with rules and he doesn't like taking medications," I explained. "Sometimes, the best you can do is provide a meal and some company."

"He is a good friend to you?" Conan asked.

"Yeah." I nodded. "Taught me a lot of what I needed to know for basic survival. Where to scrounge for food, where to find medical care, when it was a good idea to get some different clothes… even kept a couple toughs away from me once. Took a pretty hard beating for it."

"Good man." Conan nodded and something was percolating in the back of my brain.

"A very good man," I agreed.

We reached the manse on Phoenician Boulevard and let ourselves in. Kyle wasn't back yet, and I sort of itched from the sweat from my run and the smell from poor Hal had seeped into my clothes.

"I'm going to shower, baby," I said and Conan nodded, sliding the bag of our purchased books onto the wine bar's counter outside the dining room on the way into the kitchen.

"I'll put the kettle on," he said, and I smiled.

"Tea sounds lovely," I said, and he winked at me.

"Doesn't it just?"

I showered quickly and efficiently, drying my hair and opening the wardrobe in my dressing room pulled down one of the silk dresses Conan favored back at Bootlegger Head. I hadn't worn one for him in a while and I slipped it on.

While it felt good against my skin it felt… I don't know, dated? Like an old skin that while the dress was flawless and fit true to size and perfectly, at the same time it didn't feel like it fit anymore.

I found Conan in the sitting room, on one end of a settee, sipping tea from a fine china cup one of his books open in his hand, waiting for me.

This was our thing. I would lay back, my own book in my hands, my head on a pillow in his lap, and we would just read and cuddle. Kyle thought it was adorable, and almost always snapped a picture of us when he caught us at it and I loved that.

Without a word, Conan set one of the velvet pillows from the settee in his lap when I'd selected one of my new books from the low marble table top in front of him. I laid down, and he put his free arm around me, his hand between my breasts just resting there.

I smiled and opened my book, hesitating before I started reading when whatever it was that'd been percolating in my mind finally rose to the surface…

Conan Roan had bested the Chess King of Indigo City and not two hours before, *I* had bested Conan Roan…

"Oh," I uttered and closed my book as my epiphany completed itself…

"What is it, Poppet?" Conan asked, setting his own book aside.

"I think I'm ready," I said and looked up at him. He smiled, and it held both wisdom and pride. I felt my brow wrinkle and asked, "You knew?"

"Of course, we did," he said with a nonchalant shrug. "There's no need to rush things with the Escadrille so firmly rooted at the moment."

"So, what? You were just waiting for me to come into my own or figure it out naturally for myself?" I asked.

He winked at me and I laughed, and suddenly I realized what all this low-key restlessness I'd been experiencing the last several days was from. It wasn't anxiety or reluctance at all – quite the opposite. It was eagerness, *readiness.* I was ready to be on the move and for whatever our next step was going to be.

The electronic sound of a phone taking a picture came from the doorway and I turned my head, Conan looking up.

"Hello, you two. Have a nice afternoon?" Kyle asked.

He came in, tucking his phone back in his pocket and I smiled.

"Yes," I said, turning my head in Conan's lap and tipping it up. Kyle put his hand to the back of the settee and leaned way down and kissed me, an almost chaste press of lips. On his way back up he winked at Conan and asked, "You want one too?"

Conan arched a brow and said, "I'd feel left out, mate," calling Kyle's bluff. Kyle pecked Conan on the tip of his nose and Conan pushed him away laughing. "You bloody sod!" he cried and Kyle bounced his eyebrows at me. I giggled.

"So?" he asked, lifting my feet and depositing himself beneath them on the other end of the plush, velvet piece of furniture. "What'd I miss?"

My eyes practically rolled into the back of my head as he pressed a thumb into the arch of one of my feet, down low, near its start at the heel. I let Conan fill him in.

"Well, it would seem our Poppet passed her tracking and shadowing a mark flawlessly this morning," Conan announced. "A test I hadn't even thought to give her quite yet."

"You got him?" Lach asked, and I nodded in Conan's lap and almost immediately regretted it.

"Well done!" he crowed and took his hand off my foot to hold it up for a high five. I high-fived him back and set my hand back down on my book on my stomach so it wouldn't slide off.

"Walked right into The Black Watch like she owned the place," Conan agreed and chuckled. "Didn't even know she was behind me."

"I did," I agreed. "And I don't own the *place* I was there for my king." I threaded my fingers through Conan's and he chuckled.

"What else did I miss?" he asked. We recapped the rest of our day and he nodded.

"So, we're ready for phase two or whatever," he said and Conan laughed.

There weren't really any phases to any of these things. At least not yet. We needed more plans for that.

"I think so," I murmured. "Don't stop that."

Kyle laughed at me and said, "Wouldn't dream of it, just give me your other foot." I did as he told me and sighed out in bliss. Conan petted my hair.

"So, what's next, Captain Roan?" Kyle asked with a sigh.

"Next, we take the fight to them."

WE STARTED TO PLAN, BUT YOU KNOW HOW THAT GOES. THE SECOND you planned anything was the second things changed. One man changed them.

Hiram Emerson, Republican, Texas.

He'd been speaking in front of several committees, attacking the cost of the War on Drugs, and that the government had no place sending DEA agents into other countries, and doing God knew what sort of "CIA spook business" over there. Those men were needed at home, on the border, and hunting the real threat to Americans, illegals crossing the border, and the home drug trade.

Everything that happened in France was a French problem, even the suspected leader of this criminal organization was a Frenchman, and that was most definitely a French problem, a European Union problem. It wasn't something the citizens of Texas, or Alabama, or Maine needed to be footing the bill to deal with. His words were fire and acid, and then people were listening.

"You've got to be kidding," Lach said. "No one believes this asshole, do they?" He muted the small television in the kitchen but good ol' Hiram kept right on screaming, waving his papers and putting on a good show at the lectern.

"He's trending positive," Roan said. "And people *are* listening." He was back in his happy place, the kitchen, putting an impressive chiffonade on some basil for a garnish. God, his knife work was sexy... I was starting to sound like Lach.

"Why are they listening to that giant empty hat?" I asked, getting my brain firmly back on the problem at hand. "Is he supposed to look like a cowboy? I mean, what is even happening here?" I waved my hand at the television like I'd had a particularly abrasive and condescending personal shopper wave at me once.

"He's the senior senator from Texas, and it looks like in the next election cycle he's likely to become the new leader of the Republicans, if they carry the Senate, he'll be the most important person after the president," Roan said.

I looked back at the television and mouthed the word, *Gross.*

"For a Brit, you seem to know your politics." Lach gave him a snipe.

"For a Yank, you are typically unaware of them." Roan gave him one back.

"Now, *boys,*" I said, turning my attention back from the television. "If this takes the Escadrille out of the center of attention, they get to recover, and then they're a problem again, am I right?"

"You are naturally correct," Roan said. "And this feels too convenient for them to be anything like a coincidence.

"Who the fuck is that." Kyle stood up from his seat at the counter, looking at the screen. "You have to be fucking kidding me," he growled. In the publicity shot, standing six smiling faces to the left of Emerson, was a very familiar face. Her makeup was conservative, and her hair wasn't blonde, but I wouldn't forget that cunt's face even if I were struck blind.

Kaijin... the name slithered through my brain like a snake covered in cloying perfume, the taint of merely thinking it lingering long after I'd thought it. I didn't dare say it out loud, I cast a worried look in Roan's direction. He stood, knife forgotten in his hand, but his grip around the handle was a white-knuckled one.

I am so going to make that bitch pay, I thought to myself, twisting on my own stool with a mighty desire to do some violence.

"What in the actual fuck is she doing there, half of the international police people are looking for her," I said, incredulously.

"The Nazi had ties to the German government, and if it took that long for the French to move on Mont Saint Chauvignon, they must have had people there too. It shouldn't be a surprise that they have people inside our government here," Roan said sourly. He set down his knife and leaned heavily, palms flat against the counter as we all watched.

"This is a major problem, mate," Lach said, picking up the remote and turning the television off so we didn't have to look at her haughty fucking face anymore.

"No, that's an *opportunity*," I shot back, twisting my lips back and forth, the wheels in my head turning.

CHAPTER EIGHTEEN

*R*oan...

Our plans were laid out, moving as a unit to Austin, Texas with the intent of smoking Kaijin out of hiding, and then take her down. She was the closest threat and had escaped us once before. Ajahi was missing somewhere overseas, and from near as I could tell even the Cartel didn't know where he and his men were. Things had been especially ugly for them the last few months, being caught between international attention and local gunfire. Some of the other cartels had taken the outing of the Escadrille as a *carte blanche* to move in on their territory.

Some nations, formerly in various ways beholden to the Cartel, did much the same. Compounds were attacked, fields were burned, workers were liberated or killed, and in some countries their leaders preferred the latter to the former. It was an ugly business all around, though there were few tears that could be shed for corrupt governments and incompetent international agencies attempting to kill a powerful and vindictive Cartel.

On a certain level, many people supported the actions of Emerson. The news was a constant downer, each seeming victory in the war on drugs was countered with violent massacres, abductions, horrific maimings, terrorist bombings, and all the rest.

People were to the point that when that fell out of the news, and the new daily outrage revolved around a few high-profile celebrity nude leaks and some off-color jokes from people of importance just felt better. They could get properly angry about that, sign a petition, post comments on their social media, cheer it up proper. Not quite as cathartic when the new item of the day is the daughter of some foreign cabinet member being kidnapped and then returned with both of her hands and her eyes removed.

The planning dragged out, there was no looming sense of urgency, so we dawdled.

There were things that seemed to need doing before taking off on our next dark adventure.

When the phone call came, it was a complete surprise.

That they were able to find my phone number was the first surprise. The second was that were able to slip it in through even my basic phone screening techniques. The last surprise was the voice on the other end of the phone: Guillame *le Generale* Chauvignon.

"Good morning, Conan Roan," he said, his voice was that of a very tired old man.

"Aye, and morning to you too, General," I said. I brought out my laptop and started recording the call, and sending a tracer to find where he was.

"Your call trace will end at the French Embassy in Washington DC, so I will save you a little time," he said. "But I would like to make an accord with you and yours."

"An accord?" I repeated, watching the trace program run.

"*Oui*, an accord. A truce."

"What did you have in mind?" I asked. I gestured for silence and put the phone on speaker. Lach looked surprised, Sadie confused as to what I was doing. I mouthed the word *general* at both of them.

"A complete cessation of hostilities between our two interests. You have no stock in the heroin trade, and surely you have better things to do with your time and wealth…" he paused.

"What terms are you offering?" I asked.

"Complete pardons, all around."

"That's an interesting start, doesn't do much for my blown-up house or the six months I spent as one of your people's prisoner. That wasn't square with Geneva if you understand me."

"*Oui*, I understand you. You blew your own house up, and that is most unfortunately on you. The mistake I made was one of hubris, and as hubris drew the ire of the Gods, mine has drawn the ire of the world. I have made a number of mistakes, with the first being calling professionals into a family spat. That should never have happened, and everything that came after was none but by own wounded pride, my ego. My brother is dead, more men than I can count have died because we could not reconcile our opinions, and the Escadrille is a shadow of what it once was, I am certain that several billion euros in losses is more than adequate recompense for your house." His voice was scathing at that point.

"Gwendolyn Kaijin?" I asked.

"Has been relocated, reprimanded, and if she fucks up again, I will have her tied like a suckling pig and delivered to your front door with a parsnip corked up her bottom, but so long as she behaves herself, she should never cross paths with you again." He was irritated with her, and that was readily obvious.

"And if we don't accept?"

"Then I do what I must, send what men and agents I can hire with the funds remaining to me to that lovely house on Phoenician Boulevard and try again to finish what was started last year," he said, calm and icy. "I would prefer to keep as we have been for the last few months, our paths not crossing, our interests not conflicting."

"How do you know what we've been doing for the last few months?" Lach asked.

"Kyle Lachlan, I was wondering if you would be present for this. It would be arrogance to boast that I know everything, but transparency might be more prudent. You've been watched for some time. I know where you are, and generally what you are doing. I know you've been preparing for something with the guests you've had. It was time to make the call."

Lach was standing, then he was gone. Window to window, he was scanning outside to see if he could spot the watchers. He would start turning the house over, top to bottom, looking for surveillance equipment, the hidden cameras and microphones. If he found any, I would see what sort of malware I could feed back through them, see how much more damage we could do that way.

"Do you accept my terms, is this enough, or do you require more blood and death?"

"You'll forgive my lack of trust," I said.

"Completely warranted, but you and your partner have proven to be men of your words. If you say this is done, then this is done."

"Then, as much as it pains me to do so, I accept," I said.

"*Monsieur Lachlan*, do you accept?" Chauvignon asked.

"I don't trust you as far as I could throw you, but yes. I accept." His hands were fists.

"Lastly, *Mademoiselle Brooks*, I assume you are there, do you accept?" She looked startled, to have been called out by name. It was chilling. He might have been offering peace, but it wasn't surrender, he knew our real names, and our address, and even had my phone number. I would have to find out how he did that and make sure it couldn't happen again.

"You can go fuck yourself, but we accept your terms," Sadie spat.

"Excellent, I would say your reputations are sterling, but to be honest, silver doesn't make a proper comparison. Best of fortunes to all of you, and I hope that we never cross paths again." He sounded relieved.

"You still going to have us followed?" Sadie almost growled.

"*Non*, of course not. We are all men of our words," he said, almost sounding surprised. "The word of a soldier is non-negotiable. *Monsieur's*, it has been an honor to have seen such fine work, I would appreciate it much more highly if I were not the target of it."

And like that, the call was over. Sadie was oddly furious, she thought the call was a show of weakness, and now that the beast was wounded, we should move in for the kill. She didn't recognize that he could have put bullets and boots through our doors and windows, if he knew where we were, and when we did things.

Lach went through the house, looking for spy equipment.

To our collective surprise, he found several items. But given their relative age, placement, and non-internet connectivity, it was unlikely they were from Cartel sources. The batteries were dead, but it was simple enough to power them back up and access their memory devices. It was pedestrian fair, bed-and-breakfast snooping. A spy eye in the shower, another in the master bedroom, and a security camera outside the house peaking over the fence toward the backyard of a neighbor.

Most of the footage was mundane, maid service cleaning the shower stall, the last guest taking a shower, the lens steaming from poor placement. The bedroom feed was the same, housekeeping, a person sleeping. It was one of the more dismal attempts I had seen at attempted voyeurism.

He went over the house several more times, looking in increasingly deceptive places. Eventually Sadie and I confronted him, after he had taken the microwave apart, looking for a microphone. Replacing the microwave was a small price for a slice of peace.

There was also the matter that I think we were all a little disappointed with the voyeur gear we found having nothing of interest. With all the cameras the Bootlegger house had, there were a number of encounters that had been caught through the electric eye. The *thrill* of making home movies was easily dampened by modesty on Sadie's part, and my complete non-interest in being some sort of mock porn actor. The current news loop of some singing actress tart with her own line of shoes, cosmetics, and peripheral electronics throwing lawsuits and social media tantrums after her nude selfies and thirty second sex tape were leaked was just the icing on the cake.

"So, it just over now?" Sadie asked. "That's too easy, I don't believe it."

"We'll play it by ear, love," I said.

"But we're totally canceling that Texas plan." Lach nodded.

"Yes, yes we are, we have other things to do now," I agreed.

"Like what?" Sadie asked.

"First order of business is to decide if we want to remain here, or find a new location," I said, and managed to get a proper fold on the omelet.

"Here as in just this house," Lach said. "Not here as in changing cities."

"We'll stay in this area, most of our real estate investments are here," I agreed. "But if Escadrille knows about this house, it's as good as burnt."

"Not actually burned," Lach said, looking over at Sadie. "Burned as in everyone knows where it is, so it's not safe anymore."

I was trying to not look too hard at her for the moment. Sitting at the little breakfast nook table, she looked more delicious than anything I was making. I felt like the luckiest man in the world, and even the events in Mont Saint Chauvignon were becoming little more than distant memories, being neatly wrapped in a pearl of forgetfulness.

"I know what he meant." I could hear her eyes roll at Lach.

"So, we have to go house hunting again?" Lach groaned. "Can't we just get an agent to find a new place?"

"Well, that was the plan, either that or built from the ground up, but that will take time," I said.

"This place doesn't have a big enough garage," he added.

"You don't have any cars to put in the garage we have *now*," I countered.

"I know, and when are we going to address that?" he asked. "I'm tired of renting if I want to go for a Sunday drive."

"I'm sure that getting new cars is not a priority right now, but I really agree with Kyle on this, I need some fast cars to go with all this, now." Sadie grinned. High-speed driving was on her training list, and she seemed keen to get to that.

"We should celebrate somehow," Lach agreed.

"After breakfast," I countered.

"Well obviously," Sadie quipped back at me.

THE DC SHOWROOM FOR AUTOMODELLISTA WAS BREATHTAKING, EVEN to my jaded senses. The floor was white marble, veined lightly with gray and almost a hint of pink. All the fixtures were polished chrome, everything else was almost antiseptic white. It wasn't a car dealership, I felt like I had walked into Heaven, everything was aesthetic. The cars sitting on display were the sort that even felt beyond our not-insignificant resources.

The obvious centerpiece was the black-on-black Bugatti Chiron, looking like Satan's coupe, double parked at the pearly gates. The Pagani sitting to its right was some mental one-off that was all carbon fiber and Italian flag colors. To its right was a Koenigsegg Regera, as stark and opulent white as the showroom itself.

"Welcome to AutoModellista, we have been expecting you." The hostess smiled.

"You were expecting us?" Sadie asked.

"Yes, of course, we are only available by appointment. No one can just walk in here, off of the street. There is decorum to consider, plus many of the things we sell are legally registered as works of art." She gave a smile as precise and stylized as anything Lach could. "I understand you are interested in purchasing something from our midrange offerings."

"And what are these?" Sadie asked.

"These objets d'art are part of the AutoModellista personal collection. They are for display, not for purchase." She gave her precise smile.

Oh, Sadie mouthed and took a step back from the Chiron.

"We have a number of cars in storage here that might match what you are looking for, and any of them can be made ready for a test drive in an hour, at the very longest." She beckoned for us to follow. Her private office was as stark as the rest of the place, but we were offered a stop at the in-house barista, and then flipped through portfolios of cars. It was a library of Ferrari, Lamborghini, Maserati, and the rest of the exotic car offerings to be had on the East coast.

Other portfolios, all neat leather bound, lined a shelf, and our hostess declined to bring those out. It was the West Coast, and Texas inventories. Those could certainly be had, she assured us, but there was some cost associated with bringing cars across the country, and most preferred to visit those branches, rather than handle said costs. There was certainly plenty on hand here, and if nothing fit what we were interested in, then we could venture into those volumes.

We narrowed our interest down to Ferrari.

Then it was sorting through if we wanted an older Ferrari, or a newer one, and then how close to factory stock, or how customized.

Sadie did ask about the old Ferraris, and realized that those were in the highest tier, being millions of dollars each.

The final choice was a *rosso corsa*, Ferrari racing red, 488, in a convertible Spyder layout.

The final finish was close to factory spec, which suited me very well. I wasn't one for heaping praise on Italian car makers, but the 488 had near perfect lines. Its predecessor, the 458 had perfect lines, but there wasn't one available to match what we were looking for. They had 458s, but so many of them had been overburdened with body kits, aftermarket modifications, and *pimping* that they were eyesores, out of the range we were looking to spend, or were currently in negotiation to be sold to some interested rap artist, deejay, or person of alternate income. That last was a polite term for people like cartels and dealers who could pay cash for cars in the hundreds of thousand-dollar range.

We accepted delivery of the 488 after the wire transfer went through and a few other things pinged as complete. The insurance issued, and the car was covered, for all of us to drive, and the keys were handed over.

The hardest part was accepting the keys to our sensible four-door sedan while Lach took Sadie in the Ferarri. I would have my own chance later, but I knew that he was more the driver than I was. He said dinner was his treat, and all I had to do was keep up.

The drive from AutoModellista back to Indigo City was a blur. Trying to keep up with the 488 was already a challenge given its better power to weight, handling, acceleration, and driver. It was made worse because of the car groupies who would give a little chase, trying to get a pic of the car for their feeds. By the time I pulled into the lot at the Burger World on Lucas avenue, Lach had backed the Ferrari into a parking space, the boot of the car facing the constantly flowing stream that was Lucas. I parked closer to the building, but ignored the blue-and-white handicapped parking spot. Technically I could have taken it, but I refused to own one of those blue hanging tags or have a plate with the symbol on it.

It was one of my points of ego.

Inside was everything that I expected from a flagship fast-food dive: plastic counters, digital screens overhead, constantly changing between the illuminated menu and its numerical values and nearly pornographic clips of the food from their commercials. Bouncing buns, vegetables crisp with freshly misted water on them, steaming hot fries with elegantly tossed salt, and the pièce de résistance, the money shot of condiments being layered onto the burger. There was no subtlety at play as mayonnaise was artfully and almost erotically delivered to the waiting bun, just a bit leaking out the side when the well-manicured hand grabbed the burger and gave it a supple squeeze.

What was delivered on the plastic tray was far from what the monitor promised. Paper wrapped, the bun a steamed almost sodden mess, it looked like the thing had been assembled in a car constantly pulling a hard turn, causing the contents to come out over the side. I stifled a sigh; this was not my cuppa.

It was for her, and the radiant smile she had on her face.

She had eaten half of her bacon and cheese monstrosity and couldn't be happier. Even Lach had a goofy, almost boyish grin on his face. A real one, not the tactical calculated smile, but a real one. That alone made me happy enough.

I ate without complaint.

"We should celebrate, proper like," Lach said between French fries and milkshake. "The only question is when and where."

"I would say we should save serious celebration for when we are sure that the Cartel has made good on their promise, and *then* we can relax," I said.

"I'm just waiting for the other shoe to drop," Sadie admitted. "Like, it's too easy for those guys to just roll over and show their belly."

"Why is it so hard to imagine?" I asked. "I'm guessing that dealing with the three of us has cost them at least one senior member, easily a hundred or more of their lesser dead, or seriously injured. Then, after Oberhausen, with everyone from the DEA to the Pakistani government going after them, that revenge is just too expensive. They've lost more money than the three of us could even consider spending."

"I can spend a lot of money, mate," Lach pointed a fry at me, "that's Bugatti money."

"You could probably have bought AutoModellista with what they've lost in the last six months."

"Fuck em, they *should* lose everything," Sadie said. "I bet none of them have ever had to eat trash out of a dumpster."

"No, I should say not," I agreed.

CHAPTER NINETEEN

*L*achlan...

We settled on having our victory dinner at the place where all of this started, *Le Jefferson*. I hadn't been inside in well over a year now, and Sadie had never been. That was okay, she would appreciate it. Almost as much as I was going to appreciate their aviators.

Everything inside was elegant. Crisp white linen table clothes, linen napkins, crystal glasses; the works. She was elegant too, having settled on a form fitting white dress. It was something Roan helped her find, and it had a glorious high collar, but a keyhole in the neckline that drew the eye to her cleavage. Roan had rattled out some long fancy word for it, but I didn't care. She was a goddess, draped in white and gold.

Her hair was up, and she was wearing a gold net, set with some sort of obscure gemstone in it, some rich variation of topaz, maybe? I didn't care about that either, but the stones almost matched her eyes.

There were a few things that I was sure about, and two of those things included her being the most beautiful woman in the world, and the fact that in a few hours, I was going to fuck the hell out of her. I felt a shiver of excitement run from the base of my skull down to my toes at the thought.

She had been unyielding to my curiosity, to know what she had under that dress: panties, a thong, nothing? I suppressed a shudder of new nervous excitement. There honestly was no wrong answer. Tasteful white, exotic and bright colors, or nothing but herself, I didn't care, and I also hoped in a small way for any of them, all of them.

It was unfair, in a way, for Sadie.

She wouldn't have anything as exciting as Roan and I did, the joy of finding no panties, or that moment of elation when we got to see that tiny piece of fabric, or the lip biting satisfaction of finding nothing but her waiting there. What did she get, but a floppy dong? Boxers, or better fit boxer-briefs.

At least they weren't those awful tighty-whities. There was also the fact that in all the years I had been getting around, I hadn't met a woman outside of porn who looked at a naked cock with the same intensity that we showed breasts or a really nice bush.

That was kinda sad, really.

My daydreaming, such as it was, was interrupted by our cocktails. Aviator for me, cosmopolitan for Sadie, and two fingers of something brown with a gibberish name, probably Scottish, if I were betting. It was nice having the old Roan back, the one who tossed back shots. As long as that awful tangle of a ranger beard didn't come back though, that was a bad sign. *That* Roan liked to get in fights, break things, and was a bit of a bastard.

Dinner itself was perfect.

Salads served on ice cold plates, and everything was fancy as shit. No lettuce, no tomato, no cucumber, and if someone had asked for ranch dressing, the entire place would have gone silent, a waiter would have dropped a plate and then the maître's d would have come out and asked them very politely to leave.

The best answer was always *the vinaigrette.*

Mains were equally fancy shit. My steak seemed almost boring compared to her rack of lamb, complete with little paper boots on the exposed bone ends, and Roan seemed delighted scrapping marrow out of some animal's femur. I kept my shudder to myself, osso bucco was definitely not on my list of delicacies.

Everything was fucking elegant.

Three aviators with their goddamn magical crème de violette.

The flash of Sadie's tits through the keyhole in the dress.

The perfectly cooked and seasoned chateaubriand.

Not even Roan scraping the inside of that bone with a tiny spoon could ruin this.

I passed on dessert, not much of a sweet tooth. Sadie had some sort of decadent crème brûlée with three different kinds of fruit on top, I recognized none of them. Roan took a slice of a classic cheesecake and another two fingers of neat Scottish whiskey.

I'd have to line up another visit to the Meerschaum Tobacconist for them. They wouldn't be interested in the offered smokes, but the food was top notch.

Battleship gin, that was a nice thought.

There was such a sense of relief. Roan had spent the last few weeks watching everything the Cartel did. Trying to keep a tab on where Kaijin was, and a week after her back-scene appearance with the Texan senator, she left the country, private jet from Dulles to London, and then he couldn't track her. He said her next destination wasn't North American or European Union. It seemed likely that the *Generale* had done good on his problem and called his bitch back to go deal with the production side of their operation.

Good, fuck her. Maybe some highland tribal fighter would shoot her in the head.

The ceremony of getting our coats from the coat check was nice, as we waited for the ride share to show up. None of us had decided to be a designated driver, so we let Indigo City provide that option for us. We stepped outside, and while it wasn't cold, it was cool enough to justify wearing coats. It was dress-up, but that put a smile on their faces.

It was a complete surprise when there was someone waiting outside for us. For *me*.

"Stark," she said, her voice sharp. I looked up to see the less chiseled features of a woman I had met several times before.

"Pa-Pamela?" I asked. She looked like she had been awake for two days and had put on at least fifty pounds since the last time I had put my dick in her.

"Plamena, you fucking Yank," she hissed.

"Plamena, how are you?" I asked.

"I am..." She launched off into a jag of what was Russian and I couldn't follow. "You son of a bitch, you make me pregnant."

"Pregnant?" I took a step back. She looked rough, and had put on weight, but that wasn't a baby she had, that was different. "I haven't seen you in over a year, more than a year."

"Your son is a year old, you piece of..." more angry Russian followed, but the gist was fairly obvious.

"Ma'am, I think you need to calm down," Roan added.

"No, you need to shut up and give me money. A place to live, take care of your son." There was a hint of her old hard features in the sneer she gave us. It was almost completely pointed – pointed at Sadie. That made no sense. "You fuck me, you make me pregnant, you make me lose job, lose home, now have your son and you no care. Fuck you, Mister whatever-your-fake-name is!"

"Back the train into the station, this isn't possible." It would certainly be an immaculate conception, considering that as soon as I could afford a vasectomy, I'd had one. That wasn't something to shout out on the curb, but still. The fucking audacity.

"You fuck, you make baby, possible and is!" She looked over at a Sadie. "You watch out, he fucks you, make you fat, then leave you." It was a barb, hooked, and it struck home. I could see where it sank in and snared her heart.

"Look, get the fuck out of here," I growled. "You're fucking lying and I know it."

Sadie looked wounded. Fuck. Why?

She didn't want kids; I didn't want kids.

I never met a woman who could get pregnant swallowing my load.

The damage was done.

Fuck.

Fucking really?

"Mate, take care of this, I'll take Sadie home, and you can get a different ride, yeah?" Roan asked, playing cover and damage control. He would sort her out, the escorts were supposed to be on birth control, IUDs or pills, and how awkward would the conversation be where I told her that when I fucked my escorts, I painted their faces, and almost never inside them.

He tucked her away into the back of the waiting ride share and then they pulled away from the curb.

I would owe him for this.

"Listen, the escort service had rules, and if someone you managed to get nut off your face and up your snatch is on you, fucking seriously," I snapped. "Do you want money, is that what this is, a fucking shakedown?"

"Is no shakedown, but you should give me money, yes." Her eyes were hard as broken glass.

"How much for you to go jump off a bridge and to never see you again. I know I came on your face because you had that purple lipstick."

"Fifty thousand."

"Let me just pull that out of my pocket. You have any proof of this kid?" I snapped. She pulled out her phone and showed me blurry pictures of a chubby infant, a tousle of dark hair, but other than that, it was a pink beanbag with closed eyes.

"Is that a stock picture, that you took a picture of?" I asked. My God, the audacity of this bitch.

"Is no stock, is your son, a hundred thousand, or I start sending pictures to your girlfriend, she would like that," she threatened.

"Oh, you need to fuck off right now." I jabbed a hand in the direction she needed to fuck off in. "There will be a fucking paternity test before I give you any goddamn thing, this is a fucking setup and you've fucking ruined my evening!" I knew that my chance of finding out what Sadie was wearing under that dress had gone from undoubted to zero. My blood was almost boiling.

I stalked away from the front of *Le Jefferson,* and Plamena chased after me, shouting insults in a slurry of Russian, German, and bad English. The angrier she was, the more mangled her multi-lingual insults became.

"If you don't fuck off, I'm calling the cops," I finally fired at her. "Don't fucking push me."

"Call them, I tell them you fuck me."

"I'll tell them what agency you worked for, and let them arrest you. You know the cops around here and how they feel about hysterical foreigners." That seemed to throw a speed bump in her path. "If you're still out here after I cool off, I *will* call the police *and* my lawyer, and we'll sort this out with those lawyers and a bunch of needles. Oh! And fuck you if your green card isn't in order. They'll have you back in Siberia or Ukraine or wherever the fuck you came from."

She didn't follow me as I stepped into what amounted to a high-end dive bar off the main strip. I decided to have a few drinks, cool down, and give Roan time to get Sadie home and see what he could do to defuse that situation. I had my facts straight, and some of them made me look like a right bastard, but I wasn't a breeder. There was no way, being raised an orphan, my own mother likely having been a junky whore, that I would do the same thing to someone else.

I wouldn't have bastard by blows running around anywhere.

The bar didn't have anything but shitty mid-tier gin so I had a beer.

Then a second.

I texted Roan to assess the situation. A pretty waitress brought me a gin and tonic, complementary. She had a pretty smile. I returned the smile and hammered the gin. There was a bit of a weird taste to it, but it was shelf stuff, and maybe it all really tasted like that.

"Good evening, Mr. Lachlan," a woman said, sitting down across from me. I looked up at her, and my vision blurred for a moment. I wasn't buzzed or drunk enough for that to be happening. I knew that this should be alarming, but everything felt sluggish.

"Did you know that one of the very first things a woman learns while in a bar is to never accept a drink from a stranger?" There was a familiar accent, French? "Ah, yes, you are feeling it now, aren't you?"

I looked up into her eyes, and I recognized her.

"Kaij…" My lips felt thick, my tongue was numb.

"Hello, you didn't stay for any hospitality when you visited my home, that was very rude, you know?" Her fingernails didn't have animals on them now, but they were still talons, emerald green, a flourish of geometric pattern at the base.

"What…"

"Did I do to you? Surely, you've figured that out, Mister Lachlan? Kyle, may I call you that?" It took almost every ounce of willpower I had to keep my head up, staring at her.

"I've poisoned you, I thought that was obvious. You men, so stupid, you make it easier than slipping *Rohypnol* in an underage girl's coconut-flavored vodka."

Was this how it was going to go down? I had thought about my own death many times. Gunfight? Knife? Car crash, or helicopter crash? In none of those dark fantasies, almost memories now, did my end come as a glass sitting in front of me.

There was a fleeting moment of worry, would this hurt? What would Roan and Sadie do? I fumbled for my phone, to send a call, a text, anything. She took it from my hand like I was a child, and my head sank toward the table.

This…

This wasn't how things were supposed to go.

This fucking bitc…

It was cool wherever I was. My mouth felt like a bag of cotton, and my eyes were made of sandpaper, set in glass sockets.

"Oh, there you are." I heard a fuzzy voice. "I bet your head hurts like nothing else."

"Water," my voice cracked.

"You'll not have that pleasure, not yet," the fuzzy voice said again.

"Where?"

"My personal residence, it's a nice place, I think you would appreciate it under other circumstances." The fuzziness was receding. My eyes were still agony, but light and dark was starting to sort itself out. There was a feeling of cold, pressure, and the person stepped back.

"What?"

"All you do is ask questions, and it's annoying, no?" the voice asked, female, French accent. *Fuck.* "Do relax, you're only going to hurt yourself if you struggle, and that is *my* privilege. I'm going to let you come up a bit, and we'll have a little talk, just you and me."

"Kaijin…"

"Yes Kyle?"

"I'll… kill…"

"Darling, no, you won't. You're my pet now." She patted me on the cheek and then left the room.

I wasn't sure how long passed, but my head cleared, and I felt less horrible. I was able to look around. I was restrained to a St Andrew's Cross, a bit of bondage furniture that left me hanging from restraints at the wrist and ankles. My shoulders were in agony from hanging for so long and getting my feet under me was a fucking relief. Moving revealed an IV buried in my arm, attached to a bag. She had me juiced; God knew what was in that.

The fact that I was naked took longer to sink in.

How long had I been out?

She hadn't poisoned me, she knocked me out with something in the gin.

How had she found us? How had she known what dive bar I was going to be in? There was no way that she could have planned that out with such precision, there was too much chaos. What if I had gone a different direction? What if I picked a different bar? There were so many in the area… It wasn't possible for a plan to have come together with this sort of efficiency. It wasn't fucking *possible* to be that keyed in.

Not even *we* could pull off something like this.

She returned, but with no windows, no natural light, or timepiece, I had no idea how long anything took, everything felt like hours. She paused and pulled out her phone to snap a few pictures. "I see why she likes you, Kyle."

"How did you do this?" I demanded.

"Your arrogance makes you simple," she replied. She deftly undid the buttons of her blouse and slipped it off. She folded it neatly and sat it on a shelf. "I had you followed, quite simply enough."

"You aren't supposed to be here," I growled.

"You aren't the only one to use false identities. You are not at all accustomed to using a body double, no?" She undid the clasp of her bra and placed it on top of her blouse. "I found one of your former conquests, quite down on her luck. Drugs, they have a habit of ruining people's lives." I hit the end of my restraints and she chuckled darkly. "It was easy to get her to claim you were the father of her child, and no, there is no child. No woman would be as stupid as to allow herself to carry *your* seed." The muscles under her shoulders and back flexed as she continued stripping. Each piece of clothing was neatly folded and put into a single pile until she had on nothing but a piece of sheer material pretending to be a pair of panties and a pair of stiletto heels.

Her entire back was covered in ink, the same animals as before, a Chinese dragon, phoenix, koi. Feathers and scales coiled around her hips.

"You were set up. I flushed out; away from your companions, knowing you are such a simple man that the only things you use to soothe your nerves are gin and pussy. Plamena texted me, I was waiting. I knew when your reservation at *Le Jefferson* was. Then it was just putting some serious sedatives in a glass of cheap gin. You were so *easy*. Your partner at least had the machismo to fire a gun at me before taking a knee." I ground my teeth and would have spat at her if my mouth weren't as dry as a lint filter.

"So, you understand the situation, I take it? You belong to me, now. You are mine, just as your dear Conan belonged to me before." Her smile was acid. The tattoos wrapped around her entire body, and there was little of her torso unmarked by ink. It wasn't Yakuza style, not a Japanese body sleeve, it was something else. A little more chaotic, more visceral. There was almost a high-end jailhouse vibe to it, there was so much red ink, almost nothing was in black outline. Her nipples were stiff and dark, the patterns drawing the eye to them.

She patted me between the legs and I jerked against my bonds. She chuckled. "I wish I could say I traded up in this bargain, but alas..." Her lips curved in a smile that was nothing short of demonic in its cruelty.

"Fuck you," I managed in a hoarse whisper.

"In due time, yes. I will have you, like I had him." She gave me a massive smile, then. One that was startling in that it was the first time I really noticed her teeth. Several came to artificial points, not fangs like some emo vampire, but something darker and more sinister. No wonder she never smiled like an American did, those teeth. Jesus. Fuck.

Roan had said she liked to bite.

She ran her fingernails down my body and I tried to squirm away from her, but the restraints held. This amused her and it turned into raking those claws across my skin, pinching and pulling my nipples until I screamed.

How had he managed to put up with this for *months*?

Her hands went back between my legs, and instead of more sharpness, they were soft. I pressed my head back, clenched my eyes shut and tried to block everything out. This was harder than ignoring pain, knowing and hoping it would pass, like floating on the top of storm waves.

My body betrayed me, and she had my cock hard. It didn't even seem hard for her to get me up. I cursed myself, I felt weak and stupid for being so easily caught.

Was Sadie still mad at me?

Did they know where I was?

Did Kaijin know about how my phone worked, with all the tricks Roan had worked into it?

I tried to pull away when I felt something hot and wet press against my cock. She laughed, and caught me in an iron grip, I grunted and, in a few seconds, could feel my pulse in the end of my cock. "That loop will keep you up for a good while, no matter how much you try to think about baseball, or whatever it is you pick to meditate. He couldn't resist, and neither will you."

"I'm going to do everything I want to you," she whispered, grabbing me by the hair and pulling my head back. It exposed my neck and the option of headbutting was gone. I strained, but she smacked my head back and gave me a stinging slap to the face. "I am going to do things to you that are going to haunt you for what life I chose to let you have."

I had never had a woman hold me like this, head restrained, tied to a giant fucking metal X. She hooked one leg over one of the cross's leg and ground her pelvis into mine. I could feel the sheer material between us, and could imagine that she wasn't aroused, that it was venom dripping from between her legs. I grunted and strained but the chains and leather cuffs were more than I could do anything against. None of it was breakaway. When I had to relax, she went back to her previous grinding against me.

She whispered insults in my ear, mocking my cock for being smaller than Roan's. For being dumber, and easier to fool, easy to tie up, and how she was going to fuck me, what she was going to use on me, what kind of toy and where it was going. There was a particularly vile stream about what toys she was going to stick up my ass, and how I was going to cry over it.

I laughed.

"You don't know shit about the foster care system." My voice was ice.

"You don't know what I can do to your body, little boy." Her teeth grazed my ear, and I tried to pull away. "Don't mistake me for some hard-up kiddie-toucher. Do you know what I do when I find one of them working for me? The men who like to touch the little boys and girls?" Her breath was hot against my neck, and her words were nothing but poison.

"Well for one, you fucking hire them," I said through gritted teeth.

"Not intentionally, but you men are such fucking degenerates, they are just everywhere. You know that, if you were in that sort of foster care. I can guess what they did to you." I snorted a laugh.

"Was it Dean?" She dragged her teeth down the side of my neck. I felt my blood turn to the ice. "Was it Priscilla? Or someone else? A foster uncle?"

"Fuck you," I grunted.

"I think someone else, Dean, didn't seem like the sort to touch the little boys, he liked the little girls, didn't he? Did he like to touch – Sadie?" She said her name like silk. I slammed against the restraints again. I was stronger than she was, but the restraints took all of my leverage away. I let out an inarticulate rage-filled scream, and she just laughed, high and loud.

Then her phone rang. Reluctantly she untwined herself from me, her eyes smoldering. "That's probably important and I need to take it." She plucked the phone from the pile of clothing and put it to her ear.

"Hello?" She walked back toward me.

"Yes, I am aware. That is why I am in charge now, and you work for me."

"You didn't do *shit*." Her English flicked over to French, peppered with words that I knew were vulgar. I picked up a few different words, *Le Generale, revolution,* and a few others that seemed important.

I considered yelling something, but would it do any good, who was she talking to? They seemed pissed and she did too. She spoke another a machine gun fire of rapid of French, hard and aggressive, starkly at odds with how she looked, naked but for tiny panties and heels. She walked back to me, and grabbed my balls with her off and hand and started squeezing them, firm, then harder. I grit my teeth, and she squeezed harder. Her grip was constant and increased. I had no desire to give her the satisfaction but eventually she crushed a scream out of me. I panted when she released me, and I felt like vomiting. The sudden release left my head spinning.

"I will do to you what I am doing to the man who killed your team, you..." more French followed. She grabbed me by the shaft and started working me. It wasn't pleasant, but it also wasn't painful.

"Fuck off, you bitch," I managed to cough out. She ignored me, carrying on her conversation in more rapid, fluid French. She did give me a smile, and I worked up a small bit of spit but couldn't get any range on it. She stopped stroking me to smile at the small glob on her breast. She mouthed me a *thank you*, swiped it up with her fingers and used it on my shaft.

I struggled, and beat against the bonds, and trying to twist out of her grip, and the only thing that happened was her grip would tighten, relentless. I couldn't escape it, and then came betrayal. Throbbing, hard, unable to ignore basic biological function, my cock started dripping. With less friction, she went faster.

Faster.

Her tirade never slowed. The person on the other end of the phone took a verbal beatdown, and I managed to pick out a few words, and it seemed that there had been a major shakeup inside the Cartel. The details were hard to track, most of my attention was tied to the grip she had me in.

I came.

I gasped and went tense against the bonds. Most fell to the floor, but some spotted against her hip.

She never slowed and kept hammering. The sensation almost immediately went to being more than I could handle, I would have rather been slamming my balls in a car door that let her keep after me like she did. It was nothing less than fucking agony, and even when I screamed, she refused to stop.

It only ended when the person on the other end of the phone relented, apologized, and hung up. She clicked the phone off and finally stopped. I felt raw as an exposed nerve, a broken tooth buried in ice, but the nerve was between my legs.

"Well, I suppose it's time to bring you up to speed, save you asking a lot of stupid questions," she said, bringing her hand up to regard it. There were several drops from the mess I had made. She licked them up slowly, never breaking eye contact, and the intensity seemed fucking relentless.

She was a fucking monster.

How had Roan survived this sadistic fucking bitch?

"You have to realize that when Chauvignon decided to take a knee, surrender to your ilk, that he wasn't speaking for the entire organization." She smiled. "That is why I decided that it was time for him to look into retirement."

"He offered a truce," I said. "This could have been over."

"And now he's dead, and I'm in charge, and it is officially not over. I'll have my plaything back, and when I get tired of both of you, well. You'll never know when I get tired of you. What meal will be your last, which cum shot will be the last? When will you close your eyes and just never wake up again? I like to keep my pets on their toes, you see."

"You're a fucking sadistic bitch," I growled.

"I most certainly am," she said softly, and she loosened the loop and took it off. "I am a very sadistic bitch, and nothing in the world makes me happier than fucking with a man like you. So strong, so confident, so arrogant. You'll cry for me, you'll scream, you'll thank me, and you'll tell me that you love me."

"Never," I spat at her.

"Now, now, keep an open mind. You're much better endowed partner did all of those things. You'll sing, you just have to be tuned first." She unfolded her clothes and dressed. "I have to go take care of some business, running a Cartel that has been given a substantial defeat is somewhat time consuming. I will be back in a bit, you rest up, but I'll be putting that *cock*," she sneered the word like it was a joke, "to what I can get out of it."

"Let me check my appointment book. Sorry, I'm all tied up later."

"A sense of humor is good, you'll last longer." She smiled.

While she was gone a young man came into the room, carrying a bag. His smile was professional, despite the youth of his face. I tried to talk to him, but he refused anything other than giving me a half-smile.

The IV came out, and he sprayed me with something in a bottle and wiped me down, it had a whiff of alcohol.

"Man, are you marinating me?" No response.

He went through a few other things, including putting something on my dick that stung for a moment, but then the raw feeling improved. He drew blood, jammed a cotton swab up my nose, and gave me that half-smile again.

"Word of advice?" he said, closing the samples up in his bag.

"Keys would be better," I countered.

"The harder you fight, the more she enjoys it. If you give up it will be over quicker and you won't suffer as much."

"What does that matter to you?"

"The longer it lasts, the more extreme she gets. The harder it gets to clean you up and keep you alive. It isn't too difficult, but once she gets to amputation and knife play, that is messy and I do not enjoy cleaning up after it." He snapped the last latch on the case shut, stood, and left.

Amputation and knife play?

I alternated between standing, leaning against the cross, and sometimes trying to find something like a comfortable hanging position. There was nothing really comfortable, and my hands felt like they were just going away. I could clench my fists and crack my knuckles one at a time, but it wasn't the same.

A different person came in, a woman with long dark hair and well-done makeup. She might have been my type if her face hadn't been a punching bag. Her nose had been broken several times and poorly reset, and she looked more like a retired boxer than a model. She had the same silent disposition as the probably-not-an-actual-*doctor* doctor who had been in before.

It was fucking awkward as she pressed her fingers into my lower stomach. I wasn't sure this was any sort of exam, at least like none I had ever had before. Then she hit something, there was a massive sense of pressure and I pissed.

"Good boy," she said, the only words that I would hear her say.

She had a kit of toiletries and used them to shave my face, then what hair I had on my chest, and then she knelt. I had been shaved before, waxed one time at a spa. Her touch was surprisingly delicate, and she shaved me from bellybutton to taint with efficient quick strokes. The flash of the straight razor killed anything but cold paranoia.

Kaijin returned.

She was dressed differently.

Had I slept?

My shoulders hurt, and I was cold again. I think I slept.

She repeated her previous routine, stripping down out of her professional woman in a place of power pants suit down to nothing but a different pair of stiletto heels. No panties this time.

Fuck I was tired.

"Ah, you've been visited and groomed. Excellent. Have you been enjoying your stay so far?"

"I won't be leaving a five-star review, sorry." I smiled.

"You are right, you won't be leaving." She pulled the loop out, and cinched it around the base of my cock, then a second went around my balls, pulling them down. It wasn't the most pleasant sensation. "You passed the tests; you are a clean boy. No need to shoot you full of antibiotics and wait until all the diseases are out of you. Mayweather did mention that everything else was in the ideal range, lucky you with your good cholesterol and blood sugar results."

The loop had me hard fairly quickly. She started rubbing it down with lube, and with her other hand she started getting herself worked up.

"You might be the strangest fucking sadist I've ever met," I said.

"That will be later, right now you're a stunt cock." She wrapped one of her legs around me, like she had before and I felt the head of my cock graze the inside of her thigh. I tried to close it all out, I hadn't been with anyone since Sadie came back into my life, and that was something I had been personally proud of, not giving into that old desire for easy sex. She rocked back and forth a few times, guiding my head to slide back and forth between her lips.

There was a loud explosion, the house shook, and there was a waterfall of breaking glass. Kaijin jerked from her position. I blew out a breath of relief, my entire body sagging against the restraints for a long moment.

She stormed over to her clothing, pulled out the phone and made a quick call. Every word was French, fast and angry, and then she started throwing her clothes on.

I heard gunfire.

"You're fucked now," I managed to get out.

CHAPTER TWENTY

adie...

"Red Queen this is White King, perimeter is clear, you have no eyes on you." I peeked up over the low stone seawall and stood on the shore of the manse we'd tracked Lach's phone to. Somebody was going to be fired, if I didn't put a bullet in them first. Of course, there could still be the possibility that this was all a trap. *Who fucking knew?*

Roan and I had moved swiftly, tracking, getting the lay of the land, and priming me for the rescue. He was nearby, on a different approach, sitting in the back of a box truck that had been fitted as a mobile command unit. We had been planning on driving it to Texas; now it was serving us just fine on the shores of the Chesapeake, just the other side of Indigo City. Ideally, we would have had another tech person and Roan out with me, but we wouldn't wait, *I* couldn't wait, that long.

I cracked open the back of the M79 grenade launcher and eased one of the three grenades out from the strap holding them against my thigh. These three were the high explosive bad boys, the ones in the bandolier across my chest were teargas and flashbang, respectively. I did *not* want those getting mixed up with the high explosives, hence the different locations I was carrying them in. They were different colors too, but Roan said that wasn't reliable if people were shooting at me and I didn't have time to visually identify each different type.

He had gone over it with me a half dozen times, but it worked like a cartoon shotgun, break it in half, chuck a Redbull-sized grenade in it, slap it home, then point and shoot. The skull with a lightning bolt hard carved into the stock was a nice touch, Roan said the weapon was a relic from Vietnam, and that's how he had gotten it so quickly, and easily.

"White King, I'm in position." I slid the cartoon bullet home and racked the launcher back together, ready to fire.

"Repeat Red Queen, board is clear."

"Copy that."

I stood, and in the tactical crouching crab-walk thing I'd been taught, scuttled across the grass up toward the back of the house.

"Fire in the hole," I warned Roan in a harsh whisper and I leveled the *Thumper* up by my hip and fired it through the bank of windows overlooking the bay. Behind me the water lapped and beyond that, Indigo City lay in a gorgeous panoramic view.

THUMP, crash! Through the glass it went. I ran back several paces, took cover by the edge of the brick garden wall, and the night exploded in a symphony of utter chaos.

"That got someone's attention," I said with a savage glee.

"Board is in motion, Red Queen." Roan's voice in my ear held a note of consternation and I smiled in spite of it. He was worried, I know, but I had been trained by the best and my confidence was right where it needed to be at. Which was to say, I was confident, but I definitely wasn't over confident by this point.

I pulled the gasmask down off the top of my head and over my face, checked the seal was good and murmured, "Red Queen advancing."

"Don't linger," I heard in my ear and I didn't.

Several motions were made at once. I opened the Thumper, loaded a grenade off the bandolier around my chest into the tube, and went through the smoking ruin of the back of the mansion. As I advanced, my boots crunched over broken glass, I launched the round of teargas inside and to the left. Reload and thumped another to the right. The emergency lighting strobed, the smoke alarm blared its mournful warning song, and I stayed sharp, remained focused, and watched for movement as I reloaded yet again.

"Thermal imaging has six, love. Two on your ten, one on your twelve, and three coming from your three o'clock. They're coming from the front of the manse; twenty seconds."

I took cover behind the overstuffed couch, dropping Thumper it on its strap across my chest and flung the AR on my back up over my head and into my hands like Lach had taught me. I racked it, safety off, knocked it to my shoulder to Roan's tone of warning in my ear as he said, *"Red Queen..."*

"It's on, motherfuckers," I muttered and I stood, taking out twelve o'clock, *pop! Pop!* Man down. Pivot, turn to three o'clock – *pop! Pop!* The man in front went down, and I wasted no time, pulling the trigger again, twice, *pop! Pop!* I caught motion on my left at my ten hand and dropped just as the men at ten o'clock opened up.

Fucking amateurs let loose in a spray that one, went wide, two, was too high, and three wasted a whole lotta ammunition as they went full auto. I lay practically flat to the floor as Roan remarked dryly in my ear, *"Getting loud in there, Poppet."* They were dedicated marksmen so long as their targets were the sofa, walls, and windows.

"I'm fine," I grated through gritted teeth and set the rifle aside and picked up my new buddy Thumper. This thing was actually fun.

"Three verticals, closing on your position" he said tonelessly and I could feel his apprehension filter through the earpiece.

"On my own time," I said lightly, and I popped up and *Thump!* The launcher lobbed a teargas grenade into the hall where the pair at ten o'clock was hiding. They started coughing – a good sign. I smoothly reloaded as I pivoted back to three o'clock and used what I had on hand to face the man who was drawing a bead on me from that side, and fired my last loaded teargas grenade into his chest. He took it full in the body armor and flew back and Roan asked incredulously in my ear, *"Did you just—"*

"Uh, hell yes I did," I said and got back down. I reloaded the launcher, set it aside, took up my rifle and sure that it was in working order asked, "Direction, please?"

"Right, twelve o'clock leads to the foyer, staircase will be on your left, I am getting two heat signatures on the second floor, two to three doors perhaps down to your right. Reinforcements are advancing, Red Queen. You'd best make your move."

"Copy." I got up, the two in the hall at my three o'clock, incapacitated by the teargas. I double tapped them both. I wanted to feel bad about it but leaving them alive at my back wasn't an option.

Survival of the fittest, baby... I heard Kyle say in my head.

"Red Queen, you'd better move, you'd better move now!"

I slung my rifle, picked up the launcher and as the first man crested the threshold of the double front doors, I repeated the trick and launched a round into his chest, knocking him back into his companions and out the front door.

It wasn't a teargas round, this time. I ducked behind the solid staircase and squeezed my eyes shut as debris from the explosion rocked the front of the house and dirt, rock, and the smell of explosives, flew past me.

"Red Queen, Mary Bloody Queen of Scots!" came through my earpiece.

"You say the sweetest things to me, what's my count?" I asked.

"The rest out front are fleeing, there are at least two more in addition to the one with our asset. Hold your position, Red Queen – two pawns are making for the main stair."

I held my position beneath the sweeping staircase, my back pressed against the wall, and after reloading with teargas dropped the launcher to my hip, swapping it for the rifle, holding it at the ready as feet thundered down the stairs above me.

"Jesus!" one of the men said as they slowed, boot falls crunching on the debris on the bottom steps.

"We aren't paid enough for this shit, let's go." Getting a glimpse of them, they were in suits, and had pistols. No rifles, no body armor, holy fuck this was so above their pay grade.

The pawns skirted out the door and I let out a breath I hadn't realized I'd been holding.

"Red Queen, board is clear."

"Copy, White King. Advancing."

I went up the stairs, rifle at the ready.

"Blast it, I'm reading seven new signatures, possibly a shielded saferoom, end of the hallway past the door I believe to be holding our asset. Watch yourself, Red Queen."

"I've got it," I murmured, and at the top of the stair, I paused.

"They're coming right for you, Red Queen."

"Not a lot of cover, White King."

"You know what to do," he reminded me, and the surety in his voice bolstered my confidence.

I launched a teargas grenade around the corner without looking, less for the teargas to incapacitate, although that was a bonus, but more for the cover the smoke would provide me. These guys weren't pawns, unfortunately. How did I know? They didn't just open up in my general direction like the trained monkeys downstairs.

"Looks like I've leveled up, baddies just got harder," I commented dryly.

"Look alive, Poppet."

"Uh, trying to *stay* alive, White King."

I went down on one knee and made myself even smaller, predicting that when fire came, they would aim for someone much taller than I was, expecting a man, and if I made myself even smaller than that? Well…

I ducked around the corner and let loose with some rounds and took out their point man with at least three shots, two center mass which was just fucking useless – they had body armor, but the third was a lucky shot, blowing apart the top of his leg.

He fell back into his compatriots, and they moved him to the back of their ranks. They couldn't see through the smoke, clearly, or they would have aimed lower, but they didn't open up full auto like the dipshit downstairs, either… as Roan would like to say; *bollocks.*

"What's it look like?" I asked.

"They're falling back."

"K."

I ducked around the corner again and let fly, jerking back at the first sign of muzzle flash beyond the haze of teargas.

"Spicy!" I heard one of them call out and another one or two laughed.

Shit. They were *definitely* trained mercs if they were remarking on the teargas like that.

I stood up on the other side of my corner.

"You like that?" I called out.

"Poppet..." Roan's voice held a note of warning.

"Shit, it's a female," one of the men said in the ringing silence.

"What the fuck?" I heard another one say.

I ducked out, and fired, falling into a crouch as I did it and I heard one of them beyond the smoke cry out.

"That was a hit," Roan declared.

"No shit," I muttered.

"One down, one wounded and thus semi-incapacitated, at least five still on their feet."

"Thank you."

"Perhaps the last explosive round?" he asked, and I grimaced.

"I don't like that idea; the target and our asset are between me and them, the collateral damage might be more than we're willing to pay out."

"Too right, looks like they have you in check."

"Yeah, well, I'm about to put them in check mate," I grumbled.

"Going for the last explosive round after all?" Roan asked.

"Got a few flashbangs I haven't even touched, first," I said.

"Ah, a good compromise."

I lit off in their asses with all three of those flashbangs in as rapid a succession as I could pull off, rounding the corner and opening up with some suppressive fire to advance myself up the hall.

I ducked back into an alcove meant for art, shoving a statue off its pedestal and out of my way as a few rounds whizzed by. Those rounds weren't particularly aimed, which is why I was still intact – well, that and some damn luck.

"I don't think I like you taking risks like that."

"Makes you feel better, I didn't like taking it either, but I'm pretty sure our black king would have approved."

"Likely not," Roan argued. *"Less talk, Red Queen. Stay focused."*

"Next door is our lucky door, isn't it?" I asked.

"Aye."

"K. I manage to take any of those assholes out?"

"You have two still capable according to movement. Whether dead or unconscious on the rest, I cannot tell."

"Right." I loaded the launcher with the last explosive round. "Going for broke," I muttered.

"Copy that, Red Queen."

"Fire in the hole," I warned and launched the explosive cannister to the far end of the hall which was lengthy enough that I was willing to risk it.

The cannister clattered, I felt like the universe held its collective breath with me, and the explosion went off, rocking the end of the hall, the blast blowing out the side of the house, plaster dust and whatever else rolling past my alcove while my ears ringed fiercely.

"Check mate?" I asked.

"Certainly, check. Advance, Red Queen – but remain cautious."

I shouldered my rifle and worried I was getting low; I hadn't been keeping count, and I'd traded quite a bit of fire with these gits at the end of the hall.

A muzzle flash, low, a round whizzed past me, I aimed and popped off, just as I reached the set of doors, a masculine voice grunted and groaned and I watched the figure slump and go still.

"Check mate," I muttered.

"You may have won the battle..."

"Yeah, yeah, still at war."

I hauled back and kicked open the doors to the room that held Kaijin, our black queen, and Kyle, my black king and I took aim.

"Your left!" Kyle called out, and I turned and click!

"Oh, ho, ho!" Kaijin laughed at me, I looped the rifle off over my head and threw it at her to buy myself time. She snarled and leaped before I could clear the Beretta Cheetah from its holster.

I blocked, as best I could but she was both taller and stronger than me and we both went crashing to the floor.

Both Lach and Roan's voices clashed in my ears at once, but I was focused on the bitch that was grappling with me. She went for an elbow drop, I dodged and flipped her, I got a couple of good shots in and snatched the fucking wig off her head in the process, pissed that we were in an epic cat fight for the ages.

"I'm going to make it so every time you look in the mirror, every time they look at you, you all think of me!" she snarled, and I grinned savagely.

"Good idea!" I spat, and I brought my forehead crashing down into the bridge of her perfect nose. I felt that sucker crunch and she cried out, angry and reversed hold on me. We rolled across the floor, both struggling to get our hands on the other's throat and neither of us succeeding. Finally, with a rage-filled cry, her head darted forward.

I jerked my head to the side and narrowly missed her sinking her teeth into my goddamn cheek, what she did manage was to sink teeth into my shoulder where it met the side of my neck and that bitch *sank teeth*. I screamed, equal parts rage and pain as she clamped down and tried her damnedest to make her fucking teeth meet in the middle, through my fucking flesh.

I let her go in a desperate grab for the knife in my boot and I got it, and without thinking, in a miasma of rage and pain, with no real aim, I stabbed at her. Over and over, at least three or four good shots to the flank, her mouth opening in a scream as she rolled off of me and away, putting distance between me and the knife. I sniffed, eyes watering, and stood at the ready.

I was between her and Kyle, thankfully, as she clutched her side, glaring at me.

I heard the roar of multiple shotgun blasts.

"Sadie!" Roan bellowed from downstairs. Kaijin grinned, my blood coating her whore mouth, making it a feral thing, and she ducked out the door, running flat out down the hall in the direction I'd blown up.

I took off after her, ditching the knife in favor of the Cheetah.

She leaped out the bloody blasted hole in the end of the hall and I wasn't about to go after her, but you'd better believe I wanted that bitch dead.

That was twice she got away.

I turned, Roan was moving up the hall like a thunderhead, big automatic shotgun in a forward grip.

"Watch our six," I demanded and went in to free Kyle from whatever X shaped contraption she had him chained to.

"Good job, baby," he praised. "Get me off of this thing."

"Working on it," I grunted. "I sure hope I got that bitches' kidney."

He sniffed. "Not high enough and not far enough back, sorry babes."

"Next time," I promised darkly.

"Oh yeah, for sure," Kyle agreed, stepping down. I handed him the pistol after he finished rubbing feeling back into his hands and freeing himself from the bands that the bitch had him in.

"We good? Can we get out of here now?" I asked.

"Depends, you mad at me?" he asked and I shook my head. No, I wasn't mad at him, I wasn't mad at him at all. I *was*, however, so over this need to play rescue ranger. I wanted that fucking cunt *dead*.

"I don't give a fuck what you do or how you do it, but *find her!*" I snapped once we were back in the panic room. I stalked out of the room, over several dead men and went looking for the bar this fucking place had to have. I found some gin in a blue bottle and stomped back, finding Roan sitting at the computer console and Lach almost done dressing himself in the suit of one of the dead men. He fingered the bullet holes in the dark shirt before putting it on. They were mid-conversation.

"Aggro Sadie?" Roan asked, mildly.

"Aggro Sadie," Lach agreed and his tone was both grim and tired. "Any other evening this eventful, and I'd be all for it, but… bro…"

"I take your meaning perfectly, mate. I'll handle her."

"Neither one of you ever has to *handle me*," I said, oddly hostile. Kyle jerked back like he'd been slapped.

"Sadie, no. That's not what we meant."

I looked from one to the both of them and parroted Conan's words: "I take your meaning *perfectly*," I declared. I set the bottle of gin on a stone side counter of the panic room which was fairly sizeable and held all manner of surveillance and computer equipment.

"I'm going to take a shower."

I left them both, staring at one another and went and did just that. Being clean from some of this blood would be more than worth using a strange shower. They weren't in a hurry to chase after her, after all.

I found myself in the bathroom attached to the room that unmitigated cunt had been torturing Kyle in.

The bite *hurt*. Throbbing incessantly, the flesh torn and swollen like a damn tennis ball was up under there. I examined the bruised and angry skin; it was hard to see through all the sticky blood but I was betting it was going to scar. An ugly one.

Angry tears stung my eyes.

Fucking bitch, looks like you got what you wanted, I thought to myself.

Fuck. Every time one of the boys looked at it, would they see her instead of me? Every time we fucked; would she be in the back of their mind?

I wanted to scream. I wanted to take a great deep breath and bellow my rage at the marble and glass walls of this shower – but I couldn't. All it would serve would be to panic Kyle and Conan and I couldn't do that to either of them. They'd both been through so goddamn much and the last thing they needed to do was worry about me…

The last thing I needed to do was make myself into someone or something they needed to *handle* when they were already overburdened as it was, trying to handle their own traumas.

Everything is such a goddamned mess. I thought, and I was so angry, so restless, so – *gah!* I felt like I was going to come out of my fucking skin!

I stood under the shower and gritted my teeth against the pain, watching my blood swirl pink down the drain, until the water ran clear to my eye and I felt as raw, pink, heated, and scrubbed as I was going to get.

I wrapped my hair in one towel, a turban on my head, and another around my body and went to find my men starting where I'd left them… the panic room. Roan was still furiously working at the terminals and I needed to apologize.

Lach stood at the side counter I'd deposited his gin on, a first aid kit open on the granite. He was meticulously unwrapping this or that and laying everything out neatly. He turned when he heard me and scowled, his gaze zeroing in on my shoulder.

"Come here, Shady. Let me have a look at that," he said, and I sniffed and went to him. He put his hands on my waist and popped me up onto the counter. I gasped where the towel didn't quite cover and the backs of my thighs made contact with the cold stone.

Too bad it did nothing to cool my ire.

"I guess we all three have been bitten by her, now," I murmured and I wouldn't make any eye contact.

Lach smirked, the accompanying scoffing snicker a light sound heavy with derision, as he tipped some antiseptic onto some gauze. I sucked in a sharp breath at the serious sting as he covered the bite with it and pressed lightly.

"Sorry, Shady," he murmured.

"No, I deserve it," I said swallowing hard.

He stopped and cupped my chin and I looked up into his deep, night dark eyes.

"Now what makes you say that?" he asked.

"You guys have been through what you've been through and I'm being such a demanding bitch," I said. He laughed then, outright. "Just like her," I finished.

"Indeed, you're all fired up, no doubt… but no you're nothing like that bitch. It's nowhere near the same thing."

"Isn't it?" I asked.

He shook his head, gaze steady, and I waited him out. He took his hand from my shoulder and took that accursed stinging gauze with it and reloaded a fresh piece.

I swallowed hard, and he said, "She's not demanding, she *is* cruel and evil, Shady. You? You're all fire and passion, full of spirit and soul. You have needs, just like the rest of us and there is nothing wrong with having those needs met. You see yourself as demanding, and yes, to a degree – but you would set those demands aside were it required. She would not."

His fingertips were gentle under my chin where he brought my gaze back up to meet his.

"Talk to me, Shady… what is it you want? What do you need from me, right now?" I hadn't realized I'd begun to shake until I let out my pent-up breath and it came out in a shudder. I gripped the edges of the stone counter and sniffed.

"I feel like I'm out of control," I confessed. "I feel like I'm going crazy and I'm wild and all over the place. Like I'm spilling out all over," I crossed my arms over my chest and hugged myself, "and I just want one of you to put me back… I don't know, like back in my place."

"Ah, perhaps your comedown and mine complement each other then," he said and smoothed his hands over my skin, his hands warm against my shoulders and upper arms where he touched me. "I've been repeatedly told about my need to dominate whereas it sounds like you've a need for the other end of that."

I closed my eyes. "Why is this so hard to talk about?" I asked and cleared my throat which felt tight. My cheeks burned with something like embarrassment, and Kyle smiled, stroking lightly over my cheek with his palm.

"You've got trust issues, Shady, and rightfully so," he murmured. "It's always hard talking about our deepest and darkest desires in the best of times, which you and I don't have a lot of…"

I swallowed hard and nodded, and we lapsed into silence, while he carefully doctored the bite in the side of my neck, where it met my shoulder.

"Will it scar?" I asked.

"I'm not a doctor, but yes," he said with a sigh. "How bad is anyone's guess."

I felt that wellspring of eternal rage refresh itself anew. She said she was going to leave a mark that I wouldn't forget and fuck her for actually doing it.

"There may be surgical options, in a year or so, when we know how bad the damage is, yeah?"

"Yeah," I said, steel in my voice.

Roan cleared his throat, and we both turned. He stood now, facing us beside one of the saferoom's terminals, "Are you okay?"

"I'm good, are *you* okay?" I asked him. He halted and stared at my shoulder for a heartbeat too long.

I lifted my good shoulder in a shrug as if to say it was nothing, which honestly the damage was done. It would get better eventually, right?

"She'll be right as rain after a shot of antibiotics and a good dirty fuck," Kyle said, winking at me.

I felt myself color.

"Right," Conan nodded. "We should go."

CHAPTER TWENTY-ONE

*R*oan...

The home-invasion-cum-rescue-operation went many times better than expected. The house itself only had minimal security. The defenders were in most cases poorly armed, completely unarmored, and had very low morale in holding their ground. Sadie had been by every measure a female Rambo going in solo. While there were many dead and wounded, the majority of the personnel picked caution over valor, stole cars, and fled.

That was good for us.

They completely abandoned the house, every one of them.

Sadie having a near melt down over our conversation was less good. She was injured, amped up on endorphins, and Lach was right; her taking a shower was a luxury at the moment, but it was one we could afford.

The police would eventually get here, but over a noise complaint, they wouldn't hurry. No alarms, that would bump their priority down a few notches. The plus side of dealing with groups like the cartels was that they didn't call the police, and often it was uniformed officers and agencies that were the greater threat to us.

There was a security system control panel in the back of the panic room, and I went to secure the grounds, make sure we didn't have any inbound while Lach put some bloody fucking clothes on. I forced myself to focus, because the main thing on my mind was the shark bite that Kajin tried to take out of Sadie's shoulder. It was awful and bloody, but no arterial bleeding, there was time. Cleaning it would be bloody awful, hopefully the shower would help cool her off, and help cleanse the wound some too.

I rewound the digital recordings and managed to track Kaijin's egress, to the garage. Sadie wanted to know where the woman went, so it was an easy thing to find out. She seemed to be furious, I assumed that her personal car was one of those the guards had used for an escape. Two approached her, one a woman, the other a mousy looking man with a baby face.

She drew a pistol, likely taken from one of the fallen guards, and shot both of them in the face. The tape was silent, but I could well imagine the back-to-back pop pop. They both crumpled like dolls. She grabbed keys, got into a white sedan, non-descript, and drove away.

"The house is ours, all forces have withdrawn," I called out. "Police have not been notified; their alarm isn't even triggered. What a bunch of jokers."

"They really felt like jokers when I was being shot at," Sadie called from where she was sitting with Lach. They were caught in their own soft conversation, while he tended her injury.

"Touché, Poppet, touché," I admitted.

"We will need to clear out of here posthaste, even if the police weren't tagged by the security system, there is no way no one nearby didn't call the police with all the shooting and grenades going off," I said.

"She had no idea about the phone, mate," Lach called.

"That's how we found you so fast," I said. "She didn't even turn it off."

"Would that have worked?" he asked.

"It would have slowed me down a bit, but maybe ten-fifteen minutes longer." I had a little brag in that. I set the system to upload all of its data to my own cloud, concealed behind its layers of encryption. There was a ton of info not just about the house, and the record of the multiple felonies that had happened here, but also Cartel finances in North America.

There were plenty of personal files.

This was where Chauvignon had actually been living, this was his house. The son of a bitch had been practically our neighbor the entire time.

How many times had we crossed paths and never known it?

If Kaijin had her pleasure dungeon shit here, where was he?

There were too many questions and not enough time.

After the upload completed, I hit the keys to force the entire system to do a factory reset. Everything would be wiped, all the memory files blanked, it would take a government tech forensics team to get anything out of the hard drives now.

"It's time to go," I said, clicking the last few keys and shutting the place down. "Before Indigo's finest finally do get here."

Lach was dressed and only looked tired, but Sadie was pale and she was nearly coated in a sheet of fresh blood from her shoulder that stained the top of the towel she was in. Lach had managed a crude bandage over the worst of it, but that would require serious attention later. I should be able to handle it, but if it was too much, Doc Max was easy enough to reach.

"I'll come back for the command van later, it's safely parked and locked," I said. Lach was still unsteady on his feet, and Sadie stumbled a bit. Blood loss and adrenaline crash were hell on a body. I wanted to get her back somewhere safe and make sure she didn't try to go into shock. We liberated a BMW sedan from the garage and made the drive to Phoenician in what was likely record time.

LACH ALMOST FLOATED IN THE OVERSIZED TUB, AND SADIE PERCHED gracefully on the edge, their hands entwined. She had been reluctant to let me remove the wadded-up bandage and made a sobbing sound when I probed the wound. It didn't look like a normal bite, she looked like she had been bitten by a dog, or some other sort of animal.

I gave her some Tylenol, the good kind from Canada, then sprayed the bite with a local anesthetic. This would be easier than removing a bullet, but the wound was ragged and ugly. It might take a few stitches, especially on the sides of the bite. Cleaning the wound was delicate, and getting antiseptics into it made Sadie cry out, Tylenol, even with the added benefit of Codeine, simply wasn't enough I am afraid.

Lach suggested I give her some Ole Reliable.

I went and checked the improvised bar, and came back with a bottle of some local high proof whiskey, and handed it to her. "Ole Reliable."

"Ole Reliable is whiskey?" she asked, almost incredulously.

"Bottoms up, let him get to work," Lach said. She gave a half shrug and tipped the bottle back to take a hit. She coughed and hacked after the swallow, and color bloomed through her face, but she stayed steady.

"Ole Reliable," I said, and went back to work. The wound was cleaned, and I used a needle and suture to close up the sides of the bite. "How in the shite did the cunt make this kind of bite?" I asked, mostly to myself.

"Her cuspid and first molars are augmented," Lach said. "Upper and lower, I don't think they're stick-ons."

"No, I would guess they aren't," I said. Memories came back of how she liked to bite, and how her teeth had seemed so sharp against my skin, and how I had thought I was being delicate, overly sensitive. I shuddered a little at the thought, those teeth, and her going down on me, how aggressive she had been and how she seemed to enjoy choking herself, gagging herself, on me.

"Easy there," Sadie said. "Don't have butterfingers with that needle."

She turned the whiskey up again, and there was a glint in her eye.

I fucking knew that look.

I finished sewing her up, dropped a few butterfly bandages, and then covered the entire bite with gauze and tape. "It will be bloody stiff and sore later. It's not just the broken skin, but there will be a lot of subdermal trauma, and probably bruising. Everything else will go away pretty quickly."

"What do you mean everything else?" she asked.

"Bruises and that," I said. "When you're going through a firefight, your adrenalin is so high that you can be shot multiple times and not feel it, not unless it hits bone or something vital."

"Fuck, did I get shot?" she asked, a little alarmed.

"God, no," I replied quickly. "You just have, you know, some bruises, nothing major."

She had used the M79 at close range, she had been a fistfight with a sadist, how she got a bruised face had a hundred different potential answers. None of it was especially bad, and she could pass for having been in a car crash, and airbags, or really needing more sleep.

She handed Lach the whiskey and went to look in the mirror for herself.

"I can't wait to fucking kill her," she growled at her reflection. She climbed into the tub with Lach and took the whiskey back from him for another drink.

"Try to keep that bandage dry," I offered.

"Yeah, sure." She coughed again.

"There are a few things I need to attend, are you both alright for a little while?" I asked.

"I'm okay," Lach said. "And I'll keep an eye on our queen, here." She smiled and flicked him her middle finger.

"Alright, I'll be back in a few."

THE ESCADRILLE CARTEL HELD THE MANSION ON JOHN LAURENS Highway through a small holding company, Lafayette-Indigo Venture Real Estate. It was a shell company, the sort of thing that should have already folded and reverted all of its assets to another company to prevent the thing I was about to do.

Lach and I had our own holding and shell companies, places that only existed in legal documents and online assets. Setting up the hostile takeover of Lafayette-Indigo by the Cromwell-Washington Investment Group took less than half an hour, and three phone calls. I looked into what assets were also in the massive data breach that I had managed to pull off almost entirely by accident.

I emptied two bank accounts and closed them.

There was also a deposit box at a Baltimore bank vault, a list of Escadrille dealers and hubs through the eastern US, and a few businesses that were fronts for their money laundering operations.

I wondered if this was how the Vandal king Genseric felt when he defeated the Romans and burned Rome. I pillaged. I transferred the contents of their bank accounts through overseas banks, and then back into one of our accounts, letting the plunder pay for its own liberation. There was no fee too exorbitant when I was paying with someone else's money.

The lists of names and criminal operations I clandestinely leaked to different agencies. Individual documents were sent to specific detective's desks. Others went to the heads of agencies and departments. Poppy fields could be replanted, and there were always going to be third world nations in Asia that would put people in chains to grow and harvest the plants. Building distribution networks, selling the product on the end, under the police and western governments, that was what took longer to build. Burning those fields, that was how to deal damage.

I burned them.

I burned them to the ground.

It would take the Escadrille decades to reverse the damage I was doing. That was assuming that they survived this blood-letting.

And then I found it, I found the record of the coup.

Chauvignon had been completely sincere in his truce with us, and I was looking at the missives sent to stand down tracking and surveillance of us, even the names of the people who had been doing the work. They were good, grassroots operations. One of the informers was a homeless man who cased neighborhoods in exchange for smack.

He had a heart attack, very sudden.

Then Kaijin took over. There was no one to oppose her. We had killed the Nazi, and Ajahi was somewhere in Asia, or Africa, and notes indicated that Kaijin thought he was actually dead, fighting some militia or Islamic faction in the far east. There was no one to stop her, and she had put her own people in places of power, at least a dozen other former Chauvignon supporters were executed or locked away somewhere until they changed their minds.

This was going to be a problem that we would have to deal with before she came after us again. This wasn't business, with *Le Generale* it had been just that, business that got personal and then it cost him his life. I had no doubt that she murdered him.

We were next on her list.

THE NEXT FEW HOURS WERE QUIETLY TENSE. WE ALL TOOK TURNS getting cleaned up. Lach got his own clothes, and we disposed of the bloody suit he had worn. Sadie traded her blood-stained tactical gear for something that wasn't heavy on her shoulder. A bra was going to be a problem for a day or so, at least until the swelling had subsided.

I had the shortest turn around, which was to say none at all. I hadn't been soaked in blood, tortured, or wearing a dead man's outfit. When they were through with their bath and I was done with my computer work, I found Sadie in the living room. She smiled up at Kyle a little bravely when he brought her something, depositing a couple of round white tablets in her palm.

"Pain meds, from my secret stash," he said with his characteristic crooked grin that was a few shades off from his usual devil-may-care.

She smiled up at him and nodded. I moved off to both give them some room and to bring back a glass of water. The only people who dry swallowed pills were either in movies or were certifiable psychopaths.

Kyle gave her face an unexpected but tender scrutinizing. I listened this time as I drew some water from the closest tap in the nearby downstairs half bath.

"I expected Roan to come through that door…" he murmured.

"Wasn't gonna happen," she murmured back, arching her eyebrow. "It's about time I rescued you, for once."

I stepped back into the living room as he closed his eyes and pressed his forehead to hers. I very much felt the third wheel, this was something that was deeper than my relationship with her, maybe even with him.

"You save me every damn day, Shady Brooks. You have ever since we were kids. Don't you know that?" he asked.

"I do now," she said, bringing up her eyes to look at him that were starting to brim with tears.

He nodded slightly, and she let out a slight gasp right before he kissed her. She closed her eyes and I could see her letting herself go in the moment. When they parted, she drew in a ragged breath. There was a familiar flush to her cheeks and I could see her nipples pressing through the thin fabric of her light silk dress.

"Fuck her good, mate," Kyle said and pushed away, up off the couch. "I wish I was in any kind of shape to do it right now."

She smiled and said, "Raincheck." Her eyes smoldered and I knew that was a check that she would definitely be cashing in later. Lach looked over at me and gave a nod. I returned it. I knew what Kaijin's touch was like, and how sometimes when she was done, I would hurt for days after. He would make good on that check. Just not today.

"She's in good hands, mate," I said, and helped her up off of the couch.

"For sure. And now I'm going to go drink myself stupid and pretend its brain bleach." He grinned, and I nodded. He had probably already taken a few of those pain pills for himself.

CHAPTER TWENTY-TWO

---

*S*adie...

I knew when Kyle Lachlan needed space, and right now he needed the space. Maybe from what Kaijin had done to him, the feeling of being completely vulnerable. He had always valued his solitude.

Roan moved back in front of me, coming near, his proximity an intimate and comforting one.

"Best take those," he said, and I nodded, putting them into my mouth as he pressed a glass of cold water into my other hand.

I drank the pills down while he checked up on the bandaging on my shoulder.

"You want I should shag you on my kitchen counter, or up in my bed proper like?" he asked, and I smiled to myself. Not very demanding, but he wasn't the demanding one. He was used to giving and generously so... it could work though, if he would just *give it to me*, if you know what I mean.

"I don't give a fuck where we fuck, Mister Roan, I just want your dick inside me," I told him honestly, my blood heating.

He kneeled down in front of where I sat on the couch and

smoothed his hands atop my thighs, walking forward the last half a pace or two, sort of stepping into me, right up against the couch. I parted my knees as he swept one of his big hands up into the back of my long locks, threading them between his fingers before making a fist. I made a surprised, choking sound as my hair tightened against my scalp with his grip and he gently tugged my head back, peering down at me from his superior height, even kneeling as he was.

"Too much?" he asked softly, and I smiled up at him.

"Not at all," I whispered. "Not enough, actually."

He smiled and brought his mouth slowly down to mine. "Oh, I'll give you plenty, love," he murmured and covered my mouth with his.

Usually, his kiss was light, something gentle, a questing tip of his tongue against my bottom lip begging for access. This kiss was not that. Not even close. This kiss was everything I needed it to be.

He plunged his tongue past my lips and conquered my mouth with his kiss. His tongue sweeping against mine, exploring, tantalizing, teasing with promise as he swept his other arm around me and pulled me right up to the edge of my seat against his body.

He got up slowly, bending with me, his one hand never leaving the back of my hair, giving me just enough room to rise with him.

When he'd kissed me breathless and panting, he tore his mouth from mine.

"Now, I'm going to march you, my pretty little poppet, by your hair to my bed and I'm going to fuck you until you scream my name."

Oh, I liked the sound of that.

"Yes, please," I uttered and felt a lascivious grin caress my lips.

He tore the dress I was wearing down the center and tossed it aside on the floor and did exactly as he promised, marching me nude, through the house, to his bedroom. Kicking the door shut behind us and marching me over beside the bed, forcing me down by my hair onto my knees in front of him before relinquishing his hold on me.

"I want you to suck my cock," he said, pulling his black tee over his head and wadding it up between his hands.

I went for his tactical belt, and he pulled off his tank top beneath his tee, and settled his hands on his hips, his expression unreadable where he looked down on me.

I met his gaze and worked him out of his pants.

If this wasn't at all his usual thing, he could have fooled me with how hard he was. I wrapped my lips around the head of his cock and teased the tip with my tongue and he groaned, closing his eyes and throwing back his head.

I worked my way down his shaft, teasing the underside of him with my tongue and blindly worked at the laces of the boot on his good leg to get it loosened up and off of him at some point.

"Oh, Sadie, *yes,*" he praised, sucking in a breath through his clenched teeth. One hand on his hip, the other drifting to caress my hair as he slowly thrust himself in and out of my mouth. I held still for him, and let him fuck my mouth, carefully secreting my teeth away behind my lips. He let me pull his boot off and I peeled his pants and boxers down his powerful thighs, while he worked himself and I practiced breathing around him as he reached further and further into the back of my throat.

"Touch yourself," he commanded, and I parted my knees, dipping my fingers between my folds, closing my eyes at peace when I found myself so terribly wet. I teased my clit with my fingertips, plunging those same fingers inside of myself and whimpering when it just wasn't enough.

He buried a hand in my hair again and with a scathing rush of air, pulled back, freeing himself from my mouth.

"Up, on your feet," he commanded, and I got up. He tipped my head back and captured my mouth with his once again and trapped me between his big body and his bed at my back.

"Lie down, and let me look at you," he commanded, and I scooted up on the bed, laying back, and watching him watch me… *damn.*

"I didn't say stop, Poppet."

I captured my bottom lip with my teeth and smiled, letting my hand drift down my body as he worked his pants off, and disengaged his prosthetic to let all of it fall to the floor. He climbed up onto the bed beside me, propping his head in his hand and letting his free hand drift down my body.

"Make yourself come for me, darling," he murmured, and I went for broke, masturbating for him, bringing myself right up to that edge.

"That's it," he encouraged, before he dipped his head, taking one of my nipples into his mouth.

I groaned, and panted, breath becoming heavy, the air seemingly harder to drag in – thick like warm honey. The way his murmuring voice coated me with its golden warmth.

"Oh, God!" I cried, my back arcing off the bed, a shudder running through me as the pleasure coursed through every nerve and vein.

He chuckled darkly, and mounted me, sliding himself all the way in as I still pulsed around him, his big body a warm weight over mine, caging me, holding me together and keeping me from flying apart as he stroked deep and deeper still.

He delved his big arms beneath me, wrapping me up tightly in his embrace, trapping my arms to my sides as he grunted, the same grunt of appreciation he had when we sipped fine wine or a particularly nice brandy. He moaned my name and set a fierce pace.

I felt a fresh, intense orgasm brewing and oh God, how I wanted it, how I wanted him to give me everything and then some. To make me, to break me, and to remake me. His love the glue to put back the million little shattered parts of me back to rights.

"Oh, Roan," I gasped. "Conan, *yes... close, so close.*"

His thrusting intensified, and I came, crying out, the sound choked as wave after wave of searing pleasure crashed through me. I didn't even remember him letting me go, or getting off of me, but he had because when I came back to myself, his big hands were on my hips as I struggled to get my legs under me, to get up onto my knees as he was urging me to do.

"That's it," he encouraged, smoothing his hands over my body.

I gripped the covers beneath my hands and arched low to the bed, thrusting my pussy into the air and back at him in offering, my mind in that pleasant state of disconnect as he thrust back inside me.

I yowled in pleasure, the intensity of it like nothing else as he gripped my hips and pulled me back to meet every one of his forward thrusts.

He asked if I liked it and I begged for it harder until the head of his cock banged into my cervix on every thrust and it was impossible to hold back the scream that clawed its way up my throat.

God, he fucked me so damn good! He fucked the absolute shit out of me, just like I asked, just like I needed, and when I came that third and final time, it was a goddamn mess.

That's what he made of me, a beautiful fucking *sated* mess, and I lived for it – because after all of that death, that's precisely what I needed and what I wanted, the reminder of what it was to truly *live*.

"I've not drained my balls like that in quite some time," he murmured a long while later. I lay against his chest, clutched against him like a treasure as he kissed my temple. "Thank you," he murmured, I giggled a sultry and throaty sound I hardly believed came from me.

"You're thanking *me* for that?" I asked. "Thank *you*." He chuckled darkly. "Way to take one for the team," I whispered softly.

"Hey, there'll be none of that," he murmured.

"I didn't mean anything by it," I said. "Honestly."

"Hmm." he didn't sound like he believed me. That was okay.

I drowsed slightly and finally heaved a big sigh.

"We should clean up and go find Kyle… he's had enough alone time. He needs cuddles."

Conan looked down at me, and massaged the back of my neck, he smiled and said, "Your pupils are as big as saucers, love."

"Guess the pain meds kicked in," I said. "That's beside the point. I said what I said."

"Aye, and I agree," he murmured and kissed my hair.

We got up, and we cleaned up. Well… Conan honestly did most of that. I could barely keep my feet under me. I was high as fuck.

I put a hand over my mouth and giggled like a ninny as he dressed me in a long, cream, satin nightgown. One of Kyle's favorites.

Conan donned a pair of gray satin pajama bottoms, and we went off in search of our third.

We found him lying on his stomach in his bedroom… well, glorified dressing room. He had the single bedside lamp on as he stared sightlessly into a half full glass of gin, the fresh bottle of his Botanical stuff I'd brought him two-thirds empty.

"Hey," he said when we came in, his voice a bit far away. "You guys have a good time?"

"As ever, mate," Conan said gently. I went around the bed which was smaller than the one we typically shared – by a lot, but suitable still for the three of us and got in, motioning Kyle over into my lap. He turned over, and I put my back against the headboard, burying my hands in his hair.

"No." I thrust my chin on the other side of Kyle and Conan paused from where he'd been about to come around to lay on the other side of me. He didn't argue with me, though. Simply set his crutch aside and laid down on the other side of our third stretching out, and propping his head on his hand.

"This is weird," Kyle said, face buried in my lap. "Being in the middle."

"Just for tonight," I said. "I think you need it."

"Okay," he said faintly, voice small, and Conan chuckled, reaching over Kyle to rest a hand atop my thigh just above my knee, his arm across Kyle's back.

"I love you guys," Kyle said, voice muffled, and I massaged his scalp, lightly scratching with my nails and he sighed out. I wrinkled my nose slightly at the cloud of gin vapor that wafted up to me.

"We love you too, mate," Conan said genially, and his gaze met mine. We smiled.

That's how we slept that night, Kyle in the middle, me cuddled tight against his chest, his arms around me, Conan at his back, an arm over Kyle so that he could palm my hip.

I think it may have been slightly awkward for them at first, but I honestly think that quickly fell away all things considered.

Once again, we could have lost so much… once again, we were just grateful to all be here, wrapped in each other's arms.

I wondered faintly if this game of cat and mouse would ever be over, and I tried not to despair.

CHAPTER TWENTY-THREE

*R*oan...

Afghanistan had been cold at times, and there was no option to build shelters for bivouacking. Sleeping in the vehicles had been tagged as a negative since a couple of our trucks had been popped with RPGs. That would be a rough way to wake up. We would stop for the evening, break out the spades and picks and dig foxholes, like our brothers had done thousands of times before in places whose names were hallowed in military history: the Somme, Verdun, the Marne. Except that it was the twenty-first century, and while we were digging into the side of a hill that was just a number on the map, we would never be remembered. Everyone would only remember the jets screaming over, dropping bombs through the mouths of caves, and putting tons of ordnance down, blowing up camels, goat herders, and mud brick villages.

We learned that sitting by yourself was a long and bloody cold night. Best thing was to snug up next to one of your mates, back-to-back, and share body heat. Some of the lads had been averse to this, but a few nights in the Afghani highlands and they decided that having a bit of warmth was worth not being a rugged individual.

The only difference, when I woke up, was rather than being cold, I was close to being too hot. Lach was sawing out a light snore, but he was also flat on his back. Sadie had her face half buried in his neck, and a single tit popped out on his arm. She looked as soft and adorable as I had ever seen her. She was our angel, and I could barely imagine not having her, and thinking back to when she had been dropped in my lap, how could I have been cross?

Getting up was a slow process. I didn't want to disturb either of them.

Once free of the tangle of sweaty limbs I took to downstairs. Coffee was started and then I availed myself the downstairs bathroom, a piss, a shower, and a morning shave. I felt like a new man when I pulled the robe closed and returned to the kitchen. It was going to be a busy day for me, plans had to be laid.

Kaijin had to be dealt with before too long.

Sadie had been adamant about nailing the woman, but she was in transit. We weren't *The Fugitive*, our resources were limited and we couldn't intercept flights, couldn't close roads, and setting up APBs would bring us up for local police scrutiny. That was not something that we needed to deal with.

The acquisition of the Cartel's holding company had gone through, and now their assets were ours, including the house on John Laurens.

I put in a low-key call to a *cleaning service* that would go in and remove the bodies, if the police hadn't locked the place down as a gang war crime scene. They told me that I would receive updates via their encrypted network, and if I was interested, I could start the appraisal process for repairs.

I knew the guy who set that system up, good guy, had been in the same line of work as Lach and me, and decided to cash out and started his own very special service. Most of his work now came from celebrities and VIPs who had to deal with overdosed party guests, dead hookers, and some asshole snorting too much coke and shooting his mistress in the face in a paranoid fit.

There were a dozen financial pings. Almost all of them rejected by the system.

Kaijin had gone to BWI and had tried to grab a flight out of the US and back to France. None of the US accounts were active, I had already shut them down, so her attempts had been denied. I could only imagine the fury as she was rejected at the Air France ticket counter, then the concourse Starbucks, and then a refused query at an ATM must have sealed the deal there. It was the last pinged attempted transaction.

I found her location, she had managed to check into the Powhattan Hotel, north side of Indigo City, on a charge account billed overseas. I had closed all the local accounts, but she wasn't completely shut out. That was good, that meant that we could pin her down in one place, and take care of business. Hotel hits were some of the most common work we had done in the past.

All of these compound assaults, running gunfights, and car chases, that was rubbish for the movies, not what we really did.

I sent a few emails and accessed a few systems. I wanted notifications if she did anything more than take a piss. If she ordered room service or requested more towels, I wanted to know. I needed to know where she was and how safe she *thought* she was.

And how many she had with her. That was important. If she was alone, we could take our time. If she had bodyguards, that would make being quick and quiet more important than extracting maximum revenge from the job.

Sadie was the next to come down the stairs. "Any hot water left?"

"Yeah, the dark prince still asleep?" I asked.

"Mmm." She nodded and helped herself to coffee.

"He's going to be surprised to wake up by himself," I said. She shrugged her good shoulder only.

"What are you doing up?" She walked over and gave me a peck on the cheek.

"Morning business." I smiled.

"Keep your secrets then, Mister Roan." She returned my smile.

"You wanted to know where she was?" Sadie immediately stiffened and came to stand behind me, looking at the screen. "The Powhattan, room 216, facing the water."

"That fucking bitch," she hissed between her teeth.

"I shut down a lot of their funding yesterday, from their own panic room." I took a sip of coffee. "She tried to leave the country, couldn't get a plane ticket or a latte."

"But she got a hotel room?"

"International account. I wasn't able to hit anything on their European side. They were dumb, but not quite *that* dumb."

"So, she's holed up in a suite less than an hour from us, with no bodyguards, no security system, no machine guns, nothing?" There was a hint of excitement in her voice.

"Possibly," I cautioned. "She *is* armed, and we don't know that she's alone. Check-in info doesn't list the number of occupants, and the room can technically sleep eight."

"That's a damn big suite," she said offhandedly.

"It is, and expensive," I added. I thought about it and finished with, "And very public." Sadie wilted a little at the last.

"So, what is our plan?" she asked.

"I was thinking we wait for Kyle to wake up, then breakfast, and then cruise over to the Powhattan and case the hotel, see if we can find the car she took yesterday."

"I'll go wake him up, we can go right now," she said.

"Ease it down a notch, I've not even checked your bandage. She's on the run, has nowhere to go, and about the only safe place for her to go, the French Embassy, would extradite her back to France in chains, they know who she is."

"I want her, and I want her now." Her voice was hard.

"You're not alone there, lass," I agreed. "But revenge is best served cold."

"Is this really the time for those lines?"

"For this once, we have the luxury of time, and we are going to move, but not this very instant. Let me check your shoulder and see if you need any more antibiotics. Being bit by a person is almost as bad as being bit by a monitor." She made a face, but we both went to the main bathroom.

Under the bandage, the bite looked both better and worse. The discoloration and bruising were certainly more prominent and looked terrible. The swelling was still present, but not as pronounced as it had been, and the stitches were holding. I gave it a light cleaning, applied another dose of topical pain killer, and applied a new bandage to it.

She looked away the entire time, her face as soft as a presidential profile on a coin. There was more here than torn skin and bruised muscle. Kaijin had attacked her beauty, the reflection she would see in the morning, every day. This was a scar that even the best cosmetic surgery could only reduce, never erase.

I made a mental note to suggest a tattoo later. That was a trendy thing that some women did to either conceal or make their scars into centerpieces.

But not right now.

Lach wouldn't like that suggestion at all, but that too was a problem for another day.

"You'll need to keep taking the antibiotics; can't let this get infected or fester." She nodded wordlessly, and when the dressing was done, she pulled her shirt back on.

"Last night—" she started.

"Was your comedown, and perfectly normal," I finished.

"I was going to say intense, but yeah."

"That is how the job goes, once it's over, all that energy has to go somewhere."

"I like where it went." She smiled.

"You assholes let me sleep while you're down here having coffee like secret confidants?" Lach reached the bottom of the stairs, clad only in a pair of lounge pants.

"But you were so cute." Sadie gave him a scrunched-up smile.

"Bah, coffee?" He waved her away.

"In the pot." I pointed.

"Good, good, I need the caffeine."

"How are you feeling?" I asked.

"Aside from my balls feeling like someone tried to pull them off, not too bad," he said. "It's a little tender down there, and not in a good way."

"We've got her location," I added.

"Good, good, when are we going to go hang her from her own St Andrew's?" he asked.

"St Andrew's?" Sadie asked.

"The big metal X she had me tied to," he replied.

"Oh, that has a name?" She crossed her arms and gave a derisive shake of her head. "That's just weird."

"Different strokes for different folks," I said. "Kaijin had a lot of high-end BDSM equipment but she doesn't represent that lifestyle at all."

"Do you know much about it?" Sadie asked.

"I do, but it's been mostly work related, we've had contracts on a few people who were pretty deep into that scene, and you can't slip in unnoticed if you show up like a tourist." Lach nodded in agreement. I had done the research, he had worn the leather pants, it was a good trade off.

"Not to be too direct, but when are we going to move?" Lach asked. Sadie nodded in agreement with him.

"She's not going anywhere, her accounts are frozen," I said.

"She'll have help inbound, and they'll have money, cash. Lots of it. I know you went scorched earth on them, but it probably didn't take them long to figure it out. She's still a boss, and she will have people coming from God knows where. New York? Baltimore? Anywhere they had operations."

"Yeah, but those police departments were tipped off and should have moved on them already," I protested.

"They're police departments, not special forces. Telling NYPD where a heroin distribution hub is won't have them roll out a strike package like we're in Kandahar," Lach countered. "As soon as they figured out that they were burned, how many of those assholes closed shop and bolted like roaches?"

"A lot of them," Sadie added. "If we just sit here, she *will* get backup."

"My God, fine. Let's get dressed, drive over the Powhattan and go shoot her in the head," I said in exasperation.

"Excellent plan, let's go," Sadie agreed.

"I'm being sarcastic."

"I'm not." She was adamant.

Bloody hell.

AN HOUR AND A HALF LATER WE MADE A CIRCUIT OF THE POWHATTAN parking lot, and there was no sign of the white sedan Kaijin had escaped in. That didn't mean it wasn't there, we couldn't cruise through the valet parking, and that was probably where it was.

"I'm still not sold on why don't we just go in and kill her." Sadie glowered.

"Because if we do," I said, "it's loud and messy, and there are a lot of guests in a hotel, and then we'll have to deal with the police, and other guests, and a general panic," I said, not for the first time.

"We case the place, and find a way to isolate the target, and then remove them as quietly as possible. If we can do it without firing a round, we win. If guns come out, we've fucked up."

"Why don't we use silencers?"

"Because movie silencers are fiction," I said, again, not for the first time.

"I wish they worked like that, my job would be a lot easier," Lach said.

"Ugh, why can't I just shoot heeeeerrr?" She sounded like a petulant child, but by now it'd quite lost its charm.

"She's not a dinosaur in *Jurassic Park*." Lach put a hand on her good shoulder. "And as much I agree with you on killing her, Roan might be right. If we go in guns out, we get in a lot of trouble, more than if we just waited."

"We've also been spotted," I added. There was a familiar face standing at the curb, a cigarette between his lips and phone pulled out. The lens could easily be pointed at us. "Pull over, let me out, then go park. Wait for me to call." Lach looked over at me and nodded in agreement. "After I call, we'll have lunch," I said.

"IT'S BEEN A LONG TIME," I SAID WALKING UP TO THE MAN.

He tucked the phone back into his pocket. He wore an off-the-rack suit, his light brown hair close cropped. He had a shadow of a red beard coming in on his square jaw and practically no neck to speak of, it was so wide and near constricted by his collar and tie. His brow ridge, pronounced as it was, gave the illusion of stupidity but Kurt Worthington was not a stupid man.

"It has, Conan, it has," he replied.

"How are the kids?" I asked.

"You know good and bloody well I was never daft enough to plant any seeds, mate." he gave a laugh, and we shook hands. "When was the last time we saw each other?"

"Camp Bastion, Kabul," I said. "'06."

"That's right, been a long time, then."

"What brings you to Indigo City?"

"The only thing that matters; work."

"Fair, anything you care to talk about?" I asked.

"Now, *I'm* fair certain you can make a good guess."

"I was hoping it was a happy coincidence." I nodded. "Can you spare one of those?"

"When did you take up smoking?" he asked.

"There's a time and place," I said, accepting the cigarette he held out to me.

"True, looking for trouble?" he asked.

"It has a way of finding me, and keeping me well paid." I laughed, tapping the filter against the side of my hand.

"Who were your friends?" he asked.

"If you're working for who I think you're working for, you probably know."

"Right you are, as always," he said.

"I was never wrong when it mattered." I smiled.

"You were only bad at cards." He passed me a small plastic lighter. "How are you doing these days? heard you had a stint as a POW."

I placed the filter between my lips and rolled the wheel of the lighter with my thumb, sparking it to life and taking a moment to draw the tobacco smoke into my lungs.

"It wasn't pleasant, but I've still got all of my fingers, teeth, and half of my toes." I puffed on the smoke and got it going.

"You only had half your toes the *last* time I saw you," he said, taking a drag off his own cancer stick. I handed him back his lighter, and he tucked it away inside his breast pocket.

"Same number now." I gave a laugh. "Only one foot gets cold in the winter. How is your employer doing, I understand there was scrap yesterday?"

"Aye, there was a scrap." He puffed on his cigarette. "She got nicked a few times, nothing serious. She's mighty pissed off, as you can imagine." He flicked ash off the end into the gutter.

"Indeed, so what's the plan then?" I asked, taking a drag off of mine, the harsh chemicals and tobacco invading my mouth, drying it.

"Helo evac in about thirty minutes, bird is in the air and inbound. If you're going to try something you don't have long to do it," he said.

"It's danger close here, so no," I said. He relaxed the slightest amount. "Did she hire you?"

"Not like that, no. Guillame brought me in, and I was handling some of his security restructuring. Next thing I know, I'm still obligated by contract, I'm out of the command loop, and the old general's heart quit. He wasn't a spring chicken by any means, but he wasn't *that* old."

"I think he was assassinated," I offered.

"I think so, too. Too convenient him pushing daisies that quick after getting that truce."

"Kurt, did you have a hand in that?" I asked. He nodded. "The truce, aye. Not that other bit. Bad business, that."

"Aye," I agreed. "Bad business, that."

"You can't let business get personal," he said. "That's when you get sloppy and make mistakes. Like when Dobson went out with his patrol after those two Talibani shot up his buddy. Got torqued, went out mad, and got himself and six other lads shot up. I'm pretty sure he would have been court-martialed for disobeying orders and misappropriating equipment if he hadn't been so ventilated."

"He was a good lad, though," I said.

"He was, and now he's dead. I think we should both see what we can do to stay above ground," Kurt replied. He flicked the cigarette into the street. "We're flying out in a few minutes, I'm interested in trying the local barbecue where we're headed. The brisket is apparently a big deal there." He gave me a not-insignificant look. "Take care of yourself, Captain," he said and gave a minimal salute and walked back into the hotel. I likewise dropped my cigarette and ground it out. I waited a few minutes and then called Lach and Sadie.

"Go ahead and see if you can call in and grab us a table, we aren't going to get anything here today but lunch," I said. There was a fuss in the car and they both appeared out of the parking area. Sadie looked cross and Lach annoyed following after her. As they came within walking distance, the sound of the helicopter became audible.

"Where is she, who was that?" Sadie demanded.

"She's about to take her leave." I pointed up as the helicopter passed overhead and landed on top of the hotel. "She's about thirty floors up, on the roof, getting on that helo."

"If we run…" Sadie's eyes were wide.

"She has a security detail now, the man I was talking to was its commander, I served with him over in Afghanistan. Good chap. If he has control of her security, we won't get close to her now."

"I knew we should have been quicker getting here," Sadie growled.

"I'm guessing it was Kurt who got her in this place and organized the evac, but don't worry," I said, tapping the side of my nose, "I know where they're going, and what we're going to do about it."

"What's the plan?" Lach asked.

"First things first, I understand that there is a special on oysters today, and the blue crab is always fresh here," I said.

"Oh my God, *really?*" Sadie huffed.

"Yes, she's in the air now." I pointed as the helo took off again, circled the building once, and then flew away. "We can't do anything to her unless you happen to have a Stinger missile in your clutch."

"Where is she going, mate, what's the plan?" Lach asked and sounded frayed. Precisely why now was not the time.

"She's going back to Texas, and that means either the compound we've shot up once already, or somewhere associated with Emerson. He might be her patron now, no telling," I said. "But in the meantime, Sadie needs time for that shoulder to heal up, and it's time for lunch. Patience is a virtue."

"So are poverty and chastity, but I have no time for either of those either." Lach gave me his now traditional response.

I merely chuckled and led the way to the Powhattan's restaurant, knowing surely that Lach and Sadie would follow.

FOR THREE DAYS EVERYTHING WAS CAUGHT UP IN A *BACKFIELD IN MOTION* game. Tracking Kaijin's movement was difficult, even using my illegal access to the FAA, and trying to use the honest to God radar arrays that watched the US skies. To be any more precise in chasing her aircraft down would have required either hacking into ballistic missile detection radars, a definite off-limits area, or somehow gaining access to a Global Hawk drone or AWACS jet. With either of those over US soil I could have gone down to the point of finding out what color shoes she was wearing.

But I didn't have access to those, so we watched and plotted and planned. Kurt was in charge of her detail now, and it made a difference. Her digital trail vanished at the Powhattan. Her helo made a not overly long flight northeast, crossing the Chesapeake, and landing at Atlantic City.

We liked Atlantic City, the security systems were behind the curve, it wasn't a major hub, but connected to several easily, and well, Lach liked any place that had gambling. If there was gambling, escorts weren't far away. Although, with the addition of Sadie into our lives, I believe that last bit was drastically changed. Now that we had Sadie in the house, he hadn't spent a single dime chasing designer tail, and that had saved us a good bit of money. It didn't offset our finances being left on autopilot for six and a half months, or the house being leveled, but it *was* noticeable.

In Atlantic City she picked up a shuttle flight and vanished into the mess that was New York La Guardia International. My window to spot her movement was narrow, but I knew where to look, and I also checked for Kurt. He wasn't the alias sort, he wasn't a hitman, but a security contractor and personal protection specialist. He boarded a coach seat bound for Dallas Love field, with an undesignated connecting flight after that.

Unlikely, if they were heading back to Oasis and the compound there. There were no commercial flights to a city without anything larger than a municipal airport, and there were no flights registered to Oasis. They would throw tickets and overshoot their destination. Sometimes, when I was routing Lach to a target, I would have him get off at the last layover and keep the flight path going another leg. A few hundred bucks was a small price to pay to keep heat off of us. His homebound flight plans were either split between different carriers to stop easy tracking, of his layover at BWI or Dulles would just be a pause before a westbound flight. I liked to dump a lot of his destinations at Seattle or San Francisco. Kept things fresh.

"You've been doing a lot of work, in here," Sadie said, walking into the panic room. Over those three days, we had transferred our few possessions to the house on John Laurens. The view over the bay was spectacular, breathtaking, and fuck the house was worth it just for that. The first morning we had stayed, watching the sun rise over the bay, and then illuminate the place. Fucking art.

Sadie was art too, sweeping up behind me and wrapping her arms around my neck.

"Keeping tabs on our target," I said, and gave her hand a pat.

"Where is she?" Sadie asked.

"Oasis, Texas. It was where we went to start this high-profile, nation hopping, gun fighting jiggery-pokery," I said.

"Was that the place Kyle was, where everyone was all thermal imaged?" she asked.

"Indeed, it was," I said.

"It's hard to think about where I was, *who I was*, back then. It seems like another lifetime. Someone else's life." She gave a soft sigh.

"Would you change any of it?" I asked.

"If I changed anything it would be to smooth out the bad parts, like losing you for so long." She kissed my neck, and it wasn't a casual peck like her normal kisses. It was softer, and her breath almost seemed hotter and to linger against my neck.

"I would change that too." I let out a breath.

"I want to apologize about the other day, and a little for before that," she said.

"No need, Poppet," I said. She kissed the side of my neck again, her hands tracing patterns against my chest.

"If you would rather me leave you alone, I will," she said, her voice sultry like velvet. I turned to face her and aside from a pair of fuzzy socks, she was naked as the day she came into the world.

"Poppet!"

"Should I go?" she asked, hooking a thumb over her shoulder.

"No, no, you should stay." I gulped. She came and sat in my lap, pulling my hands to hold her, and twisting her head to kiss me. I wasn't sure how she could bend like that, maybe she was part cat. For a moment I forgot about the tracing I had been doing. It was just going through the motions, nothing had changed in hours, and feeling the heat of her body was much more appealing that a cold set of monitors.

"What about contractors?" I managed to ask between her intoxicating kisses.

"They aren't coming in until ten a.m., we have plenty of time, and do you think they *ever* show up early?" she asked and ground her hips against me. This wasn't like when she was on her comedown and being aggressive. This was much softer, much more enticing and seductive. *She was seducing me.* The thought manifested itself as a stiffening between my legs. She moaned into the kiss as she felt me getting hard.

"That's what I was hoping for," she whispered, before sliding out of my lap and out of my grasp. For a moment I was left in a lurch, her heat was gone, and her breasts and hard nipples weren't in my hands anymore. Her fingers were quick, undoing the drawstring of my lounge pants, the button of my boxers. She pulled me out of the front of my boxers, taking a moment to almost *admire* my cock before she started going down on me.

I came to full hardness quickly enough. Part of me wanted to pull her up off of the floor, off of her knees, but there was more to it than that. She had picked her posture and position, and it was deliberate. She took me slowly, and only partially at first, but as I was getting harder, she was going down further, taking more of me. The things she did stole my breath, and I considered one day asking her how she had gotten better at this. This was a long way from the first time she went down on me.

The thought of her practicing on some plastic toy, imagining it was me, my balls tightened.

"Sadie…" I let out a groan.

"Mmmm?" She looked up at me, and I knew that my will to resist was done. This was so nice and felt so good. This was not where I had been for almost half a year, there was no humiliation or cruelty. There was no reason to even try and pull away.

"I… I love you; you know that?" I asked her.

"Mmmm-hmmm." She smiled around my cock and I groaned again, her eyes twinkling. She was enjoying this as much as I was. Eventually she pulled back and released me. She stroked it a few times, looking from it to me, and then back to it. My ego would have groaned in pleasure if it could. She stood without letting go of me and turned her back to me.

"Do you need lube?" I asked, breathless.

"I don't think so," she said, and I saw how wet she was as she guided herself down onto me. There was a small amount of tension, but it was gone quickly, and she let herself slide all the way down onto my length. "No, I think we're…" her breath hitched. "I think we're good," she groaned.

She rode me in reverse, and her hips rolled and bucked. There wasn't a lot of up and down, in and out, but that didn't matter. I knew, somewhere in the more rational parts of my brain, that she was using me to find those spots inside her, those spots that she could focus on and make herself cum. All I had to do was sit back and hold her hips, so she didn't fall or slip out of my lap.

"How are you doing?" Lach asked, walking in front of the desk.

"I'm good, yeah." I let out a gasp.

"Fantastic, yeah?" He laughed.

"Definitely fantastic," Sadie agreed.

"Busy?" I asked.

"Oh, this is all you, mate." Lach gave me a smile. "She woke me up in the best way possible."

"What," I groaned again as she fondled my balls. "What's that? The best way?"

"Morning head, what else?" he asked.

"Ah," I managed. Sadie managed more, lifting up off of me, clenching and shaking. She came impressively and was almost panting when she sat back down on me.

"Oh God," she whispered.

"There was more after, but I'm pretty sure you can figure that out. So, what is the sit rep?" he asked, looking at the computer screen, I turned my head to look but one of the screens was still tracking flight control radar out of San Antonio and the other had gone to its screen saver mode. I tried to produce a coherent answer, but concentration was difficult.

"Um, flight, something… Dallas Love…" I stumbled.

"Mate, you are way too tense right now," he said. "How long have you been up, working on this?"

"He *is* pretty tense," Sadie said. "Especially between his legs, a lot of tension down there."

"Couple hours… three…" I managed to spit out, she was working my balls over again, and fuck. *Fuck.*

"You're working too hard, you need to take a break," Lach said, putting his hands on both of my shoulders, digging his thumbs between them. "Sadie, do you think he should take a break?"

"He should, definitely take a break," she said, and stood up. When I came out of her, my cock slapped back against my stomach, glistening and wet with her last orgasm. "He's so tense." Her words were honey and silk. She took me in her mouth again and started giving noisy, aggressive head. The sort that was hard to resist, hard to hold back from.

"Oh God, mate." I managed a half wave at Sadie. It was a perfect opportunity for him to take her from behind.

"Relax, we've already gone once this morning." He gave my shoulders a massage-like squeeze. "This is just you and her. I'm enjoying the show, though."

I felt her take me completely into her mouth, and her hands were back on my balls, giving them the business that she knew I liked. "You've almost got him, Shady, you've almost got him." He laughed.

"You are very specifically *not* helping," I managed to say.

"Mate, just relax, enjoy this," he said, gripping my shoulders and giving me a little shake. It was damned distracting, his hands on my shoulders, her eyes burning into mine, watching her slide back and forth, rocking her whole body, my cock vanishing into her mouth. There was no way, no way she was getting all of that in her.

She fell into a steady rhythm, wet, and sloppy. I groaned, and I felt things drawing tight, the tension rising into a knot. She cupped my balls and gave them an affectionate squeeze. "Oh… fuck…" and it was over. My good leg folded. Lach caught me before I fell out of the chair, and I came.

Certainly not my proudest moment, in hindsight.

At the time, I was barely aware of anything other than what felt like a floodgate being opened and almost falling.

There are different sorts of orgasms. Some brief; intense. Others longer and more drawn out. This one, this one was the sort that started strong and while each individual pulse was a little weaker than the one before it, they seemed to deal more cumulative effect. The first two or three were enlightenment, nirvana, want and desire leaving the mortal coil in strong spurts. Then the next few imitated the throes of intoxication, taking eye hand coordination with them. The last few dribbles, the ones that Sadie milked out of me, never looking away, were the ones that left me unable to walk or even do anything but struggle to remember how to breathe.

"There you go, mate, that'll set your clock right." Lach laughed, pulleing me back up into the chair and giving me a few hard smacks against the chest.

"I think I need to go get cleaned up now," Sadie said, standing up. "I'll leave you some hot water."

"My God, you two set me up." I looked up at him. He only grinned.

"You deserved it," he said and winked.

CHAPTER TWENTY-FOUR

*L*achlan…

I handled most of the drive down to Texas, manning the driver's seat of the once upon a time moving truck. The back of the vehicle was a finished mobile command center, with Roan's second computer rig, mobile hotspots, a drone rack on the top. The front half had been given over to basic accommodations. There were cots, an improvised kitchenette, and a few other basics.

"You know, in the future, we could totally do this *Breaking Bad* style," I said.

"What, get a shitty RV and cook meth in it?" Roan asked. The clicks of the push-to-talks were crisp enough we didn't have to throw *over* at the end of each line, and the fun of pretending to be truckers lasted about as long as it took to get out of Maryland.

"No, get a *nice* RV, and swap out a section of that for your mobile drone command center," I said. "We'd have a nicer bed that'd fit the three of us, a shower, a kitchen table, you know, creature comforts."

"He's right," Sadie agreed, sitting next to me. She wasn't comfortable riding back in the box, but Roan was. He was still doing more of his keyboard warrior work. "I tell you; no one is getting lucky in this rolling goodwill dumpster."

"I don't blame you, Poppet," he replied. "I was working on short notice, and trucks like this aren't very expensive and they're easy to work with."

I had to lay on the horn for a second, watching some silver import jag back out of my lane. "It's almost invisible too," I growled.

"And slow, what's this thing's top speed?" Sadie pouted out the window. "Twenty miles an hour?"

"Sixty-five," I said. "And that's going downhill." When traffic eased off, or we were on the long empty stretches of Virginia, Sadie drove. We parked at a truck stop before crossing the Appalachians on I-81, ate truck stop fast food, and slept in the back of the truck. We were on the road again before the sun rose, and we took turns driving. There wasn't much for anyone to do, so all three of us rode up front. The bench was large, Sadie was small, and Roan could pop off his leg for extra room. He didn't think this was amusing, but *did* agree it was practical.

The drive took the better part of three days, even with changing drivers. The truck was slow, acceleration was imaginary, and it handled like an oil tanker.

Our final destination was a split-level ranch house less than a mile from the Final Prophecy Center. Nothing had changed in Oasis, but it would take something dramatic like a comet hitting the planet or Armageddon to change anything in places like this. It could have just as easily been 2000, or 1985, or 1955. No big box stores, lingering mom and pops, there were only a handful of modern fast-food places and they were clustered right at the highway exit. The only things of interest in places like this were obscure museums that were bizarrely specific, like just Native American arrowheads, or the car museum that only had six cars in its collection.

We had *bought* a house in the town, and it had running water and electricity, but that was almost all it had. Sadie was the first to shower, while Roan and I worked on getting his mobile command center set up, running three extension cords to power outlets inside the house, and checking everything else.

"When is Grant going to be here?" I asked.

"He's already here," Roan replied, as he started his inspection of the quadrotors.

"Must have his camo on because I don't see him," I said.

"He's here in Oasis, got here before us. He said that he was going to get a room at the motel by the highway," Roan said, and started checking the next drone. "He'll be over in a few hours, and he said he'll bring dinner."

"Last time I was here I ate at the B&B, nice couple," I said.

"They're still open here, but the business is for sale," he said.

"Didn't expect that," I admitted.

"Someone gave them a good tip on a short stay last year, as soon as the bed-and-breakfast has a buyer. They're retiring and moving back to Mexico," he said.

"How the fuck do you know that?" I asked.

"I gave them the financial advice, after the job last year. I considered picking up the business, but it's not really valuable. Nothing here to draw tourists and guests. Hernando admitted most of their clients were traveling with the petrol industry, or people with car problems."

"Come for the gravel, stay because your radiator boiled over?"

"Accurate," he said.

Roan was taking his turn in the shower when Grant rolled up into the driveway, driving a completely inconspicuous neon green Lamborghini.

"Deejay," I greeted him as he popped out of the convertible. "I see you took low profile to heart."

"This car has a very low profile, to get a more low-profile car would have meant trying to get a Ford GT or a Caterham," he said.

"Low profile, like *blending in*," I suggested, and helped him grab some of the bags he had brought. Some were gear and went in the back of the moving truck, the rest seemed like a local barbecue joint. He was lucky Sadie wasn't one of those girls who liked to flirt with vegetarianism or veganism. She would have been left with almost sickeningly sweet iced tea and a Styrofoam cup of coleslaw.

"Grant!" Sadie greeted him with a hug. "Fries!" she greeted the bags of food, and took a bag of said fries and some sort of sandwich.

"So, what did you bring us to eat?" I asked.

"No idea, fam, I told them fuck me up with fifty dollars' worth of their food and this is what they gave me."

"I got sliced steak," Sadie said.

"That's brisket, Poppet," Roan said, walking in. "Shower is free."

"Grant's here," I said, mastering the obvious.

"Let's go get all of your gear tied into the mobile rig in the yard," Roan said. He paused long enough to dig another brisket sandwich out to take with him.

The shower was a shower, and that was about it. No real pressure, and the hot water didn't last long enough, but after that many days driving and just changing clothes rather than real cleaning, it was enough. Roan had insisted on us not stopping at any hotels, and had even gone so far as setting up a few decoys at the house on Phoenician, several food deliveries through apps, and a couple bottles of booze as well. He said the neighbor would pick it up, I didn't keep up with all the balls he had in the air when he started juggling.

I could only assume that he knew we were back on being monitored again.

He also seemed to know the man in charge of Kaijin's security detail, so I wasn't going to argue with him. I barely remembered Worthington, in the short time my unit and the Royal Marines were teamed up, I couldn't throw a rock without hitting a large man with a beard and an English accent.

Roan knew him, and that was good enough for me.

AFTER EVERYONE HAD THEIR SHIT SQUARED AWAY, WE STARTED GOING over the plan. Roan rolled out a large printed map of the Final Prophecy compound and starting laying aerial photographs that he had managed to grab with the drone while I was taking that shower and a time out for a long overdue shave.

"That explains why you wanted a fucking printer in the truck," I said, picking up a print off the table of the guard house now. The place had been reinforced, and there were two men standing there. They looked like the last wannabe cowboys who had been here, but rather than being kids in oversized hats and belt buckles, they were all older, their faces more weathered, and instead of kitted up ARs they had pistols in holsters.

"Resolution on these is really good, man," Grant said, looking at a few of the other pictures. "Like crisp *and* fresh."

"New optical filtering program on the drones, and I did what you said, and switched from LG optics to Apple. They were more expensive, but you can almost read this wanker's name on his belt buckle."

"C'mon, plan now, nerd later," Sadie said. "I want this bitch dead and I wanna go home to my big-ass new house."

"Yeah, this place is a drag," Grant agreed.

"We'll owe you one, man," I said. Having Grant run the wizard's seat, putting three of us on the ground, armed and armored? These guys didn't know what was coming.

"Lach is going to reprise his role from last time, the path you took along the perimeter and crossing the fence seems to still be viable," Roan said. "And you will be the point of the spear." I gave him a salute. "Sadie, you are going to head up the opposite side of the perimeter, and approach the blind side of the compound."

"Why didn't Kyle do that, last time?" she asked.

"Because he was carrying a small arsenal of weapons, and the wall he would have to cross would be too high. He's carrying maybe a third of what he had last time, and you'll have that fence cutting torch." I knew he was talking about the torch Sadie and I had used to cut through the fences when we were bugging out, after Bootlegger. "Once you clear the grounds, you will skirt the building, go around the sports complex and there are several glass double doors there. Those will be easy to bypass quietly."

"But I'm still bringing Thumper, right?" she asked.

"Yes, you are still bringing the grenade launcher," Roan agreed.

"You have a n00b t00b?" Grant asked grinning.

"It's a Vietnam era M-79 grenade launcher, and yes," Roan said. "She's good with it," he added. "I actually watched her shoot a guy in the chest with a teargas can." Grant grinned and gave her a high five.

"Boom!" He laughed.

"That guy thought so, too." She raised her eyebrows in amusement and gave a little half-smile that stirred something inside me.

"So, once you get through the glass doors, you'll go for the upper floor, the internal floor plan is open, and you will be able to bring down fire from above. If it gets too spicy, you can cool things down with teargas, flashbangs, or those H-E rounds you liked."

"Too bad there aren't set-shit-on-fire grenades." She tapped her chin thoughtfully.

"There are, but it would take too long to smuggle them into the country," Roan said.

"Russian?" I asked.

"Naturally," he replied.

"God bless the Russians for being kill happy and not caring who they sell it to," I said.

"So, you will be in through the side door like last time, Sadie will pincer and strike from above, and that should catch most of them in the middle," Roan said, sweeping his finger along the floor plan for emphasis.

"What are you going to do?" Sadie asked.

"I've got an automatic shotgun and a revolver that needs to be broken in," he said. "And I'm coming in through the front door. Grant will begin with the first strike option, shut down their power, alarms, and security system. While they scramble, the two of you will already be in motion. After they figure out they're fucked, I'll take out the guard shack, come in through the front, and we'll finish this like Montgomery."

"And I'm air support and comms," Grant said.

"Correct, this place is recently renovated so a lot of their equipment is borderline smart, but it's old enough that almost none of it is prepared for anything more than rudimentary cyberwarfare. You will splice into everything they have. Last time we were here, I was able to turn the lights on and off, and trigger the fire sprinklers."

"Dude, no way they haven't corrected that by now?" Grant asked.

"It looks unlikely, I ran a search on service tickets to the building and it looks like all they did was a ton of clean-up, body removal, and bribes to get local and federal officials to leave the place alone. I found Emerson's signature on a few of the items, so that's how they got the heat off of them, and this place wasn't confiscated and made government property."

"Do we need to deal with Emerson?" Sadie asked.

"I don't think so. When Grant isn't supporting us, he has the job of seeing if there is any database or servers here, get into them, and see how much of this we can blow up. It hurt them bad when I nuked Malmaison's data, and then taking out Kaijin's node at John Laurens' locked her down until Worthington bailed her arse out," he said.

"So, if this goes well, we'll burn Emerson and everyone attached to him too?" I asked.

"That's the plan," he said.

"What about Worthington, what happens when we cross blades with him?" I asked. "I know you served with him."

"I did and don't worry about it. Worst case, he is an enemy combatant, best case, I have it in the bag."

"How?" Sadie asked. "I've seen buddy action movies go bad with this sorta thing."

"Because he owes me," Roan said, more confident than his normal confident self.

IT WAS CLOSE TO MIDNIGHT WHEN WE STARTED THE OPERATION. IT WAS sooner than planned because all of us but Grant had to walk to our starting places. The low-profile Lamborghini couldn't be used as our personnel carrier, too obvious and no room to carry our equipment. It had been pricey getting all of this in hand, but Roan used the money we had stolen from Kaijin to pay for it, and expedite it. More dragonscale armor, Kevlar vests, helmets and gas masks, we looked like black clad storm troopers.

I checked my weapons and ammo. The others did the same, Roan inspecting his elephant blaster automatic shotgun, cowboy revolvers, and earpiece. Sadie was impatient, rolling a teargas grenade around in her hand. At least she wasn't playing with one of the high explosive rounds, those were tucked in a thigh bandolier and *God,* was that hot.

I knew the AR I had was ready to go, and so were the pistols.

We followed our designated paths, Grant tagging a drone to follow each of us, so he didn't have to try to chase us with one, or run the risk of losing one to wind or accidentally drifting into power lines or a fence while it was idling. As we went, he was sitting in front of four monitors, and chirped us all the guidance we needed to ghost through Oasis. I reached my target first, and scanned the building through my scope, looking for heads popped up over the wall or sticking out in the guard tower on this side. There were two, maybe three, and there were no cigarette cherries glowing, no phone illumination. It was dark, aside from a few floodlights.

Sadie was the last to check in, but had the longest distance to go.

Once she chimed in, we went into action.

I was over the fence, rifle in a forward position, and all but sprinted across the grass. There was no cry of alarm, no spotlight hitting me. About the time I met the base of the wall, the lights flickered, and went out.

Five seconds later, they came back on.

Flicker.

Then they were out again. He had mimicked a power failure in the grid, and from where I was, I could see the lights on the road and in some of the buildings had gone out. Most people were asleep, so it wasn't likely that calls would come fast, and the local utilities wouldn't come into play immediately.

My plan to slip in the side door a second time was a bust, this time it was locked. We had prepared for this, and I had a single C4 charge, a door opener. I did a countdown, and within a fraction of a second of each other, two explosions went off. The door came apart in pieces, shattering the drop bar behind it, cracking the frame, and reducing most of it to splinters. On the other side of the building, Sadie had lobbed a high explosive round into *something.* I was in, rifle up and dropped down into a shooting stance.

There was another building-shaking explosion.

Then the shouting started. Several men came down the familiar staircase right into my line of fire. I emptied the first clip in ten triple round bursts. They threw themselves into cover, and a few returned fire. I advanced a step and into the breakroom. The hall behind me rattled with more coordinated gunfire.

Then there was a familiar thump, quickly followed by a second one.

Then the cursing and coughing started. She had started lobbing gas into the lobby, and they were *not* prepared for that. Kaijin had neglected to mention it, I had to guess. *Sloppy.*

The gunfire ceased, and I heard shouted commands, and a lot of coughing, one person vomited, by the sound. I clung to the wall and advanced. Between the gas and the lights being out, visibility was awful, but I knew theirs was much worse. Hard to see through blurred vision and nausea.

Getting into the ranks was easy, and then it was close quarters with the AR, the triple pop of each burst fast and loud. It fell into chaos, and there were people shouting over their radios. They held discipline better than the Mercenary Monthly guys had last time, but they weren't on our level.

Being in some national guard or homegrown militia didn't prepare these guys for US Army special forces, or Royal Marines, or cyber-warfare, or an angry woman with a grenade launcher.

Especially that last part.

My training barely prepared *me* to handle that.

There was another thump, and I ducked as the flashbang went off, then another thump and a second one. Then there was the familiar sound of AR fire. Quick pops, three at a time.

My earpiece was alive with chatter, and the distant sound of that big automatic shotgun greeting the men at the guard shack.

Then a loud *WHUMP* as something outside went up. Aviation fuel and the helicopter, I ventured to guess. That would draw attention, certainly. Oasis only had a volunteer fire department, and that would slow their response time, and worked in our favor. If they even got the call, that was.

There was more gunfire, and I pulled back and sheltered behind the stairs.

The men who were still on their feet organized a fall back maneuver and were making for the front doors. The housing area had gotten too hot for them, caught between teargas, an elevated shooter, and a shooter they couldn't find. It wasn't the best idea, since Roan was coming up on their six, but I wasn't going to correct them.

I saw one of them hit the doors and bail out into the night.

Then I heard Sadie let out an inarticulate scream, not pain, but raw anger.

She broke from her position, and I saw her streak across the upper hallway toward the room where more than a year ago I had killed the mark that had started this entire shitshow. She had spotted Kaijin and was going for the kill.

I had to back her up, the last time these two had crossed claws, Sadie almost lost a chunk out of her neck and had ended up looking like an MMA fighter after a rough match. I had to get to her, to not let Kaijin get in the position of taking her down or captive.

Crossing the room netted me a few rounds right into the dragon-scale and sent me rolling across the floor. I came up onto my feet and raised my AR just in time for it be knocked from my hands and a follow up punch connect with my jaw. Teeth clacked together and my feet came out from under me again.

"I remember you," a big man said. I looked up into the dark and ominous face of Ajahi. This was unexpected, and while I was going for my pistol, he grabbed me. I was in the air, then crashing into a wall. *Fuck!* The force of the impact knocked the wind out of me, and I lost my pistol. I fumbled for the AR, still hanging from its shoulder strap, but as I was bringing it up, he grabbed the barrel and used it to pull me into several hammer blows to the head and shoulders. I gave up going for the gun and went to blocking. Even with my arms up, he hit like a Mack truck.

He dropped a few low body blows, but the dragonscale stopped his fists just as easily as it stopped bullets. After he realized I was armored, everything he threw came after my face. I could barely connect even the quickest jabs, and those didn't faze him in the slightest.

"Fuck, you're supposed to be in Afghan," I grunted as he hammered me into the wall.

"Last time I heard, you were screaming with ya balls in a vice," he said. He relented the blows to the head long enough to grab my mask and rip it off. The lingering tear gas immediately set my eyes on fire.

"Speaking of that," I said, and then delivered what was now in my mind, the Sadie Special, and I kicked him between the legs as hard as I could. The shell of ballistic armor over my knee gave me no impression of what I had hit, but his eyes bulged and I knew I had struck home. He staggered back, and I pursued, throwing several punches, pushing him back and onto the defensive.

I put my right foot into the bottom of his jaw and he fell back into the wall, more drywall crunching under the impact. Putting some room between us I pulled the AR forward, and was going to put a clip into him and saw that not just the scope was damaged, but the barrel was slightly bent, the shroud cracked, and the stock splintered down the side.

I would feel those hits in the morning. Each time he had put me into the wall or the floor, it had been with the gun against my back.

He stood, brushing plaster dust off of his hands and shirt.

"You fight dirty, ya," he growled and I could finally see his eyes bloodshot and weeping from the gas, and from the hits he had taken. "But ya peashooter looks broken."

"You got me there," I said, slipping the strap off of my shoulder. I tasted blood in my mouth, and his face was brightening with his own sense of victory. I didn't drop the gun to the ground, even a broken gun could still be used as a weapon.

He blocked in time, but swinging the rifle like a bat was punishing. He moved away from the strike, even as the scope broke free. He swung a punch, and went for a follow up grab, but instead took the stock of the rifle above his eye. Skin yielded to high density plastic and his face was drenched in blood. The second hit glanced off his shoulder and up into his jaw, the entire butt of the rifle, stock and all coming apart.

He threw up a block and caught my left foot in the jaw. Then right foot to the solar plexus. He folded and stumbled back, and caught the remnant of the rifle directly to the crown of his head.

He staggered a final time and crumpled to the ground.

"About fucking time," Roan said, walking up with the big shotgun barrel smoking. "I thought you were dancing with him. C'mon we've got work to do."

"You could have *helped*, mate," I said, wiping blood off of my mouth, smearing it across my hand.

"Grab a gun, we're not done." I staggered away from him and found one of the downed mercenary cowboys and lifted the AK-47 from his dead body. I racked the gun and gave him my best game face.

He pointed the shotgun down at Ajahi, the big man groaned and started pushing himself back up. The double *BOOM BOOM* of the gun was deafening and dropped the South African like an anvil.

"You could have done that anytime," I said. "C'mon, Sadie's upstairs."

CHAPTER TWENTY-FIVE

*R*oan...

On cue the night was punctuated by stereo explosions. It would take a practiced ear to know the difference between the grenade and the C4, and I could only tell because I knew who was where.

"Power is out," Grant said in my ear.

"Good job, what does the alarm sitch look like?"

"Alarms are down, and land line phones are down," he replied.

"Keep an ear on the scanner frequencies, we'll need to know when police and first responders are activated and an ETA."

"I've got your back, Guild Master," Grant said.

"What else?" I asked.

"Red Queen is inside the building, and moving to shooting position, Black King has engaged," Grant said. *"Drone in motion, White King you are clear to advance on the Black Rook."*

"The Black Rook?" I asked.

"The guard shack, I'm just getting into this chess theme," Grant said.

"Well, okay then," I said, and started up the sheltered side of the driveway. There were several more loud bangs, and I knew those to be the rest of Sadie's party poppers going off. The commotion at the

"

compound didn't cross the walkies the guards had down in the shack, and they didn't show any concern until they were unable to reach anyone. That was intentional, the takedown Grant had done should have knocked everything but their cellphones out.

As I approached the shack, I pulled the pin on a grenade and tossed it in through the open window of the building. There was a moment of silence, then panic, and then the shack blew apart with a loud bang. The air was filled with wood splinters and dust, and then quiet. I stepped closer, aiming my pistol into the ruins. One man, blood running out of his ears looked up at me, dazed. I put him down with the .45 and moved forward.

With the shack down, walking up the drive to the compound was a piece of cake. All the fuss inside had their attention wrapped up. No one was looking outside, and that was their mistake.

I reached the top of the hill, and there were two paths, one went directly to the front doors, and they branched off to where the helipad was. "Thermal?" I asked.

"Thermal positive, engines have residual heat," Grant said. I paused, juggled the options, explosive or thermite? I picked the latter, pulled the pin on the incendiary grenade, and tossed it toward the helipad. I heard a satisfying metallic clang as it hit the lid of a fuel drum. Sadie had wanted grenades like this for *Thumper,* as she had come to call her grenade launcher. I had these, I thought, pulling a second pin and then throwing the second thermite grenade. There was a brilliant flash, like welding sparks, as the first went up. It only took a second for the device to melt through a fuel drum.

There was a huge sucking *whoosh,* and the fuel went up in a pillar of flame. A few seconds passed and then the unruptured drums started lighting off. The wash of heat pushed me back. The rapidly spreading pool of flaming avgas flowed around the helo, and it quickly started burning too.

"Nice throw, man," Grant said.

"Thank you," I said. It was time to hurry now.

"I've got her, I've fucking got her!" Sadie crackled over the line, and then faded out in a peel of gunfire.

"What's going on inside?" I asked as I moved to double time toward the front doors.

"Unsure, I don't have eyes inside the building, but Red Queen and Black King are both still engaged." Grant said. *"But I think we have eyes on Black Queen."*

"Good, I'm almost to the door," I said.

"Pawns coming your way," Grant said. *"Lach has them retreating toward the main entrance."*

"Copy that," I said, racking the bolt of the automatic shotgun. It was an entirely too heavy of a weapon, but I wanted absolute show-stopping power without worrying about overpenetration. It wouldn't do for bollocks to bring a light machine gun, shoot these wankers up, and then find out I had shot my own, and then sent a few hundred rounds flying into a desolate and depressing Texas town.

Now an automatic 10 gauge? That was a different story.

They kicked open the door and staggered out into the fresh air. I could see wisps of tear gas chasing them out, and the second man who came out gulped down a lungful of fresh air, and then doubled over, violently sick.

Boom boom boom boom!

The shotgun spoke with authority, and their escape turned into a massacre. A few tried to take shelter behind wooden doors, but two or three rounds turned their cover into matchsticks. Then it turned men into spaghetti sauce.

A few managed to raise their weapons, but rifles required accuracy, and their eyes were still burning from the teargas. My gun didn't need to be accurate, I just had to get close.

Boom boom boom boom!

They fell and then there was more silence.

I kicked the ruined doors open and stepped into the main foyer of the building; the air still thick with teargas. Sadie had really let them have it. The upper staircase was smashed as well, the walls reduced to shattered slat board and two by.

And in the nearly completely destroyed center of the common area, Lach was in, of all things, a fistfight with a huge black man.

And not doing well.

I shouldered the automatic shotgun and advanced, keeping the barrel up and waiting for the two of them to get far enough apart that I could drop his opponent without filling Kyle full of buckshot.

Between an upset with an AR turned into Louisville Slugger and some of his almost-signature high heel strikes, Lach put the giant back against the wall, and then dropped him. I lowered the gun and walked up. I gave him a little bit of back-handed banter, had to keep him up and running, but he looked rough. The other man tried to get up, so I put two between his shoulders and he decided to go back to lying on the ground.

"C'mon, Sadie is upstairs," he said, racking an AK he had taken from one of the dead men.

"Who the fuck is this Goliath?" I asked as Lach walked up and stepped over his corpse.

"That was Ajahi, and now he's worm food. Let's go," he said. I knew that he was super focused now, blood and bruises. He paused over the dead man who almost beat his arse down and grabbed the gold-hilted knife stuffed through his belt. He was already taking the stairs two at a time. I grabbed the gold filigreed pistol, slipped it inside my bandolier and followed Lach.

The stairs were a ruin and shuddered as we climbed them. Half of the boards were cracked or missing, broken, just shattered. We stuck to the sides, where the framing had survived the best. Part of the rail I grabbed for stability buckled and I had to draw back or risk falling. The shotgun felt as heavy as a mini-fridge slung over my shoulder, and that was with more than half of the ammo gone.

I would need to add cardio back into my workout regimen, if this was going to become more routine.

I pulled myself up, and Kyle grabbed my hand for the last step up.

We both approached the door, and it felt like Schrodinger's Box. There was a fight inside, and either Sadie was winning, or Kaijin was winning, and for a moment, both were equally valid.

Last time they met, not that many days before, Gwendolyn Kaijin had definitely come out on top, almost taking a chunk out of her shoulder, and escaping with stab wounds, but apparently nothing terribly serious as she'd not been treated that I could tell.

"Why don't you two just stop right there?" Worthington said.

"You didn't stop *her*," Lach said, hands on his AK. Kurt had his hand above the butt of his pistol, ignoring the carnage behind him.

"If Gwen can't handle a single skinny girl, she has no right to lead the Cartel, now does she?" His fingers were open and loose. I prayed that Lach remembered that Kurt had been one of the fastest hands in the regiment, taking pride in his almost cowboy shootout lightning speed with pistols.

I held out a hand for Kyle to back down. He did, but only reluctantly.

"It's been a long time, sir," Worthington said.

"It has, Corporal," I said. "Damn shame about *Le Generale*," I added. "Things were about to get back to normal."

"It was a lot of work to convince him to let it go, and that everything with him and his brother was pride," he said.

"Frogs and humility go together like Yanks and modesty." I smiled.

"Sharp as ever, Sir," he said without a smile. Kurt wasn't the expressive sort.

"You remember that debt you owe me, Kurt?" I asked.

"Aye, and it's a black mark I never paid back." He nodded.

"Walk away and we call it even," I said, calmly.

"My contract was with *Le Generale*, not some degenerate with a biting fetish," he said. Kurt took his hand away from the butt of his pistol and gestured for us to go on. Lach didn't hesitate and bolted for the doorway. I held a moment, making sure this wasn't some sort of Fallujah feint, but Kurt was true to his word and I felt a pang of regret for not trusting him.

I charged into the room. The gold knife floated through the air, almost suspended in slow motion. Thrown.

Kaijin had a pistol in one hand, a fucking Crusader sword in the other, and looked like she had gone in and come out the other end of a wood chipper.

Sadie's armor was split across the breast, dragonscale missing and the Kevlar ruined. The sword must have had a wicked edge.

I recognized the blade in Kaijin's hand – Joyeuse, the sword of Charlamagne.

A replica to be sure, the original was eleven centuries old and held under great security somewhere in France, the Louvre, I supposed.

Each of us are only afforded a few perfect moments in our lives, as short or long as they may be. In that specific second, I knew that this was one of those such moments, for Sadie, as she plucked the blade thrown by Lach from the wall between herself and Kaijin…

CHAPTER TWENTY-SIX

*S*adie...

I was really starting to get a taste for blowing shit up. I mean, it was *fun*. Like, *really* fun. What's the old saying, though? It's all fun and games until someone loses an eye?

While I didn't almost lose an eye, I *definitely* fucked up.

I spotted her first, she was on the second floor with her bodyguard guy. I snarled into the mic that I'd spotted her and was going after her. She tucked tail and ran through a set of fancy looking doors and I thought for a moment that the man in the suit with her was going to stop me, but as soon as he'd seen she'd cleared the door and he was out of his sight? He just cocked his head like I was something interesting that he didn't see every day and hand on the butt of his pistol, he stepped aside, inclining his head.

My dumbass went through the fucking door and damn near got shot. The report went off but apparently small arms fire wasn't her thing, because she missed and I tucked and rolled, coming up behind a bookshelf or desk, or *something*. It hadn't quite had the time to register what sort of room we were in. All I knew, was that I had my back pressed up against something wood.

She shot at it, and while whatever it was slowed the bullets down, it didn't stop them. It felt like she socked me in the back twice, and I mean *hard.*

"Motherfucker!" I cursed, and she laughed.

Laugh at this, you fucking little bitch. I thought savagely, and I popped up and *whump,* pause, *CRACK!* I set off a flashbang.

Glass shattered, and she screamed. I moved away from the display case. I'd been ducked down behind the wooden pedestal that was decorative with no real substance a splintered ruin from her shots - the glass from it and several others shattered and littering the thin business boardroom carpet. They didn't like the concussion from the flashbang at all and couldn't hold out against it.

I took cover behind the more substantial, heavy wooden desk and called out, "Check!"

Pop! Pop!

The desk vibrated at my back as it took the two slugs to its top, and paper fragments rained down on top of me. I gritted my teeth. She had a weird looking semi-automatic of some kind but it was small, and it couldn't hold too many rounds. I took a gamble and popped up over the desk and she raked fire across where I was. Most of the shots missed me, thank fuck, but my overreaction to getting myself out of the line of fire knocked me flat on my ass. I hit the floor hard enough to knock the fucking wind out of myself and saw stars for a second as I tried to get my damn diaphragm to work. My mask was grazed by a round, and the faceplate was ruined. I tore it off so I could see.

I waited a second and heard glass crunch under her heels. She crept around the desk, stepped within range, but I was lying on my fucking rifle. I tightened my grip on Thumper's stock as she smirked down at me, thinking I'd been hit.

Jesus, fuck, was she a natural blonde?

She lowered her pistol right between my eyes and still with that self-satisfied smile, pulled the trigger.

Nothing happened. Her pistol had jammed and I could see the brass casing hung in the chamber.

I felt my face scrunch as I grabbed Thumper with both hands and swung, *hey, batter, batter,* cracking the short stock right into the side of her knee. She shrieked, and fell, and I crawled right the fuck on top of her, pressing her face into the broken glass on the floor making sure it hurt, grinding it down in it while she shrieked like an angry banshee.

"How you gonna like lookin' in the mirror now, bitch?" I demanded, and I threw a fist into the side of her head while she bucked under me. I didn't have the best hold on her, and between her wig sliding off under my hand and her throwing herself around beneath me, she ended up bucking me off. She rolled to her feet, gasping, her chest heaving as she got up. Her hand went to her face, and the shards of glass there. If she had been smart, she would have ignored that, cleared the jammed round, and shot me. Guess no one had given her any sort of proper training like I had.

I got to my feet too and squared off, fists up and held loose. She held her pistol in her off hand like it was going to help her, but she was fucked and I was ready to *fight.* She swung at me and I dodged. We did a little back and forth, testing limits. I knew Lach would have called it a dance.

I should have paid more attention, because she was playing me, and by the time I was hip to it, she had lunged, wrapped her hand around the hilt of the sword in the shattered display and had swung it up and back down in a sweeping arc toward me.

The dragonscale armor was *fantastic* against just about anything ballistic, probably would have done me some good against a stabbing impact, but *slicing?* Nuh-uh, it parted for the tip of that blade like the fucking red sea, and it was only by the grace of God, and the reflexes that had been brutally trained into me by Kyle, that I didn't end up flayed and bleeding under it.

I backed way the hell off, flipped my rifle up and over my head, and got it between my hands just in time to use it to stop another downward savage stroke.

It stopped the sword, but the fucking plastic shit shattered, and I didn't think I'd be able to fucking shoot her.

She had me on the run, hacking and slashing at me, but the one thing I *hadn't* been trained in – to any sort of satisfaction – was fencing, and a jacked-up AR made for a poor sword. It was holding up as a shield – barely, but barely was better than nothing at this point.

She swung, one handed, chopping at me savagely and somehow, I ended up with the metal barrel of the AR in both hands, swinging the gun's stock back at her, meeting her stroke for stroke.

"Sadie!" Kyle yelled, and it distracted Kaijin, just enough. I swung and *almost* clocked her a good one as she jerked back. A flash of gold flew between us. She reeled back from it, flinching. I didn't flinch, and I pulled the knife Kyle had thrown from the wall. It was a big bastard, but it didn't have near the reach of the sword. I hefted the awkward remnants of the AR in one hand as she shrieked her rage and swung for me again.

I brought the AR up and it jarred all the way down into my shoulder with the force she put behind her swing. I lunged and slashed across her pretty pantsuit jacket with its white silk blouse and sliced clean through the twin layers of fabric, laying a deep gouge across her stomach.

"You little bitch!" she cried indignantly, and I grinned savagely.

"I'm so kicking your ass!"

She brought the sword down and tried to run me through but it was a mistake. I sidestepped, lightning quick, and swept my arm over and down, caught her at the elbow, and locked her arm up. I exerted and felt a satisfying pop. She screamed, and the sword clattered to the floor.

I immediately backed her into the wall, bringing up my arm with the knife still in my hand to block as she tried to smash me in the face with the butt of the pistol she still doggedly held onto.

I brought my forehead forward, crashing into her nose and felt it crunch all over again, then for good measure, I brought my knee up as hard as I could right into her skanky twat. She cried out and doubled forward at the assault on her lady bits and I slashed the knife down, Norman Bates style and stabbed it deep into her shoulder. The pistol clattered to the floor as the steel knife blade parted flesh, cutting deep.

"That, was for Roan," I said, and chest heaving smiled at the glint of fear that finally arrived in her eyes. One arm dislocated, the other gouged open at the shoulder. She was fucking *done,* and it was *my* turn.

"You get off on it, don't you?" I demanded. "The power at having people helpless?" I pulled the knife out of her shoulder and she let out a strangled, gasping sob. I put it against her face, and stepped into her, pinning her against the wall behind her with my body against hers.

She had racoon eyes from our last fight. Her lips were drenched in blood from her nose, and things were already beginning to swell from the blow I'd just dealt her with my last headbutt. She looked scared, really scared, for the first time I'd ever seen it and I had to say…

"I can see the appeal." I ran the tip of the knife lightly from just under her eye, over her breast, not cutting, not yet, stopping just at the fifth intercostal space at the left midclavicular line… just like Kyle had taught me.

"I hear you like to fuck big dicks," I said, and I pushed it slightly, letting the tip bite just a little. Her eyes widened.

"I've got a real big dick for you, Gwen. I've got a real big dick and you're going to feel every. Fucking. Inch. Slip inside you."

I took my time, pushing the blade in as I spoke, wiggling it back and forth. She started to scream, and I covered her mouth and nose with my hand, remembering how helpless and powerless it had made me feel all those years ago in the bottom of that swimming pool.

I slid the fucking knife up into her body, felt the blood wet her suit and my hand and I *enjoyed* watching the light die in her eyes as I savaged her black heart with the tip.

"Fuck me and mine…" I whispered. "I fuck you back, ten times harder."

I let her go, and she slumped to the floor, her mouth gasping and working like a landed fish as her heart tried and failed to pump blood through her circulatory system. I followed her to the ground and kept shoving the knife home.

"Checkmate, bitch."

CHAPTER TWENTY-SEVEN

*L*achlan…

"Come on," I said, and grabbed Sadie by the arm. "It's done, she's dead." Her hands were still white knuckled on the gold knife. She trembled, and I knew she was still trying to push the blade deeper, and the tip had hit something it couldn't go through. Something like the bitch's spine or the floor out the other side of her.

"Shady, we won, let's go home," I said again, and tried to pull her back to her feet. She shook, but eventually stood. The knife came with her, laying out the familiar grate of metal against bone. Her eyes were large, and she was breathing rapidly through her nose. This was an intense kill, even by our standards. I had done it only twice before, the slow knife penetration.

Jesus, that was more intimate than actual fucking.

She came around eventually and was tangled in what was left of her body armor and harness. I brushed some hair out of her face that'd come loose from her tight French braid, and tried to sort some of it out, so we could get out of here. It was definitely time to go, the smell of smoke was getting stronger.

"Time to bounce, your bingo time," Worthington said.

I watched as Roan picked up Kaijin's sword, hefted it once, giving the blade the critical eye. Then he hacked down once, twice, and a third time. Her head hadn't come completely free of her torso, but the wound was horrific, and there wasn't more than a single slow pulse of blood from the carotids.

"Something that evil," he spat, "I don't trust to have a bloody fucking heart."

Sadie seemed to come back to us, seeing the absolute ruin of flesh and near decapitation. Was she expecting the woman to get back up even though she had perforated the heart? She looked around as if seeing the room for the first time and nodded. "We can go, we're done."

"Head out the north entrance, there is a secondary motor pool there and you can take one of the vehicles," Worthington said. He lit a cigarette and then used his lighter to set one of the curtains in the room on fire. "Front of the building is fully involved now. Texas grass fire, spread from the helipad to the trees and to the building. It's all going up."

"Shit," I said.

"Don't worry, there won't be anything left of this place for authorities to find anything." He sighed and flicked some ash from his cigarette on to the carpet.

"I'm curious to know what you owed Roan for him to call this even," I said, helping Sadie toward the door. We must have looked ridiculous, kitted up in slashed armor, beaten bloody, and holding each other up.

"This?" He looked around at the destruction in the room. "This is because they're three paychecks behind on payroll," Worthington said, setting another curtain on fire. "But if you want to know what I owed the Captain, take it up with him."

"Fair enough," I said, and we struggled out of the room, and into the hallway. He was right, the entire front foyer was alive with flames, and it was quickly eating its way through the building. The stairs busted by the grenade were just kindling and were already burning.

"I came up a set of stairs that way." Sadie pointed with the grenade launcher.

"You can leave that," I said.

"Fuck you." Her voice was soft. "I like this one."

"Keep the piece, but keep moving," Roan said, ushering us forward. We took the narrow stairs and went down into the inferno.

"Double back here, take the left-hand hallway," Worthington said from the rear, and we complied. We were heading up the narrow service hall when something big let go in the foyer, and it sounded like half of the building came down. We were blasted with a wind that felt right out of a furnace, and then the heat just increased, rather than dissipate. Shit was getting real.

When we kicked the single door open, the air outside was almost like a refrigerator by comparison. It was clean, clear, no smoke, no lingering tear gas. Thank God for those things, my face felt like it had gone through a windshield. There were several vehicles parked here, mostly light and regular trucks, the only thing even modestly not fleet was a short bed 4X4, faded red, with a rollbar and tubular steel front guard over the radiator.

"Don't look too hard at my ride, shark eyes," Worthington said, walking over and opening the door.

"We'll take one of the white trucks, c'mon," Roan said, opening the driver side door of one of them. A battered, dirty, ugly, fleet truck, ugh. I opened the passenger door and helped Sadie in, still clutching the gold knife. "Put the bitch sticker away, Poppet," Roan said softly. It was reluctant, but she found a place for it, tucking the blade down into the top of her boot. Roan patted her on the knee and gave a nod.

"If you're ever in the neighborhood, The Black Watch in Indigo City does know how to pour a proper pint and serves a good English Breakfast on Sunday mornings," Roan said.

"Bangers?" Worthington asked.

"Unfortunately, no, local product, but it's not bad," Roan called back to him.

"I'll give it a try, when I'm in the area. Sunday morning?"

"Aye, it's also her Majesty's VFW hall, by default. There are some good lads there."

"Then count on me visiting at least once." He gave a smile and a salute.

"Dismissed, Corporal." Roan returned the salute.

Doors slammed and we followed Worthington's GMC down a winding trail, and then through a gate that he just hammered with the front of his truck. I was certain that the steel guard on the front probably wasn't even scratched going through the chain link. Sadie leaned into me and let out a massive sigh.

"Rough night?" I asked, sarcastic, but not really digging.

"It's better now," she said. Roan shifted gears, working the pedals, and brought us out onto the pavement. Worthington turned north, toward the highway, and we had to turn the opposite direction to head back to where Grant and the mobile command center was. Roan was talking to Grant, and that was when I realized my earpiece was gone. Probably came out when I was boxing with the big guy.

I was going to be fucking dead in the morning from that, and from the rounds the armor stopped. I did *not* look forward to that. As we made the turn, we could see the blaze. The entire front half of the building had collapsed inward, and now almost the entire thing was burning, furiously. The shell of the helicopter was still apparent, but the heat damage was impressive, the rotors had sagged from the heat, and the aluminum skin had buckled, like a melting milk jug. There was a pillar of flame, a storm of sparks and embers that billowed skyward as another large structure collapsed in on itself, and then I could see the trees.

They were wreathed in flames, their few leaves blowing away.

There was something almost artistic about it.

Like it should have been in some pretentious nihilist art film, burning leaves, burning buildings, something about futility or some shit.

I liked my fires and explosions with a good sound score and the heroes walking away at the end. "Kyle?"

"Yeah, Shady?"

"You thinking about that Shady Brook?"

"I am now." I smiled.

"It's nice, I think I get it."

"I'm glad," I said, not really knowing how to reply to that.

"Kiss me, boy," she said, her voice cracking as she looked up at me. I did, a brief, soft kiss. We were both a mess, but the moment, it was there.

We drove the rest of the way to the house in silence, and Grant met us at the driveway, gesturing for Roan to follow him, through a gate into the backyard. Made sense, we were in a vehicle associated with the compound, and when the locals starting asking questions, they would see the truck and follow up on it. They would be occupied for a while, that was a hell of a fire, I could see the glow of it from the backyard of the house.

"Body checks, first aid, showers," Roan said, opening the door of the truck and hopping out like fucking airborne assault. I was slower to get out, and Sadie was no faster.

"We'll check each other, mate," I called to Roan and helped Sadie toward the bathroom. "Were you even hit?"

"Not once, mate," he said. "You take care of her, if you need anything, give a shout. I'll monitor the situation with Grant, see about breaking some of this gear down. We can go home first thing in the morning.

"Hey!" I looked at him.

"Go ahead," he said, pausing.

"What did Worthington owe you?"

"A tenner," he said.

"A fucking tenner?" I asked incredulously.

"Aye, owed me a tenner, lost a bet shooting camel spiders."

"A ten-pound note?" I echoed.

"That's what a tenner is, aye." Roan smiled.

"Fucking Brits," I muttered, and I could only shake my head in disbelief. He shrugged and waved for us to go on.

Inside the house, I started helping Sadie out of the ruin that was her kit. The shoulder and chest pieces were ruined, the sword cut straps and shredded the ballistic fiber. When I got the chest piece off of her some of the individual dragonscales actually fell out, clattering loudly against the shitty linoleum of the bathroom floor.

Underneath she was sweaty, bruised, and there was a bit of blood, but I didn't know if it was hers or not. The back piece was in worse shape, and as I dropped it on the ground, I saw the purple chrysanthemums.

She had taken two hits in the back, fairly close together. The armor stopped the rounds from going through her, but left flowers for her to remember them. Those would fade, but they would hurt like hell.

There were a few other injuries, but none as severe.

"Any surprises?" she asked.

"Two in the back, just some flowers," I said.

"I know," she said softly. "She didn't miss with all of her shots."

"She won't be fucking with anyone ever again," I said, a whisper against her hair.

"Let's see how you did." She smiled, and there was some strain in it. I let her help me out of my armor, which in its own way was in worse shape. The chest piece was rough, having stopped at least three rounds. She let the entire chest piece, front and back, fall at the same time. Her touch was delicate, as she probed where it looked like I was considering opening up a florist shop.

She pressed her lips against the bruises, kissing them.

"Shady?" I asked.

"Hmm?" she half replied, kissing more of my chest. Was this the time? It had certainly been quietly circling in the back of my mind, all the endorphins and the amped up feeling from the adrenalin. She undid the buckle of my belt and let it fall, then undid the front of my pants.

"Kiss me first," I said softly. She paused, and then did. Her kiss was hot, and I could smell the ash and blood from everything lingering between us. I didn't care, I'd never felt so alive. The bruises, the ache in my face, even seeing her as rough as the night had been on her, seemed to make the sensation higher. Her hands hadn't left my pants, and she had me out of them before we were done kissing.

She slipped to her knees and took me into her mouth.

I groaned softly, and she moaned her own approval in counterpoint.

There was no need for speaking, we needed no words. We just needed each other.

She did struggle for a moment, getting her own belt loose, and tried to get her pants pulled down, but started getting tangled up. I stepped back, and she leaned forward, and only stopped sucking me off when she couldn't reach, and almost tipped over. I helped her strip, throwing the sports bra in the corner. She managed to get out of the pants, and I pulled her into another kiss.

"Lie down," I said. She looked at me, curious for a second, but I saw her realize what I wanted to do. The floor wasn't the most comfortable place, a bed would have been better, but that was a luxury we didn't have at the moment. Fucking unfurnished house, or cots in the back of a truck…

It didn't matter, this did.

She looked up at me, waiting. Her knees parted, and she reached out and started stroking me with her hand. I kneeled next to her, letting her squeeze and tug me, and then she pulled me toward her mouth. I lifted my knee and straddled her head. The end of my cock met her lips, and I felt her tongue dancing against it. I groaned, absorbing the pleasure of the moment. She I leaned forward, braced myself on my elbows and buried my face between her thighs.

She was sweaty, and her smell filled my nose. It was irresistible. I tasted her and kissed her. Her pussy was almost dripping wet before I even touched it, and she would have quickly been crying out and howling in minutes. Instead, as I teased her clit, and sucked on her pink lips, she could only groan around my cock.

I started rolling my hips, slowly at first. She groaned, and I felt her clench with pleasure. I went a little quicker, going a little deeper. The more dominant I was, the more she responded. Faster, deeper, she dug her fingernails into the backs of my thighs. I thrust, and she groaned. She clenched and raked her fingernails, and I moaned.

She squeezed my balls, and I went lower, moving away from her clit and down toward her ass. I felt her thumb massage the base of my balls, then start slipping lower. She touched my ass, and then I came.

Everything went tight, and my balls drained themselves like it was a fire drill.

I pulled myself up, freeing my cock from her mouth, and she gave it another good squeeze. I had a bit of shudder as I changed my position. She looked at me and wiped at her mouth. "You have a double shot in you?" she asked, and goddamn it, she was my succubus.

"You'll have a double shot in *you*, when I'm done." I returned her grin with my own devil's smirk. I mounted her, driving into her with no hesitation, no gentleness. It was hard, and my pace was fast.

She clawed my back and howled.

When my arms were shaking, we changed position, and she turned to get on her knees. She arched her back and presented her dripping wet slit to me. I took her again, with the same intensity as before. The angle was different, and she seemed to enjoy it more. She clenched more, and the wet noises were louder.

"Everything okay?" Roan asked, from the doorway.

"Oh God, yes!" Sadie shouted, and I gave him a distracted thumbs up.

"You feeling tense, need a back rub, mate?" he asked. My thumb turned into an extended middle finger. He gave a laugh and pulled the door back shut.

Distraction gone; we both threw ourselves back into the moment. I could feel her orgasms, small, close together, like pearls strung on a necklace. They were getting more powerful though, a little further apart.

She started gasping out another one as I massaged her asshole with the tip of my thumb. She groaned and pressed back against me, and I knew that she was ready. I let it slide the entire way in. She groaned loudly and clenched tighter than she had before.

"Yes," she hissed between her teeth. I let my hand barely touch the bruises on her back, wishing I could take those away, but she probably wasn't even aware of them at the moment. Mine were certainly forgotten.

I swapped my thumb for my first two fingers, getting her ready for what would likely be the main event. I was thankful that I had already gone off once. Holding back right now would have been challenging. Instead of focusing on keeping myself up and going, I was well into my second wind.

My cock was glistening wet, our juices mixed. It was slick in my hand, and when I pressed the head against her asshole, she shivered in anticipation. While I wanted to tease, it was a distant feeling. I pushed forward, and she leaned into me. There was resistance, a tightness that caught my breath.

The pace started slow, and then quickly moved to a fast, deep stroke.

She shuddered when I put my hand around the base of her neck, my grip firm.

I felt her hand move between her thighs. She grabbed my balls, pulling on them for a few seconds, and then disappearing. When they were gone, I felt her shaking. While I took her ass, she furiously attacked her pussy with her own fingers.

She came.

I kept going, not changing my pace. Her next grasp on my balls was firmer, pulling me to go faster.

She shuddered, fingers on her clit, and came again.

I felt it building. It felt like it was coming from a deeper place, somewhere more primal.

Her back arched, and she started shaking, this was a big one. Her moan turned into a guttural howl, and I could see muscles in her back flexing. I buried myself to the hilt and exploded.

She held for a moment, vibrating like a tuning fork, and I heard something dripping on the floor.

We both collapsed forward at the same time, tangling in each other's limbs. I slipped out of her, and she shivered.

The only reason we got up was that the floor wasn't comfortable. Getting into the shower was an exercise in deliberate self-control. Her knees were gone, and my own body was boneless. She turned the water to what was likely highest temperature setting.

I took the soap and sponge and used it to wash her down, taking care to not press against the bruises. Then it was shampoo, and I ran my fingers through her hair, working it up to a rich lather. When she started rinsing her hair, that was my cue to get soap and sponge again, and wash her front.

We would be dead in the morning, so I stole a kiss while her eyes were closed, head tilted back to rinse. The kiss lingered, and she stopped what she was doing to put her arms around me.

When her hair was rinsed, she made a point to get the soap and sponge from me and then started giving me the same favor. Her touch was like a butterfly over my bruised chest. Her eyes smoldered as she took me in her hands and worked up a lather. After a double, I wasn't going to be up for a third, but if she kept it up, I was going to melt and run down the drain.

The hot water ran out far too soon.

We toweled dry and realized neither of us had grabbed clean clothes. "I'll be back." I gave her a small kiss, and covered only by a wet towel, I went and grabbed our bags. When Roan and Grant saw me, they both started hooting and whistling, and then I had to think about how loud we had been.

Roan tossed me the first aid kit before I managed to make my escape. I caught the kit, lost my towel, and left it on the ground. I went back to where she was sitting on the side of the tub and opened the kit. There were some cuts and scrapes to hit with antiseptic, but nothing required stitches, that was a good thing. Her shoulder was swollen, the bite wasn't done healing, but it would take a while longer to be fully healed. It least it wasn't bleeding.

"Your face will need some attention," she said. "What happened?"

"Ajahi, the big South African, he was downstairs, and we danced," I said. She took the kit and started dabbing at my face.

"You might need some dancing lessons," she whispered. The antiseptic stung cuts that I didn't realize were there. "I don't think you'll need stitches, but a few of these butterflies wouldn't hurt." She unwrapped a few and put a few on the left side of my face, at the eyebrow, and the cheekbone mostly. He had big hands and swung like a big leaguer.

She finished and put a hand against my chest.

"Yeah, nothing we can do about these but pop some painkillers," I said. She opened a bottle and shook out several for both of us.

"It's done, it's really done," she said.

"It is," I said.

"It's all done?" She leaned forward.

"Even if she was a vampire, it's done. Knife in the heart, head removed, and remains burned. The General is dead, the Cartel's inner circle is dead, we killed all of them."

"I think it'll take a while to fully sink in," she said softly.

"It's over, Shady," I said, and kissed her on the forehead. She closed her eyes and sagged against me and I held her close, carefully.

"It's over," she echoed softly, voice full of unnamed emotion.

CHAPTER TWENTY-EIGHT

*R*oan…

Flipping the house on Phoenician Boulevard was easily handled, the market was running a bit hot, and we netted a tidy profit even after covering a few unexpected repairs. Repairs at the John Laurens house were done before we made it back from Texas.

The renovations and upgrades, however, took longer.

I had certainly learned lessons from the fall of Bootlegger Head, taking the Final Prophecy Center, twice, and then storming this place once. Walls were reinforced. Roll hardened steel, packed beneath sheetrock, steel bolts anchoring everything together, strong enough to stop everything south of heavy armor-piercing rounds. Even grenades and RPGs should be stopped by that much armor.

The windows were likewise reinforced, more double pained bullet resistant Lexan.

Several rooms didn't even *have* windows – what looked like windows were large screen monitors beneath curtains. It gave the illusion of space, in the rooms that were more heavily armored. The original panic room was turned into the new nerve center for our operations. I had a new rig, one that Grant came by and helped with. Nine monitor display, multiple methods to connect to the internet, new security countermeasures, and entirely new hardware to run everything.

That only took a month to get fully operational.

The entire house was tied into it, on its own dedicated system. The lights were adjustable, temperature controlled through a dozen smart systems, everything tied into the same entertainment system.

We organized an entirely new layout for the bedroom situation. There was a master bedroom that was the master of masters. It had an Alaskan King, a massive nine foot by nine-foot behemoth of a bed. Even with three sleepers, there was plenty of room. It was our regular sleeping arrangement these days, with the room large enough for dressers and wardrobes for our clothing and other accessories. The attached master bathroom was likewise enormous, with a huge garden tub, with jets, a waterfall shower with two side showerheads, and while not the most glamorous thing, it had two hideaway toilets.

Almost no amount of closeness between us would eliminate entirely the need for privacy.

To that end, we each maintained what amounted to a personal room. Almost like a college dorm, these rooms were our individual studies, and where we kept our personal affairs, and interests. There would always come a time when a person might need or want to be alone, spend some time following their own interests. Sadie was the most resistant to this, but as much as I wanted to indulge her every whim, we had a responsibility to maintain our own autonomy, our own individuality.

To that, our old version of the time-share came back to the fore. At least once a week, we all had to fuck off on our own, do our own thing, and be comfortable just being with ourselves. For myself, that was generally Sunday, and I would start that off with a mid-morning visit to The Black Watch.

Sadie and Lach came a time or two, but it wasn't any sort of going home for them. They didn't see the Union Jack the way I did, and *God*

Save the Queen didn't mean that much to them either, any more than I had any particular bursting patriotic adoration for their stars and stripes. I didn't really keep up with what they did on their days, but that was the point, wasn't it?

The garage was upgraded, the door was replaced with what amounted to a blast door, along with all of the exterior doors on the house. It would be easier to blow a hole in the wall than take that door out, and either action would take something like a tank or a thermal charge, the sort that cut steel.

We stocked the garage with new cars, but there was a serious problem, space. We all wanted our own specific cars. The deal made was that we each had our own personal pleasure car, and there were three vehicles that were kept for general use, an armored and reinforced sedan and an SUV, for doing work. Currently one was an Audi, and the SUV was a chic Porsche Cayenne Turbo. The last was a regular pickup truck. It had no armor, no reinforcement, no tricks, but it was more for doing work things, moving things around on the property.

The groundskeepers and remodelers were pleased to have access to it.

It was also handy for being a completely non-descript vehicle for cruising into the less than opulent parts of the city or rolling through the country.

I debated, back and forth, on replacing my DB5. Another DB5 would be expensive, and there were problems I had with the car, most of which involved my stiff leg and prosthetic. I splurged and ended up with an Aston Martin One-77 supercar, in a glorious proper British racing green.

Lach wasn't going to be shown up and picked a gloss black Lamborghini Sian roadster. He was, in his own words, a cunt's hair away, from getting a Bugatti Chiron, but when he saw how much the service cost; a new set of tires, oil change, and general service could run near a hundred grand, he thought something flashier, but less demanding to own would suffice.

Not to be left sitting on the bench or riding shotgun, Sadie picked for herself a brand new Ferrari 488 Spyder, in Ferrari racing red. The cars were somewhat known, as it wasn't uncommon for us to take them down the John Laurens Highway and to track days. As much fun as they were to drive fast and wild, running on the actual tracks gave us the option for full power without dealing with regular drivers or police.

Made for fun afternoons.

We added an extension to the nerve center of the manse and made it the arsenal. Our first trophies were already hanging there. Ajahi's gold knife with its lion tooth inlay was the current centerpiece. I had to have it tested to find out what the inlay in the handle was. Next to it was his gilded Desert Eagle pistol. The replica of Charlemagne's sword *Joyeuse* had its own display. The most important part of the sword, to us, was the russet stain of blood in the fuller.

It had taken some effort to keep the blood from being wiped completely from the blade.

It was something that we would never forget either.

Sadie took a few months to fully recover from the incident – not just everything that had happened but from that kill, so close and so personal.

There was more good news for us. The Escadrille Cartel completely collapsed. Their North American operations came to a near halt, as it found itself lacking funds, burned with enforcement agencies, and when the other drug lords and cartels smelled blood in the water, they were torn apart or consumed into those other organizations.

What followed that could only be described as a blood purge.

This flared and chased the Cartel from its financial holdings in the Middle East and Europe all the way down to their poppy farms and street-level drug dealers. There were heads left on spikes in some parts of the world, and the price of heroin rose even down on the street. The damage done was almost impressive enough to affect the bottom line of the biggest drug dealing cartels in the world, the manufacturers of opioids and opioid derived painkillers. We almost made the cost of Oxy rise, and that was simply astounding, even to me.

I was glad that we hadn't done that much. That was how some of those interests started looking at who was causing the problems, and how to get rid of them.

That was how you ended up getting the Chiquita treatment. Threaten something big like prescription painkillers and you had national interests involved, and then the USMC and private military contractors were coming after you like you were public enemy number one.

The Escadrille had thousands of members, billions of dollars, and an utter ruthlessness in pursuit of its goals. However, a first world military had hundreds of thousands of people, budgets in the trillions, and had things like satellites and made men like Kyle Lachlan and me. The DEA claimed the organization dead less than three months after we left Kaijin's corpse in a burning Texas compound. They claimed that the last holdouts had been eliminated in a massive raid in Miami, netting a few hundred pounds of cash, a truckload of weapons, and half a ton of heroin, destined for market.

It was a day or so after that when Kurt Worthington turned up at The Black Watch. I bought him a pint and introduced him to the regulars.

"How have things been?" he asked, giving his pint a sip. "Fuck me, its proper!"

"It *is* proper; I told you, mate!" I chuckled. "And it's been good."

"How's your bird?" he asked.

"She's done well, took a bit getting over that sticking she gave."

"I bet, that was right in the business, up close, right up close," he said.

"She did, close enough she got blood on her face," I said.

"Fitting end for that bloody twat."

"You ever make up that lost pay?" I asked.

"No, not really," he said. "I picked up a few souvenirs, but not enough to make good."

"I hate to hear that," I said, and drained my pint, and gestured for another. "So, what are you up to now?"

"Tried the private contractor thing, and it's not been great.

Working for the Cartel took money out of my pocket, once the books were settled, and hanging out with people that push heroin, they aren't the best." He shrugged. "I was given a good recommendation for those assholes, and that the work was clean and the pay was good. Turns out wrong on both accounts."

"They had management problems, and yeah, drug dealing organizations don't attract the best and brightest." I thanked the waitress when she dropped off another pint.

"I'm looking at going into small scale security, personal protection and the like. Bodyguard work," he said.

"Big Whitney Houston fan?" I laughed.

"Bollocks, no, Kevin Costner." He laughed and finished his pint.

"Well, I wish you the best of luck, mate. Maybe you'll end up blocking for some smoking hot Hollywood starlet, and maybe shag you a piece of that."

"We call that living the dream," he laughed.

"Living the dream," I said. I thought of where I was now. Aston One-77 in the garage, Sadie in the middle of the continent sized bed, and my changed relationship with Lach. It *was* living the dream. A dream I hadn't dared *to* dream, and I couldn't be happier.

I mean, I had gone from being tied to a frame, tortured and molested, to having thrown a few test laps into a Vulcan and telling the salesman that I just didn't feel the legroom. My phone rang, and I looked down to see Sadie's smiling face on the ID. "Pardon me a moment."

"Of course, sir," he said.

"Hello, Poppet," I answered. I smiled. "Yes, of course I haven't forgotten." I looked over at Kurt and gave a nod. "At the pub, having a pint. Where else would I be on a Sunday?" She giggled on the other end of the line and I felt it get a bit hot around my collar. "Oh. Oh? In red you say?" She sent me a quick pic, and I felt a definite rise in my blood pressure. I smiled.

"I know this is a breach of etiquette, but I'll allow it." I hung up and slipped the phone back in my pocket.

"Duty calls, sir?" Kurt asked.

"Duty indeed does call, and I am afraid I'll have to cut this to my last pint, and I'll have to be on my way."

"The missus?" He gave me a wink.

"There are only three things in the world that would make me leave an unfinished pint on the bar," I said.

"The Queen calling?" he said.

"Aye, if the Queen called, I would leave a pint behind. The second would be my lady calling, which she has."

"What is the third?"

"Nazis. I would leave a full pint on the bar if it meant taking one of them out of the world." Kurt offered a toast. I clinked my pint against his and drained mine in a single pull.

"You okay to drive?"

"These cars today, they drive themselves, plus you know I have a hollow leg." I laughed.

I got into the Aston and pulled away from the curb, and turned toward the house on the bluff, overlooking the Chesapeake. It was time to go…

Home.

The End.

ALSO BY A.J. DOWNEY

The Sacred Hearts MC

1. Shattered & Scarred

2. Broken & Burned

3. Cracked & Crushed

3.5 Masked & Miserable (a novella)

4. Tattered & Torn

5. Fractured & Formidable

6. Damaged & Dangerous

The Virtues

1. Cutter's Hope

2. Marlin's Faith

3. Charity for Nothing

4. Stoker's Serenity

The Sacred Brotherhood

1. Brother to Brother

2. Her Brother's Keeper

3. Brother In Arms

4. Between Brothers

5. A Brother's Secret

6. A Brother At My Back

7. A Brother's Salvation

Sacred Hearts MC Novella

Christmas with the Brotherhood

Indigo Knights

1. Her Thin Blue Lifeline

2. His Cold Blue Command

3. A Low Blue Flame

4. His Wild Blue Rose

5. Her Pained Blue Silence

6. A Cold Blue Call

7. Her Reluctant Blue Cavalier

8. Forged Under Fire

9. Under A Blue Moon

Sacred Hearts MC Pacific Northwest

1. Over the High Side

2. Wind Therapy

3. Apex of the Curve

Paranormal Romance (with Ryan Kells)

1. I Am The Alpha

2. Omega's Run

3. Hunter's End

Indigo City Darker (with Jared KingPacal Lain)

Triple Threat

Standalones

Synchronicity

ABOUT A.J. DOWNEY

A.J. Downey specializes in writing real and relatable contemporary romance stories. She's from Seattle, WA and loves the Pacific Northwest. She finds inspiration from her surroundings, through the people she meets, and likely as a byproduct of way too much caffeine. An avid reader all of her life, it's now her turn to try and give back a little, entertaining as she has been entertained.

Stalker Information:

Website
www.ajdowney.com

Sign up for her newsletter at
http://eepurl.com/dkQiIH

Facebook Group - AJ's Sacred Circle
https://www.facebook.com/groups/authorajdowney/

facebook.com/authorajdowney
twitter.com/authorajdowney
instagram.com/ajdowney
bookbub.com/authors/a-j-downey

ALSO BY JARED KINGPACAL LAIN

Indigo City Darker (with A.J. Downey)

Triple Threat

Paranormal Romance (with Timber Philips)

The Water's Edge

ABOUT JARED KINGPACAL LAIN

Jared KingPacal Lain hails from the Great Smoky Mountains, a place of both beauty and dark things, where he explores strange fiction, hidden secrets, and venturing away from the main path to find hidden pleasures, wonders, and horrors.